THE AMULET

A Novel of Early Canada

NORMA SLUMAN
& MARNIE SLUMAN SOMERS

I hope you enjoy this book!

Marnie Sluman Somers

FriesenPress

Suite 300 - 990 Fort St
Victoria, BC, V8V 3K2
Canada

www.friesenpress.com

ISBN
978-1-5255-0480-8 (Hardcover)
978-1-5255-0481-5 (Paperback)
978-1-5255-0482-2 (eBook)

1. FICTION

Distributed to the trade by The Ingram Book Company

Other Books by Norma Sluman

Blackfoot Crossing

Poundmaker

John Tootoosis: Biography of a Cree Leader

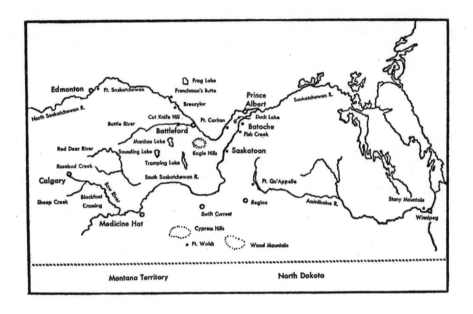

Edmonton • Ft. Saskatchewan

North Saskatchewan R.

Frog Lake
Frenchman's Butte
Bresaylor

Prince
Albert

Saskatchewan R.

Cut Knife Hill
Battle River
Ft. Carlton
Duck Lake

Battleford

Batoche
Fish Creek

Manitou Lake
Sounding Lake
Eagle Hills
Saskatoon

Red Deer River

Tramping Lake

Rosebud Creek
South Saskatchewan R.

Calgary

Ft. Qu'Appelle

Sheep Creek
Blackfoot
Crossing
Regina
Assiniboine R.
Stony Mountain

Bow River

Swift Current
Winnipeg

Medicine Hat

Cypress Hills

Ft. Walsh
Wood Mountain

Montana Territory
North Dakota

This book is dedicated to the memory of Norma Pauline Sluman, wife, mother, grandmother, and author of this book and others which we treasure as a family.

Norma's legacy is that her work lives on to inspire her descendants who love to read, are lifelong learners, and are continuing to develop their writing skills to follow in her footsteps.

Note from the Editor

My late mother, Norma Sluman, was a talented Canadian author, who during her lifetime, wrote two novels of historical fiction (*Blackfoot Crossing* and *Poundmaker*, published by Ryerson Press) and co-authored a biography (*John Tootoosis, a Biography of a Cree Leader*, originally published by Golden Dog Press and reprinted by Pemmican Publishing Ltd.).

Before she passed, Mom sent me her draft manuscript for *The Amulet*, laboriously written on a manual typewriter. She asked me to use my computer to retype it into digital format to meet the new criteria for submitting drafts to traditional publishers.

I read Mom's manuscript in first-draft format and I thought back then it was a good read. But I didn't make the time to get the job done for her. After she passed away, I felt quite disappointed in myself—that I had let her down. An important story, based on a historically significant Canadian incident, was destined for obscurity.

Years later, the light finally dawned that it was not too late to do something about it—if I just committed myself to the effort. I began the task of copy-typing her manuscript into digital format. As the chapters began to emerge, I just could not resist the urge to tweak Mom's story. *The Amulet* is still very much her story, although I have edited some terminology. I can only trust my intuition that she would approve of this mother-daughter iteration.

-Marnie

CHAPTER ONE

The District of Saskatchewan in the
North-West Territories Summer, 1884

If there *were* hidden watchers in the long grass, neither man could detect them.

"Zapristi!" the Métis swore, as he tightened his hands on the reins. "I can damn well *feel* them out there, Mac! Watching and waiting." He slapped at a deer fly biting his cheek.

"You're spooked, Gabe," said Ian McNab.

"Well, maybe." Gabe Berthier knew better than to argue with the granite-jawed man riding beside him, a nerveless and stubborn Scot who never wasted words, especially with the men who worked for him. But he noticed that McNab's eyes were more wary than usual.

The rutted trail unrolled ahead of them, but nowhere on the sun-scorched plains was there a sign of life, just tossing grass and heat-shimmers blurring the far horizons. Dust puffed with every step of their horses and those of the wagon teams behind them. It billowed aloft, where it hung like a ragged shroud against the brassy sky—a sure sign of their passage.

McNab cursed it silently as he looked back. His hard eyes stopped briefly on the girl in the first wagon, then moved back along the line of Red River carts, Speight freighters, and Concords, carrying settler families. At the end of the convoy, in a buckboard, was a red-coated policeman carrying mail and military dispatches. McNab looked at the girl again. She would have been more comfortable in the well-sprung buckboard, but McNab curtly refused the policeman's offer to drive Catherine, using the excuse that Pascal Lebret was the best teamster in the business. He was also over seventy years old.

"She's still there, boss," said Gabe, a flicker of amusement in his eyes.

Biting back annoyance, McNab managed a tight smile. "It takes getting used to, having a new wife at my age. But I'm looking at the dust and thinking about the noise we're making. We're hardly sneaking our way north." Red River carts can be heard for miles, wood on wood screeching unabated.

"Well, it's a big train, and they're staying bunched like you warned them. But that means we can only go as fast as the slowest wagon."

"Too slow for my liking," agreed McNab.

Berthier gave him a quick glance. He had worked for McNab for years, both on the trail and at his trading post in Pounding Lake. It wasn't the locals the inscrutable Scot was concerned about; it was the young woman. Like everyone else, Berthier was astonished to learn that McNab was now married after years of going it alone. He was even more astounded when he met her. She looked about half of McNab's age, nineteen or twenty. She was a beauty, with a smile that made you like her right away. But *merde*! She sure as hell would be out of place in Pounding Lake! What had happened to McNab back there in Ontario? So far as Berthier knew, the dour Scot had never done an impulsive thing in his life.

Berthier's speculation was interrupted as both horses shied violently. Carrying his rifle rather than resting it in a scabbard, he was nearly thrown. *"Nom de Dieu!* These two have burrs up their asses today, eh Mac?"

McNab agreed. "They're spooked too. Leading a circus like this one, no wonder." They rode on in alert silence, unlike the old days. Now, with the buffalo wiped out, the tribes were mean and starving. And wagon trains were fair prey. McNab wondered how these new settlers would behave if they did run into trouble. He felt pity and contempt for them. Their dreams of a new and better life would likely be eclipsed by the danger and hardships that lay ahead.

McNab's first visit in ten years to see his father in southern Ontario had been a duty, not a pleasure until he met and became hopelessly infatuated with Catherine. She was the daughter of William Matthews, his father's closest friend and an Anglican minister. But he still could not believe that he had married the girl!

A few women had drifted in and out of his life during his twenty years in the northwest; but he always stopped short of marrying any of them. McNab was a born loner; his business was his real passion. It prospered because he was shrewd and astute, with simple tastes and nerves of steel. He was set in his ways and never considered changing them for anyone. Until Catherine.

Now here he was burdened with a girl half his age, over-protected by doting parents, and 'purely ornamental', as his father, Jamie McNab, had said. He believed he would be the butt of many jokes when word of her got around the Saskatchewan country. McNab was too proud to relish that. He supposed he loved her, but she was an utter disappointment in bed. As it was, only Berthier ventured to congratulate him on his marriage when they arrived at the Swift Current railway terminal.

McNab was pleased to be riding Dundee again; the stout buckskin with his glossy black mane and tail always served him well. Despite his uneasy thoughts, the heat, flies, and choking dust did not disturb him; he was used to them. But he wondered how they were affecting Catherine. With her fair hair, delicate beauty and stylish clothes, she looked lost and vulnerable jouncing along beside Lebret in the rough freighting wagon. And lonely. The other settler women in the train were leery of her and stopped talking whenever she approached them. The Métis teamsters were shy and formal with her. She was going to need to do better than that in Pounding Lake; there were no other white women in the remote settlement!

But Lebret was enjoying her company. He was a cocksure little man with a wide, gap-toothed smile in his leathery face. Like other Métis, he wore a battered felt hat, a faded flannel shirt, a rainbow-hued sash tied twice around his waist, and beaded moccasins. He cracked his bull whip expertly and with flair, snapping flies from the sweating hides of the oxen, while rarely stinging any of the plodding animals.

"It's one of my good tricks, that one," he bragged to Catherine. He jerked his thumb back at the other wagons. "None of *them* can do anything like that. All they do is hang on, cuss loud, and follow me. That's why the boss keeps me at the head of the line. I know bulls—when to push them and when to go easy."

She smiled at him, as he was hoping she would. "It's amazing the way you snap those flies, Mr. Lebret."

He chortled. "I'm full of tricks, and don't you go saying 'mister' to me. I'm 'old Pascal'. See, if I forget that, I'd maybe whip up this here team and run off with such a pretty girl as you."

Catherine replied, "I couldn't risk *that*, so 'old Pascal' it is. But I think it should be 'old flirt' instead."

"That's true," he said. "A lot a kids in this territory look just like me!"

She seemed to enjoy his nonsense. He was originally dismayed when he was told this fancy-looking city girl would be riding with him, expecting all kinds of complaints and demands. But she spoke not a word of protest, even though she sometimes got down to walk alongside the wagon. Once he saw her tenderly rubbing her backside.

"I'll bet there's one thing the boss didn't tell you when he came courting."

"There were a lot of things he didn't tell me," she said, looking away.

Pascal went on quickly, "He plays the bagpipes, Mrs. Mac. And what a terrible howling noise it is too!"

"He does? Ian?" She laughed. "Well, I *do* like them."

"More's the pity then; you won't be putting a stop to it, looks like. Now me, I play the fiddle. *Real* music, that is."

"Oh yes," she agreed. "I love to hear good fiddlers. Do you have your fiddle along?"

"Sure," he answered. "Where I go, it goes. I'll play for you, maybe after supper."

Despite his first impression of her, the girl was beginning to win him over. He noticed that she did not burn ugly-red under the sun like a lot of whites; she tanned instead. Her fair hair was bleaching out, as she often went without a hat. The athletic way she moved made him suspect that she could run like a rabbit.

And those eyes of hers, almost purple they were, could take a man's breath away. She was too fine-boned and delicate looking to suit his taste, but she curved in all the right places. He did not find her stuck-up like the settlers thought she was; she was just ... he tried to think of a word. *Reserved*, that was it.

Then Lebret, who shouldn't think about such things but always did, wondered if she was *reserved* like that when alone with McNab in his tent at night. He thought she might be. Gabe Berthier noticed it too, once remarking, "Those two are sure polite with each other for newlyweds."

Sometimes she was quiet. She would sit with her hands clasped tightly, looking ahead at her husband. There was an odd look in her eyes then, questioning, and he thought, bewildered. But mostly she was good company. With her in the wagon, the tedious miles passed without notice. She was a good listener, eager to hear all he could tell her about her new home. And so, he flicked flies, grinned smugly at the other drivers, told her his best whoppers, and tried to tone down the cuss words. Catherine would not have minded them; she knew a few herself and was not above using them when provoked.

***

That evening, when the wagons were circled and supper was eaten, Pascal Lebret and another teamster, Gus Laronde, approached the McNab tent carrying fiddles. At the sight of them, Catherine got to her feet. "Ah, you did remember then! Ian, I think old Pascal and his friend are going to play a few tunes for us." Puffing on his pipe, McNab looked surprised, but he nodded at the two Métis. "Well. Thank you; go to it then."

They played a jig first, then a reel, moccasins tapping, their dark faces absorbed over the lively bows. Heads around the wagon circle turned, then the settlers moved closer and began to clap to the music.

The young policeman was headed their way, and McNab assumed that he was about to ask Catherine to dance. Abruptly, McNab cut in front, bowed formally to Catherine and asked her to dance. As the McNabs glided around the open space, one of the settlers drew his wife to her feet. The policeman asked their blushing daughter to dance with him, which was his original intention. Those who were not dancing sang and requested other favourites. The moon was well up before anyone retired to their tents or wagons.

***

"Ian," said Catherine, lighting a candle, "the Métis do look a bit rough and wild, but they seem so kind and full of fun. It makes me wonder about all this rebellion talk. Are the ones with us so different?"

He shrugged. "The men here have no quarrel with anyone. Nor would the Métis over at Batoche, if the damn government would give them legal title to their family farms. They are kindly people as you say, honest and good-hearted. But they are also reckless and too easily led. Their leader, Louis Riel, can tell them anything and they believe it. And when they get to drinking, they get to brawling. Just grown-up children, a lot of them."

Catherine kept him talking, because she knew what would happen as soon as they put out the candle. It happened nearly every night. McNab was a rough and demanding man in bed. She still flinched when she remembered their wedding night. All she knew about the facts of life consisted of veiled hints from her embarrassed mother and giggling misinformation from girlfriends at school. She summarily discounted all eligible suitors in Rosemere as immature and lacking in ambition, quashing any opportunity for romantic experience.

During their whirlwind courtship, Catherine learned nothing from her husband. He did no more than hold her hand and kiss her politely, once telling her that he could not trust himself, if he did more than that. She wanted to be held and caressed by this virile and exciting man. But on their wedding night, without any preliminary, he abruptly forced himself into her. Ignoring her pain and shock, he thrust with what she thought was insane fury until he was spent and rolled away from her. Upon seeing blood, the frantic girl was sure that she was gravely injured. Sobbing, she arose to attend to herself. Only then did he attempt to reassure her.

"Lass, that means nothing, only that you were a virgin. Lord knows I didn't want to hurt you, but I knew I would. I thought it best to do it quickly.

Now stop that sniffling and come to bed. It won't hurt like that the next time."
She huddled on the far side of the bed away from him for the rest of the night.

Now in the small tent, she gazed intently at the man who was her husband. He
was not the same man who had courted her so ardently at her home in Rosemere.
From the day they stepped off the train in Swift Current, he became a remote and
preoccupied stranger. Just another one amid all the other strangers in this wild
and unfamiliar land. He was sitting on their bedroll, smoking his pipe again,
still wearing his boots and trousers, although his shirt was stripped off revealing
broad heavily muscled shoulders. There was not a spare ounce of fat on him, nor
a sign of grey in his mahogany hair or sweeping moustache. His face was as lean
and rugged as his body, unlined but weathered from years of exposure. It was a
hard but handsome face, despite a scar across the bridge of his nose, where it had
been cut and broken.

He looked at her. "Do I pass inspection then, Catherine?"

She pretended to think about it. "I haven't quite decided, Ian. How did
you get that scar on your nose?"

He ran his finger over the mark. "In a stupid drunken brawl, if you must
know over a ... but no, I'll not be telling you more about it."

"Over a woman, no doubt. I thought you said it was the Métis who did the
drinking and brawling. But now tell me about the Indians. You have night
guards posted, and you all seem very watchful."

"Indians, is it now? Well, no white ever gets to *really* know and understand them, though some claim they do. There'll be flare-ups with them here
and there. They're close to being finished without their buffalo, and with the
sicknesses they catch from us. It won't be long before they're gone too, just
like the buffalo."

"You sound so cold about it. They *are* people."

"Being sentimental doesn't change a thing, Catherine. Time is running out on
them, that's all. And on us right now. I'm not going to sit up talking all night." He
got to his feet, unrolled their bedding, then looked down at her, his face inscrutable. "I suppose you'll want the candle out before you get undressed, as usual?"

"I ... no ... It doesn't matter, Ian." She started to unbutton her dress.

"Yes, it does," he said. "And I don't know why. You've a beautiful body, meant to be looked at. But have it your way." He snuffed out the light and came to her. "You've got a lot to learn about pleasing a man, if you ever care to try." He undid the rest of her buttons and shoved her dress off her shoulders. She was bewildered by his anger, but he gave her no time to think. He began to kiss her hungrily and roughly stripped off the rest of her clothes. Already aroused, she could feel him hard against her. She wanted to love this man, but she felt trapped and wanted to struggle free. His arms were almost crushing the breath out of her. It was not the first time she had panicked in the darkness with him. When he entered her, she forced herself to lie quietly under him until he was done and rolled off. Her once-rigid body began to relax, as she waited for his breathing to confirm he was asleep. She was, once again, reminded of her mother's concern about her impetuous decision to accept Ian's marriage proposal.

"Be sure!" Mrs. Matthews had told her. "If you marry this man, you'll have made your own bed and you'll have to lie in it!"

***

They moved out again at dawn. It was cold and Catherine drew her shawl closer as she took in the magnificent sunrise. The empty plains had an austere beauty all their own, with the sky aflame like this. The land caught and held the shifting colours like the stained-glass windows of some eastern cathedral. Along the trail, the ground was littered with buffalo bones, stark and bleached, with grass growing up through them.

Pascal's slingshot was tucked into his sash, and he kept a bag of stones handy. Sometimes he handed her the reins while he shot at the massive horned skulls, hitting them squarely between the empty eye sockets. But she cringed when he killed magpies with the same lethal pellets. She thought the big birds were beautiful, with white flashes on their black wings and their long sweeping tails. Pascal noticed her distress when he downed one.

"Don't pity them, Mrs. Mac. They're bad birds. They can kill the young of horses, cattle, deer. Say one gets a wound somehow. Magpie, he sinks claws into that place, tearing out meat with his beak. Only way the poor animal can get him off is to roll, but that damn bird comes right back. Never goes away once he starts. Terrible way to die, slow and hard." Catherine shuddered.

The country was changing. It was more rolling, and bluffs appeared, dotted with scrub pine. She could see willow trees marking the courses of meandering creeks. There was much less dust; here the air was clean and fragrant with mint, sage, and clover. They halted after fording Eagle Creek and McNab rode up into the hills. Soon she could see him on at the top, scanning with his field glasses.

"He's looking for Indians," Pascal said. "We're on Mosquito's reserve now. They're Assiniboines. Tough customers. They'll be wanting food from us for going on their land, if they spot us. And that would be trouble. So, what your man wants to do is see them first. And if he does, we go the longer way, moving fast."

"If they are so hungry, Pascal, why don't they hunt or fish?"

"They would if they could. But there's too many reserves around here, so too many hunters. Nothing left to shoot, creeks all fished out. Even snakes, gophers, their dogs ... all gone. Some eat grass now. Seen that more than once."

"My God! Do the authorities know about this?

"No real man's going to sit back and watch his folks starve to death, when others around him got lots to eat. And these are fighting men, born and bred. Only the treaties have kept them quiet up to now, which is maybe all they were meant to do."

McNab cantered up to the wagon. "No sign up ahead; looks like we can go straight through. You'll be in Battleford tomorrow, Catherine."

Still stunned by the idea of people eating grass to stay alive, Catherine felt as though she was an entire world away from her tranquil life growing up in Ontario.

CHAPTER TWO

After the long trek across the featureless plains, Catherine was surprised that Battleford was such a large and bustling settlement. She looked around eagerly. It was located along the banks of the Battleford River, just west of the point where it flows into the North Saskatchewan. Both rivers were teeming with rafts, barges, canoes, and majestic steamboats, carrying freight, supplies, and passengers to and from other settlements.

Across the Battleford River, on high ground, the police fort loomed behind palisaded walls. "That's D Division," Pascal told her, "biggest in the northwest it is, over two hundred men. But on this side, it's called the 'old town' where folks first built homes along the trading trails." She stood up to see better. The riverside dwellings were mostly small cabins made of rough mud-chinked logs.

Their wagon turned onto the busy main street, where Pascal identified the Indian agency and Land Registry offices, side-by-side with general stores, specialty shops, blacksmiths, livery stables, and boarding houses, all doing a brisk business. On a rise, east of the main street, were more substantial and neatly landscaped homes belonging to the affluent merchants and professional men of the area.

Suddenly the wagon train began to break up. The settlers, waving goodbye, followed the signs to the campgrounds. The Métis traders on the Red River carts headed for the docks; the policeman went to the post office to deliver the mail. McNab led his own wagons to a livery stable. As their wagon groaned to a halt, Catherine turned to Pascal.

"I *will* see you again, won't I?"

Pascal nodded his grizzled head and patted her arm. "Sure now, Mrs. Mac. Me, I live in Pounding Lake too. And I'm the one the boss wants you to drive with."

"I know," she said smiling at him, "because old Pascal is the best driver around. I won't tell him what a terrible flirt you are." She started to climb out of the wagon, but McNab was there. He lifted her out effortlessly and set her on her feet.

"We'll be staying with friends of mine," he told her. "John and Jenny Appleton. John and I were partners for a while. I telegraphed them from Swift Current, so they are expecting us."

Caught off guard, Catherine looked down at her dusty, rumpled clothes in dismay. "Oh Ian, I thought we would be staying in a hotel. I'm such a mess to take to meet anyone."

"No one comes in off the trail any different, and not many as bonny as you are. You'll be a bit of a surprise, I'm thinking."

"You are just full of little surprises," she said. In her annoyance, she almost refused to take his arm, but the planks of the boardwalk were rough and uneven and she relented. They turned off the main street into the residential area. It was nearing the supper hour and not many people were to be seen. The wind had died down and a faint blue haze of smoke from cookstoves, sweet and sharp-smelling, hung in the air.

***

Jenny Appleton threw her door open and ran to meet them, both hands extended in welcome, her round, grey eyes fixed on McNab. Then she looked at Catherine, and her smile vanished. "Why you are just a bit of a girl!" But she recovered quickly and her smile was back as she took McNab's arm. "You did pull a fast one on all of us, didn't you? We could hardly believe it when we got your telegram. Imagine Ian McNab married!" Then she spoke to Catherine. "Are you hungry? I'm a good cook, as you can tell by looking at me." She led them inside. While Jenny was not fat, she was a square-built, big-breasted, wholesome woman in her mid-thirties with a high nervous voice. Still clinging to McNab's arm, Jenny said, "I have your favourite chicken stew cooking, Ian, and fresh-baked bread, which you should enjoy after all that awful bannock."

To Catherine's surprise, McNab responded with a light kiss to Jenny's flushed cheek and said, "Thank you Jenny."

For a moment, Jenny's face stilled; then she spoke again. "John is supposed to be coming home any time. It won't hurt to close the store early for once, I told him. Now Ian, how is your father?" As McNab and Jenny chattered on, Catherine stood quietly looking around. They were in a big comfortable parlour, with an overstuffed sofa and matching chairs grouped around a stone fireplace. Bright braided rugs and a bearskin warmed the gleaming floors. Jenny and Ian were still deep in conversation, so Catherine proceeded to inspect the many framed pictures on the walls. Most of them were tin-types of rigidly posed people gazing sternly out at the world. There was also a striking portrait of Jenny, beautifully etched; her round eyes and small neat mouth seemed so lifelike they almost seemed about to move. The artist had not signed it, but there was a tiny image of a crested bird in the lower corner. Moving on, she was confronted by a sepia-toned print of a glowering, bearded man in a clerical collar. He looked as though he had been born preaching hellfire and brimstone.

"Catherine, my dear, we have been neglecting you. But you know how it is with old friends." Jenny beamed fondly at the print Catherine had been examining. "That is my father, rest his soul, one of the first clergymen in these parts. He is greatly missed."

"I am sure," Catherine said, wondering if it was with sadness or a sense of relief. "My father is a clergyman too."

Jenny did not reply. She turned and looked across the room toward a noise at the door. A florid man, with a shock of silvery hair stuck to his forehead, hurried into the house. "Well, at last," she said, "John, where have you been?"

"Got held up, honey," he said, then looked at McNab, his face alight with pleasure. "How are you, you old son-of-a-moose? What a sly stunt you have pulled on us. Now, where is this lady who finally got you haltered and broke?"

As he peered around, Catherine came toward him, instinctively liking the paunchy little man. "Oh now, say no more," John cried, taking her hand in both of his. Then he took off his glasses and began to polish them. "Had to do that, they got all steamed up!" he added, bellowing with laughter at his own joke. "All those years we were out on the trail together, old Mac here never gave a sign of having a speck of romance in his soul. And now he has found himself a beautiful bride."

Jenny interrupted. "Catherine, you must want to wash up." She turned to a raven-haired girl setting the table at the end of the room. "MaryLou, take Mrs. McNab to the guest room."

The girl's voice was low and very soft. "Yes ma'am. This way please, Mrs. McNab."

***

Catherine was not tired, but her feet were. She followed MaryLou into the bedroom, then sat on the bed and began to unbutton her tight shoes. She stripped off her hose and wriggled her toes blissfully. MaryLou poured warm water from a jug into a basin; her glossy black braids fell to her slim waist. Although she wore a plain cotton dress, she was wearing a pair of beautiful beaded moccasins.

MaryLou pointed to a dressing table, "Soap, towels, the other things you will need are all there. A man came to the house with your bags. I will bring them."

When she was gone, Catherine took off the rest of her rumpled clothing with relief. She splashed water over herself then spread the lather over her damp face, around her shoulders, down her tanned arms, and over her white breasts. She was suddenly aware that the door was open. Jenny was standing there, with eyes scurrying over Catherine's body like busy grey mice. Catherine reached for a towel and covered herself. "I didn't hear you knock!"

"No? Well, you *were* splashing away. My, you are the skinny one, aren't you?" Jenny came into the room and set down Catherine's bag. "You'll need more flesh to get through a winter at Pounding Lake."

"No, I don't think so," Catherine retorted. "Ian seems to be quite happy with me the way I am."

Jenny's face blanched; her eyes hard as marbles. "Supper is ready as soon as you are," she said, and left the room.

Catherine stared after her. *So that's how it is,* she thought, *our Mrs. Appleton has quite a yen for Ian. Well, let her go to bed with him the next time; maybe she...* The thought came so unexpectedly and resentfully that she was shocked. Was there something wrong with her that she was beginning to resent the nightly ritual of marriage? After all, it was Ian's masculinity, his arrogant self-confidence, and the way he looked her over so appraisingly, that had sent tremors through her at their first meeting.

***

Catherine had accompanied her father to call on Jamie McNab during a brief illness. Ian McNab answered the door, invited them inside, then stared at her as if he had never before seen a woman. He then informed her father that Jamie's doctor decreed that his patient could only have one visitor at a time. Quite untruthfully, he had admitted to Catherine much later. He led her into the parlour and stared at her with that bemused expression again.

"Are you going to ask me to sit down, Mr. McNab?" He took her hand and led her to a chair.

"I think I'll do more than that, lass," he replied in all seriousness. "I'm going to marry you and take you home with me!"

"Mr. McNab!" she gasped, then began to laugh. "I never accept proposals from men I have known for less than fifteen minutes."

Ian glanced at the clock on the mantel. "Then it seems we have about ten minutes left, Miss Matthews, to discuss less important matters."

In addition to her amusement, Catherine was dazzled by this bold, virile man with the lilt of highland ancestors in his voice. That all seemed like years ago, now.

She suddenly realized that she should be dressing, not standing there lost in memories. She slipped into her remaining set of clean clothes and pinned up her hair. It was a funny memory, she told herself. Why then was there an ache in her throat and a silly tear slipping down her face? She had no idea.

***

Downstairs Catherine noticed that her husband had also washed and put on a clean shirt. John was pouring a shot of brandy for him.

McNab accepted it, giving his friend a quizzical look, "Bootlegged, is it, John?"

Appleton laughed and rolled his eyes at Jenny. "With her around? Not likely! No, you can get a permit for it by swearing it is for medicinal purposes only. Lord, don't you folks drink up north?"

"We do," grinned McNab. "Most of us make our own and the smuggled stuff gets in sometimes. No policemen in Pounding Lake, remember?"

Jenny looked at her husband reprovingly, "Bring your *medicine* to the table then. Ian and Catherine must be starving by this time." It was a bountiful meal. Chicken stew brimming with fresh garden vegetables, warm crusty bread to eat with it, and a Saskatoon berry pie for dessert. Afterwards, MaryLou cleared up the table while they sat talking. Jenny's eyes were, more often than not, intent on Ian over her knitting.

Accepting another glass of brandy from Appleton, McNab said, "I hear you had a nasty upset with Poundmaker at his reserve last month."

"Upset? Mac, it came within a hair of being an all-out shooting war. Our militia unit got called up when things got too hot for the police to handle alone. Touch and go it was for sure."

"That bad?" McNab lit his pipe. "You know, Poundmaker is all talk and bluff as I see him. Any other damn Indian as troublesome as he is would be locked up by now. Spoilt as hell he is, by the way everyone kowtows to him."

"He *is* Crowfoot's adopted son," Appleton reminded him. "The folks in Calgary, close to the old chief and all his followers, wouldn't be happy if Poundmaker got pushed around. Can't say I blame 'em."

"Mr. John," MaryLou's soft voice emerged from the background, "Chief Poundmaker and his father made peace for the first time between the Cree and Blackfoot people. You whites couldn't have settled here safely if that hadn't happened."

Jenny frowned at the interruption, but Appleton smiled with obvious affection. "True, MaryLou. But your 'peacemaker' scared the *hell*, pardon me ladies, out of most of us during that ruckus. He was carrying a war club with three steel blades embedded in it, and he's over six feet tall. None of us were crowding him, you bet!"

Catherine was listening wide-eyed. Her husband caught her look. "Catherine, we're talking about Plains Crees and Assiniboines. The Indians in Pounding Lake are Woods Crees, not at all like the ones John is talking about."

Giving her husband a pointed look, she replied, "I find this fascinating!"

"What started all this?" asked McNab, turning to Appleton again.

"Several of the local bands were holding a Rain Dance, against government orders. The policemen were sent to put a stop to it, and all *hell*, pardon me again ladies, broke loose."

MaryLou spoke up again. "The people had a reason to be angry, Mr. John. They were in the midst of a very sacred ceremony. Then the police came, shouting and tramping all over the place. How would you like our people to interrupt one of your church services that way?"

"Really, MaryLou," began Jenny, but her husband interrupted her.

"The girl's right. We can't take *everything* away from the Indians."

Annoyed, Jenny put aside her knitting, "Well, you two can sit here all night if you want, but I am sure *poor Catherine* is exhausted. MaryLou, get a lamp and see Mrs. McNab to her room."

Poor Catherine could not think of any polite way to contradict her hostess. Like a dismissed schoolgirl, she followed MaryLou to her room.

***

MaryLou put the lamp on a table and turned to leave, but Catherine stopped her. "You speak English so well; where did you learn to do that?"

Catherine thought that MaryLou was not going to answer, but after hesitation, she did. "A man who lived here in town paid for my brother and I to go to a school in Winnipeg."

Catherine smiled at her. "How kind. An education like that will give both of you a much better chance in life, I'm sure."

"I have this work here, if you want to call that a better life. Enough to eat, clothing and shelter. I can even send my starving relatives a little money for food."

There was a coldness in her voice, and Catherine responded to it at once. "I'm sorry. It was rude of me to pry and then comment about something I know nothing about. All this is so new to me. And after the talk downstairs, I am really wide awake."

"No, you're not. Mrs. Appleton says you are exhausted, so you are. Mrs. Appleton is *never* wrong." Catherine was startled, then she saw MaryLou's lips twitch and suddenly they both laughed. "I don't mind you asking really. When my brother Jay and I were very young, we were with the Big Bear band. Then Clear Sky, our father, went away, because he caught our mother with a Métis man. He was a Christian, and he didn't want to kill the man, and that is why he left us. Our mother was very sad and ashamed, and she waited a long time for him to come home again. Then she heard that he had died. The Métis man still cared for her, so he brought my mother and us to live in Battleford. But she died too, not long after that."

Catherine was shocked, not by the story, but what it might be costing MaryLou to tell it. "Don't feel bad, Mrs. McNab, all this was a long time ago. My stepfather worked for the Hudson's Bay Company for years, and had the money to send us to school in Winnipeg, instead of the Indian school here. A few years later, he died too, so we were sent back to Battleford. The Appletons took us in. Jay worked in the store, and I worked here in the house. Jay made quite a bit of extra money by painting and drawing pictures for white people. He did the one of Mrs. Appleton in the parlour."

"Oh, I saw it! It is a wonderful likeness. He is much too talented to be working in a store."

MaryLou looked amused. "He's not there now. Jay is not a *tame Indian* like me. He went back to Big Bear's band. But I see him when he comes into town to sell some paintings. He is in Battleford now. You will know him if you see him. He is very tall and handsome. All the girls in town, even the white ones, want to pose for him."

"If he looks like you, I am sure he is appealing," said Catherine.

MaryLou gave her a searching look. "You are very nice, young Mrs. McNab. Too nice I think for Pounding Lake." Then she was gone.

Catherine began to undress, pondering that enigmatic statement. She could hear a murmur of voices from the parlour, Ian and John and the shrill voice of Jenny. The woman had gotten rid of her very neatly, she thought, half-annoyed and half-amused, as she unpinned her long hair and began to brush it out. She was still sitting at the dressing table when Ian came into the room, his face flushed. He had a half-finished glass of brandy in his hand, which he set down very carefully. Then he came up behind her and looked at her reflected face in the mirror.

"My God, you are a beauty," he exclaimed. He put his hand on the lace straps of her chemise, pushed them off her shoulders and down her arms, baring her breasts. She was so surprised that she did not move. His voice sounded thick and different. Then, a little uncertainly, she lifted the chemise to cover herself again.

"Don't do that!" He slid his hands under her arms to cup her breasts, tearing one of the straps. She pushed his hands away and turned to face him angrily. He stared at her puzzled, then took a few steps backward and dropped into an armchair beside the bed. "I think old John's brandy has done me in." He leaned his head back and closed his eyes.

"Damn it, Ian, why can't you just be gentle with me? We are supposed to be people in love, not rutting animals!" A benign snore was her only reply. She sighed and turned away from him. The glass on the table caught her eye. She picked it up and the smell of it reminded her of over-ripe peaches. She took a sip, and though it burned her throat and made her gasp, the heat sliding down felt quite nice so nice that she drank the rest of it.

"That is a *damn*, excuse me ladies, a very *good* drink." Catherine whispered, then took off the rest of her clothes. She donned her nightgown, turned the lamp low, and slipped into bed. Relaxed and comfortable, she looked at her husband sleeping awkwardly in the chair, his long legs stretched out in front of him. "We will have to get us some of this brandy. Goodnight Ian."

CHAPTER THREE

Catherine was ironing the clothes she had washed and hung out that morning. MaryLou insisted on helping her while Jenny took her early afternoon "siesta", as she called it. McNab was at the livery stable, checking out his livestock and wagons.

The two women were sweltering as the fire in the cook stove was needed to warm the flatirons they were using. MaryLou held up a lacy chemise. "The strap on this one has been torn somehow. Shall I mend it for you?"

"I yes, please if you don't mind. I caught it on ... something." Catherine knew she sounded silly, and the girl gave her a quizzical look before going for her sewing kit. Since talking last night, they were more at ease with one another, although they shared tacit agreement for the need to be formal and polite when Jenny was nearby.

"Oh, let's go out to the pump for some cold water," Catherine gasped as she finished her husband's last shirt. MaryLou got two glasses and headed out for the water, as Catherine replaced the flatirons on the stove.

The women sat on the back steps, enjoying a cooling breeze, bird songs, and the spicy scent of flowers wafting in from the garden. Beyond that were rows of flourishing vegetables, and then the stable where John Appleton kept his stylish carriage.

Suddenly the peaceful scene was disrupted. A magnificent bay stallion cantered down the driveway, and then stopped. A man dropped silently to the ground. He tied the reins to a hitching post, and strode over to where they were sitting. He moved with effortless grace. She knew at once who he was from MaryLou's brief description, and he looked like his younger sister, very tall and handsome. His unbraided, raven-black hair was held in place by a colourful headband. He wore a red cotton shirt over deerskin leggings, the shirt pulled in at the waist by a leather belt. His high-boned features were dominated by fierce, wide-set, black eyes. As he bent down to greet his delighted sister, he smiled. It altered him from arrogant and almost surly-looking into a much more likeable young man.

He said something in Cree, and MaryLou corrected him immediately. "My brother, this lady with me cannot understand you. You will speak English, please." Jay Clear Sky had been so intent on MaryLou that he seemed unaware of Catherine. For the first time, he looked at her, and she felt an odd sensation as his piercing eyes locked on hers, cool and searching. She took a deep breath, trying to shake off the impact. He seemed as surprised as she was. Neither of them spoke, but just stared at one another.

"Jay! Remember your manners! This is Mrs. Ian McNab. She and her husband are resting here before going on to Pounding Lake."

Clear Sky looked confused. *"You* are McNab's wife?" His speech was as precise as MaryLou's, although a bit more accented and musical. "The word has gone around town about you. I see the talk is true." After this enigmatic statement, he turned back to his sister.

"I am here because I heard you had some trouble on the street the other night, with the man Sol Lemaire."

"You hear a lot of things! Yes, I did, but it was nothing I could not handle. I scratched his face and got my knee between his legs. Hard. He had been drinking."

"He has more than a scratched face and sore crotch now. But what were you doing out on the street, at night and alone?"

"Mr. John had to work late. Mrs. Appleton asked me to take supper over to him."

"She should know better than that! And so I'll tell Mr. John. Look, I traded him a painting for this." He reached into his shirt and took out a package.

"This handgun is small but good at close range, and there are bullets for it. The next man may not be as drunk as Lemaire. And use it if you need to!"

Catherine blanched at this ominous warning, but MaryLou nodded. "I will carry it at night. This town is not as safe as it used to be, despite all the policemen."

"Watch out for some of them too," he said. "I can't always be here to protect you myself. Big Bear has sent for me. He and Poundmaker are going to a chief's conference at Duck Lake. They want me with them as an interpreter. They don't trust the government ones."

Just then, Jenny arrived at the door, "Whatever are you doing out there, MaryLou? It's tea time!"

MaryLou retreated to the kitchen. Catherine stood up. She and Clear Sky were staring at each other again. She became aware of his obvious masculinity, and it unsettled her. This young man, albeit handsome and well-spoken, was an *Indian* she reminded herself. She had learned enough about customs in the northwest to realize that just standing there with him would be considered highly improper. Perhaps he read her thought.

As Clear Sky turned to leave, he said, "You be careful too, Mrs. McNab. You are safer alone than a girl of our people would be, but maybe not much."

***

Several minutes later, Corporal Peter Gray of the North West Mounted Police, smoothed his brass-buttoned scarlet tunic and checked his gleaming leather boots for dust. Finding none, he knocked at the door of the Appleton house. MaryLou answered and fixed him with that stoic look she reserved for policemen.

Gray's darkly tanned face and vivid blue eyes offered a friendly expression, but MaryLou was unimpressed.

"Yes?"

"Mr. Ian McNab, please."

"He is not here."

"Is Mrs. McNab in then?" he asked.

Reluctantly, she opened the door. "Yes, come in." The corporal removed his hat and stood erect in the dim room, trying to adjust his eyes from the outside glare. He was nursing a headache from playing poker in the barracks nearly all night. Then he forgot his headache. The policeman on postal service had told him the new Mrs. McNab was a looker, but he had not expected anyone like the young woman now approaching him. She smiled, and he almost forgot why he was there. Catherine held out her slim hand, and he was not sure if he should take it or bow over it. For a wild moment, he felt like kissing it gallantly. Then sanity returned, and he shook it instead.

"I am Catherine McNab," she said, when he did not speak. "You are...?"

"Excuse me, ma'am. Corporal Gray. I have a message for Mr. McNab about his return to Pounding Lake."

"He is at Peterson's livery stable, Corporal. May I pass the message along to him?" Her softly modulated voice suggested at least a middle-class background, perhaps private schooling. Coming from that same background himself, he recognized it immediately.

Before he had a chance to answer, Jenny interjected from a chair by the fireplace. "My stars, Peter, stop your staring! Come in and sit down, we are just having tea." He followed Catherine across the room obediently, thinking that Jenny Appleton was not in one of her better moods today. He sat down and accepted tea from MaryLou.

"Mrs. McNab, we have some men going out to relieve the Fort Pitt detachment this week. Superintendent Cooke would like you and Mr. McNab, of course, to travel that far with us. Reverend Wilson from Camas Lake plans to do the same. The Indians seem to have settled down again after the recent trouble, but it is best to be careful for a while."

"Yes, I am sure Ian will agree to that," she said and smiled.

"Don't be too sure," offered Jenny. "Ian is very independent."

"I can speak for my husband, thank you Jenny." Jenny's face reddened and her knitting needles clacked noisily.

Good for her, Peter thought before breaking the awkward silence. "Actually, I have two messages. Superintendent and Mrs. Cooke would like to meet you before you leave Battleford, Mrs. McNab. They hope that you and your husband, along with Mr. and Mrs. Appleton, might like to join them after the dinner hour, tomorrow evening."

Jenny dropped her knitting, suddenly looking much happier. She answered before Catherine. "Of course, Peter. Tomorrow night, did you say?" Her voice had lost its sharp edge, and Peter smiled to himself. The ranking police officers were the cream of society in the northwest, and such an invitation amounted to a social coup. But Mrs. McNab seemed to have no idea that it was anything out of the ordinary.

"Will you be there too, Corporal?" Catherine asked.

"Oh, no ma'am," he answered, really amused now. He did not look at Mrs. Appleton, but he could imagine the scandalized expression on her face. "But I will be with the men going to Fort Pitt. I will have the pleasure of seeing you again, if you do come along with us." Then he stood up. He was on duty, and afternoon tea with two married ladies was not his idea of a good time. Catherine followed him to the door. He looked back as he untied his horse from the post. She waved, and he gave her a friendly grin and a snappy salute. Then he wondered what on earth a girl like her would think of life in Pounding Lake.

***

Back in the house, Jenny look flustered. "Really Catherine, I know you are new out here, but corporals do *not* hobnob with senior officers!"

"I'm sorry, Jenny. I had no idea that social distinctions were so rigid in the northwest."

"Well, they are," snapped Jenny. "But how *could* you know? Ian never seems to tell you anything. As for Peter, he probably will be an officer some day. I understand he comes from a prominent Ottawa family." Catherine sat down, and Jenny resumed her knitting. "You certainly dazzled him! I suppose you must have the same effect on Ian, though how you managed to get him to propose is beyond me. He's hardly the marrying kind."

Catherine laughed at that. "I didn't *manage* it, Jenny. One of the first things he said to me after we met was that he was going to marry me. I thought he was crazy!"

Jenny stared at her knitting. "I think you're right. He must be, to take a girl like you to Pounding Lake. It is totally isolated and surrounded by Indian reserves."

"He did tell me about that. But I agreed to make it my home too, and I don't intend to give him cause to regret our marriage."

Jenny sighed. "I still can't imagine him as a married man. I first met Ian and John when I was fifteen, coming here on a wagon train from Winnipeg. They were partners, taking trade goods north, and agreed to guide and hunt for us. They got us to good grass and water every night and provided all the meat we needed. You know how young girls are. I thought they were so romantic and dashing in their fringed buckskin coats, fancy boots, and cowboy hats. They used to tease me, and I enjoyed that. My father was a good man, but stern and ... unsmiling." Catherine looked up at the tintype of him, and the departed man glared back malevolently.

"Ian and John often helped us," continued Jenny, "when our teams or wagons broke down. After we got to Battleford, they used to come and visit us. Then John built the store here, and they ended their partnership. Ian was not ready to settle down yet. I married John soon after that." Her last sentence came out flat.

Instead of the man you really wanted, thought Catherine. Later, as she was helping MaryLou with the tea dishes, Catherine told her about the invitation to the fort.

"I heard, Mrs. McNab," she answered. "I know most of what goes on around here."

"I guess you do, but I wish you would call me Catherine."

MaryLou looked pleased but shook her head. "That would be even worse than Corporal Gray *hobnobbing with officers*," she replied in a shrill voice, perfectly imitating Jenny. Both women giggled at that.

***

That evening, as they were dressing, Catherine asked her husband, "Did you ever think about marrying Jenny yourself, Ian?"

He was struggling with the buttons on his starched shirt. "I hate these things," he grumbled. "How John can wear one every day ... what did you say? That's a funny question."

"I know it is," she admitted. "But tell me, did you?"

He looked uncomfortable. "No, I did not; it was John all along who was taken with her. A much better choice for her than I would have been. I told her it would be a hell of a life for a woman out on the trail with me, and I wasn't about to stay in one place. Not back then."

"You told her that? Why?" Ian gave up the battle with his shirt, and sat down on the chair beside the bed. Catherine went to him and did up the top two buttons.

He was frowning. "I didn't mean to say that, but since I did ... I might have led her on without meaning to, or knowing it at the time. But she took my liking her for more than it was, and I needed to set her straight. Not long afterwards, she got smart and married John. But that was years ago. It's all forgotten now."

"And now you are married to me," said Catherine, thinking that Ian really believed what he was saying. Men were strange, obtuse creatures. She drew a lace collar around her neck and fastened it with a diamond and sapphire pin, a gift from her wealthy aunt on her eighteenth birthday. The flashing sapphires were deep blue the same colour as the silk dress she was wearing. In this light, her eyes held the rich fire of the gems.

McNab finished knotting his tie and looked at her. "Yes, I'm married to you, lass. And you'll do me proud tonight."

THE AMULET

***

Catherine enjoyed the drive through town and over the bridge in the Appleton's stylish carriage. It was still daylight and the view from that vantage point was magnificent. In the sweeping valley of the two rivers, the waters were turned to liquid gold by the setting sun. Yet overhead, the sky was a soft blend of violet and blue, with the first stars twinkling. The ponderous gates of the fort opened and they passed through the palisaded walls. She looked around curiously at the rows of buildings, the immaculate grounds, and the smartly uniformed policemen. They stopped in front of a large house, where Superintendent Cooke was waiting to greet them.

Cecil Cooke was a balding man with cool, cobalt-blue eyes, a jutting prow of a nose, and a waxed, fierce-looking white moustache. But when he greeted Catherine, his frosty expression was warmed by a smile. "We have a daughter about your age back in England, and a son at Sandhurst Military College. You make me realize how much we miss them." Laura Cooke was also waiting for them at the threshold. She took Catherine's arm and led her into the parlour. She was a handsome woman of about forty, with a genuine smile, and a noticeable English accent. She took Catherine at once to meet the other officer in the room.

"David, meet the lovely bride we have all been hearing about. Mrs. McNab, this is Inspector Kingsley, in charge of the detachment at Fort Pitt." Kingsley was not at all like his commanding officer. He had a diffident, almost shy manner, and he looked too thin for his uniform. There were deep furrows creasing his narrow aristocratic face, and his skin had a yellowish tinge. His dark hair was salt-and-pepper streaked, but it was his eyes that caught Catherine's attention. They looked like melted chocolate, not the cool, hard eyes of a military man.

"So pleased to meet you, Mrs. McNab. As Laura said, we have all heard about you. Lovely ladies are not all that common in this country, particularly in that part of it where you are going."

"How kind of you, Inspector," she replied, noticing that his eyes revealed a flash of she was not sure what. *Concern? Anger?* He stroked his sparse moustache and changed the topic.

Catherine looked around curiously. The room was cluttered with memorabilia. The obligatory print of Queen Victoria stared grumpily from over the fireplace. A tiger skin, complete with mounted head, was on the floor in front of it, looking only slightly surlier than Her Majesty. In another corner, sets of engraved brass bells were strung on silken ropes. She looked at some photographs: Mrs. Cooke in a howdah on the back of an elephant, and a much younger Cecil Cooke with a polo mallet in hand, astride a splendid white horse.

"Quite the beauty that one," said Cooke, joining her and looking fondly at the horse. "I got him from the King's stud in Njed, Arabia. Stamina, heart, speed ... he had them all." Catherine, who loved horses and rode quite well, looked more closely.

"How elegant he is! That small head and arched tail!"

"Yes, typical of Arabs. Notice the concave face. It's called the "dish" or "jibbah". I see traces of it in some of the mustangs, throwbacks to the Arabs brought to America by the Spaniards. I've tried to get one ever since coming here, but the Indians won't part with the best ones."

Catherine thought momentarily of Clear Sky's beautiful bay stallion. "You were in India, of course. It sounds so exotic. Were you there for long?"

"For several years. Seventeenth Cavalry Bengal Lancers, as was Inspector Kingsley. It is exotic, as you say. Colourful, mysterious, and teeming with humanity, most of whom are, sad to say, incredibly destitute by our standards."

"Speaking of India," said David Kingsley, smiling at Catherine. "It was quite a change for us to come to Canada. It has a much healthier climate despite the cold winters. This yellow skin of mine doesn't indicate a Chinese ancestor. I am just back from sick leave after a recurrence of malaria—my less romantic souvenir of India," he said, looking at her with undisguised admiration.

***

A bit later in the evening, Catherine noticed her husband and Cecil Cooke standing together. McNab's face wore that stony look indicating that he was annoyed, and the policeman's eyes were icy. Neither man raised their voice, but she could hear them.

"I have been in this country longer than you have," said McNab, "and feel I can assess the possible danger as well as anyone. I must go to Pounding Lake to attend to business. And I did not bring her all this way to abandon her here in Battleford for the winter."

"Mr. McNab," said Cooke, "I have access to confidential reports intended for the Indian Department, as well as constant contact with my own men in the field. None of them are hysterics, or prone to exaggeration. My advice to you is sincere, but it is up to you, of course, to accept or reject it as you see fit."

"What do you have to say, Kingsley," demanded McNab, "more of the same?"

"I would, if I thought it would serve any useful purpose to argue with you. Since it would be futile, I propose this. You are well-known and respected in the northwest. If men like you would impress upon the politicians to treat the Indians more humanely, especially regarding the food-rationing system, we may yet avoid serious trouble. But, if the policies remain as they are, we are in for very serious trouble. One thing in our favour though is that both Fort Pitt and Pounding Lake are a long way west of the rebellious Métis settlements."

After refreshments, it was time to leave. Thanking the Cookes for the pleasant evening, both couples decamped to the waiting carriage. Superintendent Cooke and his wife stood in their doorway waving goodbye as the carriage left the fort.

"It didn't work, Laura," said Cecil Cooke grimly. "He's determined to take her there. And I sense there's something very wrong behind the peaceful façade of Pounding Lake."

CHAPTER FOUR

In a chilly pre-dawn mist, McNab led his wagons full of trade goods and a new buckboard across the bridge and up to the fort. Old Pascal was driving the buckboard, while Gabe Berthier was teamster for the wagon. McNab had replaced the oxen with faster teams of horses.

Catherine was happy to be with the old man again, and to see the buckboard, equipped with comfortable padded seats. But she noticed that all McNab's drivers had rifles handy, in slings beside their seats. They seemed to be even more wary now than on the trail to Battleford.

The night before, while helping Catherine to repack, MaryLou handed her a letter. "Give this to the Indian Agent's wife in Pounding Lake. She's my cousin, but we're more like sisters. It might help you to get to know Melissa. You may not be able to make friends with her though; she has little to do with whites."

"But isn't the agent, Mr. Burr, a white man?" asked Catherine.

"Jim Burr? Yes, he's white, maybe that's why she doesn't like them! Oh, they had a great flaming love affair when they first met. He is a charming man, as you will see, and she is a beauty. But it takes more than that to be happy together. I think she is as lonely with him as I am here. But I said some nice things about you in the letter, so she might unbend a bit. She told me once that there are some odd people in Pounding Lake, some nice, some not so nice."

Catherine's thoughts were interrupted when a wagon pulled up beside them. She could hear a baby wailing peevishly.

"That's the Wilsons, heading for Camas Lake," Pascal said. A woman in the wagon leaned out to wave at them, and they waved back. "Her name is Emma. Nice lady. The reverend though, only thing he ever enjoys is funerals."

Just then, the fort gates rumbled open and police carts appeared, followed by a troop of mounted, red-coated riders who divided into two groups, one ahead of the lined-up wagons, and one behind.

Pascal chuckled. "A reg'ler parade we are, Mrs. Mac. I see they got their guns handy, too."

John Appleton, who had ridden out to see them off, pulled his horse up beside them. He handed Catherine a parcel. "Jenny sent this to eat along the way." Noticing the teamster, he added. "Lebret! Are you still around raising hell, pardon me Catherine, all over the Saskatchewan?"

Pascal assumed an innocent look. "Sure. But I slowed down some when the boss gave me Mrs. Mac here, to see to."

John did not smile. "You'll do that, won't you, Pascal?"

"You can bet on it." Then Pascal's face went blank as McNab rode up.

John turned to his friend. "I almost wish I was going with you."

"I wish you were too. It's been a long time."

The first group of policemen started to move out. The two men shook hands. McNab spurred his horse into position behind the Wilsons, and beckoned to Pascal, who released the buckboard's brakes and flapped the reins.

***

It was hot when they stopped for the noon break. Catherine went into the bushes to relieve herself, happy to be on her feet again. They were moving too quickly for her to walk for intervals, as she had done on the trail to Battleford. When she returned to the buckboard, Emma Wilson was there with her baby in her arms. She was an apple-cheeked woman with china-blue eyes, and wisps of auburn hair that had escaped from her bonnet. She brushed impatiently at them as she greeted Catherine.

"Hello, Mrs. McNab. Welcome to the wild west! What do you think of it so far?"

Catherine looked at the tree-clad hills rolling like great sea waves to the north, then back to the grassland sloping down on the south side of the valley. "It is so wild and big and empty. Awe-inspiring. I now understand why Ian was so anxious to get back."

"It is," Emma agreed. "And it can be cruel and savage too. I'll ask you that question again when you've spent a winter here."

McNab started a fire to heat water for their tea. When Catherine saw how much food Jenny had packed for them, she invited Emma and her family to share it with them. However, as Emma went back to gather her brood, McNab frowned at Catherine.

"Emma and the children are fine, but Charles Wilson is as useless a man as I ever met. I could have done without his company."

The Methodist clergyman, dressed in a black suit and tall hat, looked amazingly like the late American president, Abraham Lincoln, but there was no hint of humour in his long melancholy face. Emma was still carrying her baby and holding one of her boy's hands, while she called to the other one. The reverend ignored them.

"Well, McNab," he said, "back to work, I see. Mrs. McNab, I hope you'll be able to persuade your husband to attend my services more often than he has in the past."

"It's twenty miles each way," McNab reminded him.

After eating, McNab doused the fire with the remaining tea. Emma opened her blouse to nurse her baby. Shocked, because she had never seen a woman do that in such a public way, Catherine gathered the dishes and cutlery and went to the creek to wash them. Reverend Wilson sat silently, lost in some ponderous thoughts of his own, although everyone else was busy. Teamsters and policemen watered and grained their horses. Inspector Kingsley smiled at Catherine as he rode by, followed by Corporal Gray, fair-haired and taller than most of his men. McNab watched the policemen narrowly.

"What I would like to know," McNab muttered on Catherine's return, "is why they are so edgy? I know duty at Fort Pitt isn't relished. No social life, a lot of monotony, and there's a hell of a lot of Indians out there for twenty-five men to keep tabs on. Especially the ones under Big Bear. But these men are nervous. No laughing or fooling around. That corporal you met Gray, is it? he's usually an easy-going lad, but he's cracking the whip today. Maybe they know something we don't."

"Like what, Ian!?"

"Like maybe the damn Big Bears are somewhere in the area. There's a lot of old die-hard warriors with him. They were the last band in the northwest to take treaty. And then only because they were starving and needed to have government rations to stay alive. Mind you," he added, seeing Catherine's concern, "they don't come around Pounding Lake. They're Plains Indians, horsemen and buffalo hunters, and they get spooked by woods and hills like we have at Pounding Lake. The Indian Agency is located there, but when Jim Burr has to deal with them, he goes to Fort Pitt."

***

A few hours later, the wagons halted abruptly. Pascal swore under this breath, reached for his rifle then stood up, shading his eyes with his free hand to see what was ahead. "We got company," he said, "Indians, coming this way. No, Mrs. Mac, you stay sitting." The pitch of his voice changed. "Not Big Bears though; it's Chief Poundmaker, his brother Yellow Blanket, and their war leader, Fine Day. Don't know the others ... there's one Big Bear; see the young one in the red shirt? Jay Clear Sky. Interpreter, he is."

The men came up out of the river valley at a leisurely pace. The policemen fanned out along the south side of the wagons, facing them. Inspector Kingsley and Corporal Gray moved out ahead of the other men. The one pointed out as Poundmaker surprised Catherine. Extremely tall, he was younger than she had imagined, about her husband's age. His wide and handsome face was framed by long braids bound by copper wire. He did not look fierce, his full lips affirmed a man who smiled easily. Yellow Blanket resembled him, but he was older and his expression was cold and foreboding.

Jay Clear Sky looked as he had in Battleford, except for the streaks of red paint across his cheekbones. He rode beside Poundmaker, listening to the chief, nodding from time to time. Again, Catherine admired his beautiful stallion. He left the other men behind and came forward to greet Kingsley.

"*Tanse*, Inspector. You are heading for Fort Pitt?"

"*Tanse*, Clear Sky. We are. I assume this is not an accidental meeting?"

The young Cree smiled, and Catherine was struck again by the way it transformed his otherwise ferocious face. "We did not go out of our way to meet you, but we did not avoid you either."

"I see. Now, tell me what you are doing off your reserve."

"It is no secret. The chiefs of all the Cree bands are going to Duck Lake for a conference."

"For what purpose?"

"You should know that, Inspector. Last winter, many children and old people in the bands died of exposure and starvation. Do you expect us to sit quietly and let that happen again? The conference will decide how we can change things."

"I know you have had a hard time," responded Kingsley. "But try to be patient a little longer. The police, missionaries, and prominent citizens are trying to get the government to increase your rations."

"The government," said Clear Sky, "has no use for us now that they have our land. We are not stupid; we know that. But we also know that the police do not make such decisions. Fat men in fine offices in Ottawa do. So Chief Poundmaker has asked me to say that you can put your guns away. No one will trouble you between here and Fort Pitt." There was arrogance in his voice and posture, as his eyes raked the line of policemen and wagons. Just for a moment, his piercing eyes stopped and held on Catherine. He smirked. "Not this time, anyway." As soon as he finished speaking, the men moved off, heading east.

"That insolent young bastard could use a lesson in manners," McNab said to the inspector.

"Maybe," said Kingsley, "but since he was with Poundmaker, I'll wager Big Bear and his war chief, Wandering Spirit, are somewhere nearby, but didn't want to talk to us."

McNab was still scowling. "Do you think the rest of the way is open?"

"Yes. Poundmaker always talks straight. We will stay on the alert, of course, but I'm a bit happier now."

***

An hour before sunset, they stopped by another small creek. After McNab raised their tent, he went to help the teamsters picket the horses. They had eaten, and were having a second cup of tea, when the Wilsons joined them. Their two boys were laughing, frisking and shouting at one another, but Emma looked tired as she sat beside Catherine.

"Any idea where we are?" Reverend Wilson asked McNab.

"I have. This is an old trail, and I have used it many times. We are past the last reserve, Little Pine, to the southeast. We'll make it into Fort Pitt about the same time we stopped here, day after next."

They were interrupted by the Wilsons' oldest boy, Danny, who came running to Catherine with a furry bundle in his arms. "Look, Mrs. Mac! You don't have a baby, so I found you a puppy!" She ran her hand gently over the tiny grey body. It looked half-dead. It lay inert in her lap, slowly blinking its sunken eyes.

"That is a wolf cub you have there," said McNab. "Lucky it isn't a bear cub, Danny, or we could be in big trouble. Give it here, Catherine, I'll get rid of it."

"No!" she snapped, as the boy howled in protest. "Let me see if I can bring it around. Danny, hand me that pot, we still have some stew left." The boy complied and she began to spoon some warm liquid into the animal's mouth. It swallowed feebly.

"Catherine, that is a damn wolf. It won't be cute and helpless for long, even if you do revive it."

"Well, it won't have grown much by morning," she retorted.

"See that you keep it out of the tent, then," he said, shaking his head, "It's probably crawling with fleas."

When the Wilsons had left, and McNab was in the tent, Catherine wrapped the cub in an old shawl and put it in the buckboard. She heard a small noise, and turned to find Emma Wilson.

"Catherine," she whispered, "you will think I'm crazy, but it is such a pathetic little thing." She handed her a cup. "This is what it needs, some of my milk. I have more than enough for the baby."

"Good Lord," said Catherine. "What would Ian say to this?"

"Don't you tell," Emma implored. "Charles would have a fit."

They shared a conspiratorial laugh. "You have my word," vowed Catherine, suddenly liking Emma very much. She put the tin cup on a stone near the fire to keep the milk warm. Twice during the night, she crept outside to spoon more milk into the pup. She was happy to find it still alive in the morning.

***

On the move again at sunrise, Kingsley beckoned to Corporal Gray and Sergeant William Porter, who rode out ahead of the other policemen. Porter was a stocky man with stiff military bearing, hiding a nurturing trait. The "mother hen", as the men called him, was usually expressionless, but now his eyes were twinkling.

"Are you going to share your joke with us, Sergeant Porter?" asked Kingsley.

"It's not a joke, sir, but it tickles my funny-bone. The new Missus McNab found a wolf cub somewhere, and insists on keeping it. McNab is hopping mad. Had quite a scrap about it, they did. And she's got spunk. She swore and stamped her foot, and damn, if he didn't back off."

"Why would he mind?" asked Peter Gray. "He didn't pay for it." All three men smiled, knowing McNab's reputation as a tightfisted Scot.

"Well, now that we are up to date on the morning gossip," said Kingsley, "I want to discuss another man with you: the Indian Agent in our territory. Jim Burr worries me. Superintendent Cooke did everything he could to get him transferred out, to no avail. I don't know him. Can either one of you tell me more about him?"

"I have met him, but I don't know him well," said Gray. "He is a big talker, I remember that, and was said to be a skirt-chaser at one time, but I've heard that he is now married to an Indian girl. A beauty they say, but that news surprised me. I got the distinct impression that he had no use for Indians at all."

"I know him," said the sergeant. "I was assigned to escort him for the treaty payments last year."

Kingsley looked impatient. "This is off the record, Sergeant Porter. I do need to know about him."

"Yes, sir. Well, he has the devil of a temper and is vain as a peacock. He is right sociable with his equals or superiors, but I wouldn't want to work for him. His hero is George Custer, so that shows you how Burr thinks. He admires a general who got himself and his whole command wiped out at the Little Big Horn. Not too bright but lots of nerve. I saw him insult Chief Big Bear one day for no reason. Can't stand the man, myself."

Kingsley looked bleak. "It makes no sense. They detach twenty-five men to keep a lid on Big Bear's outfit, yet leave a man like Burr in charge of them." The other two men glanced at one another. They agreed with Kingsley, but it was a lapse for an officer to criticize government policy, especially to his own men.

Kingsley caught the look and resumed formality. "The white men in Pounding Lake seem oblivious to the danger they could face if a rebellion breaks out. McNab is an example, too pig-headed to take advice. Unfortunately, they don't know all the facts, because they are still confidential. The Indian Department is trying to talk Big Bear into wintering at Pounding Lake on the promise of increased rations."

"Christ!" exploded Corporal Gray. Then he reddened. "Excuse me, sir."

"Certainly. My own reaction exactly. The idea is, if trouble does break out in the Métis settlements, Big Bear and his militants will be too far away to get into it. But now I need to put a detachment up there. I can only spare six men at the most, but I want you, Peter, in charge of it. There is a vacant house in the town you can appropriate for barracks and an office. The agency operates a sawmill, so you can get what lumber you need to adapt the house and stables."

"Yes sir! I can do that, but I'm going to need five very good men," countered Gray.

"Pick your own. You'll need them. Pounding Lake may be a very tough assignment."

***

Catherine was thrilled by the sheer grandeur of the country surrounding the old trading post. Fort Pitt was on the north bank of the river, dark and slow-moving in late summer, below a bluff covered with dense stands of pine and willow. There were few trees across the river; instead she saw sweeping, undulating terraces rising one above another until they blurred together into the hazy distance. The Hudson's Bay buildings dominated the settlement, which was not really a fort any more. Once it had been protected by bastions and palisaded walls, but they had crumbled and many of the old logs had been used for firewood.

As the column started down the bluff, people were seen waving eagerly up at them. Everyone waved back, and even the small cub on Catherine's lap raised his head. They were well down into the valley when the first people greeted them: two identical girls with flaming red hair and brilliant green eyes.

"Ellen and Connie MacKenzie," said Old Pascal. "Their pa is the Hudson's Bay trader here. Your man, he worked for him when he first came here." One of the girls climbed up on the seat beside Catherine, then leaned across her to kiss the cheek of the old teamster.

"We are *so* glad to see you," she cried. "No one has come through here for such a long time."

Pascal grinned at her. "Now, Miss Ellen, don't go wasting kisses on an old-timer like me. Go kiss some policeman."

"Well, even you look good today," she retorted, "So you can tell how lonely we are." Then she turned to Catherine. "Who are you?"

"Catherine, Ian McNab's wife. We were married about a month ago."

Her eyes bugged wide. "McNab? Married? My Lord! Hey Connie," she shouted, "Mac's got married, of all things!"

Connie, coming alongside the buckboard, looked just as surprised. McNab was riding just ahead of Peter Gray, and she flashed him a taunting grin. "Finally wearing the old ball and chain, eh? About time. Hello, Peter, it's really good to see you."

Peter gave her a wounded look. "How come that old mule-skinner gets all the kisses around here?"

"We'll take care of you later," Ellen warned him. "Since slippery Mac here is out of the running, you're the next one on our list."

The column came to a final halt and was swarmed by the Fort Pitt people calling greetings and shaking hands. The next thing Catherine knew, she was in a big kitchen full of the smells of good food, still holding the cub. She apologized for bringing it inside, but Leslie MacKenzie, an older version of her twin hellions, waved it off.

"Don't fret about that, we're used to strange pets here." She pointed. A crow was perched on the back of a chair, shaking his feathers at the new-comers. "Meet Lucifer. Our daughter Ellen found him several years ago with a broken wing. He's fine now, goes south every winter but come spring and he's right back again. Just walks in whenever he feels like it." While Leslie MacKenzie was talking, she set the table and checked the contents of the pots on the stove. Suddenly she stopped bustling and looked directly at Catherine. "You keep your little wolf, my dear. You can always use another friend in this part of the country."

CHAPTER FIVE

They had a two-day stopover in Fort Pitt. A wagon had a cracked axle to be replaced, and McNab wanted to catch up on the local news with the MacKenzies. Leslie and George were delighted to have the company, and the twins kept Catherine busy. They took her riding and were pleasantly surprised to see that she could handle a horse as well as they could.

"My aunt owns horses," she explained at the supper table. "I spent my summers as a child riding at her stables."

"Mac, you must get her a horse," declared Connie.

"No, I don't plan on that," he said. Everyone stopped eating and stared at him. "Buying and keeping a saddle horse just for pleasure seems too extravagant to me." Catherine could feel her face flushing in the awkward silence that followed.

George, a shaggy bear of a man, intervened. "Well, quite apart from the pleasure involved and women have little enough of that out here it makes sense for them to ride. And to know how to use a gun too, way things are these days. My ladies are good shots; I see to that." McNab did not answer him. After supper, Peter Gray came calling. Catherine had not seen him out of uniform before. Although he looked younger, he seemed weary.

"It's been a busy day," Peter told them. "Have you heard yet that I've been assigned to Pounding Lake for the winter?"

"Oh, no!" protested Ellen, "Whatever for?"

"I just follow orders, honey, you know that. I'm taking five men with me. We've been all day packing our gear and getting ready."

"Six policemen in Pounding Lake?" McNab was stunned. "When we've never had one before? I don't see the need for this at all."

"And how am I going to get you to propose to me," pouted Ellen, "if you're going to be away all winter?"

"Why pick on me all the time? There are at least a dozen other fellows in the detachment trying to get your attention."

"Well," Ellen replied, counting on her fingers, "One, you're a corporal and make more money, two, you are the best-looking one, and three, you are the only one I have to chase; the rest of them chase me."

Peter feigned injury, as the rest laughed. "I noticed my dollar a day topped that list. You might have mentioned my good looks first."

"I'm a true Scot, Peter. I have also considered that you get a kit and clothing along with all that money."

"There could be a problem there. I could share my drawers and undershirts, and my four pairs of socks, but I only get one set of braces, one shaving kit, one plate and cup…"

"And one *palliasse*," interrupted Ellen.

"Yes," replied Peter, "that too. But maybe they have double ones. I might consider your proposal if they do."

Everyone smiled at that but Catherine. "What on earth is a … *palliasse?*"

"That, my dear," replied Ellen, "is a piece of ticking folded lengthwise. It's sewn on the sides and one end, leaving the other end open for stuffing with straw, dried grass, or whatever else is available. It provides an easily maintained and portable if dreadfully uncomfortable mattress for barracks or patrol duty."

"A mattress? Oh, Ellen, really!" Catherine's face flushed, and they all laughed again.

***

But there was no merriment on the morning they left Fort Pitt. The six policemen looked glum, Reverend Wilson looked more cranky than usual, and the twins were woebegone. Ellen and Connie rode with the wagons until they reached the top of the great valley, where they waved goodbye. Catherine felt a sense of loss. She was going to miss them.

Peter Gray stayed with the twins briefly for a private farewell. Catching up, he pulled even with the buckboard and spoke to Catherine. "You know, I think I'll have to marry that Ellen, Mrs. McNab. She's wearing me down!"

"You are as willing a victim as I ever saw," she told him. "And please, call me Catherine." She had the cub on her lap again. He was lying on his back, pawing at her teasing fingers. She looked up at him. "You would be a very lucky man to marry Ellen. Perhaps you should speak up for her soon, if you are serious. I think every young man in the fort is smitten with her or Connie."

"You should hear what they are saying about you!" he said in reply. "You bowled them all over, even Inspector Kingsley. But I *have* spoken for Ellen. We've talked about getting married at Christmas. I've been in the force long enough that getting permission won't be a problem, but this posting has delayed that. I wouldn't take her to Pounding Lake."

"Why not?" she asked. "Peter, what is it about that place?"

He silently cursed his slip of the tongue. It was not yet certain that Big Bear's band would consent to spend the winter there, and there was no point in upsetting the townspeople unless they did. Pascal listened too. Whatever the constable said was bound to go the rounds in the town. Peter answered carefully. "I suppose people think about the isolation. It isn't on a main trading trail like Fort Pitt. In deep winter, hardly anyone comes or goes. And you'll be the lone white woman there.

"No, she won't," said Pascal. "Didn't you hear in Pitt? They've got a new farm instructor, Bert Simmons. Married. His wife's a nice lady, they say."

"Good!" replied Peter. "At least Judd Bolton's out of there."

"Just in time, too, else you might have had a murder case on your hands! He was asking for it, that shit!"

Trying to change the subject, Gray said, "One reason I won't take Ellen there is that I don't relish sharing a honeymoon with five other men. But it is a pretty place. I was there last year, chasing a horse thief."

"Didn't catch him either, did you?" cackled Pascal.

"Not that one," he admitted. "Maybe I should have looked in your stable?" Gray cued his horse lightly with his spurs, and moved up the line to rejoin his men. Riding ahead of the buckboard, McNab shot a belligerent look Gray's way as he passed.

Pascal alerted when he saw it. "Mrs. Mac," he said, "remember that bay stallion Clear Sky was riding? Best horse in these parts it is. The Cheyenne Stallion. It's got some fancy Indian name, doesn't come to mind. Clear Sky stole it from a Cheyenne chief back when them things was fun instead of a crime. Seems that partic'lar chief had captured it from a band of wild horses. I bet he'd like to get ahold of Clear Sky some day! You never saw wild horses, I guess. It's some sight, old boss mare out in front, stallion driving them from behind. Like a storm they are, running before the wind, manes and tails flying, hooves drumming like thunder. Old stallion thumping into them, biting, kicking, making the mares leave the foals if he has to. Stallions will fight hard and cruel, and even kill each other to keep their mares. And the Lord help any young upstart looking like he wants one! And the older and stronger they are, the more watchful and easier to rile the stallions get. Now you take bears. They're different again, loners they are..."

He went on talking, but Catherine, having grasped the old man's meaning, was lost in her own thoughts. She looked ahead at her husband, so athletic in the saddle ... and so hard-eyed and remote. She still did not know him, and she wondered if she ever would. She looked at the wedding ring on her finger, a circle of diamonds, and suddenly she had a terrible pang of loneliness. She wanted her mother. She wanted to go home, to warmth and laughter. Her eyes were stinging with unshed tears. Pascal stopped talking about bears, and reached over to pat her hand. It was such a kind gesture and so unexpected that the tears did spill over and she turned away, so that he would not see them. But he did.

"It'll be all right," Pascal said quietly. "It's just that it's all so new and strange here, and you're a young'un too. You'll do all right. You just need a bit of time, is all."

She wiped quickly at her eyes. "Will you tell me more about Pounding Lake, please Pascal?"

"Well now, it's pretty, like Corporal Gray said, hills all around "

"No, I don't mean that. What about the people ... that man Bolton you were talking about?"

"*Him*? Well, don't go letting on I told you. No good he was, always after the Indian women, knowing how hungry they and their kids was, trying to buy them with food. Made plenty of bad feelings. Came close to taking a shot at him more than once, I did."

"You really mean that?"

"Sure, the worst kind of trouble that is. All we needed, with the local priest a bit funny up here." He tapped his forehead. "Though my sister, Marie Scott, says it is just bad nerves. *Merde!* I say to that. Then Jim Burr, is he a snake in a sack! You get some like that, all locked in close. In a long winter, it can get bad. Folks get mad easy and quick, do mean things, go looking for trouble." He paused, trying to find the right words. "See, like a bear does in deep cold, Indians and us Métis, we slow down, curl up, and wait it out. But whites can't seem to do that. Your man is better than most; he don't mix much anyway, and he's got you now. The way I see it, too many white men without women in that little place, and..." His voice trailed off as he looked at the policemen. He sighed. "And now we got us six more of 'em."

***

It was noon when they got to Camas Lake: a tiny, bleak settlement with log cabins scattered haphazardly around two churches one Catholic, and the other, Pascal told her, Methodist. Two houses were more substantial than the others: the Wilson home and one occupied by the local farm instructor, Tom Bradley. South of the village, the lake was as uninviting as the town, edged with rank weeds and green scum on the shoreline. They were soon slapping at hordes of voracious mosquitoes.

McNab rode up beside Pascal. "Laronde wants to get back to Fort Pitt; he's got word one of his children is sick. I'll pay him off, and you take over his wagon. Keep on going with the police detachment. I'll take over the buckboard, and we'll stop off for a while with the Wilsons."

Pascal shrugged, hopped down from the wagon, and walked back to Laronde's. McNab tied his horse to the buckboard.

"Why are we going to stop with the Wilsons?" Catherine asked, as her husband climbed into the driver's seat.

"They invited us to lunch. And I want you to myself for a while, instead of sharing you with a crowd of policemen and half-breeds." His voice was brusque. Catherine felt tears stinging her eyes again. *I'm having my period,* she told herself. *I'm never this weepy.* McNab had been very disappointed about that too, this morning. He'd hoped she was already pregnant.

As they turned off the main trail, and stopped beside the Wilson house, Catherine felt a quick flush of anger. "Damn it, Ian, don't you think you might have asked me about this? I'm tired of you making all the decisions, and then springing them on me. I am your *wife,* not your hired help."

"Get off your high horse," he replied. "What I really wanted was to be alone with you when you saw your new home for the first time."

She thought about that. "Well, why didn't you just come out and say so? Women *like* to be told things like that. It means you care." The clack of a pump handle interrupted them, and she turned to see Emma Wilson filling a pail with water. "I'll go and give her a hand."

Ian watched her get down from the buckboard. "Catherine?" She looked up at him, shading her eyes from the glaring sun. "Look, lass, I guess I do need some educating on how to treat a wife."

"Well, Ian, I don't seem to know much about husbands either."

***

They had just finished lunch with the Wilsons when the Bradleys arrived, eager to hear any kind of news from the outside world. Tom was a stringy weather-beaten man with unkempt hair; Daisy looked tired and care-worn. A large bulge under her apron proclaimed that another Bradley was about to join their brood of five. Catherine glanced at her husband, sitting transfixed and looking bored. She thought again about his decision to stop here for lunch. She recalled the anger in his face after he saw her talking to Peter Gray. Old Pascal had noticed it too. Ian was a jealous man, and it was whittling away at his self-assurance. She would need to be more careful not to make him feel that way. McNab got to his feet, and after thanking Emma for the meal, he took Catherine's arm and led her out to the buckboard.

The women, always lonelier than the men in the northwest, watched and waved until the McNabs turned back onto the main trail.

Emma smiled at her friend. "I'm glad to be back, Daisy. I wanted to be with you when the baby comes."

"I'm not looking forward to birthing it; I had a real time with the last one. Then it died."

"We'll be sure to get Marie Scott from Pounding Lake when your time comes. She's the best midwife around."

"Tom says he's going to do that. And speaking of Pounding Lake, isn't that some lah-de-dah wife McNab's gotten himself? And half his age, too! I never would have thought it of him; he always seemed such a sensible, steady man."

"Catherine's a nice girl, Daisy, just a little out of her element."

"She's stuck-up. Putting on the sweet little-girl voice!"

Emma laughed. "Oh, you're in a snit, honey. But I know how you feel. At eight months, you don't need someone as pretty as her around."

"It's not just that," Daisy insisted. "I heard her and Mac scrapping outside when they got here, and she was watching him real funny when we were talking. Probably thinks she's too good for him. Sure, he's older than her, but he's got plenty of money they say, and he's a fine-looking man. He could warm up *my* bed anytime." Emma shook her head at her friend, and laughed again. It was good that Charles had not heard that little speech!

***

Catherine could scarcely believe her eyes when they got to Pounding Lake that afternoon. It was the loveliest village she had seen since leaving home. It was tucked into a valley rimmed by tree-clad hills, threaded by a sparkling creek flowing from the lake north of town. To their right, a white church topped with a spire and cross came into view. Beside it was a house. Both buildings were framed by a dense stand of dark green pines. McNab stopped the team and pointed to a hill north of the church. "That's where all the Indian Agency homes are. The employees have a farm back of that, where they grow crops and keep livestock. They also run a sawmill and the warehouse."

She was fascinated. "That big building with the two flags in front, it looks like it's blocking the road."

"That's my competition, the Hudson's Bay store, run by Dan Scott. Back this way, you can see an old house, looks like the police are going to use it." They could see the police carts and tethered horses. "That little place south of the house is Jerry Dunn's carpenter shop. I've just had a lean-to on my store up to now, but as soon as we got married, I sent Jerry a telegraph to build two rooms onto the store and make us some furniture. Soon we'll be seeing our home for the first time." From where they were sitting, Catherine could also see a scattering of small cabins. "The little places belong to the Woods Crees and Métis who live here." He clucked to the horses. "Now here, lass. Saved the best for the last."

The team turned into a driveway, flanked by two huge poplar trees. They were facing a large L-shaped building. She stared, trying to take it all in at once. She could hear children playing in the nearby creek, and closer, sawing and hammering coming from the police barracks. Wild canaries called and flitted overhead. Gold and green dappled light cascaded from the poplars onto the driveway. As she stepped down from the buckboard, her eyes sparkled with delight.

"Ian, I never imagined it would be so pretty here! Why didn't you tell me?"

"I didn't know how it would seem to you, lass. It's no Rosemere."

"I didn't expect it to be," she replied. He led her to the long arm of the L, where a porch ran its full length. Several rough-looking men were squatting on their heels or lounging on the railing, looking at her curiously. The Métis touched their hats, and the other men nodded in silence. Inside Pascal and Gabe Berthier were already unpacking and putting away the newly arrived trade goods. The one long room was lined with shelves piled with a bewildering array typical of general stores all over the country. She was interested in the store, but even more anxious to see her home. Sensing this, McNab steered her through it quickly, and pointed to a door at the back corner. "This used to lead to the lean-to. We can go in that way."

The instant McNab opened the door, they were struck by a flood of sunshine and the smell of damp, fresh-sawed lumber. There was a window on each side of the door, providing an attractive view of the church on the opposite hillside. Across the spacious room was a new black and silver cook stove, which McNab had shipped in from Winnipeg, the stove pipes already in place and flanked by boxes of firewood. The rest of the room was filled with bales of household goods waiting to be unpacked. There was very little furniture, just a worn couch McNab had used in the lean-to, a square wooden table, and some wall shelving. The anteroom had a sturdy new bed frame, a chest of drawers, and a wash stand.

"We'll need some more furniture, I know," said McNab, watching her closely. "Decide what we need, and I'll get Jerry Dunn to make it. He was probably hard-pressed to get this much done before we got here."

"He did very well," said Catherine, bravely dismissing a fleeting memory of the gracious and elegant home left behind in Rosemere. She absently stroked the wolf cub she had brought in with her.

"I can't wait to unpack our wedding presents and the things we bought in Winnipeg. I can make curtains and a new cover for the couch to match. I saw some blue gingham in your store that would match our blue china. Can I have that? And hooks. We'll need them to hang our pots and pans handy to the stove and…"

He laughed, interrupting her. "Are you going to take off your hat and put down that damn pup before doing all that, lass?" She had never seen him looking so openly pleased. She realized then how concerned he had been about her reaction to her new home. She was moved.

She took off her hat, put down the pup, and laughed with him. "You won't know this place in a few days," she promised, then she went to him and put her arms around his neck. "I'm sure we'll be very happy here." For a moment, he was motionless, then he drew her closer and kissed her with bruising intensity. "No, Ian," she said, "just hold me and be gentle, like you were before we were married. I need that, too."

To her surprise, he loosened his grip and smiled. "All right, but it's not easy. Have you set a spell on me, then?"

"That I have, Ian McNab," she told him, imitating his Scottish lilt.

He began to stroke her hair. "I'm just not used to having a wife, and now a home and maybe children of my own." She rested her cheek against his shoulder.

Then she laughed and pointed. The little wolf cub was standing by the door, watching them and wagging his tail, standing over a puddle. "I think I am going to have to train both of you."

"If I do that, you can always tie me up outside."

"Don't think I won't."

***

Their intimacy was broken by a knock at the door. It was the new farm instructor, Bert Simmons, and his wife. They were both carrying parcels. McNab had already met Simmons. He introduced him to Catherine, then put the parcels on the kitchen table, while Simmons introduced his wife.

"This is Julia, also from Ontario, Mrs. McNab. We have brought you eggs, butter, and milk from the farm. Also, one of Julia's cakes, which you had better taste before thanking her. She tries, but she's not the best cook in the world."

Julia flushed and her voice caught. "I'm not, but we did want to welcome you and congratulate you on your marriage. Having another white woman here will make quite a difference." Catherine had never seen a more timid-looking person than this freckled, ginger-haired woman.

"Thank you," Catherine said. "Why don't you sit down on one of these boxes, or on the couch over there? Your cake looks fine."

"Just a bit lop-sided," agreed Bert. "The police told us you would be in today, so we've been watching for you. You're a happy surprise, Mrs. McNab, and a lovely one at that."

McNab sat on the couch and lit his pipe. Studying Simmons through the haze, McNab asked, "Bert, how are you doing, making farmers out of the Indians?"

"It's like trying to make an ox out of a wild deer. They try, but Judd Bolton left me a pile of trouble. Maybe they think I'm as low-down as he was, but I get chills up and down my spine when I'm out alone with them. Corporal Gray says he'll send one of his men out with me when I make my rounds, at least until they get used to me."

"You might be a bit fanciful there," said McNab. "The Indian Agent can handle them. I've no doubt."

"Burr? He's a swaggering bully. He deliberately provokes and insults them every chance he gets. He's the last agent in the department I would have chosen to work for."

"Oh, Bert, watch what you are saying, please."

"That won't go out of this house," McNab told Mrs. Simmons. "But Bert, she's right. It's best to be close-mouthed in a small place like this."

"McNab, I've just been here for a month, but already I can say you towns-people have been too close-mouthed about the way Jim Burr treats the Indians. Much more of it and they could turn on him, and that could mean turn on us, too."

McNab shrugged. "Burr's been dealing with them for some years, and it hasn't happened yet. I know he likes his mean little games, but the department must think he can handle the job or they would have fired him. Like they did Bolton. Besides, I'm a trader, not a politician."

"You and old Dan Scott, you're a pair. He says the same thing. And that reminds me. He's missed your pipes at sunset, and wants to know if you'll play 'The Galway Hills' for him tonight?"

"That I will, if I can find my pipes in all this mess. How about you Mrs. Simmons? Do you have a request?"

She gave him a shy smile. "I love 'Highland Lassie!'"

"I'll play it. And we thank you for your kindly welcome," he said, as they rose to leave.

Catherine suddenly remembered MaryLou's letter. She took it out of her handbag and gave it to Bert. "If you go by the agent's house, would you give this to Mrs. Burr?"

"They are right next door to us. I'll do that."

***

After they left, Catherine unpacked the container of kitchenware. McNab went to the store for pot hooks, then surveyed the wall behind the stove judiciously. "I think the griddles over here and the pots on the other side." He screwed the hooks into the wall, hung the cast-iron ware on them, and stood back to admire the effect. "How does that look, Catherine?"

She hid a smile at her husband's first attempt at domestic chores. "Just fine. I'd say you have real pot-hanging talent."

He took her seriously. "I copied how Jenny had hers arranged."

After supper, they sat on the steps of the new addition, while Ian tuned the bagpipe reeds. As the sun began to go down, he rose, set his lips to the chanter, and started to play. As he paced back and forth to the wild skirl of his music, she watched him intently. Again, he seemed almost a stranger. Would she ever get over that feeling?

"The next tune is for you," he said, "'My Love She's But a Lassie Yet'."
It was a beautiful lilting melody. Catherine sensed that her husband could
perhaps express emotions with his music that he was reluctant to put into
words. As the light faded from the sky, and shadows grew long across the
little settlement, he played the old hymn, 'Abide With Me'.

She was deeply moved, barely able to speak. "That was beautiful, Ian."

"I guess I could say I meant the hymn for you, too. Come, abide with me,
Mrs. McNab." He took her hand, and they walked into their new home and
closed the door. It had been a happy day, in all respects.

But towards morning, Catherine writhed in the throes of a vague but
terrifying nightmare. Heart pounding, she was drenched in sweat. Danger,
violent death, and horror all lurked there with her in the silent room. She
had called out to Ian, Peter Gray, old Pascal, but no one was there to help her.
At last, someone appeared. Of all people, it was Jay Clear Sky. At that, she
came fully awake, wondering at the terror and strangeness of it. It was a long
while before she fell asleep again.

CHAPTER SIX

Pascal Lebret's sister, Marie Scott, who was once Marie Dumas, sat at her kitchen table looking at her husband, Dan Scott, or Scotty as he was often called. He had finished his noon meal and was having a quick smoke before going back to the store. He was a lean man, almost bald, with a bleak expression that belied his easy-going nature. He felt more than saw her keen black eyes on him, and looked back warily. "Let's have it, old woman, what have I done now?"

"Nothing yet today that I know of anyway. No, it's what I am going to do that I'm thinking of."

"Let me guess. With all the talk about McNab's new wife, you, nosy as usual, are going to see her. I wondered how long you could hold out."

"Nosy? Not me, Marie! But polite, yes. It is only polite to welcome new-comers. I should have gone before, and you should be nice about it instead of insulting me."

"The only reason you haven't gone snooping already is because you were sick in bed."

She smiled at him then, and while the smile drew many lines, her broad face was still beautiful to the man across the table. But he did not smile back. "I don't know about this, Marie. You know how some white women are. I won't be having you snubbed."

Marie surged to her feet, and put her hands on her ample hips. It was just as well she was tall or she would have been a completely round ball of a woman. Under her voluminous print dress, her breasts, belly, and thighs blended into an impressive pillar of femininity, one to keep a man warm in his bed and happy in his head, as Scotty often said. Now sixty, she had been pretty in her younger days, and it still showed. "What is this?" she demanded. "You think I would be bothered by a snub from a girl as young as some of my own grandchildren?"

"No, I said that *I* would care. Now sit down, and tell me why you are feeling so polite today."

"Oh, I am nosy and that is the truth of it, although you could pretend to believe me sometimes. That Ian McNab imagine! Married to a city girl half his age!"

"You don't know that she is a city girl," chuckled Scotty.

"All easterners come from cities," she insisted. "Now why on earth would he bring a girl like that out here, I wonder?"

"I guess he had to, once he married her. And don't say 'a girl like that'; you haven't even laid eyes on her yet."

"I hear things," she said. They sat in companionable silence until Dan finished his pipe. Marie cleared the table and set three fresh places. Dan went back to his store and sent his clerk, Tom Adams and Joe Two Horse, his handyman, back for lunch. Suzy Two Horse, Joe's wife who helped Marie, came from the bedrooms where she had been dusting and sweeping. Like Marie, the she wore a loose cotton dress and moccasins. Her long black hair was neatly braided. Copper hoops dangled from her ears and encircled both her wrists. She was a tiny, bird-like woman, and she and Marie were close friends. Joe and Suzy were Woods Crees who lived with their three children in a cabin close to the store. Marie watched them demolish rabbit stew, mounds of potatoes, and fruit pie.

There was little conversation over the meal, as Suzy could not speak English, Joe spoke it poorly, and Tom Adams could not speak Cree. Tom's eyes often squinted in pain. A fall from his horse while he was with the North West Mounted Police had broken his hip and it had not mended well. He was very lame, but like Joe and Suzy, he liked working for the Scotts. They would never get rich on the pay, but the Scotts were good people. And Marie's cooking was famous from Battleford to Edmonton. She cut three more wedges of pie and refilled their teacups, always amused to see little Suzy pack away as much food as the men. She often wondered where it disappeared to in her tiny body. When the pie was gone, Suzy asked Marie if she was going to visit the new arrival today.

"I have to see this one for myself," she nodded. "You should hear the way my brother, Pascal, talks about her. Real taken he is, the old coyote."

"Are you talking about Mrs. McNab?" asked Tom. "I met her when she came in for her mail one day. She is one nice-looking lady."

"Well, don't you go making eyes at her, young man," warned Marie. "McNab may seem like a dry stick of a man, but when that kind decides on a woman after years of going it alone, he has to be very taken with her. Pascal says he watches her like a hawk."

Tom looked thoughtful. "No woman is pretty enough to make me tangle with McNab. He's been quiet enough since he came to Pounding Lake, but I heard some wild stories about him when I was in the police force. I wouldn't cross him even with two good legs."

"That's smart," approved Marie. "There's a fighting streak in the Scots. My Scotty is one of them. They don't say or show much, but dear Lord, watch out when they do."

***

An hour later, Marie eased her stately body along the footpath leading to McNab's store. It was hot and dry; no rain had fallen for two weeks. The grass was yellowing and covered with dust, and cattle were bawling plaintively, thirsty this early in the afternoon. She hated walking. Ordinarily, with her baking done and her kitchen tidied, she would have been in her rocking chair, sewing, knitting, or more likely, napping. She had done a lot of living in her time, and she felt it. She had given Rene Dumas seven children before he died. That was back in '64 and she had married Dan Scott five years later. Those had been hard years, during her widowhood, but with the help of old Pascal, she had managed to keep body and soul and her family together. Scotty, never married, was a man of warmth and humour under his crotchety manner, and after the hard years, she was very happy with him.

He was a good man, she reflected, with few faults to her way of thinking, and even some of them were endearing, but she did wish he were more outgoing. He and McNab were as alike as two peas in a pod, late-marrying, closed-mouthed, and keeping to themselves. But then too many people in this town meddled and gossiped. She stepped up onto the porch and knocked at the door of McNab's new home.

Marie had been prepared for a pretty woman, but she was still taken aback when Catherine opened the door. Her sun-streaked hair was tied up and back; she was wearing an apron, and had a wet mop in her hand. But she looked, Marie thought, as fresh and lively as a spring flower. She had never seen eyes that colour, almost purple, fringed by long silky lashes. When Catherine offered a welcoming smile, Marie knew there would be no snub for her here.

"You must be Mrs. Scott! How nice to meet you at last! I have heard so many nice things about you."

"And they are all true," said Marie, smiling.

"Please, do come in, but be careful not to slip on my wet floor." Fortunately, by this time, the boxes had been replaced by sturdy chairs. Marie sank into one gratefully her feet hot and tired after the walk. As Catherine put the kettle on for tea, Marie looked around approvingly. Blue gingham curtains framed the windows, and McNab's old couch had a new matching gingham cover. There were family pictures on the walls, books on some of the shelves, and good blue china pieces on another. The glass chimneys on the lamps were polished, and a bouquet of wild flowers graced the table. The place was a far cry from McNab's old lean-to.

Marie handed Catherine a covered pail. "Here's some pea soup made from my famous recipe. And some honey scones. I waited until you had survived whatever Mrs. Simmons brought you," she said, her black eyes twinkling.

Catherine kept a straight face. "She brought us a lovely cake."

"She sent me one too, while I was sick. It got me out of bed fast though; I was afraid she'd bring me another one!" Marie's laugh was so hearty that Catherine had to laugh with her.

"Mrs. Scott, it wasn't *that* bad! Now I'll be afraid to let you taste my cooking."

"Well then make some tea, child. Your kettle is boiling, and I'm thirsty after the walk. Oh, dear Lord, what is *that*?" Catherine had been reaching for the tea canister, but she turned swiftly at the genuine fear in Marie's voice. She was staring in horror at the wolf cub, who had just pawed open the door. Catherine picked him up and scratched his ears gently.

"This is a souvenir of our trek from Battleford. He was half-dead when we found him. He is quite tame now, but he thinks he is a watchdog."

"But that is a *muhekun*, a wolf! And me, Marie, I am even afraid of dogs and cats."

"I'll put him in his box. He'll stay there while we have tea."

Marie accepted the cup, along with one of her own scones, keeping a wary eye on the small bundle of fur. The pup, unaware of the impact he had made, curled up in his box and went to sleep.

"Well, child," Marie asked after taking a few sips. "What do you think of Pounding Lake?"

"I had no idea it would be so pretty."

"It is that. They can say all they want about Fort Pitt being so open and grand. But here we have the hills for shelter, and many kinds of wild berries. Good water too, with whitefish in the lake and creek. All the wood we can use and still more to sell. And we are far from any trouble spots."

"Are we really? Mr. MacKenzie and Inspector Kingsley in Fort Pitt don't seem so sure of that. They gave me the impression that they were at least ... uneasy."

"These are troubled times," admitted Marie. "As far as my people are concerned, the new white settlers get land, but we can't get title to ours. To the government, we are just in the way. The Indians are confined to reserves, and very poor and hungry."

"In all this huge and empty land, there must be a way for everyone to live together peacefully."

"You would think so, but the government can't be bothered with us, and that's the truth of it." Marie's brown face had sunken into sombre lines, but with visible effort she rallied. "But as I said, it is quiet here in Pounding Lake."

"Is that really true, Mrs. Scott? I heard about that awful man, Bolton, who taught farming before Mr. Simmons replaced him. I have heard some odd things about Mr. Burr, and even about the mission priest. And why do we suddenly need six policemen here, where there were none before?"

Marie pursed her lips, giving Catherine a pointed look. "That seems odd to me too, but when I tried to talk to my Scotty about it, he said it was just politics. And when I say how bad Jim Burr is to the Indians, he says to mind my own business. But I don't know. If you close your eyes to the things you don't like, you might miss something you should see. But Scotty thinks that is just my excuse for being nosy."

"That's the way Ian thinks," said Catherine. "They remind me of ostriches." Marie looked puzzled, so Catherine added, "Big birds over in Africa. When they are afraid, they are said to stick their heads into the sand. When they can't see, they think there is no danger, so they feel safe." Marie liked that story. She slapped her knees and chortled.

"The next time Scotty calls me nosy, I will call him an ostrich and let him try to figure *that* one out! I will have a little more tea, child."

Marie looked thoughtful again, as her cup was refilled. "Maybe those policemen know something that we don't. And I don't like that idea much."

Catherine decided to change the subject, although she was not sure how to put her next question. "Mrs. Scott, everyone says that you are a very good midwife like a doctor, almost."

"I am. I've birthed too many to count them any more. Why, child? Are you pregnant?"

"No, but I do wish I was. I can't seem to get that way, and Ian is anxious to have children. He is getting a little ... upset about it."

"Dear Lord, if that isn't like him, waiting all these years and then wanting a child right away! Don't let him get you anxious about it. I've known that to *stop* a woman getting pregnant. You'll get that way when nature says you will and not before, and that's the truth of it."

Marie noticed the girl looked both relieved and embarrassed. "Those Scots! Once they get their mind on something..." She began to laugh. "I'll tell you a story about Scotty. I'm a Catholic, but he isn't, so we weren't married in a Catholic church. Now that really bothers Father Lafarge. He's always scolding me about being a bad Catholic, and saying that if Scotty really cared for me, he would convert so we could get properly married. I guess that got under his skin after a while. One day, Father Lafarge was at it again in the store, and my old man yelled at his clerk, Tom Adams, to open the door. He grabbed poor Father by his collar and the seat of his pants and threw him out right into a pile of snow!"

"I'm not sure he should be entirely blamed for that. He must have been very provoked."

"Provoked! Dear Lord, we all hung on to him to keep him from going after Father and beating him up! He could have done it too, him being so mad and the little fat priest a bit winded." Marie chuckled, apparently not too depressed by her sinful state. "Yes, Lafarge does strange things at times. Then we had Bolton busting the buttons off his pants every time a woman came anywhere near him. We *are* an odd bunch come to think of it. My son Giles works at the sawmill for Alex Richards, and more than earns the bit of pay he gets. The carpenter, Jerry Dunn, seems all right, but he joins right in when they get to teasing and playing tricks on the dummy. Cruel it is."

"You said ... 'the dummy'?"

"You haven't heard about him yet? He is either a Blood or Blackfoot Indian, they say, but no one knows how he got here, just wandering aimlessly, I guess. There is no knowing in his eyes; he walks all funny and can't talk, but there's no harm in him. You'd think grown men had more to do than make fun of him. Even the priest does it. When that happens, the Indians, who call him 'As-a-Child,' will take him away for a while, but he always turns up again. You'll know him when you see him, but no need to be afraid."

"I won't be," said Catherine. "My young brother had brain damage at birth, and he too 'walks all funny' although he speaks well and is very intelligent.

We never allow anyone to mock him or play tricks on him. As my father says, life itself has done enough of that to him."

Marie's dark eyes were filled with sympathy. "That's the truth of it. You know the Indians are very gentle to people like that, for all their wildness. Some believe they have special powers, and they share what they have with them to share in that power. Even the Plains Crees, who scare nearly everyone. Melissa Burr is one, and you will see what I mean when you meet her. She can stare holes right through you."

"I know two Plains Crees," said Catherine, and told her about meeting MaryLou and Jay Clear Sky in Battleford.

"You met him? He is well-known as Big Bear's interpreter and often his courier. Some consider him one of the real troublemakers. He comes here sometimes. Big Bear is under Jim Burr's agency, and can only talk to the government through him. So young Clear Sky, who speaks English, and Burr doesn't speak Cree, acts as a go-between. He visits his cousin, Mrs. Burr sometimes, bringing her news of their family."

"Maybe I will see him again, then," said Catherine, remembering her strange dream of seeing his face so vividly.

"Be careful there," warned Marie. "The white men here don't like him. It wouldn't do for you to ever be seen talking to him. It's all right for me as a Métis. Chief Big Bear himself is an old friend who comes to visit Scotty and me. The whites can accept that, if grudgingly."

Then she heaved herself out of the chair. "Dear Lord, child, how we have talked! Mac will be in here to charge me rent if I stay any longer." She approached the door cautiously, her eyes fixed on the sleeping cub. *"Muhekun!"* she said, shaking her head in disbelief. "Do come and see me soon, child, but leave that *terrible beast* at home."

"I'll do that Mrs. Scott," she promised, smiling to herself as she looked fondly at *the terrible beast*.

***

Over supper, McNab asked about Marie's visit.

"I enjoyed it. She is quite a lady. That's her famous pea soup you are eating, you know."

"And men have killed for less, so she says. I used to eat with the Scotts when I got tired of my own cooking. She's a good cook and doesn't mind letting you know it. A good doctor too, with medicines for every ailment of man or beast. She spends most of the summer collecting herbs and drying roots for her concoctions. I suppose you got all the gossip?"

"Some. We talked of many things. I notice she speaks English better than old Pascal."

"He's a lot older. I don't think he went to school. He told me he was out freighting, at the age of ten, by the time she was born."

"She gave me a Cree name for my wolf: *Muhekun*."

"She likes giving out nicknames. Mine interprets loosely as 'Crazy-Man -Pipes'."

"That's all right," she laughed. "I have given her husband one too, I think."

"And what would that be, now?"

"I happened to tell her about ostriches, how they are said to stick their heads into the sand to avoid seeing danger."

"So, she thinks that is what Scotty does, eh? And probably me too. It must have been quite a conversation."

"It was interesting."

But it was disturbing too. Marie was a smart and knowing old woman, and she cast doubt on the supposed tranquility of Pounding Lake.

That night, Catherine had the terrifying dream again, just as vivid and horror-filled as it was the first time the same in every detail.

CHAPTER SEVEN

Summer lingered on in Pounding Lake. It was mid-September, but there was no hint of oncoming winter. By this time, McNab had realized that Catherine's air of delicacy was deceptive. He was very annoyed one day when, bored and restless, she asked if she could ride Dundee.

"He is a big stubborn horse, needing a man's strength to control him," he snapped.

"I have ridden far more fractious horses than Dundee," she told him, but decided not to push the issue further.

What she did enjoy was berry-picking, root-gathering, and herb-hunting with Marie and Suzy, although they once encountered a fat and lazy bear. They dug the roots of coneflowers and purple flags, burdock, snakeroot, and camas. They took the inner bark from willows and picked chokecherries, crab apples, and Saskatoons. They collected milkweed down and seed (used to dress burns), plantain, mint, and wherever they found it, sweetgrass for Suzy. At home, they made jam, pie fillings, and jellies with the fruits found on the wooded hills.

Sometimes, on rainy days, she visited Julia Simmons. Catherine could knit and sew but Julia taught her to crochet. She was delighted with this new interest. She made lacy edgings for towels and pillow cases and even her dish cloths.

McNab was unimpressed, "You'll be sewing it on my underwear, next thing I know."

She enjoyed long walks with Muhekun too. They sometimes went to the shallow stretch in Pounding Creek where the children played. On one warm afternoon, she tied the wolf to a tree and delighted the little ones when she removed her shoes and hose, and hiking up her skirts, waded into the water with them. One of the boys shyly gave her a bouquet of wild flowers. She smiled her thanks and wondered if someday her own child would come to play in the creek, with endearing brown-skinned tots like these. Then her smile gave way to a sigh. She was still not pregnant, and her husband was not at all happy about it.

***

One day, Ian came to get her, looking harried. Gabe Berthier had gone to Fish Creek to see his mother, and Pascal Lebret was driving a load of lumber to Fort Pitt. Several customers were waiting, and he needed her help in the store. She responded eagerly. With so much time on her hands, she had thought of offering to do that. But her husband had been so testy lately that she had not cared to further annoy him. For the first hour or two, she had trouble finding things and had to ask questions constantly, but soon she began to work more efficiently. With three reserves nearby, they had plenty of customers bringing in furs to exchange for ammunition, traps, and blankets. Women exchanged beaded leather work and basketry for flour, tea, sugar, and yard goods. Catherine found the Woods Crees pleasant and easy to deal with, invariably soft-spoken and polite with shy smiles. Few of them spoke English but communication went well with pointing fingers, nods, shrugs, or shakes of the head.

It was almost closing time when a tall, regal-looking woman came into the store. She had a finely chiseled face dominated by ebony eyes. But *she* did not smile; her eyes were stone cold. She wore a curious mixture of moccasins and blue glass beads, while her dress was that of a stylish white woman, a yellow gown ruffled at her neck and wrists with a small shawl of the same colour draped around her shoulders. A little girl was with her, also in a yellow dress. Her neat curled ringlets were tied back with matching ribbons. The woman went at once to the yard goods section without looking at or speaking to any of the other Cree women.

"Melissa Burr," said McNab. "You look after her." Catherine walked over to her, then stood a little uncertainly, as the woman continued to study the bolts of material. Finally, her long slim fingers touched a roll of dimity (a thin cotton European fabric), woven with a heavier yarn forming tiny, raised roses.

"You must be Mrs. Burr," Catherine said. "I am Ian McNab's wife."

"I know who you are," she said, still considering the dimity. "I want some of this for Lizabet's Sunday dress. Cut enough please." As Catherine cut and folded the cloth, she realized the woman had not asked the price of it. She wrapped it and handed the parcel to her.

"Tell McNab to charge it to Burr," Melissa said, then looked at Catherine for the first time. "You saw MaryLou in Battleford. How is she?"

"She looks well, but she is, I think, a little lonely."

"She doesn't belong there. She should go back to our people like her brother Jay. But I am the *last* one who should tell her that." Then taking her beautiful child's hand, she turned and walked out of the store.

When McNab was locking up, she asked him about Mrs. Burr. "Is she always like that? So aloof, almost hostile?"

"Always. But she did speak to you, so consider yourself lucky."

"She is as pretty as they say. I have never seen a lovelier woman."

"I have," replied Ian. "Just one though, and I married her." Catherine was surprised at the compliment, since he had been so moody lately. "Mrs. Burr does have her problems," he added after a moment. "She knows the Woods Crees have no use for her husband. No doubt she misses her own people, who hate him even more than the Woods Crees do. And she won't mix with white people. She has isolated herself completely."

"It seems so strange that those two did marry one another."

"It is quite simple; she is a beauty and Burr has an eye for that, and he had lived alone too long at the time. Human nature won out over good sense. A man who despises Indians, and an Indian who hates whites, ignored all that and rushed into marriage. They probably regret it now, but at least they have a child."

Catherine blanched. "You know how much I want to give you one. Ian. It hurts, when you say things like that to me." She turned away from him and went back to the kitchen. As she prepared supper, she was both resentful and depressed. "So, nature won out over good sense..." Was that how he felt about his own marriage now? Muhekun, sensing her distress, gazed up at her and wagged his tail. She picked him up and hugged him. "I'm so glad I have you," she whispered.

***

When Ian went outside to play his pipes that evening, she did not follow him as usual. When he finished, she heard him talking to someone. He looked at her closely when he came back. "Your friend Corporal Gray has invited us to a dance at the barracks Friday night. Since you like him so much, I assumed you would want to go, and I accepted."

"Does my liking a nice young man who has been pleasant to me deserve that sort of sarcasm, Ian? For your information, he is in love with Ellen MacKenzie and plans to marry her."

"I thought that was just fooling between them. Well. He'll be getting a little hellion then, but I bet she'll keep him warm on cold winter nights."

"I'm sure." After a while she added, "The dance might be fun. I may see people I haven't met yet, like Father Lafarge and Mr. Burr. I'm curious about them."

He lit his pipe before answering. "You haven't missed much. Burr can be a charmer when he feels like it, but I can't say even that much for the priest. The Agency interpreter, Paul McRae and his wife, Louisa, are a Métis couple, but decent people. They have *nine* children."

Catherine rose abruptly, scraping her chair back. "I'm going to bed."

He gave her a hard look. "Do something for me, Catherine. Don't wear that damn nightgown of yours tonight." She drew in her breath sharply, but did not answer him. Her hands were trembling as she undressed. She took down her hair, brushed it, then splashed water from the china jug into the basin and washed quickly. She reached for her gown automatically, then withdrew her hand, turned back the covers, and slipped into bed. The cool sheets felt strange on her naked body. The last thing in the world she wanted to do was to lie there and wait for him. She felt like a trapped animal. Her instinct was to run outside, into the darkness anywhere away from him.

He came into the bedroom as soon as he heard the bed creak, bringing the lamp with him. Then he set it on the chest of drawers and stood looking at her. "Catherine," he said evenly, "did it ever enter your mind that some women *like* to have their man make love to them?"

"Ian, I like…"

"No, you don't. Just look at yourself hanging on to those covers for dear life." He pulled them away from her and threw them to the foot of the bed. He sat down beside her, put his hand on her hip then ran it up over her body until it cupped one of her breasts. He ran his palm roughly over the nipple and felt Catherine's body tense. He drew away from her immediately, his eyes angry. "How can any woman have a body like yours and yet have no feeling in it?"

"I don't understand…"

"God, Catherine, how long are you going to play the innocent with me?" He rose abruptly, starting to leave the room, but stopped and leaned against the doorway looking down at the floor unhappily. "It's me, isn't it? I'm not what you want?" She sat up, trying to think of anything she could say to please him. Then got out of bed and put her arms around his waist, resting a cheek against his tense back muscles.

"The day I met you, I thought you were the most handsome and exciting man I had ever seen. I was more than happy to leave my home and family to come out here with you. You *are* what I want. I am so sorry that I am not what you seem to need in bed. I can't help it. I don't know what is wrong with me."

"What is wrong with you is that you won't give it a chance to be good. I damn well have to pry your legs apart to get into you. A man gets tired of that little game after a while."

She stepped away from him, her throat constricting with hurt and anger. "A *game*? Is that what you think it is? Well, it's a hell of a rough one to me then. It hurts me, sometimes very much, but you don't care! You just keep

66

pushing into me harder and harder until you're satisfied, and it doesn't matter a damn how I feel, does it?"

"It still hurts you? I can't believe that, after all these months."

"So, I play games about something like this, and then I *lie* about it!?" she gasped, angrier than she had ever been in her life. "Why do you bother with me at all if you see me like that? What I can't understand is why you expected me to know anything about making love, if that is what you call it. Until our wedding night, I had never seen a naked man. I had no idea of what to expect or what I was supposed to do! And you've never tried to help me or talk to me about it. Now here you are, finally doing it with anger and accusations instead of kindness! Maybe other women, who like to have their men make love to them, get a little more than that. If all you wanted was a baby-making machine, why didn't you marry one of them?"

Sobbing, she flung herself into bed, pulled the covers over her, and turned away from him. Ian remained where he was for a while, and then he stripped off his clothes, washed, and sat on the far side of the bed. He looked at his wife; he was hurting too. It was an ugly quarrel and he had started it. He knew he should take her in his arms and hold her tenderly. He also knew he should tell her he was sorry, that he would rather have her than any other woman, even if they never had children! But the longed-for words were too securely locked behind his wounded pride. He turned off the lamp and got into bed, looking up into the darkness. He felt that something wonderful they might have had together was slipping away. It was a long time before he closed his eyes and slept.

***

As McNab and Catherine walked to the barracks on dance night, they saw that a large crowd had already gathered. Everyone was dressed in their best clothes, the Métis men in white shirts and sashes, their women in brightly coloured full skirts, and plaid shawls. The police were in their scarlet dress tunics, and McNab and Dan Scott wore their tartan kilts. Catherine was wearing her best blue silk dress, the one she had worn in Battleford. She had not pinned her hair tonight; instead she had tied it back with a blue ribbon, allowing it to cascade in rippling curls past her shoulders. She looked beautiful, but pale and withdrawn.

Inside the old converted house, three fiddlers had everyone whirling to a waltz. Nearly all the dancers wore moccasins, the sound of their soft shoes swished across the wooden floor. That was all she could take in before being seized and swept off into the swirling dancers. Her partner was as tall as her husband. She looked up into a pair of laughing hazel eyes in a lean, tanned face, adorned by a luxuriant mahogany moustache.

"Let me guess," she said as the music stopped. "I have just been abducted by Mr. James Burr." She had guessed this based on what she'd heard about him: that he had an eye for the ladies. He was living up to his reputation, appraising her so boldly that she became annoyed.

"I do trust you find me presentable after this inspection?"

"Indeed, I do, lovely lady!! Purple eyes, by God!"

"Blue," she corrected him, as her husband reappeared.

"Catherine, the sandwiches you brought have disappeared into the clutches of the law. And the next dance is *mine*."

Burr made a mocking bow. "I yield, but reluctantly, McNab."

The fiddlers started up again. As they moved onto the dance floor, Catherine looked back and watched Burr as he claimed a blushing Julia Simmons. "He does fancy himself, doesn't he?"

"Yes, as the Lord's gift to women and the Indians."

The police detachment had done well refurbishing the old house. The walls were whitewashed, the floors cleaned and waxed, and tables pushed back against the walls. Crepe-paper streamers were twisted from the centre of the ceiling to each corner for a festive look. Some lanterns hung from hooks overhead. At the back of the room was a temporary platform where fiddlers, Gabe Berthier and Pascal Lebret among them, were sawing away, feet tapping, absorbed faces beaded with sweat. For the next dance, a policeman with an accordion replaced the fiddlers, and Catherine was asked to dance by Corporal Gray. She was amused to see that he wore the distracted, anxious look of an inexperienced host at his first party.

She tried to reassure him. "Everything looks lovely, Peter. I heard the men even baked a cake for the occasion. How did it turn out?"

He grinned. "Not too bad. Cam Forbes, that's him with the accordion, did drop a layer of it after it was baked, but it stayed in one piece, even bounced back onto the table, so no harm done. Look." They stopped at one of the tables decorated with more crepe paper. The centre-piece was a huge cake with red icing and a glob of yellow in the middle. "That's the Mounted Police crest," he told her with a straight face.

"Oh, I knew that right away," she lied, then they both laughed heartily at the lurid confection. It was good, thought Catherine, to be having some fun again. Some of the aching hurt of the last few days seemed to be draining away with the sounds of music, laughter, and dancing.

But Peter, earlier noticing her pallor and downcast look, was concerned about her. *This bloody town,* he thought, *it does things to people. Or is it that possessive and grim husband of hers dimming the gay spirit in the girl I met in Battleford?* He had never liked McNab. He liked him less now.

Clicker Lang, a young constable, claimed her for the next dance: a slow waltz. He had a long, horse-like face with soft friendly eyes and a toothy smile. Catherine asked him, "Is Clicker your real name?"

"No, Mrs. McNab, I got it because I'm so skinny that I rattle when I walk. They keep me this way because I ride the fastest race horse in the detachment. I'll bet they won't even give me a piece of that cake we made. Then again," he said thoughtfully, "who would want one?"

It was getting very warm in the crowded room. When Catherine decided to sit out the next dance, Father Lafarge came to sit beside her. He was a cherubic-looking man of about forty, rotund and sandy-haired. His predatory-bird eyes were fixed on the dancers, until the music ended. Then he spoke to her.

"I assume you are not a Catholic, Mrs. McNab, since this is the first time we have met."

69

"I'm not, but I would like to attend one of your services some Sunday. I miss doing that in Pounding Lake."

"As you wish," he said in a detached voice. "Ah, Louisa and Paul McRae, this is McNab's wife."

She gave the priest a reproving look. "I do have a first name, Father," then she shook hands with the Métis couple, remembering that he was the agency interpreter. "I'm Catherine. But surely you can't be the Mrs. McRae with *nine* children?" Louisa was about thirty-five with dark skin and grey-streaked hair. She had an amazingly voluptuous body, and was exotic looking, with velvety brown eyes and a sensuous mouth.

"At last count, it was still nine," Louisa said. "It is nice to meet you at last, McNab's wife!" Her eyes flashed as she made a face at Father Lafarge. Paul McRae was a burly, full-bearded man who bowed to her in an oddly formal way, as he welcomed her to Pounding Lake.

"I hope you are not finding it too wild and uncivilized here. It must be a far cry from your former home." He spoke with a distinct Scottish burr.

"Oh, no, Mr. McRae, it's very ... quiet and peaceful here."

"Let us hope it remains that way."

"*Paul*, this is a party, remember?"

Paul grinned sheepishly at his wife's remark, and they gave each other a tender and affectionate look. Catherine's heart felt a pang. Would she and her husband ever look at each other that way? *Maybe,* she thought, *after our first nine children!*

There was a burst of applause. Turning, she saw that her husband had mounted the platform, bagpipes in hand. The people were calling out requests, as Dan Scott approached and claimed her for the reel. Her first impression of Marie's husband had been that he regarded the world unemotionally, through a haze of pipe smoke. But as soon as the piping began, he was as nimble as any man in the room, wild and spirited, abandoning himself to the haunting music of his highland ancestors. By the time the reels were over, and McNab stepped down, the room was stifling. She heard a chuckle as McNab carefully stored his pipes on one end of the tables. Jim Burr was standing beside her.

"You could steal McNab's wife before you could lay hands on his pipes, by God!"

"Perhaps someone has stolen yours," Catherine retorted. "I have yet to see her tonight."

"You'll never see her at a shindig like this. She hates Pounding Lake. She may adjust to it in time, but until she does, I leave it to her to come or stay away as she chooses."

"Oh, I didn't know that, Mr. Burr. I wondered if I had missed her amidst all these people. I met her in the store recently, and saw your little girl, too. She is very beautiful."

"She is," he agreed. "Looks just like me."

Ian joined them, along with Julia and Bert Simmons. The policemen were at one of the tables setting out the refreshments contributed by the women of the town. The fiddlers started up again just before Burr issued an angry exclamation, as he looked at the open doorway.

A bedraggled figure in threadbare clothing had lurched inside, bewildered, with a hesitant smile turned up on one side as he looked at all the people. His wandering attention was caught by the music, and he began to clap his hands.

"Now who let him in?" Burr exclaimed. "I thought we were rid of him. Come on Simmons, let's get him out of here." But the crowd decided otherwise. With hoots of laughter, they formed a circle around the shambling figure, clapping with him, urging him to dance. He appeared frightened and turned toward the door on his own, but someone gave him a hard shove back into the circle again. He nearly fell. He tried for the door again. To Catherine's astonishment, it was Father Lafarge who blocked him this time, and pushed him back. A howl of raucous laughter filled the room. Catherine looked at her husband imploringly. His look was cold and forbidding, as he shook his head at her.

"Dance dummy, dance," they began chanting. Surely someone was going to put an end to this! Catherine looked around but Dan Scott had a frozen expression, Burr looked resigned, and Simmons was laughing with the crowd. White-faced, she took a step herself toward the cringing and terrified man, but her husband seized her arm in a steely grip.

Peter Gray broke suddenly into the circle, and very much the policeman now, cleared a path for the dazed man to the door. Ignoring several catcalls, Peter led him gently outside. The fiddlers started a new tune, couples paired off again, and the dancing resumed as if nothing had happened.

Catherine was grateful when refreshments were finally served, ending the party. It was good to go outside into the clear cool night.

***

As they walked home after the party, McNab lifted the lantern he was carrying and looked at her.

"Did you have a good time, lass?"

"*Fine!* Thank you!"

"All right then, let's have it out. You think I should have broken up that business of teasing the dummy, don't you?"

"Yes, I do. And don't call him that. I can't believe that even Father Lafarge took part in baiting that poor man."

"What else can I call him? As far as I know, he has no name. And listen, this is a very small place. You can't start trouble with your neighbours and customers over every little thing. No real harm was done. The dum... well, whatever he is, has probably forgotten all about it by this time. I saw Paul McRae take him out some food when the dancing started again, if that makes you feel any better."

"Ian, the poor man was terrified. He looked so trapped. Thank God Peter stopped it when he did. Those people were turning mean, I could feel it. How long would you have let it go on?"

"Look, Gray is the policeman, not me. Lafarge is the priest supposedly upholding the moral and spiritual values in this place, not me. And Burr is the agent, so Indians are his responsibility, not mine. It was up to one of them to stop it, and Gray did. Now I'll hear no more about it."

"You won't. I want to forget I ever saw people acting like that, in the name of having a good time."

They walked in silence the rest of the way. McNab went to bed as soon as they got home. But Catherine sat in the kitchen for over an hour, staring into the darkness. She had never felt so lonely in her life.

CHAPTER EIGHT

"Catherine, would you like to take a trip to Fort Pitt?" McNab asked. She was working in the store, weighing glass beads and sorting them by colour. She looked at him in pleasant surprise.

"I would love to see the MacKenzies again."

"I have to go there next week. It's treaty-payment time my best chance to make cash sales. Indian Affairs always makes quite a ceremony out of it, 'showing the flag,' as they say. They pow-wow with the Indians, and we get to catch up with the news of the rest of the country."

"Thank you for asking. I'll enjoy the change," she replied.

"I think we could both use one; I've not enjoyed living with a polite stranger this past week."

"Nor have I," she admitted, looking down at the beads again.

***

A week later, they climbed into the buckboard, waving goodbye to Gabe Berthier, who was to remain in charge of the store. Pascal was ready in the freighting wagon, loaded with trade goods. They were joined by Peter Gray and two of his constables, along with the Burr family and Paul McRae.

"McRae is needed as interpreter, and police are always assigned to escort the agent," McNab offered. "Burr will be handling thousands of dollars. And since Plains Crees will be there, Melissa will be visiting with her family … the Blue Quills."

"This is the first time I've seen the Burrs together," said Catherine, as they moved off. "They do make a handsome couple."

"I suppose they do, for whatever it's worth," McNab replied. "Her father is a councillor in the Big Bear band. They are registered with the Pounding Lake Agency, although they haven't taken a reserve yet. A very tough and independent crew they are, too. No one is all that happy to have them around. They are arrogant as hell, but all right if you know how to take them. They can be high and mighty one minute, and the next thing you know, they'll be joking and fooling around and telling tall tales that would curl your hair."

As the miles passed, they could see that Jim Burr was having trouble with his team. Twice, it seemed, the snuffy pair were close to bolting, and they could hear Burr swearing at them.

"It serves him bloody well right," said McNab. "Bert Simmons warned him about that mare. She's dangerous. Kicked her stall apart last week. He'll be in a fine mess if she takes off with Melissa and Lizabet in the buckboard. But, as Bert says, you can't tell him anything."

***

Peter Gray had noticed the trouble Burr was having with his team. Catherine watched him walk over to the horses and soothe the jittery mare. "This wire bit isn't doing her any good, Mr. Burr; it has her mouth bleeding." Catherine had heard about Burr's famous temper. He whirled on the policeman, and even from a distance, she could see the fire in his eyes.

"I don't need your advice, Gray. You stick to telling your own men what to do. That uniform doesn't make you a God-damn expert on everything."

"I never said it did. But we are taught how to look after horses, as part of our basic training." Gray turned away, his face expressionless, although he and the two constables exchanged disgusted looks as they sat down by their fire.

Catherine had tea ready by this time, and unwrapped the lunch she had brought. They ate and sipped strong, hot tea without saying much to each other. Afterwards, McNab and Pascal went off downstream, as Catherine helped herself to another cupful.

A gentle breeze was stirring, fragrant with the scent of drying grass and clover. Overhead, large flights of geese were beginning to gather before heading south to their winter feeding grounds. Occasionally, she could hear them trumpeting their wild and haunting music. All around her were the last fall flowers; Lizabet was picking daisies. Although it was October, the brittle stems were still flexible enough for Catherine to show the enchanting child how to make them into a chain. It was so peaceful and quiet that Catherine wished she could stay for the rest of the afternoon. Finally, she stirred herself, poured the rest of the tea over the coals, and headed toward their buckboard.

The peace was suddenly shattered. Burr's balky mare screamed and reared, striking out with her hooves just missing Burr's head. He lost his hold on the harness. Fighting the tormenting wire bit in her mouth, the mare lunged forward, taking the buckboard and the other panic-stricken horse with her, heading straight for Lizabet! Only Catherine was close by. She dropped the kettle and ran to the child, managing to catch a fold of her dress in her hand. She pulled back so sharply that they both fell. Instinct and her own agile body kept her moving holding Lizabet, clawing and scrabbling across the ground away from the murderous hooves and oncoming wheels of the careening buckboard. Rolling, twisting, a deafening crack...then silence. Darkness.

After a while, she became aware of light again. There were sounds, a woman sobbing, men shouting. Somewhere a shot. Someone was probing at her face, and it hurt. She twisted away peevishly. Silhouetted by the sun, she saw heads in a circle above her, looking down.

"Catherine! For God's sake, lass, answer me!"

"Lizabet," she mumbled, and tried to sit up.

"She is safe, only scratched and half-frightened to death."

"Oh my, that was close," she quavered. "My nose hurts." This time she did manage to sit up. She blinked at her husband, kneeling beside her, ashen-faced. He was holding a wet cloth in his hand, and she reached for it. "My nose is running."

"Bleeding," he told her. "You must have taken a fair rap on it, but I don't think it's broken. How are you feeling now?"

"Cold. A bit shaky. Are you sure Lizabet is not hurt?"

A woman's voice answered. "Here she is, Mrs. McNab; you can see for yourself." Melissa Burr was holding her child and trembling with shock. "How you got her out of the way, I will never know."

"I'm not quite sure myself. Give me a hand up, please, Ian." She felt better on her feet, and tried to smile at the circle of concerned faces, including Peter Gray, old Pascal, and Paul McRae. "What about the horses?"

"Burr shot the mare," answered Peter. "His buckboard needs repairs, but we can get it to Camas Lake. The ladies there can tend to you and Lizabet." He took her hand, ignoring McNab. "You are one brave girl."

McNab turned abruptly to Melissa. "You'll come with us to Camas Lake. Your rig will have to be towed there. The child doesn't need another scare, which she will get should it fall apart on the way." He helped the two women and the child into his buckboard, then went around and climbed into the driver's seat. He looked at his wife with a mixture of pride and concern. "That's my lass, now. They won't be calling you 'that city girl' after today."

***

At Camas Lake, Burr borrowed the Wilsons' team and carriage to continue to Fort Pitt. Emma Wilson cleaned up Catherine and Lizabet, while Melissa watched intently. When they were about to leave, Melissa touched Catherine's arm gently—all the former aloofness gone.

"I will never forget this, Catherine." Her eyes were filled with tears. "My Lizabet would surely be dead, but for you."

"I just thank God I was close enough to her, Melissa."

By the time they reached Fort Pitt, both of Catherine's eyes were black, her nose was puffy, and she felt sick and dizzy. It was a good thing, she told herself, that she had not had a chance to think before the rescue. Still, she was not above enjoying the role of heroine, and she was even more pleased that she and Melissa were now apparently friends.

***

Fort Pitt was swarming with people. Independent traders had set up a temporary village of their own at the northwest corner of town, raising tents beside their wagons and picketing their horses behind them. Ian drove past them slowly, looking over the outfits to see who was there, and finally directed Pascal into a position at the end and a bit apart from the others, closest to the fort.

Farther west, a mile up the Saskatchewan River, a huge encampment could be seen. As soon as they came to a stop, the McNabs could hear pounding drums, and more faintly, the sound of singing. More people could be seen arriving, coming down off the tree-clad rise to the north. Ian pointed to a white tent with a flag flying in front of it, halfway between the fort and the camp.

"Tables and chairs will be set up and the officials will make the treaty payments, with the police standing by," he explained to Catherine. Then we'll be in business." He helped Catherine down from the buckboard, then spoke to Pascal. "I saw Buck Breland back there. If you hear anything about him selling booze here, let me know. That's one son-of-a-bitch I wouldn't mind turning over to the police."

Pascal nodded, then cocked his head at his boss. When Catherine stepped away from them, Pascal spoke quietly.

"I saw Dorrie Barker back there too."

"Christ!" said Ian, shooting a look back at his wife. "Look, as soon as you can, go to Barker to tell her to stay away from me and tell her why."

"She'll likely hear, but I'll have a word with her anyway."

Catherine heard nothing of this exchange. Her head and body were aching, and she was vastly relieved to be out of the jolting buckboard. Ellen and Connie came running to meet her.

"We have dinner waiting for you," they said in unison, then stepped back in dismay. "What happened to you?"

"You go along," said McNab, before Catherine had a chance to reply. "We'll get our tent set up, so Pascal can set out the goods, and then we'll join you."

***

Now in the MacKenzie kitchen, as Leslie examined her bruised face, Catherine suddenly burst into tears. Leslie put her thin freckled arms around her and patted her comfortingly.

"There now, dear, that will make you feel better. A good cry after such a bad fright is the best medicine there is."

After supper, McNab and George MacKenzie sat smoking, while the twins cleared away the dishes. George leaned back in his chair and put his feet up on a stool. "I'm not surprised about the accident. Burr always had a mean hand with horses, as well as Indians. Did he tell you about the chiefs' conference in Duck Lake in July?"

"No, we don't have much to do with one another. What about it?" asked McNab.

"Well, the chiefs claim they can't control the warriors much longer, unless conditions improve. If that doesn't happen, next spring they'll just take whatever they need to stay alive."

"Any official reply to that?"

"The usual one. The government says they have no reason to complain. No changes are planned. I can't understand it, Mac. That's an outright threat. There is a breaking point, and I think they're damn close to it."

McNab glanced uneasily at Catherine.

Leslie caught the look. She shook her finger at him. "Don't try to keep her in the dark about this, Ian, it isn't fair. She's not stupid, and the Lord knows, she's no coward. We women are right in the middle of all this, so we have the right to know what's going on, and what we might be up against."

"Oh, come now. I never expected to see you folks so spooked. George, you were born out here. When in all your life have you ever been in any real danger from the Indians?"

"Never yet, and you worked for me when you first came west, so you know why. I don't cheat or lie to them, and I treat them with respect. At first the government did too, but not anymore." He paused, then leaned toward McNab, looking very serious. "There's something out there that never was before. I see it like this. You mind how in the old days, when the boss buffalo bull of the herd was ousted by a younger one? He accepted it. His fighting days were over. He'd go out and graze on the left-over pastures remembering maybe, but knowing the glory days were finished. Not asking for much but enough food, a good mud wallow, and to be left alone. But sooner or later, the wolves would come for him. He'd be hurt or old and stiff, or backed into a corner. But it was just not in that old warrior to lie down and die, even though he knew what was coming. Down would go that battering ram of a head, and he'd go to charging and hooking those wicked horns of his and trampling the wolves he'd gored. When the dust settled, he'd be down and finished. But by God, those wolves were bloodied and had paid dear for their victory. *That's* what is out there, Mac. The Indians are cornered. They're hurting bad. The quiet time is over. The horns are down and waiting, and they're getting set to charge with all the old fire burning in their eyes." McNab's face was set stubborn as George finished speaking.

"You can't accept that, can you? Or won't! Listen, I'm not saying the fighting has to start. It's folks like us who have to get the wolves held back. I'm firing off warnings to every big-shot in the territory. "Feed them or fight them!""

McNab smiled at him. "George, you sure do have a way of putting things; I'll hand you that. I'll have a chance to judge things for myself in the next few days. But now I want to get my lass here settled down. She's had enough excitement for one day, and it's an early start in the morning for all of us."

As they rose, George winked at Catherine. "Don't let Mac here take all the money from the Indians. I'd like to do a little business too!"

"Fat chance I'd have of doing that with you around."

Before they could leave, George took McNab aside, "I have word that Buck Breland brought Dorrie Barker and two of her girls."

McNab's face did not change. "Barker and I haven't seen each other for a couple of years. We are at opposite ends of the line-up. And she'll be getting a warning to stay away. It'll be okay, George."

***

As the McNabs walked back to their tent, the night reverberated with the singing, dancing, and drumming from the camp.

"How long do they keep that up?' asked Catherine.

"Probably all night, but don't let it bother you. They're just enjoying a social get-together while they have the chance. Soon they have to scatter for the winter. But now it's fun time and a feast tomorrow. They always get a steer or two to keep them in a good mood. I'll bet they look forward to that as much as they do their yearly five dollars."

The bed was made up, and Catherine slipped into it with a deep sigh of relief. She thought that the drums' pounding might intensify the pain in her head and keep her awake, but she fell asleep almost at once.

***

When Catherine awoke, it was full daylight and she was alone in the tent. She arose and winced at her sore muscles, then opened the door-flap. It was another fine day bright sun with little wind. McNab and Pascal Lebret were sitting by the camp stove with steaming mugs in their hands. Jim Burr and Paul McRae were going by, carrying books and bundles towards the tent where the treaty money would be paid. They appeared to be arguing, but whatever McRae was saying was being rejected by Burr. His face was grim, his eyes cold and angry. She shivered, hurried into her clothes, then went out to join the men for a cup of hot tea. They were both watching the agency men, now well on their way toward the big tent.

"I wonder what's going on between those two," remarked McNab.

Lebret looked worried. "Burr's looked real mean since the accident yesterday. Gray looked at the dead mare. He said there wasn't much wrong with it; Burr just shot it in a fit of temper. But McRae looks upset, and he don't upset easy." The agency men were at the tent now, and some men had gathered around them, gesturing angrily.

"I'm going over there to see what's up," said Ian. "Come on, Pascal."

"Let me come too!" said Catherine.

McNab looked doubtful. "I'm not sure. If there's trouble…"

Pascal interrupted him. "If there is, Mrs. Mac's best off with us."

By this time, Inspector Kingsley was passing by, along with several of his men. George MacKenzie. McNab, Lebret, and Catherine joined them. They could see that some of the men who had talked to Burr were now running back to the camp, but several remained. One of them was now doing the talking, speaking English. He was not shouting but his voice carried clearly.

"I think you must be crazy, Agent," said Jay Clear Sky. "You are making big trouble for sure."

"What the hell?" said Kingsley, "Mr. Burr, Clear Sky, what is going on here?"

"Keep out of this Kingsley," snapped Burr. "This is Indian Department business, and I am in charge, as you damn well know."

Inspector Kingsley turned to Sergeant Porter. "I don't like the look of this. Go back and alert the men, but don't bring them here yet. Just close enough to move in should any violence start."

By this time, many of the other traders had joined the spectators. The inspector and his men moved out in front of them. Clear Sky saw them. His black eyes were glittering angrily.

"Is this dog-agent really in charge here, Inspector?"

Kingsley nodded uncomfortably, looking beyond Burr to a large crowd approaching from the encampment.

George MacKenzie nudged McNab. "I see Big Bear; they must have gone to get him. And, oh Lord, Wandering Spirit, Little Poplar, Ayimasees … a whole war party, it looks like."

The famous old chief surprised Catherine. Big Bear had a worn and tired-looking face with pouched eyes, framed by wispy strands of grey hair. A Hudson's Bay blanket wrapped around his thin shoulders, he looked like he had just been awakened. He spoke to Clear Sky in a voice that was strong and deep despite his frail appearance.

Clear Sky translated. "The chief wants to know why you have refused to give us a steer for our treaty feast, since this was promised to us, and it has always been the custom. He wants an explanation."

"You tell him that only bands who have reserves and have moved onto them will get any meat from me." Clear Sky translated and the crowd responded with an angry growl.

"You know why we have not taken one yet," said Clear Sky. "We want one with good water, grazing, and hunting, and land that can be farmed. Not swamps like other bands got. Then we can provide our own food. But we have not been offered one like that. The chief thinks you are doing this just to make yourself feel important."

"You tell him," shouted Burr, flushing at the insult, "that I don't care what he thinks! You won't get meat from me until you take whatever damn reserve we choose to give you, and then stay there!"

"Inspector," said George angrily, "he's decided all this on his own."

83

"He's bucking for promotion," answered Kingsley. "If he can report that he was the one to get Big Bear on a reserve, he could end up as Assistant Indian Commissioner."

"Sure," replied George, "and General Custer wanted to be the American president. He ended up very dead."

Clear Sky had been listening to a dignified elder, nodding his head. "Blue Quill says it is a long time since white men came and killed off all our buffalo. This is no small matter. We need this meat; it is not just for a party. He says that you have no right to break the promise of the governor. He asks you again to give it to us."

"You'll get no meat from me!" shouted Burr. Big Bear spoke again.

"He is asking you for the third time," said Clear Sky.

"Inspector," whispered MacKenzie, "he'll be asked once more, making it the ceremonial four times, and if he refuses, then we *are* in trouble. I'm going back to my place and kill one of my own steers for them. Burr may be in charge here, but that doesn't give him the right to start a war, damn it." He sprinted back towards the fort.

A sudden roar of pure rage came from the crowd that chilled the blood of every person who heard it. Catherine was terrified and clung to her husband's arm. Burr had made the fourth refusal! The men were swarming around him like angry hornets, although Big Bear was holding up his hand, trying to calm them. Wandering Spirit, the war chief, was shouting above the tumult, and his voice had an odd ringing pitch, so that he could be heard clearly. He was a big, muscular man in mid-life, with a cruel scar on one side of his face. He was ignoring Burr, talking to the people and brandishing a wicked four-bladed war club, as well as a rifle.

***

Paul McRae left Burr and hurried over to speak to Kingsley. "You'll have to call your men in on this, sir, they're out of control now."

The policeman did not take his eyes off the crowd as he answered. "I have twenty-eight of them. There's twice as many warriors over there and more coming. If my lads come charging into this mess, shooting will start for sure. Hang on, Paul."

McNab put his arm around Catherine, and Pascal stepped protectively in front of her. They all seemed rooted to the spot, not knowing what to do. Then the din died as Big Bear called for silence. He faced Burr with a look of infinite disgust on his weary face.

Again, Jay translated. "You people have long wanted to get rid of me. So, I will die today, if you will feed my people." The old man's hand went to his belt, drew a knife, and raised it to his throat. But just as the point drew a spurt of blood, Clear Sky seized him and spoke rapidly in Cree.

"He is telling the chief that his life is worth more to the people than one steer," McRae whispered to the horrified spectators. Wandering Spirit glided up to grasp Big Bear's raised arm, and he took the knife.

Paul's dark face was shining with sweat. "The war chief is telling Mr. Burr to go back to Pounding Lake and keep the government money. They won't accept it from him now."

McNab exploded. "Well, *that* isn't going to do business a whole hell of a lot of good!" Catherine looked at him incredulously.

One of Kingsley's men did the same thing. "I don't believe this man!" he muttered, before he was silenced by a hard look from the inspector.

But now Wandering Spirit was advancing on Burr. He had dropped his other weapons, but he still had Big Bear's knife in his hand, and it was raised. Many people began to cheer him on. The agent just stood there, rigid and poker-faced. Then Clear Sky jumped so quickly between Burr and the war chief that the glittering arc of the knife grazed his shoulder before Wandering Spirit could arrest it. Blood ran down Clear Sky's muscular arm, as he argued with the older man.

"Nom de Dieu!" blurted out Pascal. "That took nerve!"

McRae hushed him.

"He has just told Wandering Spirit that the Crees need him as much as they need Big Bear. If he killed Burr, he would hang and for no good. Another man like Burr would be sent to replace him." The war chief considered this, looking murderously at the agent, then reluctantly he nodded and turned away. Suddenly Clear Sky himself confronted Burr. With a furious gesture, he seized his shirt-front in his fists and shook him violently. They could all hear him.

"I said it once today, and I say it again. You act like a crazy man! But you listen to me. If you treat us like this when we go to Pounding Lake for the winter, I won't do a thing to save you. Not even for Melissa. You'll get yourself killed for sure!"

"What the hell does he mean 'when they go to Pounding Lake for the winter?'" McNab's angry question was drowned out as one of the men fired a shot over Burr's head. Kingsley gave a signal, and the rest of his men, rifles ready, joined them on the run. The air was filled with whining bullets and furious shouts. McNab pushed Catherine to the ground, and dropped down beside her, since he did not have a gun on him. Within moments, the crowd headed back to the camp, still firing guns and whooping loudly. Burr watched them go. He smoothed his shirt-front, stroked his moustache, and smirked.

***

The spectators got shakily to their feet as a wagon came speeding up to them from the fort, driven by George MacKenzie. A freshly killed steer was in the back of it, the blood of the animal dripping to the ground. The trader slowed as he passed the Indian agent.

"I'm taking this meat to the Indians!" he shouted at Burr. "And don't you try to stop me! Then I'm going to ask your superiors to pay for it, while I tell them how you just risked the lives of every man, woman, and child in Fort Pitt!" He sped off.

Inspector Kingsley strode over to the sputtering Burr. "I agree with Mr. MacKenzie. You deliberately created an emergency here. We may very well have to resolve it with force. I therefore declare myself to be in charge, superseding whatever authority you held previously. Now, you stop and think what your posturing has done. If my twenty-eight men and the other people here, maybe sixty-five in all, including women and children are attacked, how long do you think we can hold out in an old ruin of a fort against hundreds of armed Indians?"

"Really got the wind up, eh Inspector?"

"I'll be backing up Mr. MacKenzie's report to the hilt. That is, if he comes back out of that camp in one piece, no thanks to you."

"You seem to be overlooking the point that, if I can get the Big Bear band confined to a reserve, this whole country is going to be a lot safer for *everyone*. Including you, of course." Catherine could hear some muffled but angry words from the policemen at that.

Kingsley flushed. "It is a waste of time talking to you."

"Well, at least I'm not afraid of the Indians. They can kill me, but they can't scare me."

At that point, Kingsley's icy control slipped for a moment. "You have just revealed yourself as a very stupid man, as well as irresponsible." He spoke to his men and the other watchers. "I want you all to go back to the fort, where you will be assigned defensive positions, at least until we hear from Mr. MacKenzie."

"Come on, Catherine," McNab said.

"You bet," agreed Pascal, taking her other arm. "We take ourselves there pretty damn quick." As they hurried past the traders' tents, Catherine noticed three frightened-looking women huddled together.

Catherine paused. "I haven't seen them before. They're white, aren't they? Ian, who…"

"Never mind that now," said McNab. They stopped at their own tent just long enough to pick up their guns and ammunition, although McNab grumbled that the unguarded wagons would be an open invitation to looting. Then they took Catherine to the MacKenzie house, where Leslie and the twins, white-faced, were taking rifles out of the gun rack.

"We are going over to the barracks until George gets back," Leslie told Catherine. "When we get there, I will show you how to clean and load one of these things."

They went outside and joined the people streaming toward the flimsy protection of one of the Hudson Bay warehouses, which now served as barracks for the Fort Pitt detachment. And the waiting began.

CHAPTER NINE

Inspector Kingsley and Corporal Gray were on their horses west of the fort, facing the camp. It was late afternoon, and George MacKenzie was still out there.

"What do you think, sir?" asked Peter. "If you want news of him, I'll volunteer to go."

The officer's tense face lightened briefly. "Thank you, but I think we should sit tight a bit longer. He knows them as well as any white man. And he has a lot of common sense. But damn it, *I'm* the one being paid to take the chances."

"He made the decision to go on his own, and I don't think you, or anyone else, could have stopped him. You know what store he sets on his three ladies. He saw that as a way to protect them."

"You seem close to the MacKenzies," replied Kingsley. "Would that have anything to do with your request for permission to get married? I saw it on my desk last night."

"Yes, sir. I'm lucky enough to have been accepted by Ellen."

"Good man. Don't do what I did and wait so long to find your ideal lady that, when you do, you are either too old for her or she's married to someone else or both." There was a wistful tone to his voice.

"I don't know about the age part. McNab didn't let a difference of some twenty years prevent him from marrying Catherine."

"But I am not Ian McNab."

"It's just as well, sir. One of him is enough."

"He *is* an odd one, Peter. There was Big Bear this morning with a knife at his own throat, all hell breaking loose, and what was McNab worrying about? Not his wife. Just the possible loss of business!"

"He doesn't deserve her, and I don't think he's making her happy. You notice things like that, sir, in a small place."

"I hope you're mistaken. But I had a very bad hour with him this afternoon. He's furious about Big Bear wintering in Pounding Lake. I tried to tell him, we don't make policy, we just carry it out. He wouldn't buy that. We're a bunch of conniving bastards, in case you aren't aware of it."

"It *is* bad news for the people of the town, no doubt about that," said Gray. He suddenly felt sorry for the man. He had a rough assignment in Fort Pitt. He was the only officer, which in itself was a lonely situation. Former British officers were not popular with the native-born Canadians in the force, because of their ingrained reserve and formality—some called it snobbery—and he had far too few men for the vast area he served. The men he did have were edgy and restless. They were not choirboys. They lacked recreation and female companionship. Two of them were on charge after a rowdy fist-fight in Dorrie Barker's tent last night. To top it off, Kingsley looked unwell. He was a sickly colour, and much too thin.

Kingsley interrupted Gray's thoughts. "Thank God, here he comes! I'll ride out to meet him. You go back and let the MacKenzie ladies know he's on the way. It must have been a long day for them." He intercepted George at the pay tent, who stopped so Kingsley could tie his horse to the wagon and climb into the seat beside him.

"How did it go out there, George?

"I think I was able to undo some of the damage. The meat I took to them was my best argument. Clear Sky did my talking. I speak some Cree, but not enough for that. Big Bear was willing to let the matter rest, but Wandering Spirit was still furious, and the others are as put out as I have ever seen. One thing though. They refuse to go back to Jim Burr for their treaty money.

"I was afraid of that. So now I have several thousand dollars in government money that the Indians won't take."

"Well, I did manage to talk them into a compromise. But I'm not sure you'll want to go along with it."

"I'll approve of *any* idea to settle them down. Tell me about it."

"I asked them if they would take the money if Burr came to their camp to give it to them. At first, they refused, but Clear Sky argued that the agent wouldn't like that at all. If Burr was made to do it, he would be humiliated. They liked that idea. I told them that you would need to be sure that Burr would be safe with them. They claimed he would be safer with them than he would be in his own mother's arms."

Both men chuckled with a certain amount of relish. They knew the men well enough to know that the agent would be treated with such mocking solicitude and exaggerated courtesy that he would be doubly insulted.

"Burr isn't going to like this at all, Inspector."

"He'll do it though, or I'll threaten to send him back to Battleford with the money under guard, charging him with…let me see…disturbing the peace, dereliction of duty, public mischief, and incitement to riot. I may even think of a few more, reminding him that, even if the charges are later dismissed, they would not enhance his standing in the Indian Department."

"A little polite blackmail?" asked George.

"Exactly!"

Back at the barracks, Kingsley advised the traders to return to their wagons. "I don't want to have to arrest any of the Indians for theft," he explained. He also called for a general meeting in the barracks to explain the altered procedure for making the treaty payments.

***

Catherine returned to their tent, her head aching and almost sick with fatigue. She stretched out on the bed fully clothed and fell into a deep sleep.

When she reopened her eyes, it was total darkness. Sensing she was alone, she felt around for matches and lit a lantern. Then she went outside. Just one other tent was lit up, and that was at the far end of the line-up, where she had seen the three women that morning. They seemed to be having a fine party there. She could hear shouts, and then some raucous laughter. But apart from that, there was not a sign of another person. There were just a few dogs tied to wagons, barely visible in the moonlight, dimming and brightening as clouds scurried by.

"Ian?" she called. There was no answer. She could see a large fire in the other camp, but the wind had shifted and only a faint sound of drums could be heard from there. There were a few lights in the fort; the barracks were well lit, but other than that, nothing. She really *was* alone!

She was almost as angry as she was frightened. "Well, damn you, Ian McNab! Where the hell are you?" Her heart was thudding and sweat sprung out on the palms of her hands. "You really don't care much about me, do you?" she asked the night. "Why didn't you put a rope around my neck and tie me to your wagon, so that I could be a damned watch dog?" Suddenly she realized how foolishly she was acting, and stopped. Her anger drained away, leaving only the fear. The dog tied at the next wagon over had lifted his head and growled, then stared into the darkness beyond Catherine. Someone was out there! She did not know if she should run back into the tent or stay motionless and invisible where she was. The voice, when it came, was almost expected, so acutely had she sensed another presence.

"I was going to tell you not to be afraid. But you sounded so angry that I had to say it to myself instead." There was amusement in the deep voice. All she could make out was a tall shadow as he moved in closer. She had heard that voice before. Then she realized who it was. A sudden flood of moonlight revealed Jay Clear Sky. She felt an overwhelming sense of relief. But she waited a moment until she could speak calmly.

"Good evening, Mr. Clear Sky." She held out her hand, before it occurred to her that he would not see it in the darkness. But he did. He hesitated, then shook it once. She resisted the impulse to pull away from his touch. His hand was warm, but hers was icy-cold, revealing how frightened she really was!

His voice was gentle when he spoke again. "You have nothing to fear from me, Mrs. McNab. I saw MaryLou's letter to Melissa Burr, and I know that you saved Lizabet's life at great risk to yourself. But I am surprised that you remember me."

"Of course, I remember you, from Battleford and when I saw you on the Fort Pitt trail. And then during that awful quarrel you had with Mr. Burr this morning."

"Yes, I saw you there too."

"You saw *me?* But how could you with all that going on "

"Mrs. McNab, a man would have to be blind not to notice you. My eyes work very well, even when I am ... busy." He surprised her again with the compliment. She felt a little uneasy, yet pleased, too.

She had thought him very alien and formidable this morning. But at this lonely moment, he was just a shadow and a friendly voice.

"How is your arm, Mr. Clear Sky?" she asked.

"My arm? Oh, yes, a small cut; I had forgotten about it. But I am not a 'mister'; that is a white man's title. I am just Clear Sky, or Jay, as you wish. They tell me that a jay must have come to look at me when I was born. They found a blue feather in my hand. So ... that is my name."

"Then my name is Catherine, please." *I really don't believe this,* she told herself. *Perhaps I am still asleep and dreaming. How can I be standing here, having a chatty conversation with one of the notorious Big Bear Indians?*

"Catherine? I will if you wish, but not in front of your friends, if we should meet again." She saw a flash of white teeth. "They would be very shocked by that, you see. Catherine, you should go and put your light out."

"Why?"

"Someone could mistake your tent for that other one."

"Where those three women are? I saw them this morning, but I haven't met them yet."

There was a long pause, and then he spoke even more quietly. "The women you saw, they are here to sell themselves to many men. And the men looking for them will head for a tent with a light on." Catherine ran into the tent and turned off the lantern. The man must think her an absolute idiot! He was still there when she came back outside.

The wind picked up; dry grass tossed, and she could smell wood smoke. Crickets shrilled and nighthawks thrummed overhead. In the distance, the sustained howl of a wolf blended with the music of the night. The clouds dispersed, the moon washing the camp in silvery light. Again, she had a feeling of total unreality. Clear Sky was watching her. Whatever he was thinking did not show on his impassive face. In this light, he was more like a stranger again, with his long black hair whipping in the wind, high cheek-bones smeared with red paint. He tensed. There was more screaming and shouting coming from the far tent, and it was heading towards them! With no hesitation, he pushed her inside the tent, came in behind her, and blocked the doorway.

"Don't move or speak! You want no part of this," he said.

***

"You come back here, Miss Dorrie," a man shouted desperately. Catherine knew that voice at once: Pascal.

"You go to hell, Lebret," a woman screamed. "The nerve of that son-of-a-bitch McNab, telling me to stay away from him! No one talks to me like that. He should know better. I laid a bottle across his nose once before, and by God I'll do it again! I got another one ready right here. I saw a light in that tent, and I'm going in after him. I'll lay it on good, and there'll be one for that little hotsie-totsie of his too, just you watch me!"

Sounds of a scuffle, then, "No. You was seeing things, Miss Dorrie," panted Lebret. "McNab's over at the barracks with all the rest of them. Saw him go myself, I did." More scuffling. Without being aware it, Catherine was clinging to Clear Sky's arm.

"Don't worry," he whispered. "If she gets past the old man, I'll have her out and back up the line before they know what's happened."

"He's in there. You're a lying bastard, you old fool!" Dorrie shouted. "You always was!"

"I'm talking straight now. Give me that bottle. Hey, look Miss Dorrie, it's half full. Come on back with me, and we'll share this instead of wasting it on McNab." Silence for a moment.

"Well, maybe. But I'm not scum, just because of what I gotta do to make a living. I've got feelings too." She began to sob harshly. "That isn't the kind of message he used to send me in the old days; remember, Lebret?"

"I do, but that was then, and this is now. Come on, Miss Dorrie." Pascal and the woman were moving away, voices dwindling as they went.

"Oh, dear Lord," gasped Catherine. "I feel sick." She ran out of the tent, fell to her knees, and retched. Clear Sky helped her to her feet, an arm around her to steady her.

"Catherine, listen. What she was talking about ... that was a long time ago. When white men came here, they had to turn to women like her, or to our women. It's not like that now."

"Yes, I can see that. I ... just didn't want to know about it."

He was looking at her intently, then he seemed to come to a decision. "Can I call you Cate? That would be *my* name for *you*." She nodded mutely. "All right, Cate, I am supposed to be on the way to take a message to Inspector Kingsley from Big Bear. That is what I was doing when I heard your voice and stopped. I must go now. But before I do, I want to give you something. It is very old and has been handed down through generations no one knows how many. It is said that the one who holds it knows when it is time to pass it to another. My father gave it to me just before he went away forever. It has a very strong power to protect the one who wears it. Will you promise me that you will wear this amulet night and day, if I give it to you?"

"You can't part with something like that," she protested, as he gently curled her fingers around a small object.

"If you are asked about it, you can say that you have it because Crees honour brave women as well as brave men." Then he was gone, back into the night.

***

She stood there looking at the empty place where he had been, feeling a sense of loss. Too much had happened to her in the last forty-eight hours. Too much that was violent, shocking, frightening, and painful, leaving her completely dazed. Gradually she became aware that the doors of the barracks were open and people were coming out. Many of them were carrying lanterns and some were coming her way.

When McNab returned to their dark tent and put down his lantern, he was surprised to see her sitting on the bed, looking at him. "Awake, eh? When I left for the meeting, you were so fast asleep that I thought best not to disturb you."

"Thank you, Ian. Your concern overwhelms me."

"What's this?" He gave her a sharp look. "I was sure I would be back before you woke up. Were you nervous? No need to be, you know. With food in their camp, no Indians will be hanging around here."

"Why do you assume I need only fear the Indians? There are a lot of *other* rough people around. I was very frightened."

"Why? Lebret is in the wagon. He turned in early. All you had to do was call out, if you wanted someone."

"I *did*. If Pascal is there, he didn't hear or answer me." McNab took the lantern and went outside. When he came back, he looked amused. "He's there all right, snoring away peacefully. From the smell, I'd say he's had a wee nip or two. I could have been robbed blind, leaving him on guard." She looked away from him. He didn't even realize what he'd just said.

He began to undress. "Come on, Catherine, it's been a long day." She did not move as he got into bed. "No harm came to you, did it? Stop your sulking, lass."

"In a minute," she replied. He rolled away from the light and was almost immediately asleep. Only then did she open her hand to see what Clear Sky had given her.

It was a wolf's head carved from a piece of white antler, beautifully detailed. *It looks old,* she thought, its patina well-established by use and time. It felt oddly warm, and in the golden glow of the lantern light, the eyes and ears of the wolf looked almost alive! There was a metal ring on the amulet, centred between the wolf's ears.

Catherine was wearing a gold locket, a gift from her parents. She took it off, and then, with a wordless apology to them, she removed the locket from its chain and replaced it with the amulet. It slid into the cleavage between her breasts. Because of its triangular shape, it fitted perfectly. *There,* she thought, *it will keep me safe from now on.* Amused by her own fancy, she turned off the lantern, undressed, and went to bed.

***

The next morning, a fuming Jim Burr went out to the camp to make the treaty payments, and for three days after that, all the traders did a brisk business. Although their customers were not as friendly as usual, no further incidents occurred.

McNab, Catherine, and Pascal were eating breakfast, before leaving for Pounding Lake, when George MacKenzie came out to say goodbye to them.

"Did you hear about the message that came from Big Bear to Inspector Kingsley, the night of the meeting?" he asked McNab.

"No, what now, George?"

"Clear Sky brought it. The chief says that, from now on, if the Indian Department wants to tell his young men what to do, they will have to make them do it. He can't anymore, because he can no longer offer them a future. I asked Clear Sky myself what that meant, and he was tight-lipped. He just said that was the message. He knew no more than that. But it sounds to me like a warning and Kingsley agrees. Big Bear could be stepping down as chief on his own, or he has lost his influence, and the warriors are taking over."

After talking a few more minutes, the two men shook hands. MacKenzie gave Catherine a bear hug and went back to the fort. Pascal went to hitch up the teams. Just then, McNab noticed the wolf amulet she was wearing.

"Where did you get that? They won't usually trade those pieces."

Catherine sipped at her tea. "It came from Melissa Burr's family. Perhaps because I rescued Lizabet."

"Let me see it," he said, holding out his hand. Reluctantly, she took it off and handed it to him. He studied it intently.

"This is genuine, one of the old ones. You have been very honoured, Catherine. You could get a lot of money for it."

"You mean ... sell a gift? What an odd idea!"

"No, I'm commenting on its value. But that's what's going to open up this country, bartering, trading, buying, and selling. Some people will make big money when the Indians and half-breeds are dealt with. Maybe you and me, lass."

"What do you mean 'dealt with,' Ian?"

"Well, I don't like the idea, but I think George is right; there's going to be fighting sooner or later. There's got to be an end to the kind of trouble we just had here. When it does break out, we'll see how damn fast the government can move when it has to. It won't last long, and as soon as it's over, settlers will flock out here and the whole territory will be one big boom town."

She put down her cup. "I hate it when you talk that way. We are doing very well as things are. Do you really want to make a lot more money by destroying the Indians and Métis?"

"Catherine, you're so unrealistic!" He looked exasperated. "Things are the way they are, and I can't change them. It was good out here in the old days, and maybe I would go back to them if I had a choice. But we can't do that. All we can do is look ahead. And there's no point to moralizing on how bad and cruel it all is, because that doesn't change a single damn thing. Can't you see that?"

"Oh, I know that you see yourself as practical and realistic," she answered. "But aren't you overlooking a point? If fighting breaks out, it won't only be the Indians and Métis who will be shot at and killed. Have you thought of that?"

"Look Catherine, give me credit for knowing something about this country and the people in it, after all the years I have lived here. The trouble will start at Batoche, and that is where it will end, pretty damn quick. You trusted my judgment when you came out here with me. Don't you do that anymore? But I'll tell you what. If I hear about George MacKenzie packing up his ladies and getting out of Fort Pitt, then I will pack us up and hightail it out right after him. Now, I'm going to help Lebret." McNab rose, and Catherine stood up with him.

"Ian, the amulet, please?"

He had apparently forgotten about it. He looked down at it in his hand, then tossed it back to her.

"A little extra insurance is it, Catherine?"

She replaced the amulet around her neck as he walked away.

"Yes, I think you could say that."

CHAPTER TEN

"We've been kinda busy here in town, while you were off relaxing in Fort Pitt, Pete," said Constable Cam Forbes.

Corporal Gray raised his eyebrows. "I thought we had all the bad guys with us."

"Wait 'til you hear. First, there was what I call 'the case of the awful offal.'"

"That sounds good for a starter; suppose you tell me about it."

"You won't believe it, but okay. It seems that Father Lafarge had instructed his hired hand, Sandy Ellis, to slaughter one of the steers in his herd. Ellis asked what to do with the innards, which the priest usually ignores, and he was told to discard them. So, Ellis followed directions, shot the steer, opened it up on the spot, and began to dress it out. Then he noticed some Indian kids sitting on the corral fence, watching him. On an impulse, he called the kids over, and gave them the liver, heart, tripe, and the rest. Well, you can imagine what kind of windfall that meat was to people living mainly on whitefish! Those kids ran home like conquering heroes with their trophies. But it happened that Bobby Red Plume was one of those kids. His father and the priest had some argument a few days previously, over Lafarge's method of disciplining his pupils in the mission school. He's gotta keep them in line, a' course, but when Red Plume saw welts on his son's back, he took exception and went over to bawl the hell out of the priest. So, when Sandy Ellis casually mentioned that he had given the innards to some Indian kids, Lafarge had some kind of fit, stamping and shouting that Agent Burr didn't want any civilians interfering in agency business, which includes feeding the Indians."

"Better for them to have it than the flies, isn't it?" asked Gray.

"I'd a' thought so. But the priest demanded to know who the kids were that had 'stolen' his meat, and when Bobby Red Plume's name was mentioned, Lafarge really exploded. He went roaring over to the Red Plume's place, burst in through the door. Seeing a pot already set up on the cooking fire with tripe in it, he grabbed a fork, and hooked the tripe out of the water. He told Bobby and his father that he was going to have them both arrested, then went off as fast as he had arrived, taking the tripe with him."

"You're right," said Gray. "I *don't* believe it."

"There's more," said Forbes with a smug smile. "Poor Red Plume came running over here in a terrible state, thinking he was about to be arrested. I couldn't understand him, since Paul McRae was away with you, so I took him over to Marie Scott, and she got the story out of him and got him settled down some. I took him home, then went over to see the priest. He was still livid; he'd even fired Sandy Ellis over the stupid affair. And he told me that none of this was any of my business. I said it was, if he was claiming a theft. I pointed out that he had entered the Red Plume house without permission, which was trespassing, and had stolen one of their forks! I said I was considering laying a charge against *him!* That cooled him off fast. He agreed to forget the whole thing, but of course, the whole story was all over the settlement by nightfall."

"Well, I'll be damned," said Gray, then both men began to laugh.

"There was a sad aftermath, though," said Forbes seriously. "Most of the Indians have withdrawn their kids from the mission school."

"Oh boy," said Gray morosely. "Okay, what else happened while I was gone? You said you were busy."

"Yeah. The carpenter, the sawmill foreman, and Bert Simmons got after the dummy one afternoon. Marie Scott came running to tell me. They sure must be hard up for their jollies. They'd got hold of some firecrackers and were tossing lit ones at him. They were too small to hurt him, but the poor bugger didn't know which way to run to get away from them. He was so scared he pissed his pants! I broke it up and gave them a real tongue-lashing. Told them if it happened again I'd charge them with assault."

"Jesus!" swore Gray softly. "What the hell gets into people? I'd like to get those three jokers and three firecrackers, and I know just where I'd shove them before I lit the fuses! So what *else* happened?"

"Well, this one was more routine. Do you recall an Indian named White Bear? He's a Big Bear man, about my height but wide-built, husky. He's got a round face and speaks some English."

Gray thought, then shook his head. "What about him?"

"It seems he had his cap set for Theresa Blue Quill, Mrs. Burr's sister, a real good-looker, too. As soon as he got his treaty money, he headed right back before the rest of you, took the girl to Father Lafarge, and asked him to marry them. He couldn't do that, since White Bear is a lapsed Catholic, not entitled to sacraments like matrimony. But Theresa is very religious and wouldn't get hitched without a church ceremony. White Bear got so mad, he took a swing at the priest. Gave him a good welt across the cheek. Sandy Ellis came running for me; I took White Bear to the guard room and fined him two dollars for assault." Forbes began to laugh. "He's a funny one, Pete. He paid up real cheerful. Said it was worth a dollar to find out that the Blue Quill girl didn't think much of him after all, and another dollar to take a poke at Lafarge! Of course, I warned him that, if he assaulted anyone again, he would end up in jail, and advised him to stay out of town for a while. Haven't seen him since."

Gray chuckled with him. "All the interesting things happen while I'm away. Now it will get dull again."

"Yeah, and it's going to be a damn long winter. There's an odd twist to this White Bear thing though, and it explains why he can speak some English. Dan Scott told me White Bear was orphaned as a child, and Father Lafarge raised him for several years. Then they had a falling out, and White Bear left him and joined the Big Bear band. He took back his Indian name and left the church. No one knows what caused the split, but there seems to be some real bad feeling there."

"Just one damn thing on top of another," said Gray. "All of them making a bigger fence with 'us' on one side and 'them' on another. I can look back to when the treaties were signed, and we called each other 'brother.' I guess that 'brotherly love' died with the buffalo herds. Hard to believe it's all happened in just eight years."

***

Summer was long gone. Snow had drifted over the settlement and cold bone-chilling winds were blowing on the day, early in December, when the people of the Big Bear band came riding into Pounding Lake. They came in unannounced, and the townspeople threw on their coats and came out to watch them going by on their way to the agency. They were a grim-faced, hard-eyed cavalcade, armed, all mounted (although sometimes two to a horse), clad in worn skins, furs, or Hudson's Bay blankets, dragging the travois that held their lodge coverings and the rest of their worldly goods.

Catherine had never seen them 'en masse' and this closely. The look of them, so different from the pleasant soft-spoken Woods Crees, sent a chill down her spine. Their faces were painted. All the men, the older boys, and some of the women carried guns, and she could see some of the evil-looking, three- and four-bladed war clubs. They kept passing by like a river of silent humanity, ignoring the onlookers. There was just the thud of unshod hooves, the odd clink of metal and creak of harness, or the snort of a horse to be heard above the moan of the wind. Catherine looked for Clear Sky, and found him at the end of the line, with a group of other young men. For just a moment, their eyes locked in recognition. He passed by, and she watched after him, wishing that they could have spoken.

Burr was waiting outside his office with his staff and the hastily assembled policemen. After a short conference, the people rode out of sight into the woods north of the town. There they would set up their lodges, homes for more than four hundred people. Only two people followed them, Melissa Burr on horseback and the man they called the dummy, shambling along in his awkward gait, perhaps dimly realizing that they were buffalo hunters, the fierce warriors from whence he had come, and for some unfathomed reason, lost to him.

How many years had As-a-Child been wandering aimlessly, Catherine wondered, searching, perhaps seeking them, but drifting in whatever direction his feet happened to be pointing? An inarticulate call came from him, and he held out his arms beseechingly to the place where they had disappeared. Catherine could not bear to watch him any longer. She went back into the house and closed the door.

***

An hour later, restless and unsettled, she went for a walk with Muhekun, now her constant companion. She had a sudden desire to see Marie. She tied the young wolf to the porch railing and knocked on the door. Marie was delighted to see her, throwing her plump arms around Catherine in her warm and welcoming way, smiling broadly.

"Come in, child, and join us. This is my day for company!" Inside the kitchen, warm and filled with the aroma of baking bread, Bert and Julia Simmons were having tea.

"Well, Mrs. McNab," greeted Bert Simmons, "what did you think of the big parade?"

"I don't think they look any happier about being here than we are about having them."

"That's the truth of it," agreed Marie, pouring tea for Catherine. "Poor things, herded around like cattle, their precious buffalo all gone. They are prairie people, used to plenty of room. Up here, jammed into one small place with so many Woods Crees and us townspeople … why they must feel like fish caught in a trap."

Julia looked at Marie with frightened eyes. "You don't think that will make them even more surly, do you, Mrs. Scott?"

Bert interrupted. "Of course, it will! No one is safe in Pounding Lake now. If it didn't mean I'd be out of a job, I would get out of here. As it is, I'm requesting a transfer." *Poor Julia,* thought Catherine, *if she needs reassurance, she won't be getting it from her husband.*

"Now Julia," said Marie, "I know they look strange and wild to you, but underneath they are just the same as the rest of us. You take Big Bear, who is called every name there is. He's been a friend of mine for years, and any time he will come walking through that door to say hello, have a smoke with Dan, and enjoy a big bowl of my soup. I'd trust him as much as I would *any* white man in this town."

"And maybe more than some?" asked Catherine.

Marie chuckled. "You stop reading my mind, child, but that's the truth too."

Bert was not amused. "It's no laughing matter, you know."

Just then Scotty came into the kitchen. When he saw the visitors, his seamed face broke into a pleased smile. "A wee bit spooked by the newcomers, folks? Settle you down now, no need of that. If we don't provoke them unnecessarily, try to bother their women, or toss firecrackers at them, we should get through the winter still wearing hair."

At the word 'firecracker,' Bert turned brick-red and avoided Scott's eyes. He changed the subject quickly. "What is all this talk about a horse race, Scotty?"

The older man looked at his wife with a twinkle in his eye. Then both started to laugh, although Marie shook her head, "That boy of mine, Giles! He has this horse, a roan gelding, named Buster. Dear Lord, how he loves that horse; I think he kisses it goodnight! But it is very strong and fast, and he loves to race it. Now the police here, they have one they call Trooper. They have already raced once and Trooper won, but just by a nose. And Melissa, she brags about her cousin's horse, which he stole from the Cheyenne a while back. That got to Giles, so he talked her into asking her cousin, when she was in Fort Pitt, to run in a three-horse race, and Clear Sky agreed. They are going to start a mile south of town with the finishing line in front of the Burr house. The betting that is going on!" Marie rolled her eyes in pious dismay. "It is sinful!"

"It is," agreed Dan solemnly. "I hear Father Raymond is coming here from Camas Lake, not really to help judge the race, but to hear all the confessions about gambling, before Communion next Sunday. Yours too, I am thinking, Marie."

"Where did you get that idea?"

"I heard Joe and Suzy talking about how much they are going to enjoy one of your suckling piglets when you lose it to them on the race."

"It is not really gambling when you bet on a sure thing," retorted Marie. "Giles says that Buster had an off day when Trooper beat him the last time, so my piglet is safe. And I will be wearing new rabbit-fur slippers made by Suzy; you wait and see."

"I haven't heard anything about this," said Catherine.

"Didn't Mac tell you? Marie's brother, Pascal, tried to talk your man into betting his bagpipes on the race. Of course, that didn't work, but he promised not to play them for a week if Trooper loses. But if Buster loses, Pascal has to work for Mac for two days without pay."

Even the Simmons were more relaxed by this time, and they were all cheerful when they left the Scott home.

***

Catherine untied Muhekun and began to walk home. "I would bet on the Cheyenne horse," she told the wolf. "He looks fast even when he is standing still." He wagged his bushy tail at her.

"No one is betting against the Cheyenne horse, Catherine." Startled, she looked around for the owner of the unexpected voice. Corporal Gray was standing in front of his make-shift barracks, leaning against a cottonwood tree. His sky-blue eyes were twinkling.

"Oh, but they are, Peter! Marie has even risked one of her precious piglets on Buster. Why are you shaking your head?"

"Because they are betting on which horse will be second or third. The Cheyenne stallion is one of those horses they call a 'living legend'. There is some exaggeration to it, but they don't get that kind of name or fame without good reason. I do know that American cavalry officers tried to buy him to use at stud, but the Cheyenne chief wouldn't part with him at any price. That was before Clear Sky horse-napped him."

"Then why would you and Giles Dumas put your horses up against him?"

"This is horse country and nearly all of us are horse fanciers. Everyone likes to get a chance to see good horses in action. Of course, I suspect Clear Sky has only agreed to the race because Father Lafarge, still smarting a bit over a silly incident while we were away, is awarding a side of beef to the winner."

Catherine changed the subject. "Peter, I want to ask you something. I hope you won't mind, and you needn't answer if it is awkward for you."

His smile vanished. "Ask away, Catherine."

"About the Big Bear Indians. Ian was furious about them being sent here. You policemen are here because they are. Bert Simmons is going to ask for a transfer. And they don't look at all friendly or happy. Do you think they will cause us any real trouble?"

"Between you and me, Catherine, okay?" She nodded. "It could be touchy. There are some very formidable men with Big Bear. They are Rattlers, members of a warrior society who have served as protectors of their people back beyond memory. In times of crisis, they set up what they call a 'soldiers' tent' and prepare for action which might, or might not, be defensive in nature. I am to notify Inspector Kingsley at once if there is any sign of that. But Big Bear is so influential that he and the other elders may be able to talk them out of it. Unless things get so far out of hand that they no longer have a choice. Even then, I trust the old man to send me word of it, giving me time to get the people out of here and down to Fort Pitt. The trick, and that's my job, is to see that things *don't* get out of hand. I can't, now, see any reason why they should, especially if I can keep Burr from provoking them like he did in Fort Pitt. So, to sum it up, we shouldn't have trouble, but if we do, we'll have time enough to get out of here."

"Thank you, Peter. That makes sense to me. You're a good friend and, I'll say it even if it sounds forward, a dear one. I'll not repeat what you've told me. Now I must go and get supper started."

"See you at the races," he said. But as he watched her walking away with the young wolf trotting at her heels, he felt a pervasive sense of unease.

I'll do all I can to keep a lid on things here, little lady, he promised silently. *I just hope it can be done.*

CHAPTER ELEVEN

On race day, the sky was clear, but raw and windy. The McNabs had been invited to the Simmons' house so they would not have to wait in the cold for the race to begin. Catherine had visited their house several times; the visits always made her a bit homesick. Julia was not much of a cook, but she had made her home a small oasis, plucked almost whole from southern Ontario and recreated in the rustic settlement.

Julia had never said so, but obviously she had come from a wealthy family. Her parents had sent her rugs, fine china, books, and rich velvet drapes. There were plump cushions on the sofa, petit point stools in front of the chairs and embroidered samplers on the walls. An iron heater warmed the parlour. Surprisingly, Julia did not fuss around her guests; she sat quietly and enjoyed them.

Catherine was beginning to realize that the marriage of extroverted Bert and timid Julia was not as incongruous as it seemed. Bert was domineering but protective and concerned about his frail wife. She, in turn, gave him a gentle and trusting affection and admired him extravagantly.

Jim Burr came in after them, smiling broadly. "It'll be a while folks," he announced, as he took off his coat. "I told Alex Richards to close up the sawmill. He'll let us know when the Indians show up."

"Good!" exclaimed Bert, rubbing his hands. "Then we have time to warm ourselves on the inside. We have coffee on the stove. I'll slip a little of my 'coffin varnish' in it, for medicinal purposes, of course."

When he went to get it, Catherine whispered to her husband. "What in heaven's name is 'coffin varnish'?"

"It's a brew Bert ferments from potatoes. Don't have more than one and drink it slowly. You'll feel it, even though he'll make small ones for you and Julia." She accepted her cup doubtfully, though the men smacked their lips appreciatively.

"I went over to the Indian camp earlier," said Bert. "Their horse is all they say it is. He has that wild-eagle look that the best stallions have. He cut up bad when I came close though; like with most Indian horses, the smell of whites spooks them."

"I didn't know horses had that keen a sense of smell," remarked Julia.

"They do," Bert assured her. "They can scent water, or a mare in season, from miles away. Jim, I hear this one had a band of about thirty mares when the Cheyenne first laid eyes on him."

"True," said Burr. "You can imagine how the Cheyennes felt losing him to the Crees after all the trouble it was to capture him from the wild. Melissa's father says that, for a couple of years after that, Clear Sky expected to wake up some night to see a Cheyenne chief bending over him."

A rap at the door interrupted him. Alex Richards stuck his unshaven face in through the doorway. "The Indians have just gone past your place, Mr. Burr."

"Excellent timing," said Burr, setting down his empty cup. They all hurried into their coats and boots. Catherine felt warm and a bit giddy. It was more exciting, she thought, to see a race knowing something about the horses and riders. She had never seen so many people in the street of the town. Many of them were standing by Burr's house, where the race would end, but the Plains Cree band was farther down the road.

Burr pointed at them. "That's confidence for you! They think they know which horse is going to win. They just want to see the run."

McNab said, "Well, I know horseflesh, and if I were a betting man, my money would be on Trooper!"

Catherine smiled to herself.

***

Two posts had been set up to mark the finish line. A cord, tied at intervals with strips of coloured cloth, stretched between them. Father Raymond was at one post, Father Lafarge at the other. They were to be the judges, in case it was a close finish. The side of beef was decorated with a big red ribbon and bow. The policemen, all decked out in their red tunics, were unable to maintain their usual objectivity, and were a bright cheering section for Trooper.

From a half-mile to the south came the sharp crack of a rifle, signalling the start of the sprint. Every head turned in that direction, as if pulled by a single string. It was only a moment before the three racers were visible, riders flattened against their backs, heads bobbing, legs reaching and devouring the ground, manes and tails streaming. The sound of the drumming hooves came to them clearly. At first, the three riders were apace with no clear leader visible. Then, as they reached the edge of town, Catherine felt someone touch her arm. It was Melissa, her face alive with excitement.

"Watch Cloudwalker ... *Now!*" she shouted. Clear Sky seemed to compact himself and the horse altered his long rhythmic stride to a shorter, harder, and faster gallop that impelled him forward with blurring speed. All as one, the onlookers let out a roar of surprise and awe as the bay stallion surged into the lead. A length—two lengths. Then he ran over the cord that marked the finish line and vanished momentarily into the trees behind the agency. The other two horses pounded across the now unmarked line in what appeared to be a dead heat. The two priests conferred and announced their decision. It *was* a tie between Trooper and Buster! Melissa was still jumping and clapping, and others were cheering themselves hoarse.

***

Down the road, the people were dancing in circles, shouting whoops of victory. By this time, Clear Sky had turned his horse around and was back to claim his prize. Catherine was pleased for him when she saw the smile on his dark and handsome face.

"Cloudwalker goes at two speeds," Melissa exclaimed, "very fast, and then faster than any other horse. Jay just has to ask him." The stallion was prancing, tossing his head, eyes rolling and nostrils flaring. He looked as though he would welcome another run. Clear Sky dismounted and handed the reins to a tall man with a roach headdress and a cruel scar on his face. He looked familiar.

"Is that Wandering Spirit holding Jay's horse?" Catherine asked Melissa.

"That's him, leader of the Rattlers. Some say he is a very bad man; others swear they would follow him into hell if he led them there." There was a chilling aura about the man, which set him apart from the people around him.

"I don't think I would care to pick an argument with him," Catherine said, suppressing a shiver.

"No, but Jim does," said Melissa. Her eyes were troubled as she looked at the war chief. "They hate each other with a passion and have for years. Some day, I feel it will explode."

"It must be so hard for you, in the middle between your husband and your own people," said Catherine. "I felt bad for you when we were in Fort Pitt." Melissa did not answer for so long that Catherine feared she had overstepped her tenuous bond of friendship. Then she saw that the woman's dark eyes were filled with pain.

"Come for a walk with me," Melissa said unexpectedly. They went by the Burr house and stopped for a minute to congratulate Clear Sky, who smiled back at them.

"I knew we would win. And my people *really* need that side of beef." When he looked at Catherine, she again felt the impact of the man's intense presence. "Hello, Mrs. McNab, I hope you were cheering for me?"

"Of course, I was! I had to with Melissa standing right beside me." She knew her face had flushed, as she and Melissa left him and walked on to the woods. Melissa had noticed nothing; she seemed deep in thought.

***

The two women stopped at the ice-rimmed edge of Pounding Creek and looked down into the swirling water.

"It *was* very bad for me in Fort Pitt," Melissa offered. "Even my parents want nothing more to do with Jim. But I insisted on choosing my own trail. Now I can do nothing but follow wherever it goes."

"Yes," agreed Catherine. "There is no going back after you do that, no matter how much you wish you could."

"You also, Catherine?"

"Well, there are times. I know I have disappointed Ian in some ways. I wish I was more ... knowing ... about men."

"Knowing?" repeated Melissa. "What do you mean?"

Catherine took a deep breath, then blurted it out in a rush. "I am not very good in bed. I can't seem to do anything right."

"Oh, so it is *that*. Your husband says so, and you believe him. If McNab had wanted a *'knowing'* woman only, he could have had one long ago. There are enough of *them* around. It may be that he is not very knowing about you. Have you thought of that?"

"Oh no, Melissa, it is me. I...I even cried on our wedding night, when he was just trying to get the first time over with quickly."

Melissa stared at Catherine. "That isn't love-making, you foolish girl, that is " she caught herself in time. "Oh, there is no use putting the name to it. So many people think badly about my Jim, but he wouldn't do that. He knows how to make a woman want him ... too much so, perhaps. I think I am pregnant again." Catherine was about to respond, but something in Melissa's face stopped her. "I am not sure we should have more children. Jim loves Lizabet, but we even quarrel about her. I want her to be proud that she is half-Cree. He wants her to forget about it."

They were silent for a while, both a little abashed that they had been so frank with each other.

"It is true, Catherine, that my cousin has given you his amulet?"

"Yes, I have worn it ever since. It is beautiful, but strange, too. At times it gets quite warm, at other times it is cool, almost cold. When it is warm, I can see it even in the dark, but not when it is cool. You will think I am very fanciful, Melissa."

"No. That means it still has the power and will work for you. I did wonder about that. But he must have thought it would when he gave it to you."

"Can you tell me more about it?"

"I am not sure of the legend myself. Such things are spoken of only at certain times. I do know that it is not really given, only loaned to one who has real need for it. In turn, that person will know when it is time to pass it on. Jay wore it secretly when he was in the white school in Winnipeg. And when he stole Cloudwalker from the Cheyennes. Since then, it has been cool and resting."

"I wonder how he could bring himself to part with it," said Catherine.

"He must believe that you are going to need it. We will know why some day, I am sure." After that, the two of them turned away from Pounding Creek and walked back toward the settlement.

CHAPTER TWELVE

It was Christmas Eve in Pounding Lake. Northern lights 'The Dancing Spirits of the Departed' to the Crees, were flaring, fading, and streaming out again, like a sheer, radiant fabric flung over the blue-black sky above the tiny hamlet.

People arrived at the church, singing as they came from all directions for midnight Mass, their lantern lights creating a crust of brilliant diamonds over the new-fallen snow. Catherine and Ian could hear them from across the valley, as they stood at their door to welcome guests not attending the Catholic service. Tom Adams entered with three of his former comrades in the police force: Peter Gray, Cam Forbes, and Clicker Lang. Dan Scott arrived, accompanied by Julia and Bert Simmons. Marie Scott was at the church with her son Giles and his family.

Earlier, McNab brought in a small fir tree, and they decorated it with strings of popcorn and glass beads, coloured satin bows, and silver sleigh bells. There were gifts under it for Tom and the policemen, made by Catherine, Julia, and Marie, of knitted scarves and socks and made-up boxes of cookies and Christmas candies. Cam Forbes brought out his accordion, and soon they began to sing some of the familiar carols. It took "Away In a Manger" to remind McNab and Simmons that the horses should have some apples and carrots. When they came back in again, they swore there was a big bright star over the top of the stable.

"It was your own noses you were seeing," said Scotty, detecting a whiff of 'coffin varnish.'

Wearing a red velvet dress trimmed with white crocheted lace at her neck and wrists, Catherine passed food and wine to her guests. She could see that the younger men, while joining in, were also looking a bit wistful. She understood that this must be a lonely time and place for them, so far from their families and loved ones.

Peter Gray went to her and took her hand, kissed her on the cheek, and smiled down at her. "Thank you for looking like an angel and inviting us to share your Christmas. And I will say it, even if it does sound forward, you *are* a good friend and a dear one." They both laughed. She had said exactly those words to him. She looked around to see how her husband had reacted to Gray's affectionate gesture. But he and Simmons had disappeared again. It was just as well, because Adams, Forbes, and Lang enthusiastically followed Gray's example, ending with Lang proclaiming to the world that he would never again wash the lips that had touched Catherine's cheek. After a few more carols and a final flurry of Christmas wishes, the guests took their leave, just as the people began to stream out of the church across the valley.

***

The minute the door had swung shut behind the last of them, McNab swept his wife up into his arms, staggered into the bedroom with her, and collapsed onto the bed, laughing. "What a Christmas! And to think that last year I went over to the church so I wouldn't be sitting here alone. And me a Presbyterian! Did you enjoy yourself, lass?" He gave her a bear hug that almost knocked her breathless.

"Yes. And how many drinks did you have this evening?"

"I'd not be able to say for sure; Bertie and I did have a wee drop or two when we went out to see the horses."

"And you were out there more than once I noticed. How sneaky!"

He got up and began to strip off his clothes. "Wasn't it? Now come on, my girl, it's Christmas, and I'd like my real present now."

She began to unbutton her dress, then she thought suddenly of the day she had talked intimately with Melissa. She tried to imagine what it was about Jim, a man she really did not like, that would make his wife say, 'He really knows how to make a woman want him.' He liked women, that was obvious. He flattered and teased and talked easily with them. That was all she could think of to explain it. Her husband was watching her. She looked directly into his eyes, as she dropped the last of her own garments into the chair and loosened her hair.

"You will have your present, Ian, but I want one too. So, tell me that you love me, say nice things, and just hold me close for a while first."

"What are you talking about, lass? You already know I love you, why else are we married and here in our bedroom together?" When she did not answer, he took her hand and drew her down on the bed beside him. He kissed her and his hands began to move over her hungrily. Her breasts were flattened against his muscular chest, and she could feel his full arousal, hot and hard against her.

"You know by now that I can't talk about my feelings. As for holding you first, I'll try. But the look and smell and feel of you makes me wild. Why doesn't that please you? Other women understand that."

"I am not 'other women', Ian. I am Catherine, your wife."

"Yes, you are. And I'll say it then. I love you, I do." He crushed her even closer, and his mouth came down on hers, searching and demanding. He began to move against her. Catherine was careful to open her legs for him. She kept her arms around him, and tried not to wince when he pushed into her. Perhaps due to the drink, he climaxed quickly, rolled away from her, and was almost immediately asleep.

***

Catherine wished they could have talked for a while. She had been warmed by the happy evening, but the house was cooling off. She rose, pulled on her robe, and padded back to the other room to lay some wood on the embers. She sat down at the table and read again the letters that had come with the gifts from her family and Jamie McNab.

The one from her brother Billy had, of course, been dictated. The spasmodic movements of his hands did not permit him to write on this own. His world was necessarily small, and he was missing her. Her mother's letter worried her. Billy was sleeping a lot. He was very thin. He now asked their parents to read to him rather than reading himself. He often asked if she would come home for a visit soon.

She dropped the letter and tears stung her eyes. From the day he was born, that tiny feeble baby had claimed her entire heart. She crossed her arms on the table and put her head down on them. "Oh, Billy dear," she prayed softly, "I'll come just as soon as I can. Wait for me. Don't go yet, please."

CHAPTER THIRTEEN

In January, the dreaded cold came. The temperature fell to forty-five below zero. Catherine had never experienced this kind of weather. At night, she could hear explosions outside, trees being torn apart by expanding ice locked into the living wood. Catherine learned by telegraph that her dear Billy had slipped away sometime in the early hours of Christmas morning. Wracked as she was by Billy's death, the ominous cracks sounded like guns from a ghostly guard of honour, firing a last slow salute to her dead brother.

Everything creaked, groaned, and snapped. Ice formed on inside walls around the door and windows, and Catherine melted snow for water as the pump was frozen. The snow was not soft and giving, like snow in Rosemere; when she walked on this snow, there was a crackling sound like broken glass. The police and agency men who had to be outside wore buffalo coats that came to their boots—brown furry mantles that made them indistinguishable from one another. McNab's horses were blanketed in the stable and fed an extra ration of grain for body heat. Muhekun, past the puppy stage by now, was growing a splendid white coat, accented with mesmerizing yellow eyes and a coal black nose. He no longer came into the house. He had burrowed a cozy den under the snow by their doorway. Although he was free to come and go at will, he seldom went off for more than a day at a time.

The Woods Crees began coming into town from their reserves, gaunt and hollow-eyed, asking for food. Catherine was shocked and distressed to see them. Because of the wolf, they avoided the McNabs, all but one: As-a-Child. For some reason, Muhekun accepted the bone-thin shambling man.

Burr gave the townspeople a stern warning. They were not to give a *crumb* to the Indians. If they did, they would soon have whole families beseeching them for more to eat. But with her grief for Billy a continuing heartache, Catherine ignored his edict in the case of As-a-Child. She gave him hot soup and chunks of bread or bannock. He would hunker down beside the house to gulp the food, while Muhekun watched him, nose resting on his big front paws. Once, horrified by his lack of protection against the deadly cold, she brought him an old horse blanket from the stable. Someone else had given him a pair of worn mukluks and tied them on for him. When Catherine draped the blanket around his thin shoulders, she thought she could see a faint smile of gratitude on his ravaged face. She had no compunction about disobeying Burr's order. As-a-Child could not tell anyone about his meagre windfalls. One thought troubled her though. Was she doing him any real favour helping him to survive? But that worry was no worse than the all-too possible prospect of finding him frozen solid some morning.

In this punishing cold, the confinement and resultant boredom frayed nerves and shortened tempers. Burr was constantly quarrelling with the Big Bear people. He flatly refused to alter the dates set as ration days, no matter how hungry they were. Since the game had been hunted out, there were no hides or furs for them to use to make warm clothing. Without it, they could not stand hours of chopping through the ice, then more hours of crouching over the holes to fish. So whitefish, the one remaining staple of their diet, was denied to them. That meant total dependence on the agency.

***

In February, Burr announced a new policy. Until Big Bear's band decided on a reserve and gave him formal notice of their choice, the Plains Crees' heads of families would have to work at the sawmill to qualify for rations. On ration day, they would need a note from Alex Richards to prove they had turned up for work. This was chopping cord wood, frozen iron hard, peeling bark, or piling logs. The last was invented labour because the next day, they were often told to re-pile the logs back in their original location. But like the Woods Crees, they had no warm clothing, nor on their scant rations, the stamina and energy for it. Nothing like this had been mentioned last fall, when the band had been asked to winter in Pounding Lake. The few band members now coming into Ian's store were surly and tight-lipped.

On St. Valentines' day, Bert Simmons came to the McNab house. Without polite preamble, he asked Catherine to get Ian from the store. When she went to get him, she said that Bert seemed very upset.

Ian nodded, "I'm not surprised." He left the store in Gabe's charge and followed Catherine back to the house. He sat down and lit his pipe. "What's on your mind, Bert?"

"Look Ian, Jim is playing his games again. You know about his idea of making the Indians work at the sawmill? Well, I was just out there. It's forty below and they have hardly enough clothing among them to keep one man warm. They're doing useless work. Some of the older ones look like death. What if they do start to die, what then?"

Ian went on smoking, his face impassive. "How are they taking it?"

"To my mind, far too quietly. They say nothing, they won't even look at us. Not even when old Two Guns started coughing up blood and it splattered all over the snow. Not even when I took the old man inside the mill to let him rest. Ian, I just can't reason with Burr at all, and neither can Peter Gray. He told Jim that he had reported his unauthorized new policy to the Department, but that didn't faze him."

Ian studied Bert's face intently. "But you said yourself the Indians are quiet. No threats, I take it?"

"That's my whole point! They're too quiet. It's against human nature to take treatment like that, especially when we consider who these Indians are. Alex Richards and Giles Dumas are scared worse than I am. Richards is wearing a gun and Dumas says he is quitting; he can't take it anymore, Ian. Something's got to be done!" Bert said, banging his fist on the table to emphasize his point.

Ian frowned, drumming his fingers on the table as he did when he was upset. "I don't know, Bert. You could be misreading all this, seeing it as worse than it is. Anyway, what can I do about it?"

"I'll *tell* you! You, and all the other men in this town who don't work for Burr, have got to confront him, then send a protest to the Indian Department. I'll see what I can get the employees to do."

Ian thought that over. "I don't know," he said again. "I think all that would do is just get Jim's back up. And then he would be more mulish than ever, and it would not do any good in the long run."

"Can you talk any sense into him, Mrs. McNab?"

"Ian can be every bit as mulish as Mr. Burr. As far as I am concerned and apart from the danger involved, you are obligated by simple concern for your fellow man to tell Burr that sick people should not be starved and frozen. And that promises given should be kept. It is moral cowardice not to do so."

"Oh, damn it, Catherine, snapped Ian. "It's your father who's the preacher, not you! You know it's not my way to go minding other people's business. But I might have a word with Scotty and Gray to see how the land lies." Simmons did not look too happy with Ian's ambivalence as he stood up to put on his coat.

"Do it soon then, Mac," he warned as he went out the door. After Bert was gone, Ian sat on there, smoking his pipe and tapping his fingers, deep in thought.

"Well," he said finally, "back to work," and he returned to the store. Catherine was both surprised and dismayed that he had not gone to see Dan Scott at once.

***

As long winter days went by, and Ian made no attempt to see Dan or Peter, Catherine confronted him. He turned on her furiously.

"Why does it have to be *me*? I'm not the guardian angel to the whole damn town. There is a priest here and six policemen. It's their job, and I intend to let them do it."

Catherine glared back at him. "Ian McNab, you know damn well that Father Lafarge backs Jim Burr to the hilt! He wouldn't give a hungry Indian his garbage! And Peter has already tried to reason with Burr, to no avail. Bert came to you for help. Are you going to let him down completely?"

"Don't nag me, woman! I warn you, I'll not stand for it! *If* I speak up, I'll do it in my own way and in my own time."

Her face blanched. "I don't think you will. You'll risk the danger. You'll tolerate Burr's arrogance and cruelty. You never intended to do anything about it, did you?" He did not answer her. He went stamping out, slamming the door behind him with a force that shook the house. She had never seen him so angry.

She went to the window, shaken by their bitter words. The amulet felt warm, and she touched it absently. She suddenly realized that she could see the pretty church across the valley. For days, the panes had been completely frosted over. The weather must have moderated, and her first thought was relief for the men working at the sawmill. She went to get her boots and coat. She wanted to talk to Marie Scott.

***

It was good to go outside after being shut up for so long. The sky was a clear polished blue. The ice crystals on the snow glittered, and she could breathe without feeling that her nostrils were going to freeze shut. What fun it would be to go tobogganing or skating with her husband on a day like this, instead of arguing with him!

When Marie answered her knock, she took Catherine's hand. "I have an old friend here today. Come in and meet him." An elderly man sat by the stove. "This is Chief Big Bear, Catherine." Then she said something in Cree to him, and he rose and took Catherine's hand, giving it one firm shake. He looked at her with a kind and interested expression. Until today, she had only seen him at a distance. Now here she was, face-to-face with one of the most notorious men in the northwest. And he looked for all the world like any other elderly gentleman, except for his swarthy skin and his attire. He was only a little taller than her and painfully thin. He looked tired but there were old laughter lines by his eyes. When he smiled, as he was doing now, it was impossible not to smile back at him.

He said something and Marie laughed. "He says that you are very pretty, and if he was a young man, he would steal you away to be his favourite wife." When Catherine laughed with Marie, he gave a nod of approval and returned to his perch by the stove. Marie refilled his cup and offered Catherine tea, but she declined. The big Métis woman was not her usual genial self, and Catherine suspected she had interrupted a serious conversation. She decided to leave them to it.

"No, thank you, I'm on my way over to see Julia," she improvised. "I just poked my head in to say hello."

Marie nodded. "I always like to see you, child, but the chief here has brought bad news. Another old friend of ours has just died: Two Guns. He was one of the band councillors and very respected. The people are in mourning."

"I'm sorry to hear that. I'll be on my way then." She stepped outside again and headed for the Simmons' house. She was puzzled. *Two Guns?* Then with a sinking heart she remembered. He was the old man Bert had mentioned, who had coughed up blood at the sawmill! She recalled Bert's anxiety also. *"What's going to happen when they start dying?"*

***

Julia was obviously glad to see Catherine, but she appeared more upset and flustered than usual. She kept blinking and brushing her ginger hair back from her temples. As soon as Catherine sat down, Julia hurried into her kitchen and came back with coffee. Then she made a startled sound. She had spilled some of the hot liquid down the front of her dress.

"What is it, Julia? You seem upset."

The other woman dabbed at her dress with a crumpled hanky. "Oh, the usual thing. Jim Burr is on the rampage again. Someone told him we had given a little food to the Indians. He was over here a while ago making a terrible fuss. He is going to report Bert to the commissioner. I tried to tell him I was the one to blame, but he paid no attention. Then Bert lost his temper.

He said the Indians have been out of food for two days, and that sticking to prescribed ration days, under the circumstances, is both cruel and stupid. We know that Melissa's father, Blue Quill, and her uncle Lone Man, came in to try to reason with him. But that didn't do any good, of course." She lowered her voice. "After they left, the Burrs had a terrible fight. She was just screaming at him! We could hear them over here."

"Well, Ian and I were doing some of that ourselves today," sighed Catherine. "On the way over here, I saw some of the agency men riding out toward the Indian camps."

"Maybe he *is* going to call them in for early rations then. Lord I hope so! But Catherine, it will be awful for Bert if he is discharged. He has the idea that he must give me all the things I had at home. I've tried to tell him that if those things were so important to me, I would never have left them. Why can't he understand that?"

"It's just plain foolish pride. Ian has more than his share of it too. It addles their heads at times." They sat quietly, each thinking their own thoughts. Catherine decided not to tell Julia about the death of Two Guns, as she was upset enough already. When they heard voices outside, they hurried to the window. McRae, Richards, and Dumas were dismounting from their horses. Burr and Bert were outside talking to them, and their voices were getting louder.

"I'm going to see what's going on," said Catherine, reaching for her coat. Julia hesitated, then decided to go too.

***

It was so bright outside, with the sun glaring on the snow, that the women were forced to shield their eyes; then they gasped. People were converging on the agency from all directions. From the north came the mounted Plains Crees. From east and west, the Woods Crees were moving in on foot as fast as they could. Some policemen came hurrying, pulling on their coats, apparently caught by surprise. Townspeople were also appearing. McNab and Gabe Berthier were coming up the street along with Father Lafarge. Scotty and Tom Adams came out of the Bay store. Big Bear reappeared from Marie's kitchen and walked out to the middle of the road; the people streamed past him as though he were invisible.

Julia was close to tears. "Oh, thank God! He has called them in for extra rations!" A wagon was standing outside the office, and Burr climbed up on it, motioning to Paul McRae to follow him. When he looked out over the huge crowd, it was completely silent. His eyes glittering, Catherine had the impression that he was enjoying himself. The eerie silence gave the whole scene an aura of unreality, frozen in time. Burr began to speak, pausing after every sentence for McRae to interpret his words.

"I sent my men to bring you people here for a very good reason. Not for extra rations, as you may have assumed, but because I won't have any more misunderstanding on your part. I will *not* have any of you, no matter how important you may think you are, coming in to me and making demands, as you have been doing this past while. I have told you when the next ration day is, and that is when it's going to be. Not today. Not tomorrow, but on the day I have set!"

Like a poked hornets' nest, an angry hum rose from the gathering. Catherine had a sudden recollection of George MacKenzie saying, *"the quiet time is over. The horns are down and waiting, and they're set to charge with all the old fire burning..."*

Burr spoke again. "If I fed you people every time you came in asking for food, there would soon be nothing left. I was sent here to see that this does not happen."

A Woods Cree elder came forward, and pointed to the agency warehouse. McRae interpreted. "He says that they know there is more than enough food in there to feed the people until spring. Yet they are forced to go through the town dump looking for scraps."

Wandering Spirit urged his horse forward, beckoning Clear Sky to follow him. The war chief's ringing words were sharp as a whiplash. When he was finished, Clear Sky looked at the men in the wagon, his own face an angry, contorted mask as he interpreted. "He says you must enjoy telling lies, dog-agent, since you do it so much. But you do not fool anyone. You want us to take any poor piece of land you offer, and so you are trying to starve or freeze us into doing it. But we must think of our children and those who will come after them. We cannot do that. If you were any other man, we would ask you to come to our camp and see the suffering for yourself. But you would enjoy that even more than the trick you have just pulled on us. So, stay away."

Burr was so infuriated that his angry gesture nearly knocked Paul McRae out of the wagon. "*I am the one doing the talking here!*" he shouted. "I will cut off the rations of the next man who speaks! As for *you* two," he glared at Wandering Spirit and Clear Sky, "make any more trouble and I will have the police arrest you and take you to Fort Pitt!"

At that, Big Bear came out of the crowd. His voice was very deliberate as he spoke, then paused for Clear Sky to interpret. "He says that you can keep his rations, but it is his duty as chief to speak. His young men told him that you could not be trusted, before he brought the people here. But he thought that even *you* would have to keep the promises made to us by the governor himself. He sees now that he was wrong, that he gave his people bad advice, and he is ashamed."

Big Bear looked old and sick as he turned his back to Burr and spoke to the silent gathering. They heard him out, then in grim silence began to disperse, casting looks of pure hatred at Burr as they left.

The agency men and Father Lafarge went into Burr's office. The policemen, their faces stiff and expressionless, eyed the Plains Crees who appeared reluctant to leave. Wandering Spirit made a sign. As one, they turned their horses and headed north toward their camp. As Clear Sky passed Catherine, he checked Cloudwalker and looked directly at her. He seemed about to speak, but then he shook his head and moved on after the others.

Catherine shivered. The sun was still bright and giving off warmth, and there was no wind, but she was ice-cold with fear. Julia looked pale and horrified.

"This has been a rotten day all around," said Catherine. Unable to speak, Julia just nodded and walked back into her house.

***

After supper, Peter Gray came to see McNab. He took off his boots and his buffalo coat, setting them beside the door. "Did you approve of that show Burr put on today, McNab?"

"Of course not."

"Well, my men think Burr was thoroughly enjoying himself. I wasn't there, because I was in Big Bear's camp taking a man into custody. They *do* have sick and dying people out there. It might have saved some of the energy they need to stay alive, if our friend Burr had gone out to them instead of calling them in. I suspect that was his way of getting even with them, for having to take the treaty money out to their camp last fall. He is a very cruel man, McNab."

McNab nodded. "You say you made an arrest?"

"I did. An informant told me that some Métis from Batoche were there, trying to get Big Bear's men to promise to join them when the rebellion breaks out. They took off when they saw me, but I managed to nab one of the them. I'm taking him down to Fort Pitt in the morning."

"I see," said McNab, tapping his fingers on the table. "Why have you come here to tell me this, Gray?"

"Because we've got real trouble on our hands, unless we do something right now about Burr. This town was in enough trouble even before he started this sawmill thing. I never saw a bunch of people, all in one small place, trying so hard to make trouble for themselves. But now Burr has turned it into a powder keg. I have reported him once, and I'll do it in Fort Pitt again tomorrow, but reports take time, and I'm wondering how much time we have."

"What are you proposing we should do?"

"Give him an ultimatum from all the white people here. Tell him to stop the sawmill work and increase the food rations. If he refuses, and you are all behind me, I will arrest him, take him to Fort Pitt, and let McRae take temporary charge of the agency until we hear from the department. He knows Indians, and his head is on straight."

"That's a drastic suggestion, corporal."

"Damn it, man, those Batoche men were talking *war*, not offering to play tiddlywinks! I'll bet a month's pay that if, or more likely when, a rebellion does break out, they want the Big Bear people to break into the warehouse and the two stores here, and take whatever they need for an attack on Fort Pitt. And after that, to move east and join up with Poundmaker. Then the combined bands could move on Battleford."

"That is pure speculation," retorted McNab. "I have lived in this country a lot longer than you have, and so has Scotty. We know what we're doing. We're on good terms with the Indians. Their quarrel is with Burr, and I don't intend to get involved in it."

Gray rose and pulled on his boots again. "You are already involved just by being here. But I see I have wasted my time." He spoke more quietly to Catherine, as he shrugged into his coat. "I'm sorry if I have upset you. I felt it necessary."

***

After Gray left, Catherine stared at her husband.

"Tell me something, please."

He looked at her warily. "What is it now?"

"Are you afraid of Jim Burr, Ian?"

"What? Me afraid of Jim Burr? Where do you get these ideas of yours? I rarely have anything to do with the man. Why would I be afraid of him, or any other man in this town for that matter?"

"Because I think you should be," she answered, "and for a very logical reason. He is the one who is dangerously crazy here, and not that poor man you all call 'the dummy.'"

CHAPTER FOURTEEN

Marie was sitting in her rocking chair beside the stove, still mightily upset by the ugly confrontation on the previous day. Someone began pounding on her door.

"Mrs. Scott! Mrs. Scott! Come quick!" She was on her feet at once, reaching for her boots. She heard that call too often not to know that it meant a medical emergency.

Paul McRae poked his head inside, his eyes wide with alarm. "It's Mrs. Burr! She's had a fall down stairs. Burr says she's pregnant, and he's scared as hell!"

"So he should be," she replied, checking the contents of her medical bag, then hurrying into her coat. "You wait and help me over there, Paul. If I slip and fall on that ice outside, I won't be much use to anyone. What happened?"

"Don't know for sure. I was in the office with Burr," he panted, trying to keep the big woman on her feet. "We heard Lizabet screaming, and he ran back to the kitchen; then he called me to get you. She's bleeding real bad."

"Poor girl," huffed Marie, "she's having a bad enough time with that madman she's married to without this."

***

Marie did not wait to knock on the door. She hurried past the office and the parlour on the other side of the hall. Melissa was lying on the kitchen floor, breathing in shallow gasps. Her face was beaded with sweat and her eyes glazed with pain. Her skirt was twisted up around her knees and her slim legs were smeared with blood. Marie went to her knees beside her and took her hand.

"It's me, Marie, child. Tell me what happened?"

Her voice was barely audible. "I've been having some pain all morning. When I was coming downstairs, after getting Lizabet up from her nap, I felt a bad pain and missed the step."

Marie bent over her then checked under the sodden skirt. Her face was very serious when she looked back at the two men. "Bring that couch over here by the stove. We need to keep her warm." She pulled Melissa's skirt down, wrapped it around her ankles, then helped the men lift the semi-conscious woman onto the couch. Lizabet was whimpering with fear.

"Paul, take the child over to your Louisa. Mr. Burr, I need a blanket and some clean cloths." The ashen-faced agent ran up the stairs while McRae soothed Lizabet and eased her into her outdoor clothing. Marie went to the stove, poured hot water into a cup, and shook powdered herbs from her medicine bag into it. She handed the cup to Burr, who had returned with the blanket and a sheet. Without waiting a moment, Marie began to tear up the sheet as she whispered to him.

"Your wife has lost her baby, but not all of the afterbirth. I will do what I can about that. While I am working on her, you get as much of the hot medicine into her as you can. We have to stop that bleeding quick or we could lose her."

They very nearly did. Half an hour later, Burr sent McRae out to Big Bear's camp to fetch Melissa's parents. At midnight, Marie sent for Father Lafarge. But Melissa was young and healthy. By the next morning, an exhausted Marie reassured the frightened family that she was coming around and would be all right, as long as infection did not set in.

***

A few days later, Catherine decided to visit Melissa. She knew that the Blue Quills, wanting nothing to do with Burr, had returned to their camp.

She set out after lunch, carrying a pot of stew and some bread, hoping that Melissa would not consider her visit an intrusion. She also suspected that she was the only other person, besides Burr, who had known that Melissa was pregnant. She paused, then began to walk briskly again. If Melissa did not want company, then she would just leave the food and go home again.

Burr answered her knock. He looked haggard but insisted she come inside. He accepted the food gratefully.

"This is very kind of you, Mrs. McNab. Father Lafarge is upstairs with Melissa now, but he should be down soon. You look half-frozen."

"It is terribly cold, but I won't stay if you think it best. I wanted you to know how sorry we were to hear the sad news. How is she feeling now?"

"Quite down in the mouth, but she might perk up a bit if she sees you." Just then the portly priest appeared.

"Good afternoon, Mrs. McNab. Jim, my boy, the best possible thing for your wife would be to get pregnant again as soon as possible. There is nothing like a successful pregnancy to take a woman's mind off one that didn't work out."

Burr nodded respectfully as the priest put on his coat. *How strange,* Catherine thought, *that Burr is so submissive to the priest!*

***

As soon as Father Lafarge left, Burr directed Catherine to their bedroom. Melissa was sitting wrapped in a blanket, her elbow on the arm of her chair, resting her forehead in her hand. She looked pale and infinitely desolate. Catherine noticed a tear slide down Melissa's thin arm.

"Melissa, may I come in?"

Startled, she looked up. "Catherine? Yes, of course. Over there," she added, pointing to another chair. But Catherine went to her first, and took Melissa's hands in her own. They were hot and dry. Catherine looked directly into her lovely tired face.

"I came to tell you how very sorry I am about the baby. How are you feeling now? Is there anything I can do for you?"

Melissa brushed her glossy, black hair back from her face. "Yes, just sit and talk to me for a while. I'm all right; it's just that I have a headache, and I hurt here." She touched her breasts and winced. Another tear slid down her face. "Oh, Catherine, my life is such a mess, isn't it?"

"It's only natural you're feeling depressed, after what's happened, Melissa."

"It's not just losing the baby. It would have been a boy, Marie said. I was far enough along for her to tell. But it's that man downstairs, too. I care about him, perhaps I always will, but our life together is destroying me. I tried to ask the priest's advice, but all he would say to me is to have another baby. I thought he was going to send Jim up to start right away!" She managed a half-smile at that. "Father tries, and he means well, but he is not good at being a priest. Not like Father Raymond at Camas Lake, who told me once I should go back to live with my family for a while, to think things out."

"Perhaps that's good advice, Melissa."

"I have told Jim more than once that I want to do that. He tells me I can go, but he won't let me take Lizabet with me. I *can't* leave my child."

"Of course, you can't. But I wonder, have you ever talked to your husband about doing something else ... changing his work maybe?"

"I've begged him to do that. But he won't hear of it. So here I am, trapped. None of my own people will have anything to do with me any more, except for Jay. Since the band moved to Pounding Lake, he comes to see me nearly every day. I don't know what I'd do without him."

Catherine was surprised. "Yet he calls Jim the 'dog-agent'? And they obviously don't like one another."

"That doesn't stop Jay; he knows I need him. I know the whites think he is a trouble-maker, partly because being an interpreter makes him so visible. Both he and his friend, White Bear, spent some years with whites. Our people say that makes them both a little crazy. But none of that makes him a bad man, Catherine."

"I never thought of him as that. I see him as very brave and honest. And he was so kind to me that night he gave me the amulet. I was alone and very frightened, but somehow I knew I didn't need to be afraid of him."

Now Melissa smiled a real smile. "A lot of the girls in our band would have traded places with you quite happily. We tease him by saying that he *had* to steal a horse as fast as Cloudwalker to get away from them."

"He is good-looking," agreed Catherine, "although, he can look very fierce too."

The two women chatted a while longer, then Catherine rose to leave. She promised Melissa that she would come to see her again soon.

"Please do, I feel better for talking to you. We'll stay friends, won't we? No matter what happens?"

"No matter what!" Catherine assured her.

CHAPTER FIFTEEN

McNab was uneasy. *There've been no Indians in the store for two days.* He went to see Scotty about it, but the trader had gone to Fort Pitt on business. Tom Adams was as puzzled as McNab was. "No Indians have come to the Bay store either," he admitted, "Not even the friendliest of the Woods Crees!" As McNab left, he saw some men on horseback in front of the agency office. He recognized them: Chief Big Bear himself, his son, Ayimasees, Wandering Spirit, and Clear Sky. Curious, he walked over to the agency instead of returning to his own empty store.

The men ignored him. They were staring at the agency's office door. After an interval, broken only by a stomp or nicker from the horses, Burr emerged, his face set and angry, followed by Paul McRae.

"Why are you here, disobeying my strict orders?" Burr demanded.

Clear Sky replied. "I am here to tell you that there is no food anywhere in our camp. Some of our people will not live until ration day. Unless you give us a little food for them, *you* will have killed them."

"If you want to use up your rations too quickly, knowing how long they are meant to last, that is your problem, not mine."

"You will give us nothing for those who are dying? Say it, agent. We want to be sure that you know what you are doing."

"I am giving you nothing," said Burr, staring down Wandering Spirit. McNab winced as a look of deadly hatred passed between two humans. Big Bear had seen it too. He moved his horse forward between the war chief and the agent. Then he spoke urgently to the men.

McNab could hear Paul McRae talking to Burr. "The chief is telling them to go back to the camp now that you have made your decision. He says he knows what is in their minds, but he asks them to wait. He is going out to a place called End-of-the-River. It came to him in a dream that a moose is wintering there. He says he will kill it and bring it to them."

"That's a lot of crap, McRae," snapped Burr. "What the old man *will* do is get himself froze to death in this weather. Then they'll be blaming *me* for that, too." Burr walked into his office slamming the door behind him. The delegation rode away in single file.

***

McNab walked slowly down the street, pondering that scene. The look that had passed between Burr and Wandering Spirit had sent a chill down his backbone, and he was not a fanciful man. Maybe, he thought, slowing down, he should go back and urge the agent to relax his damn rules, even if only for this one time. But Burr was not likely to listen to him, the man never listened to anyone but Father Lafarge. Then McNab changed direction and walked toward the church on the hill.

The priest did not attempt to hide his surprise when he opened his door to find McNab standing there. He invited him inside, smiling wanly.

"I don't imagine you are here to be converted to the true faith, McNab?"

"No, that's not exactly what I have in mind, Father. But I do want to ask you something." Then he told him about the meeting he had just witnessed. "There's no doubt they're in a bad way. I think it would be a smart move on Jim's part to send some extra food to them."

"Why are you telling *me* this, McNab? *I* don't run the agency."

McNab felt very uncomfortable. "I hope you might put the idea to him. He'll not listen to me, but I know he respects your judgment."

"No, I don't agree with your idea at all. The only way Jim can control all those Indians is by never backing down from them. They would see such a move as a sign of weakness on his part. The man knows what he is doing

135

and doesn't need any of us undermining his authority. I am surprised at you, McNab."

McNab opened the door again. "I'm surprised at myself for that matter. My wife told me once that you and Jim Burr were two of a kind. I should have listened to her. Young as she is, she saw you better than I did." He left the priest's home without another word.

***

Corporal Gray was on edge that night, as he stood by the window in the barracks. He had been away on patrol during the confrontation that morning. But Clicker Lang had told him all about it. And two of his men, Cam Forbes and Slim Anderson, were overdue from Fort Pitt with the mail and dispatches.

Lang and two other constables were playing poker at the mess table, which they had pulled close to the stove for warmth. Lang threw in his hand with a snort of disgust and did some figuring on a pad at his elbow.

"That's okay, Clicker," said one of the players, grinning at him. "I know how much you owe me. Just two dollars under a month's pay."

Lang groaned, then looked at Gray. "Cam and Slim won't be travelling this late at night. They're probably having a nice visit with the MacKenzies right about now." He winked at the other two men. But when Gray did not answer him, he looked puzzled, then went to join him. "What's the matter, Pete, did I say the wrong thing?"

Gray shook his head. "No, it's not that. Let's just say it's my policeman's instinct working overtime. There's trouble. I can smell it coming."

"Me too," agreed Lang. "That was bad, this morning. How strong did you make your last report to the inspector about Burr?"

"I asked him to telegraph Battleford about the situation here. I came right out and said that I think Burr is mentally unbalanced."

It was nearly midnight when they heard horses coming fast. "That might be them now," said Gray going to the door. In the bright moonlight, he saw the two men muffled in their buffalo coats and fur hats. One of them came hurrying to him, while the other lad led the steaming horses to the stable. Forbes handed Gray the dispatch case. His frost-covered face was grim.

"It's war, Pete! They got the word at Pitt today by dispatch rider. The telegraph lines are down, and when patrols went out to find the break, they were fired on, so they were expecting bad news."

Gray opened the dispatch case at his desk. Inspector Kingsley's precise hand relayed the details of a fight at Duck Lake, with shocking casualties to the police and civilian volunteers. He added that he was deeply concerned about the white people in Pounding Lake. A letter was included to Indian Agent Burr, advising him to tell them to evacuate to Fort Pitt as soon as possible, escorted by the Pounding Lake detachment.

"Get dressed, Clicker. This letter must be delivered to Burr right away. Wake him up if necessary." After Lang left, Gray opened a note addressed to him, a personal one from Kingsley.

"Spare no effort to get them to come here," he read. "We can't order them to do so, but it is the only sensible thing, and I could certainly use you and your five men. Send me a reply as soon as possible."

The policemen looked at one another with grim faces.

"So, we're in for it now," said Forbes gloomily. "We didn't get the names of the casualties, but the dispatch rider said that Superintendent Cooke got shot in the face. He's expected to recover, thank God."

***

As Ian and Catherine were eating breakfast, Gabe Berthier came to the door and told them the news.

"Corporal Gray wants everyone to meet at the barracks as soon as we can get there." They left their meal and hurried into their clothes.

The barracks were crowded when they arrived, and all the men were carrying rifles or revolvers. Some of them were dismayed and silent, while others were excited and questioning. First, the corporal read the dispatch describing the bloody fight at Duck Lake. He concluded by repeating the advice from the inspector, that they should all go to Fort Pitt as soon as possible. There was a long moment of silence.

"I'm staying put," said Jerry Dunn. "Don't care what the rest of you do! What the hell, we're safer here; that so-called fort is nothing but a fire-trap! It's got high ground on three sides, so attackers could shoot down from good cover. It's too far from the river to go for water under siege. The old place was never meant to be more than a trading post, so what's the advantage of making the move?"

"There's strength in numbers, Mr. Dunn," replied Gray. "If we can get all the policemen there, and then if we can recruit every settler and loyal Métis who can handle a gun, we can hold out until the weather breaks and then head east. There's nothing wrong with the fort in Battleford."

"That's too many 'ifs' for me, Gray." Dunn's face was set and stubborn.

"I can't go, Corporal," said Tom Adams. "Much as I respect your advice, I can't leave my post here without Scotty's say-so, and he's in Fort Pitt. I'll wait until he gets back and then decide."

"As for me," said Bert Simmons reluctantly, "and the other agency men, we'll have to do whatever Mr. Burr says."

"Not so," Gray informed him. "This is an official dispatch advising you all to go to a safer place to protect yourselves and your families, if you have them. That frees you up to make your own decisions, right Mr. Burr?"

"Now just a moment here, before everyone goes off half-cocked," replied Burr. "Father Lafarge and I have been up most of the night doing some hard thinking. He believes that we should stay here to show the Indians that we're confident of their friendship. I agree with him. I also believe that, if I leave, the Indians will break into the warehouse and help themselves to whatever they want."

"We'll stay," said McNab calmly, "and for the same reason you have given, Jim. My unmanned store out there at the edge of town would be an open invitation to the Indians to loot it." Catherine stared at her husband in shock. Obviously, it never occurred to him to ask for her opinion. He did not look at her even now; he was arguing with Gabe Berthier, who it seemed was angrily opposed to his decision. Peter Gray was looking at her, and she could see her own shock mirrored in his face. Everyone was talking at once.

Gray held up his hand for silence again. "Listen to me, all of you. Most of you know that I have been in the police force for eight years now. In my job, you develop an instinct for trouble, and while I don't want to frighten you, that instinct tells me that you will be in certain danger if you stay here. I'll speak bluntly, Mr. Burr, Father Lafarge. Your confidence in the friendship of the Indians for the people of this town is entirely unfounded and unrealistic. I don't have the authority to force you to leave, but I warn you, it would be very foolhardy for you to insist on staying. However, if you do, I will send word to the inspector, asking for more men."

Father Lafarge answered him this time. "On the contrary, Corporal, we do not want *more* policemen here. Several of us were discussing it before this meeting. We think it would be best if you and your men leave here as soon as you can." The policemen looked at one another in total disbelief.

"You can't possibly mean that," said Gray.

"Of course we do. You are overlooking something. It was the police who were attacked at Duck Lake, so obviously *you* are the focus of hostility in this territory. With you gone, we will have eliminated the major irritant to our Indians."

"I can't think of any sane response I can make to such illogical, wishful thinking," said Gray, white-lipped with anger. "The focus of hostility, whatever it may be elsewhere in the northwest, is not the small police detachment in *this* town. And *this* is where you are. Now think. There is a real shooting war going on, and it could spread like wildfire, since it has been pent up for so long. As you know, the most militant Indians in the entire territory are camped just two miles from this spot. They have had a very bad winter, aggravated by your harsh and unfeeling policies, Mr. Burr. You are proposing to eliminate not a major irritant, as you put it, but your only protection against almost certain trouble. This uniform we wear reminds the Indians that we are the Queen's men, with whom mutual promises of peace were exchanged. There is still a real reluctance on the part of many Indians to break those vows."

"An eloquent lecture, Corporal," said the priest. "Of course, you totally overlook the influence the missionaries have had in converting the savages. But then we are accustomed to the arrogance of the police in that respect."

"Must I remind you, Father, that there are very few converted people in the Big Bear band? A mere handful."

Burr interrupted impatiently. "It's time to put both questions to a vote. How many of you white people want to stay here in Pounding Lake?" All the white men raised their hands. "Good! Now, how many of you townspeople think, as Father and I do, that the policemen should leave as soon as possible?" To Catherine's utter astonishment, almost everyone again raised their hands. She looked at Julia. Hers was raised. As far as she could see, only Gabe Berthier, looking like a thundercloud, kept his arms folded. McNab, his hand held high, was looking at her expectantly. She clasped her hands tightly in her lap and looked away from him.

"Carried, then," said Burr. "Corporal, I assume you and your men will get ready to go right away?"

"I still can't believe this, but we will. Under protest. But I have one more thing to say. I strongly urge Mr. McNab and Mr. Simmons to send their wives to Fort Pitt with us."

"I want to stay with Bert," replied Julia immediately.

"I want to go," said Catherine. "But I won't without Ian." Peter would not leave it at that. He turned to McNab. "I would like to hear from you, sir," he insisted, his eyes challenging the older man.

"I must rely on my own experience and instinct in thinking that my wife and Mrs. Simmons are safer here than in Fort Pitt, which is after all, a military objective. I think the Big Bear people will move out of here as soon as weather permits."

"Very well," retorted Gray. He stalked into his office, angry and frustrated. The room was at once buzzing with conversation. Everyone seemed oddly elated, convinced that they had made the right decision and the gallant one as well.

"I have to get back to my office," said Burr, smiling around at them. "I am due to meet some of the Indians there." He went over to shake hands with the policemen, but the first one he approached, turned his back to him and looked out the window. Shrugging, Burr beckoned to Paul McRae, and the two men left the barracks.

***

Burr found Wandering Spirit, Ayimasees, and Blue Quill waiting for him.

"I want to see Big Bear, too," he told them, through McRae.

"My father has gone hunting, as he said he would," replied Ayimasees, his face drawn into bitter lines.

"He *did* go out in this weather? Why did you let him do that?"

"You should know why," snapped Blue Quill. "We are starving. How many times do we need to tell you that?"

"I don't know why you don't eat a horse or two, if you are so damned hungry," responded Burr.

"We eat the ones that die," said Ayimasees. "But we do not kill them. We know we are going to need them soon."

Burr ignored that. "McRae, tell them to go get Big Bear and bring him in to me. I have news I want to discuss with him."

Ayimasees looked furious, as he replied to the interpreter. "He says that even you should know that they do not interfere when a man makes his medicine." The three Crees stalked out of the office.

"They may go for him, Mr. Burr; they are worried about him. If so, I hope they find him for the sake of all of us in this town, and that they find him alive." McRae, too, turned and left the office.

CHAPTER SIXTEEN

Corporal Gray was still livid as they prepared to leave Pounding Lake. He had little sympathy for the men of the town, but it was the thought of the families that enraged him. The Métis women could probably make it through whatever might happen here. *But, my God,* he thought, *what about Catherine and Julia?* He was being forced to abandon them in the potentially lethal trap of this place.

They left a number of things behind: clothing, food, even Cam Forbes' beloved accordion. They finished by concealing all the ammunition they could not carry with them behind the privy.

"Lord," Constable Lang said, as he mounted Trooper, "I won't be sorry to leave this crazy place, but there is something so wrong about going off like this." There were murmurs of agreement from the other men.

"It's insane," replied Gray curtly, "but we don't have any choice." Single file, they trotted silently out of the corral and turned south on the rutted, hard-frozen trail to Fort Pitt. The sun was just appearing over the edge of the horizon. The town seemed huddled and asleep, all shades of grey in the cold light. Suddenly Gray checked his horse. A small forlorn figure waited in front of the McNab store, to say goodbye. Each man touched his hat as they passed her. Gray gestured to them to keep moving, then dismounted.

"I'm so sorry about this," Gray said, considering Catherine's lovely pale face. He could hardly speak.

"Peter," she said softly. "Don't blame yourself. You did all you could yesterday. Just wait, we will all be together again soon, probably dancing merrily at your wedding." Now he *knew* he could not speak. Instead he put his arms around her and kissed her cheek. Then he remounted and moved off to rejoin his men. He looked back once and waved. He felt an eerie premonition that he would never see this beautiful girl again. How could any man worthy of the name, value a pile of damn merchandise over the safety of his own wife? It was beyond him, and he was sure his men were thinking the same thing.

It took the unexpected sight of a northbound rider to snap Gray out of his black mood. It was Father Raymond, from Camas Lake. He appeared dumb-founded when he saw the six policemen.

"Where are you going?" he asked.

"This trail leads to only one place, other than your little settlement," replied Gray. "By the same reasoning, you are on your way to Pounding Lake. May I ask why, in God's name?"

"You don't need to invoke the Almighty to get your answer, Corporal," said the priest mildly. "Tomorrow is Holy Thursday, and Father Lafarge asked me to assist him at the service. Since the people of Camas Lake have gone to Fort Pitt, I see no reason to refuse his request. *Now*, may I ask why you are out here instead of in Pounding Lake?"

"We have, to put it crudely, been kicked out of town."

The priest's mouth dropped open. "I don't understand."

"Nor do we. But I am glad to hear that the people of Camas Lake have shown some sense. I advise you to come to the fort with us."

"I am tempted," Father Raymond replied. "Without you, Pounding Lake will be completely vulnerable. But I do feel it is my duty to assist at Mass tomorrow."

"Okay, Father," said Gray. "But if you can, will you try to get Father Lafarge to see it your way? He is the one who talked them into staying put and asking us to leave."

"He did? Well, I'll certainly try. But Father is not an easy man to influence. He is downright pig-headed, to also put it crudely. But I'll talk to him, then come to Fort Pitt after the service and let you know how it went."

"Thank you, Father. And good luck to you."

"He'll need it," said Clicker Lang, as they watched him go around a bend and out of sight.

***

Catherine leaned against the porch railing and felt tears slipping down her face. She could no longer see the six men, but she could still see Gray's stricken look as he waved his final goodbye. She swiped her hand across her wet cheeks and sighed.

"Does your heart go south with the leader of the policemen?" She recognized the deep accented voice even before she turned to see Clear Sky, looking at her intently from where he stood on the Fort Pitt trail.

"Oh, maybe a small piece of it," she said, trying to smile at him. "Just as it would if I saw you going away. It is hard to say goodbye to friends in times like these."

Clear Sky tied Cloudwalker's reins to the hitching rail and joined her. He took her hand when she offered it to him, but he did not shake it in the customary way, he just held it in his own for a moment.

"Cate," he said softly. "I am your friend. I wish I could be more than that." She went very still, looking into his dark eyes. It was there again, that strange empathy she felt with him. "I shouldn't have said that," he added immediately. "Please forget I did."

I don't know that I want to, thought Catherine, but she nodded her head at him, astonished at her own reaction. Was she getting as crazy as some of the other people in Pounding Lake?

"Why are you here?" she asked after a while.

"I have been looking for As-a-Child. Do you know who I mean?"

"Yes, of course."

"I lost his tracks among all the others on the road. But I know that he sometimes comes to you."

"He's not been here lately. Jay, how do you know he's been coming here?"

"By the blanket you gave him, and because he is still alive. I tried to keep him away from town after the white men threw the little exploding sticks at him. It didn't do him any good, that little game."

"Yes, the firecrackers. I don't know how grown men could do such a thing."

"To them it was a little fun to pass the time. And *my* people are called the savages." Then Clear Sky looked past her. "There he is now. Just turn around quietly. He is talking to your wolf." Her eyes widened when she saw him, because that was exactly what he seemed to be doing. He was on his hands and knees making soft noises. Muhekun, his yellow eyes fixed on him, was tilting his head first to one side, then the other. Then he inched forward, and licked the human face so close to his own.

"Muhekun *does* seem to be answering him!"

He was not looking at the man or the wolf; Clear Sky was looking at Catherine again. "Yes, he is able to talk to animals, although he cannot talk to people. We don't know how he does it, maybe in his wanderings he has lived with animals. But he has the power. Even when an animal is in great pain, it will go quiet and listen to him."

"Then he is not as lonely as I feared; he does have friends."

"Yes, and I am talking to one of them." He changed the subject. "Cate, do you have a horse you can ride?"

"There is just the team and Ian's saddle horse. Why do you ask?"

"Get one of them now, and ride away from here. It is not too late; you could catch up with that policeman who is your friend."

"I can't do that," she replied quietly. "Not without my husband."

His eyes flashed angrily. "You worry more about him than he deserves. If you were my woman, I would have had you out of here days ago. He is as blind as the agent. He is not even as smart as that one," he said, indicating As-a-Child. "At least *he* knows when to run away."

"You think there is going to be trouble here, don't you?"

"It has a way of coming when people keep asking for it." He took her hand again. "If you won't leave, then be sure you wear the amulet. That is the best I can do for you now."

"I am wearing it, Jay. I have ever since you gave it to me."

Clear Sky no longer looked angry, just tired and resigned. He untied his horse and taking As-a-Child's arm, he led them north through the deserted street of the town.

***

McNab went back to his store after his mid-day meal to find a distraught Gabe Berthier pacing back and forth in a towering rage. He was surprised. He had employed the good-natured Métis for years and had never seen him like this."

"Are you still all riled up about us sending the policemen away?" he asked, raising his eyebrows.

"You white men here are all crazy, every one of you! I would quit working for you right now, Mac, but I am too worried about your wife to do it."

"What the hell are you talking about?"

"Look," said Berthier, stopping to give him a bitter stare. "Paul McRae was just in here, looking like a ghost. The men brought Big Bear in from his hunt, and the old man is furious. Burr wanted reassurances from him, since fighting had started at Duck Lake, that his band will stay quietly here ... that the townspeople are safe and that he wouldn't be making any 'unreasonable' demands under the circumstances. Big Bear said he couldn't do that, after all that has happened here. He did have a suggestion though. He asked Burr to give him one agency steer to try to quieten the camp, at least for a day or two. Of course, Burr refused, and then all hell broke loose, close to a riot over there. *Merde!* He has said 'no' once too often! Wandering Spirit said, 'No more talking. That is finished now!' Which means the Rattlers are taking over."

"And that has you all steamed up like this?"

"Mac, you never did bother to learn much about Indians, apart from how to trade with them. Do you know what this means? *The soldiers' tent is up!* We couldn't get out of Pounding Lake now, even if we tried. Those warriors will be turned loose on us at any moment. My guess is tonight. Now, pay attention to what I'm telling you. Get your gun and pack up your lady and hightail it over to the Simmons' place. Stay with them for the night. Then you and Bert keep a sharp watch out. I'll stay here and guard the store, because knowing you, you'll refuse to go if I don't."

"I don't know…"

"No, you sure as hell don't! If you won't go, I'll get Mrs. Mac and take her over there myself and leave you here with your store. Decide what you value most; it's up to you."

McNab could hardly believe this was Berthier talking to him. He was too surprised to be angry. "You mean that, don't you?"

"I mean it. But it's better for me to be here than you. The Indians might come raiding, probably will. But they don't hate us Métis. We might get roughed up some, but I don't think they'll shoot us."

For the first time, McNab began to feel a prickle of genuine alarm.

***

McNab closed the store an hour later, leaving the keys with Berthier. Carrying their few overnight needs, the McNabs walked silently toward the agency, Catherine pale and wide-eyed, her husband dour and silent. They were tense and nervous. After supper, the two men discussed their situation.

The Simmons were happy to see them, but neither man could understand why the Métis were so apprehensive.

"Don't you think it's possible," asked Catherine, "that they understand the Indians a little better than we do? I know Clear Sky gave me a very serious warning this morning."

"Damn it, Catherine," exploded McNab angrily, "why is it that you pay attention to everyone else but me?"

"I don't do that! I thought this was an open discussion."

At ten o'clock, McNab and Simmons took the extra precaution of locking the doors and windows. Then they banked the fire for the night and went upstairs to the bedrooms with their wives, leaving their rifles leaning against the wall beside the kitchen door. It did not occur to either man to stay on guard through the night. None of them heard the stealthy sounds all through the settlement before dawn began to dispel the inky darkness.

CHAPTER SEVENTEEN

Someone was pounding on the door so loudly that the blows seemed to shake the whole house. Catherine, finally asleep after a restless night in a strange bed, came fully awake and sat up in alarm. McNab was sitting on the edge of the bed, hurriedly pulling on his clothes.

"Wh-what is that?" she asked, brushing back her tumbled hair.

McNab turned up the lamp. "That's what I plan to find out. Something must be going on; it's only five o'clock." He opened the bedroom door. Simmons was already going downstairs with a lamp, still in his nightshirt, muttering impatiently. Leaving the other lamp with Catherine, McNab followed Simmons, who went to the door and unfastened the lock. Paul McRae, wild-eyed and shaken-looking, jumped inside.

"There's trouble!" he shouted, trying to shut the door.

"Where?" asked Simmons blinking, still not quite awake.

"Right here!" McRae gave up the losing battle with the door, and it flew open again to reveal a painted warrior standing there pointing a gun at them. "There are no horses in the stables," McRae panted, and the hay and grain has been taken. I heard a brawl going on at the Burr house, so I ran over here to warn you. Looks like I wasn't fast enough." The man walked inside, pointing the gun at McRae. A second armed, painted man followed him in, took the interpreter's gun away from him, and looked around. The rifles belonging to McNab and Simmons were still behind the door. As more men came crowding in, their rifles were snatched up.

***

At the top of the stairs, Catherine and Julia, clinging to one another, looked on horrified. The first intruder spoke and McRae translated to the two stunned white men. "They are going to search the house for any more guns and ammunition. They say as long as you stay quiet, there won't be trouble." McNab looked up at his wife, and his face was as white as his shirt.

McRae said, "It might be best if you came down here. They are going to be all over the place."

The women obeyed, clutching their robes around themselves. As soon as they were off the stairs, a pair of men brushed by them, going up to the bedrooms. McRae was again talking to the man who had led the others into the house.

He gave McNab and Simmons a warning look. "This man is Ayimasees, and he's one tough customer, a Rattler. Don't try anything; his finger's itchy on that trigger. The agent is their prisoner, and they've broken into Dan Scott's store. No word on yours, Mr. McNab. They want food."

"What will we give them?" quavered Julia.

"Anything you have in the house, Mrs. Simmons. You'll have to get it in the kitchen, but bring it in here to them. Stay as close to us as possible." Then he spoke to Ayimasees, asking him if they were prisoners too. The big warrior answered curtly. "We are, it seems," McRae told them, "and so are all the other whites and the Métis who work in town." The three men jumped, as Julia gave a little scream. She was cutting bread and meat at the dining table, when one of the men snatched the knife from her hand and started hacking at the left-over roast himself. Ayimasees kept his gun pointed at the prisoners, while the other men crowded around the table and began to wolf down the food.

Catherine returned from the kitchen with a teapot and a tray of mugs. Her hand was shaking as she tried to pour the tea, and she spilled some of it on the table. One of the men pushed her away and filled his own cup. She was close enough to her husband to whisper to him.

"I got a look out of the window. There's a crowd of them down at the barracks. They've broken in there too; I saw a boy running off with Cam's accordion."

McRae interrupted her. "They're going to take the three of us over to the agency office for a meeting."

"Bert!" wailed Julia. "Please don't leave us alone with these savages!"

"Honey, we just don't have any choice," he replied, looking helpless. "Paul," he added, "I feel like a fool standing here in my nightshirt. Ask the boss-man there if I can get dressed." Ayimasees gave his assent, then swung his rifle so that it was pointed at Julia.

"That means," said McRae quietly, "that if you try anything, he will shoot your wife."

"Jesus!" Bert exclaimed, "I won't. Julia, I'll be as quick as greased lightening." He ran up the stairs taking them two at a time. Julia's freckles were dark blobs on her ashen face, but suddenly she began to laugh. It was high-pitched and strained, but a real laugh and not hysterics as Catherine had instantly supposed. She was pointing at the table. The rest of the food was gone but the cake she had baked yesterday was still untouched.

"I know I'm not much of a cook, but am I really *that* bad?" Catherine stared at the cake for a moment, then she, too, began to giggle. Ian looked at them as though he doubted their sanity, but McRae approved.

"Good girls! Don't let them see that you are frightened." Simmons came running back down the stairs, doing up his belt buckle. He shot a quick look at his wife, then another one at McRae.

"What about Louisa? Is she all right?

For the first time McRae smiled faintly. "The last time I saw her, she was back of our house trying to hide our money and the silver, and she said, to bury the first Indian who came near her. And, Mrs. Burr is out of this. I saw her with Lizabet and Clear Sky, while the row was going on in the office. She was hysterical, but he got her and the child into a cart and off toward the Indian camp."

Ayimasees interrupted the talk by seizing their coats and tossing them at the two white men. McNab said nothing, as he bent over to pick his up. He looked dazed and disoriented.

McRae was eyeing him curiously. "How come you two didn't have your rifles at hand? Between the three of us, we could have blasted Ayimasees back out of here and put a stop to at least this part of their little spree."

"We ... misjudged the situation," answered McNab.

"A lot of us did. Now they tell me they're going to leave a man here to guard the women, then let you rejoin them after the meeting."

Julia began to sob. Ignoring the levelled gun, her husband went to her and held her close for a moment. McNab started toward Catherine, but their captors intervened and took the three men outside. The man remaining on guard pushed the door shut behind them.

Catherine felt like crying too, but she tried to comfort Julia. "Come on, dry your eyes now; remember what Paul said about not showing fear. Let's see if our keeper here will let us get dressed too." She pointed upstairs, pantomimed putting on clothing and raised her eyebrows at him. He nodded indifferently. As soon as they were out of sight, Low Horn went to the table, ate some of the cake, and washed it down with tea.

***

At the agency, the men were in an ugly mood. As soon as they were inside, McRae and Simmons were shoved roughly toward Burr, who was standing pale and tight-lipped at the other end of the room. The two priests were standing in a corner with Sandy Ellis, the farm hand. Jerry Dunn and Alex Richards were being held. Richards was ashen-faced; his captor was holding a pistol six inches from his ear. Tom Adams was standing alone. McNab sidled over to the former policeman.

"What's going on here, Tom?" he asked in a low voice.

"Damned if I know. There's been no interpreter here until they came in with McRae, so it's just been a lot of pushing and yelling to me. Looks like

Father Lafarge got banged around some." The priest did not look happy. He had a livid welt across his nose, and it was bleeding. He was wiping at it with a crimson-stained cloth. Tom Adams spoke again. "I was asleep when Joe and Suzy Two Horse came running to warn me. I ran over to the store, but they were already inside turning everything upside down. What a hell of a time for Dan Scott to be away!"

"How is Marie doing?"

"Better than the rest of us, that's for sure. When they took me past the Scott's house, I saw Big Bear sitting with her in the kitchen. Making sure no one bothers her, I would guess."

"I should have taken Catherine to her. We spent the night with Julia and Bert, and they caught us flat-footed this morning."

Adams stared at him coldly. "It's beyond me why you didn't send her out of here with the police detachment."

"I don't own a crystal ball," retorted Ian.

"You didn't need one. Corporal Gray laid it out right on the line for you and Bert."

"Okay, Tom. Nothing you can say to me could be half as bad as the things I'm saying to myself. Look what I've got my lass into. What will they do with her, if something happens to me?" McNab's face, usually so impassive, was rigid with apprehension.

"Just pray that it won't," said Adams.

A commotion was going on at the other end of the office, where the agency men were cornered. Wandering Spirit was pacing back and forth shouting at them. McRae, his face beaded with sweat, was trying to interpret, but the noise was almost too much for him.

"He says for you to give them meat now! Or he will tell his men to go out and shoot all the agency cattle."

"Why don't they then? They have all the guns," challenged Burr.

"Mr. Burr, you have baited them; now they are returning the favour. They want *you* to give it to them, after all your previous refusals. For God's sake, do it or they're going to turn on all of us."

Burr glared at them with an almost demented fury in his eyes. "All right! Interpret! I am asking if we have an inferior steer in the herd. One that is old and past his prime."

McRae gave him an uncomprehending look. "You want me to interpret that? Not on your life!" McRae spoke to Wandering Spirit, then to Jim. "I've told them only that you are giving them one."

"All right," spat the agent. "Someone, you Richards, go out and get it for them."

"Oh, sure," retorted the sawmill foreman. "Pick on me, with this guy standing here with his gun in my ear, itching to blow my head off! Try again, Burr."

"I'll go," volunteered Sandy Ellis. "Me not being an agency man, it might be better that way."

McRae spoke to Wandering Spirit, and although the war chief's hard and frozen face did not change, he gestured to Ellis, who brushed by McNab and Adams without looking at them. His eyes were wide with fear as several warriors followed him.

Father Raymond approached the group at the end of the room. "Mr. McRae, will you ask them if Father Lafarge and I can hold a church service? Say that this is a holy day to us, and that we wish to pray together." In a lower voice, he added, "it may have a calming effect on everyone." Wandering Spirit considered this, then replied, smiling coldly.

"He says yes, and that we had better pray hard today. We can all go except for you, Mr. Burr. He says ..." McRae hesitated.

"He says what, McRae?" demanded the agent.

"He says that our God does not deserve to be bothered by someone like you." Burr shrugged with a show of indifference, as McRae continued. "They will take all of us who are prisoners to the church. And they will go and get our families and bring them there, too."

At that point, most of the warriors left the office, including the one who had been holding the gun on Alex Richards. The beefy man sank into a chair, as though all the strength had drained from his legs. He was glaring malevolently at his employer.

"You know who that guy is, Mr. Burr? It's Two Gun's son. He says we killed his father by making him work at the sawmill. And that crap you tried to get McRae to repeat, about an old and useless steer! You'd rather see us all dead than come down off your high horse, wouldn't you?"

"You're fired Richards, as of now," snapped Burr. "I'll see to it that you never get another job with the department!"

Richards laughed harshly. "Christ! You still don't know what you have got us all into, do you? I'm worried about my *skin*, not another job."

"Come on, friends," said Father Raymond. "This isn't doing us any good. They're beckoning to us. I think we can go over to the church now." As they were led outside, they could see a stream of people ahead of them, going south, flanked by armed men.

Simmons cautiously edged his way over to McNab. "What do you think of our chances, Mac?"

"I'm sweating," he admitted. "I've never seen Indians acting like this, almost joking one minute, mean as hell the next. It could go either way. It'll blow over or blow up, depending on what happens next. Look, there's Julia and Catherine in the group ahead of us."

***

The men were at the church before the two women saw them and ran to them, crying in mingled fear and relief.

"I wasn't sure I would ever see you again," whispered Catherine to her husband.

"We'll be all right, lass," McNab told her. "Burr is giving them food, and they have agreed to this church service. For today, we're going to be good Catholics, I'm thinking."

"Very good ones. Ian, Jay Clear Sky came to the house after you left. He was sort of shouting at us, but that was for the benefit of the guard. He said that the warriors were very edgy and we should go along with anything they tell us to do. He said that, if we can do that for a day or two, after they have had a few good meals, they will likely cool down and the worst will be over."

"Well, that was decent of him. But, without guns, we don't have much of a chance to do anything else." He saw Gabe Berthier and his wife in the crowd and went to shake hands with them. They were each carrying a child. Berthier was much calmer than yesterday.

"They did break in, Mac. Took all the food they could find, guns, bullets, powder, all the blankets. The horses are gone. I tried, but with so many of them, there wasn't much I could do."

"Except get yourself tied up all night," said his wife. "Look. We are to go into the church now."

Once the prisoners were inside, they slipped quietly into the pews. Armed warriors were ranged all around the side and back walls, their faces as still and implacable as death itself. Wandering Spirit was the last to come in. He blocked the door, his unfathomable eyes fixed on the two priests, his rifle resting butt down on the floor beside him. His cheeks and forehead were streaked with yellow paint. There was a prolonged silence. An early spring bird call sounded with a harsh sound like the screech of chalk across a slate. Father Raymond, in front of the altar, looked composed but jumped at the sudden cry.

"Dear friends," he began, forcing a smile to his stiff lips. "We have decided not to celebrate Mass. Not in a church filled with armed men, who might interrupt or mock the service, and not with Father himself suffering some distress. But we do wish to lead you in prayers for your safety and for the deliverance of your loved ones gathered here today." His voice was strong and steady. Catherine thought of her father, who would have been very moved by the simple dignity and sincerity of the words that followed. She took her husband's hand. Like hers, his was damp and cold. She looked up at him. His eyes were fixed on Father Raymond. When the prayer ended, the priest smiled at them again, this time more easily.

"We are not all Catholics here, but I am sure we are all in the care of the same Heavenly Father. I am sure that we are all familiar with the beautiful words of the Twenty-third Psalm, which has comforted Christians in times of sorrow and peril down through the centuries. Will you join me in letting it do that for us now? The Lord is my shepherd..."

Their watchful captors did not move or make a sound. Catherine repeated the sonorous words as the others did, but she found little comfort in them. When she came to the phrase "...walk through the valley of the shadow of death ...", she wondered if that was exactly what they were doing. Slowly, the people of Pounding Lake rose to their feet. Those who were Catholics crossed themselves, as the priest blessed them. Abruptly the warriors followed Wandering Spirit out of the church. The townspeople eyed each other apprehensively, not knowing if they should follow them or remain where they were.

"My God," whispered McNab, "I was so blind and stubborn! Why didn't I see this coming?" Catherine saw a flash of agony in his eyes. "I swear I'll spend the rest of my life making it up to you, Catherine."

She squeezed his hand. "Just think of the stories we can tell our grand-children about all this!"

***

Everyone in the church went quiet again. Clear Sky had just entered. After a brief conversation with the two priests, he faced the townspeople.

"I am asked to tell you that we have moved our camp across Pounding Creek to a better place west of the Hudson's Bay store. The warriors want you to move over there too, until they decide what to do with you." There were outbursts of protest and everyone seemed to have a question for him.

"Be quiet!" he bellowed. "You got yourselves into this. All winter we watched you in your warm clothing, full of good food, while we froze and starved before your very eyes. Our babies died because mothers had no breast milk for them. Elders died because they gave their food to the young people. The agent abused us, and no one here tried to stop him. And then you sent the police away." His eyes were glittering, and for a moment, he looked like a younger version of Wandering Spirit. But with visible effort, he brought his anger under control and spoke more calmly.

"I am going to say this on my own. Be very, *very* quiet. Try to make yourselves small and invisible. Challenge no one. Go to the camp across the river. In a few days, you may even be allowed to return to your homes, if you do that. Our quarrel is with those who run this country, not with people like you. You half-breeds, leave the church now. After that, the white people can leave together."

***

The first person to speak after Clear Sky left was Gabe Berthier.

"Too much of what that young man has just said is true, and his advice makes sense. Today we do what we are told, eh? Come on, my friends." He led his wife and two children outside and the other Métis followed; old Pascal left last, and he winked at Catherine cheerfully.

The ten white people went slowly to the door, loath to leave the church and yet afraid not to. It was mid-day, and the sun was glaring off the snow, dazzling their eyes. The Métis were well on their way toward the agency buildings. Ayimasees and about thirty warriors were waiting for them. The man who had held the gun on Alex Richards earlier now prodded him in the back with it, and he and Jerry Dunn started out together. Bert and Julia Simmons followed them. McNab, taking Catherine's arm, fell into step behind them. Tom Adams and Sandy Ellis were next, and the two priests brought up the rear. *Just like a line of well-behaved school children,* Catherine thought. They moved along slowly, with their watchful captors surrounding them, on and up the valley. A cloud suddenly obscured the sun. *The valley of the shadow of death,* thought Catherine again, and shivered. They were all so silent! Just the sound of feet crunching the snow.

The white people were approaching the Burr house when Alex Richards and Jerry Dunn came to a standstill. Richards began to swear softly, almost under his breath, but they could hear him. Then Dunn turned and gestured to the rest of them to stay back. They stopped in their tracks.

Burr was standing in front of his house, hands in his pockets, glaring defiantly at Wandering Spirit. Because there was no interpreter, the war chief was making hand signs, pointing to the new camp going up on the west side of the creek.

"No, damn it!" shouted Burr, "I'm not going over there and no one else is either! I forbid it!" He was shaking his head, to be sure he was understood. "I've been pushed around all morning, and I'm not taking any more of it! I'm not budging from here, and you can do what you like about it!"

"Oh Ian," whispered Catherine frantically, "Jay warned us not…"

"I know, lass," he replied, putting his arm around her and looking back at the forlorn straggle of white people, all of them slack-faced with fear. Wandering Spirit shouted something back, and once again pointed west. Some of the warriors came running up the line to see why it had stopped. Bert Simmons moved to put himself between his wife and the running men. Julia put her arms around him and closed her eyes.

"I told you 'NO!' *Nummu!*" The agent's eyes were blazing, and his lips were drawn back in an ugly parody of a smile.

"Stop it, Burr! Right now!" McNab called out sharply. "This is no bluff, you damn fool!"

"They can kill me if they want!" shouted Burr. "But I'm not going across the creek to their God-damn camp!" Those were the last words he would ever say.

Wandering Spirit dropped his blanket to the ground, raised his rifle, and pointed it at the agent. Burr continued to shake his head. With no sign of emotion, Wandering Spirit sighted along the barrel of the rifle and pulled the trigger. The heavy bullet smashed into Burr's chest, and the terrible force of it, at such close range, lifted him off his feet and drove him backward, where he fell into a snowbank beside his doorway. Blood from his shattered chest spurted out over him and into the snow, changing it from white to a lurid crimson in an instant. One dreadful groan came from him, audible over the crashing echo of the fatal shot. Then noise rolled over them: the shrill war cries of the Rattlers and shouts of fury and hate; then more gunshots, screams, and shouts.

The war chief was reloading. He turned, looked at the rest of the white people, and now his painted face was as rigid as a stone statue. He shouted a command and pointed at them. Another shot. Alex Richards took it in the belly, and he staggered back past the Simmons and almost to the McNabs, screaming in fear and agony, his arms windmilling as he tried to keep to his feet. Then he went down. The tumult became a sustained roar punctuated by cries and groans and pleas for mercy.

Clinging desperately to Ian, not wanting to look but unable to turn away from the engulfing horror, Catherine saw Father Raymond run past them toward Wandering Spirit, his arms outstretched and beseeching. A shot from behind jolted the wide-brimmed black hat from his head and knocked him sideways. One from the other direction knocked him the opposite way and toppled him into a bush. He hung there, kicking convulsively. Big Bear came running out of the Scott house, shouting mightily, trying to stop the carnage.

Catherine, with Ian's arms tight around her, felt a violent shock go through him. Hot blood sprayed down over her, and then, very slowly, he sagged and fell, carrying her down and pinning her to the ground underneath him. Through it all, she could hear Julia screaming wildly. Ian jerked spasmodically as another bullet crashed into his prone body. Catherine lay with her face pressed hard against the icy ground, blinded by his blood. She could hear people running by, and more shots and screams. A horrible gasping sound nearby.

"Ian," she whispered. "Ian, answer me! Help me, I can't see!" But he did not move; nor did he answer her. She tried to free one of her hands so she could wipe her face with her shawl. One eye cleared, and she could see Tom Adams lying face-up close beside them. The horrible sound was coming from him. He had a bullet through his throat. She watched him for a time, with her one dazed eye. After a while, the sound slowed and stopped. His contorted body finally went limp.

"Oh, dear God, dear God, dear God," someone was moaning. It was her own voice. Although she was still pinned, she found that she could lift her head. "Ian?" She struggled to shift his inert weight slightly, and twisted to look at his face. *Oh, Ian,* she thought sadly. *Poor Ian, your head is all broken.* His unseeing brown eyes were staring up directly into the cruel sunlight. One of them was bulging out in the strangest way. She put her head down again. This proud man wouldn't want her to see him this way.

She was feeling very weary and gave a tired sigh. It was much quieter now. She closed her eyes and drifted off into merciful oblivion.

CHAPTER EIGHTEEN

When the white people started walking toward the agency, Clear Sky had closed the open church door and leaned up against it, watching them. His mind was racing. What could he do now? Earlier he had gone to the Simmons' house to see Catherine, but it had not been possible to get her out and away, even if she had been willing. Low Horn was on guard, and the whole agency area was swarming with his people.

It was the same way in the church. He could not look at her, as he gave the frightened people their instructions. There was no definite plan to harm them, but something could explode at any moment. There was so much pent-up anger and resentment!

It was a cold day, but standing there protected from the wind, he could feel warmth in the brilliant sunshine. He was tired. He closed his eyes and thought about her again. It was something he had been doing much too often, and for months now. He could not understand it, or himself. During his years in Winnipeg and Battleford, he had never seen white women as being particularly beautiful. Melissa was, and Theresa, and his sister MaryLou; many Cree women were.

But then he had talked to Catherine McNab, and touched her one moonlit night, and he had never been able to get her out of his mind again. A white married woman! It was irrational ... impossible. Perhaps it was just as well all this trouble had started, at least for him. If the white people got out of this predicament safely, they would go away, and he would never see her again.

***

The first shot shocked Jay out of his inertia. Rifle in hand, he was running before the next shots and the screaming began. He could see little but a mass of seething people in front of the agency. But as he came closer, he could see bodies stretched out on the bloody ground. Father Lafarge. Three Stars was bending over him. When he saw that the priest was still breathing, the Rattler calmly shot him in the head. Sandy Ellis was next, sprawled face-down, his straw-coloured hair riffling in the wind. Father Raymond was off to one side, his body caught and held by a leafless bush. Alex Richards was flat on his back, arms and legs flung wide with blood and matter still welling from a gaping hole under his ribs. Then he saw McNab, fallen over and partially concealing Catherine's body. Tom Adams lay crumpled beside them.

One of the warriors was pulling Julia away from Bert Simmon's broken body. Her face was as vacant and unfocused as As-a-Child's. She kept falling to her knees, reaching and calling out to her husband, only to be pulled back to her feet again. Past them, and near the body of Burr, Jerry Dunn lay curled up like a sleeping child. But Jay took all this in with only a fleeting glance. He was only too aware of Three Stars examining the bodies with his pistol in his hand.

Catherine was smeared with gore. Clear Sky was almost certain that she too was dead, but he had to be sure. He pushed McNab's body aside with his foot and went to one knee beside her. His heart lurched. Her eyes were slightly open and her face was chalk white, but she was breathing in short little gasps. He had seen dying people before, and he was afraid he was looking at one now, but he dropped his gun and blanket and pulled her free.

People were running and shouting all around him, but they were caught up in their own frenzied excitement, paying no attention to the bodies on the ground. No one was looking at him or coming his way. Three Stars was now crouched over Sandy Ellis.

Jay picked Catherine up and ran toward a thick stand of aspens and wolf-willows, expecting discovery at any moment. But he made it into the trees and then dropped down, his breath labouring, his heart thumping hard in his chest. He was strong and well-muscled, but he had been hungry for so long that he was incapable of any sustained effort.

After a few minutes, he looked back through the trees at the milling people. No one seemed to have noticed him, and his racing heart slowed down a little. He was not a Rattler and had no right to take a prisoner himself. He hoped that, if anyone thought to look for her, they would assume that she had been taken as Julia had, by the warriors.

He looked down at Catherine as she stirred. She was staring up at him, but her eyes were blank with shock. He wondered how badly hurt she was. He took part of her shawl, and using snow, wiped her face and neck. She had no wound there that he could see or feel under her matted hair. She had blood and tissue, brain matter, and pinkish shards of bone all over her shoulder and down one side, but that must have come from McNab, whose head had been blown apart. He touched the amulet lying askew at her throat and nodded. It was very warm.

"Can you talk to me, Cate?" She blinked, but did not answer. He wondered what he was going to do with her. He could think of nothing and was getting desperate about it when he heard her voice.

"Will they kill me when they find me?" she asked. Her eyes no longer blank, but filled with horror instead.

"I don't know," he answered truthfully. "But I will keep you hidden as long as I can. Are you hurt anywhere?"

"I don't think so, but oh God ... look at all this blood!" She moaned, trying to twist away from the sight of it. She retched and began to tremble violently. He leaned over her, gripping her shoulders.

"Hang on, Cate! Look, I dropped my gun and blanket when I picked you up. I must get them or they will realize who has you. I need to get you out of here. Will you stay very still while I go back to get them?"

She did not appear to take that in. "Ian! He is dead, isn't he?"

"Yes, they are all dead." He did not want to leave her, but he had to get her away before they were discovered. "When I go to get my things, I will look again at him to be sure. But I won't do that unless you promise not to move. Not even to raise your head."

"I won't move."

"And you won't make a sound?"

She shook her head. He scooped up an armload of twigs, snow, and dead leaves and threw them over her. Luckily, she was wearing a brown dress. If she remained still, as she was now, she was well camouflaged. He took some snow and wiped away the blood that had smeared his chest and backed away slowly. Then he stood up and ran back toward the path where the bodies lay.

***

Jay ran past a line of Woods Crees and Métis with their wagons, tents, and household goods, beginning to move to the new campsite. In his haste, he stumbled into two blanketed women.

The taller one scowled at him. "Have we not gone through enough today without getting knocked off our feet too?" It was Marie Scott with her friend Suzy Two Horse. Relief flooded over him. He took her arms and spoke rapidly in Cree.

"I have her, Mrs. Scott, McNab's wife."

Her mouth fell open. "What? You mean the poor thing is not dead too? What have you done with her?" He motioned her to silence and looked around cautiously before answering.

"She is hidden, but not very well and she may be hurt. Can I bring her to you?"

"My Lord, if only Scotty was here I could say yes, but I am with Joe and Suzy, and I can't put them in that kind of danger "

"Bring her to our tent when we get it up," interrupted Suzy. "Joe will want us to help her. We are feeling so sad about poor Tom Adams. Enough people have died here today."

"Bring her then," agreed Marie. "We will be watching for you."

***

Without another word, Jay took off toward the crumpled bodies. He picked up his blanket and gun and glanced briefly at McNab's shattered head. He had died instantly. Pieces of his skull were lying beside him like a broken eggshell. He turned away, stepping over Tom Adam's body. As he passed Burr's corpse, he stopped for a moment, feeling a rush of anger at the vain and self-obsessed man who had caused all this carnage. He got through the slow-moving line of people again and into the trees without attracting attention. He dreaded to look at the spot where he had left her, but she had not moved.

"I am back," he whispered, so that she would know who was coming. She struggled to her feet. Her eyes were like purple bruises in her pinched face, and he knew what she was waiting to hear.

"I'm sorry. He is dead. I made sure. He died quickly, maybe he never even knew he'd been shot." She almost went down again. He threw his blanket around her, covering her head at the same time as he tried to steady her. Then she was clinging to him frantically, her face under the blanket cold and wet against his chest. He put his arms around her and again felt anger, this time against the man who had been her husband. They had been so wrong-headed, those dead white men! And they had been taken so easily! At least the Métis had been up and on guard, and some of them like Gabe Berthier, had been full of fight. Not McNab. He had been respected in the north-west, if not well-liked. But he had completely failed this terrified girl, who was weeping and grieving for him with only a well-worn blanket between her and almost certain death.

"Come, Cate," he said quietly. "If you hold this blanket over your head and around you, no one will suspect you are not one of our women. I have found a place to hide you in the camp across the creek."

She was still clinging to him. "Do we have to go there? Oh, please, can't you and I just go away from here?"

"No. I know what would happen if they caught us. If I was a warrior, I could claim you as my prisoner, but I am not a Rattler. The best thing to do is hide you with friends who will take care of you until the trouble is over. Now, you walk along behind me. Keep your head down, and go where I go. We must walk slowly."

They walked out of the trees at the fording place and mingled with the other people who were crossing the creek. The line-up was quiet, but back in the town, the drums were pounding and wild singing could be heard from the new camp. The creek water was waist deep and icy. She gasped and faltered at the shock of it as it swirled around her. Although Jay heard her, he did not turn around. She had to make it on her own. Once out of the water, they climbed up the churned and muddy track on the far bank. Beside the tall tepees of the Plains Crees, another circle had formed, consisting of tents, wagons, and Red River carts. It was into this smaller circle that Jay led her.

The smell of smoke was sharp in the cool air. Some of the women were cooking on open fires or on camp stoves just inside the tents. They were all subdued and quiet, in marked contrast to the noise and frenetic activity in the other camp. Suddenly Joe Two Horse materialized and pointed to his tent. Catherine had seen none of this with her head down, eyes glued to Jay's moccasins. Utterly rigid with terror, she stumbled inside.

**

"Give me that blanket, child," said Marie. But Catherine was holding it so tightly that they were forced to pry it out of her icy fingers. She cringed away from them. "It's all right now," said the warm comforting voice, as a pair of ample arms went around her. She tried to break away, calling out wildly until her eyes focused on the familiar broad and kindly face. She was still for a minute, then she dropped to the ground as though struck down. She had fainted.

Jay, still sweating from the nerve-wracking walk, picked her up at Marie's quick order and put her limp body on a bedroll at the back of the tent, not easily visible from the door-flap.

"Dear Lord, look at the mess of her," gasped Marie. But even as she spoke, she was wringing out a wet cloth to bathe the face of the unconscious girl. "We will have to see if she is hurt. Suzy, help me get these clothes off her. And

Joe, a cup of hot tea with plenty of sugar." While this was going on, Jay went back to the camp stove and poured himself a cup. Seeing a piece of bannock, he wolfed it down.

"When did you last eat?" asked Joe Two Horse.

He looked puzzled. "I'm not sure. Oh ... I had some cake this morning when I went to the Simmons' house."

"And before that?"

Jay shrugged without answering.

"Look, Mrs. Scott made soup earlier. We were having some with Big Bear when the shooting started. I brought it over in my wagon with other things." Joe went to the stove and took the lid off a pot. He dipped a cup into it. "Here, have this. Not too fast or you might get sick." He took it gratefully; he had never tasted anything so good!

"Well, she is not hurt," announced Marie. 'This is all someone else's blood."

"McNab's. They nearly blew his head off," Jay said, as he looked over at the two women. They were busy folding Catherine into a dry blanket. She had regained consciousness, because they were supporting her shoulders and giving her sips of the sweet hot tea.

Joe was looking worried. "They took all our guns away. I can't do much, if they find out she is here and come for her."

"I will stay close by. When I rest, I will get White Bear to watch."

"You would need to tell him why," objected Joe. "Can you trust him?"

"He is my best friend and backs down to no one. He is just crazy enough to enjoy putting one over on the Rattlers."

Both men alerted suddenly and jumped up to face the door-flap. Jay had his gun at the ready. A small head poked through and then blinked up at their wary faces. It was Paulette, a young daughter of Paul and Louisa McRae, who then entered, followed by one of the Two Horse boys. The girl came to relay a message to Marie. It had cost her father several blankets and some money, but he had talked Julia's captor into giving the white woman to him, and now her parents were trying to find out about Catherine.

"You can tell them she is here with us," said Joe sternly. "But you must tell no one else. Do you understand?"

The girl nodded. "I know why," she said importantly. "My father is the only agency man left alive, and my mother was very frightened when he went to get that white woman. She cried. But he came back with Mrs. Simmons, anyway. Then she got *really* angry when he told her about trading the blankets. With so many people in our tent, there were not enough blankets for all of us. My father asked her how twelve people in one small tent could get cold? Then my mother said that, if he ever took a chance like that again, he would find out. Then he asked if she would really do that to him, and she threw a dish at him! It was very exciting!"

The women had come to listen to Paulette. For a minute, the four adults looked at one another blankly, then began to smile for the first time that day. During all the tumult outside, the fatal shootings and the ever-present danger, this child could still see a minor domestic tiff as 'exciting.' It provided a welcome and silly bit of relief.

"We will send two of our blankets back with you," Marie said, patting Paulette's head. Joe got them, then went with the child to see her safely back to McRae's tent. Marie and Suzy poured themselves some tea, then sat down. They were both exhausted.

"I wish to speak to Mrs. McNab," Jay told them. "I will tell her that her friend is safe. She cannot have understood the Cree words."

Marie looked up at him, frowning. "She is still very shocked and may not understand. Speak to her, but not for long. She needs to be quiet." Catherine was lying very still in the shadows at the back of the tent, but there was enough light for Jay to see that her eyes were open and her face wet with tears. When she saw him, she brushed at her eyes.

"Mrs. Simmons is alive. And safe for now. She is with the McRaes."

"Oh, thank God! I was sure she was in terrible trouble." She sat up then, forgetting or not realizing that the women had stripped away her ruined clothing. The blanket fell away from her shoulders and down to her waist. Jay had never imagined that she would have such full and beautiful breasts, with nipples the dusky pink of wild roses. But even as he looked, he leaned forward and lifted the blankets on to her shoulders again. She wrapped it around herself, but although confused and embarrassed, her eyes held steadily to his.

"Thank you." Then she reached out and took his hand. "You have always been so kind to me. Ever since we first met. But today ... I know you risked your life to save me. How can I thank you for that? I can't think of the words to tell you how I feel."

Very still, he could only look back at her as her hand remained so trustingly in his. Although he was tired and tense, he could feel his body responding to her touch. He always had this feeling for her, but never with the intensity that he knew now. He wanted to put his arms around her and comfort her as he had earlier in the day. Perhaps she sensed what he was feeling. Now she had gone very still. He had to say something quickly.

"You don't need to thank me. Mrs. Scott says that what you need is to rest and be quiet."

"I can't. Every time I close my eyes, I see and hear it all again: the shooting and the screaming and the blood "

"Then keep your eyes open and try to remember happier times. After a while, you'll be asleep. You look very tired."

"I'll try to do as you say." He withdrew his hand gently from hers and rose to his feet.

She looked frightened. "You're not going to leave, are you?"

"I can't stay here, but I will come back soon. I'm going to get my friend White Bear. Between the two of us, we can keep trouble-makers away from this tent." He saw that Marie was frowning at him again. He could think of nothing more to say, so he obeyed the older woman's unspoken command and quickly left the tent into the clamorous night.

***

In Fort Pitt, David Kingsley was at his desk, re-reading the letter from Agent Burr, explaining why the townspeople had asked the police to leave Pounding Lake. His face was drawn with strain.

"None of this makes any sense to me, Corporal."

"Nor to me or my men, sir. All it does is confirm my very strong impression that the man has mental problems. The Indians, especially Big Bear's men, are in a very unsettled mood. Yet," Gray shrugged, "the other white men followed Burr's advice like sheep."

"Maybe they're all a bit crazy. In a couple of days, whether Burr likes it or not, I'll take some men up there myself to check out the situation."

Gray looked relieved. "Do that, sir. They might be more inclined to listen to you after a few days on their own."

At dawn, two days later, a chalk-faced Métis rode in from the north, demanding to see the 'boss-man' immediately. Sergeant Porter would have made him wait until the inspector had finished his morning coffee, but the man's frantic urgency convinced the sergeant to admit him immediately.

As soon as he saw the inspector, the Métis started in. "See, I been workin' at a lumber camp half a day's ride north of Poundin' Lake. Had a row with the boss, and I told him what he could do with his damn job. Packed my gear and got out, and got to the town just about sunset last night." The man stopped, his face stricken.

"Go on," said Kingsley, bracing himself.

"There's a bunch of dead white men all shot to hell, lyin' along the path to the agency. And there's a big Indian camp west of the creek, soundin' like it was full of all the demons in hell. Never heard nothin' like it; never want to again. Wasn't a soul in the town not live ones, anyway. All the buildin's is busted open. I got to hell outta there quick as I could."

David studied the man's grizzled face, feeling sick. "You saw bodies, you say. How many of them?"

"Dunno. Ten maybe. Two priests."

"There were two white women in the town. Any sign of them?"

"Oh, Christ!" groaned the Métis, then shook his head.

"Sergeant, take this man to the mess, then hurry over to George MacKenzie's place. Dan Scott is staying there. Bring both men and Corporal Gray."

Within minutes, MacKenzie, Scotty, and Gray were in Kingsley's office.

"Sit down, please." Kingsley's face was composed, but there was a look close to agony in his eyes. "There is no easy way for me to tell you this. I'll just have to say it the way it came to me. I have just received word that most, perhaps all, of the white people in Pounding Lake, including Father Raymond and Father Lafarge, have been killed by the Indians." His listeners sat in frozen silence staring back at him.

Finally, Gray spoke. "Reliable word, would you say, sir?"

"I'm afraid so."

"Oh, my God!" blurted MacKenzie, his face drained of all colour.

Scotty was on his feet again. "And here's me, hanging around down here while all my friends...Oh Lord, *Marie!* I've got to go there. George, come and give me a hand hitching up my team."

"No," objected Kingsley. "You can't go there now. If they have killed all the others, they won't spare you. You'd be going to your death, man!"

Scotty gave him an iron-hard look. "Inspector, not you nor your whole damn detachment is going to keep me from getting back to my old lady!" The old trader left the room abruptly.

"I could put him under protective custody," said Kingsley. Halfway to the door, MacKenzie stopped.

"Don't do that, Inspector. Scotty is doing what he must, what we would do in his place. Let him go. If he can get through, and the two white women are still alive, he might be able to do something to help them. Remember, he's been a trader and lived among Indians most of his life."

Peter Gray was slumped in his chair, head down, his hands clasped between his knees, thinking of the last time he had seen Catherine, small and forlorn in the cold grey dawn, waving goodbye to him. And then recalled his own premonition that he would never see her again. He was choked with grief.

"We can't go there," said Kingsley, resting his hand on Gray's shoulder for a moment. "If they are on a rampage, they could be heading this way any time. We are their next logical target. We must guard this place and get it ready for siege. Corporal, you and Sergeant Porter, assemble the men immediately." When they were gone, the inspector had a moment to confront his own grief. He had cared more than he should have for Catherine McNab.

Scotty's team was hitched to the wagon, and he was ready to go. He looked down at MacKenzie. "George, don't look so worried. I'll get in, all right. Big Bear is a good friend, remember? Since the Indians have probably now got all the food they need, they won't be so mean by the time I get there. I'll get word back to you, if I can." Then he flapped the reins and was on his way.

MacKenzie watched after him for as long as he could see him across the valley, until Scotty took the northward turn to the Pounding Lake trail.

CHAPTER NINETEEN

It was Easter Sunday. The bodies of the men who had died on Holy Thursday were still sprawled where they had fallen. Joe Two Horse and Paul McRae admitted this to the distraught widows. They also insisted that nothing could be done about it.

"I don't care what they do with me!" Julia screamed at McRae. "But I want poor Bert's body laid to decent rest! Your children say the bodies are being kicked aside and mocked by those wicked fiends as they pass by, and the magpies are pecking at them!"

"Look, Mrs. Simmons," snapped Louisa. "Don't you care that Paul has already risked his life to rescue you? Isn't once enough? As the only survivor of the agency staff, the last thing he should do is attract attention to himself. So, stop going on about it."

It was Catherine who got the chance to do something about the bodies, when Big Bear came to see Marie and discovered that she was protecting McNab's widow. Through Marie, he expressed his great sorrow over what had happened. She was sure his sympathy was genuine; there were tears in the old man's eyes as he talked to her.

"Mrs. Scott," she said in a small voice, "ask him if he can do anything about Ian's body lying out there." The chief looked disturbed by the question. He sat deep in thought for a while.

"He says to tell you that his people are now at war with the white men. In times of war, it is the fighting men who make the decisions; he can't tell them what to do. But he will try to get them to take Mac's body into the church. The two priests have been taken there, and he will try to have Mr. Simmons' body put there too. They may burn the church later, but that is the best he can do for you." Catherine held out her hand in gratitude to the Chief.

"That would be better than where he is now," she replied.

***

An hour later, Joe Two Horse came on the run to tell Marie that Scotty's wagon was coming. She jumped to her feet, shaking in fear.

He tried to calm her. "The warriors are quieter now. I think they will let him come in unharmed." And he did get through.

Soon a tearful Marie was hugging and scolding him at the same time. "Where have you been all this time, old man? Letting me go through this alone, like you did! Maybe you were off chasing some woman. You are never around…"

"Marie," he interrupted, "stop this nonsense! I never would have left if I thought there was going to be trouble. And I will never forgive myself for not seeing it coming. But I came back, through men who have killed my friends. And here it is you, not them, giving me a bad time." He spoke sharply, but his eyes were gentle. Scotty knew his woman, and that she was scolding him out of pent-up fear for him. Then he turned to Catherine, who was watching them wordlessly.

"Thank God you are safe, lass, though Ian is gone, poor man. I hear his body has been taken into the church. I saw fires as I came in. They are burning the town."

"Why are they doing that, Mr. Scott?" she asked.

"It's war now. They won't be staying here, and they don't want to leave supplies and shelter for their enemies to use."

"Can I look over there? Please. This will be the only chance I have to say goodbye to Ian." The Scotts looked unhappily at one another. They knew they should keep her hidden, but neither one of them could bring themselves to refuse her pathetic request.

"We'll disguise her like Clear Sky did," decided Marie. She picked up a blanket, wrapped it around Catherine, then went outside with her.

***

Columns of smoke writhed up into the clear sunlit afternoon. As the upper winds caught them, they started to meld together and made a dark pall over the settlement, dull red on the underside, reflecting the ravenous flames seething through the wooden buildings. Everything was burning. The church was a pillar of fire. Catherine watched, as she reflected upon how they had prayed together there on that last terrible day, repeating the Twenty-third Psalm which ended with "and I will dwell in the house of the Lord forever."

"And now you will, Ian," she said to herself. The store and her house were aflame too. She could see it in her mind, the blue china on the shelves, the gingham curtains she had made, the sturdy black stove and the pots on the hooks that Ian had so carefully set up. The tiny bedroom where she and her husband had slept together during the brief months of their often-stormy marriage. All burning, along with the man who had brought her here. He would never again herald the sunset with his beloved bagpipes. She hoped they were burning too, and not looted as Cam Forbes' accordion had been. She thought of their books and her blue party dress and their family photographs and then gasped Muhekun! But no, he had not been around that last day. He was free now. Maybe some evening, she would hear his song without knowing it.

Random thoughts kept flitting though her mind as she watched the flames leaping higher into the sky, burning away her naiveté, her plans, her dreams, her home, her husband, and the life she had tried to make here.

The Scotts took her back to camp, and she sat where they put her, hands clasped tightly on her lap over the voluminous skirt of one of Marie's dresses. Scotty watched her, his face a mask of sorrow and pain.

***

As feared, word was getting around that Catherine was in the Two Horse's tent. That evening, the notorious bootlegger, Buck Breland, showed up demanding to see her. Joe and Scotty went out in response. White Bear lounged nonchalantly nearby.

"What in hell would a man like you have to say to Mrs. McNab?" Scott demanded.

"Just doing her a favour is all," replied Breland, trying to arrange his coarse face into a friendly smile. "I happened by when they were going through her house before burning it. So, I went in to see what I could save. I got something for her." Neither man believed a word of it, and they were reluctant to let him inside. Scotty opened the door-flap, understanding that if they refused and the big brawler insisted, the probable uproar would create far too much attention.

Catherine had been mute since seeing the burning town. When she looked up at the hulking brute smiling slyly at her, she was more puzzled than alarmed. He threw something into her lap. She gazed down at it curiously, then gasped. It was her diamond and sapphire pin!

"Maybe you want this back, eh?" he asked.

"Oh, yes," she stammered. "This is very kind of you. I don't quite know how to thank you."

He leaned over her and whispered. "I can get you out of here. By morning, we can be far enough away so they'd never catch us. I own a fast horse, and I can get the gelding your husband rode for you."

"I don't understand," she said, frowning at him. "Are you offering to take me to Fort Pitt?"

Breland began to laugh. "You think I'd give you back that gew-gaw and risk my damn neck to take you to the police? Not on your life! What I'll do is get you out and treat you well enough. We could go down over the border until all this blows over and then…"

Catherine jumped to her feet and backed away from him. "I'll take my chances with the Indians. I'd rather be killed by them than go anywhere with someone like you!" She threw the pin back at him. He caught it deftly, his eyes slitted. Scotty and Joe watched warily. Breland ignored them.

He glowered at Catherine. "Before you are many more days in this here camp, Miss High-and-Mighty, you'll come crawling to me. You think the Indians are going to let an old man and his tame Cree keep a pretty little thing like you to themselves much longer?"

It was Marie who acted first. She picked up a teapot filled with boiling water and advanced on Breland with flashing eyes. "Get out of here, you maggot, or you'll get this right in the face!"

He glared back at her, deciding she meant it and headed for the door, pocketing the pin as he went. As he hurriedly exited, Breland ran smack into White Bear, rifle in his hand.

Catherine was trembling. "What did he mean that I would go crawling to him? What is going to happen to me?"

"Nothing lass," said Scotty. "We'll keep you safe. With my old lady on your side, we can do that all right!" He looked fondly at Marie, still brandishing the teapot. "And, I don't know who that Indian was, but it looks like we have some outside help, too. Catherine sat down slowly, wondering if there was ever going to be an end to this nightmare.

***

Melissa Burr's nightmare had ended. This last month had drained her so emotionally and physically that she was numb from losing her baby, the long restless nights expecting the warriors to come for her husband, and all their bitter quarrels over how he was treating her people. She was heart-sick about his violent death, killed as her mother had said, by his own crazy pride, as surely as he had been by Wandering Spirit's bullet. But now it was over. She was where she belonged, back with her own people. One agony remained. Jim had taken eight other men with him, and it was affecting her profoundly. She prayed that she would never again have to face her friend Catherine, or the other white woman, Mrs. Simmons.

The only one Melissa could really talk to in the days following her husband's death was her cousin Jay. He had passionately opposed her marriage to Burr, but he was being especially kind to her now, ready to listen whenever the sorrow, bitterness, and pain could not be contained. On the evening the fires were set in Pounding Lake, she and Jay walked along beside the creek, looking at the awful smoke and flames still raging, and inhaling the acrid odour.

"I know I never should have married Jim," she confided, "but he was so handsome with those teasing green eyes and that smile of his ... that was all I could think about. It sounds crazy now, even to me, but I would have given the rest of my life, if necessary, for one night with him! Jay, I hope that kind of craziness never happens to you."

"Maybe most people feel something like that, at some time or another," he said.

"Do you think so? Well, I paid for it. He hated for me to speak Cree, and he wanted me to dress like a white woman. So, he taught me to speak English and wear the dresses he bought me. But I could not change my hair, or my eyes, or the colour of my skin, even if I wanted to. And our child, although he loved her dearly, is a still a half-breed. I believe he resented that and regretted our marriage, although he never said so.

"You may have imagined that, you know."

"No, you know how proud he was. He always seemed uncomfortable when we were with his white friends, afraid I think, that I would say or do something to embarrass him. So, after a while, I just stayed away from them, especially the white women. The men were usually polite to me and often flattering, but the women resented me! I had *dared* to marry a real 'catch', one of their own ... handsome and educated! They were careful to be polite in front of their men, but were never friendly."

"Cate McNab is not like that."

"True. We were getting to be good friends before her husband was killed. That poor woman!" Melissa sighed, as they turned around and began to walk back toward the camp. "Not that she was all that happy with him. She should no more have married McNab than I should have married Jim. He was a hard man, that one. We talked about it one day. At least Jim, for all his faults, was kind and gentle when we went to bed together. McNab was not."

Abruptly, Jay stopped walking. He looked back at the raging fires with an expression she had never seen before. He was silent for so long that she touched his arm tentatively.

"What is it, Jay? You look ... upset. Am I talking about Jim too much?"

"No," he said as they began to walk again. "Talk to me whenever you need to." He smiled down at her. "Some day you may have to listen to all this from me. It is a good thing that we are cousins, not brother and sister."

She knew what he meant. While male and female cousins could laugh and tease, joke and play tricks on one another. In the Cree tradition, brothers and sisters were required to be more formal with one another.

"When did you start to call her 'Cate'," she said. "I just noticed that."

"I forget. Oh yes, perhaps on the night I gave her the amulet. You remember, she had been injured when she got Lizabet out of the way of the horses."

"Of course, I remember," said Melissa.

"Well, McNab had left her alone out in the trader's camp." He told her about the incident with Dorrie Barker. "I made her hide in her tent. I don't know what might have happened if Barker had found her."

"Nothing good. Jay, that girl just does not belong out here! Now that McNab is gone and when this trouble is over, I hope, for her own sake, that she goes back where she came from."

"She probably will," he said, "*if* we get this trouble over with. I don't think we will. This band has killed nine white men, including two priests. It does not matter who killed them, we will all be blamed. We may win a few fights, but in the end, with all the men and weapons they have, they will come after us and we will be finished. I can't see it ending any other way."

*****

Melissa and Jay were back at the Blue Quill lodge by this time. The entire family was inside and White Bear was with them. Jay gave him a questioning look.

"It is all right. Everyone was watching a meeting of the Rattlers," his friend assured him. "Even the troublemakers."

"Including you," agreed Blue Quill, smiling at the heavy-set young man and then everyone else smiled. 'Troublemaker' was the word most often used to describe men who had been in difficulty with the police. Just a few months ago, when White Bear tried to marry Theresa Bull Quill, he had been fined and ordered out of Pounding Lake after striking Father Lafarge. The romance had since cooled, but the Blue Quills liked him, and as Jay's friend, he was still welcome.

Outwardly, the two friends seemed very different. Jay was intense, with the speed of a big cat, while the shorter White Bear, wide-bodied and thick-muscled, had the explosive temper and slower perceptions of his namesake. Jay's lean face was dominated by his piercing eyes and quick flashing smile. White Bear's face was round, flat, and deceptively innocent. But they shared the subtle, often raunchy wit of Cree men, and they were both artists, Jay with his paintings and White Bear with words. What pictures White Bear could create with his range of voices, gestures, and his expressive face! He loved to tell about We-sak-a-chuk, the mythical, rascally Cree trickster who was tricked himself, as often as not, by the birds and animals he invariably tried to victimize.

Throughout that past miserable winter, he had regularly called the cold and hungry youngsters together with his favourite saying: "Children need to laugh." Then he would launch into one of his interminable tales until the little ones would double up and sometimes roll around on the ground with great hilarity. No matter if they had heard the story before, White Bear would always add new embellishments. The children in the band were firmly convinced that We-sak-a-chuk looked exactly like White Bear!

But now, White Bear was preoccupied with the plans for an attack on Fort Pitt. "We are going to leave our families and the prisoners here," he said.

"They would slow us down. We can take that old fort quickly. It is so poorly fortified and located that the advantages are all with us."

"Will there be more killing then?" asked Melissa, interrupting the talk of the men. Blue Quill gave her a reproving look, but her sad eyes stilled his annoyance. He was a fond and indulgent father, and their estrangement during her years with the Indian agent had wounded him deeply.

"It is not the plan to kill them," White Bear answered. "We will give them the option to surrender. What happens after that is for them to decide. But we are going to destroy the fort." Then he looked at Jay. "We need to be sure that Buck Breland goes with us. He tried to get away with the white woman while I was near the Two Horse tent today. The grandmother chased him off with a pot of boiling water. But, if I know him, he will be after her again."

At that, Blue Quill gave his nephew a searching look. "I heard strange talk at the meeting. They are saying that you took the McNab woman away from the shooting and that you hid her afterwards." Blue Quill's wife, Rose, Theresa, and Melissa were all astounded by this news. White Bear, belatedly aware that he had said too much, assumed his most innocent expression. Jay remained silent.

"Why would you do a thing like that?" persisted his uncle. "It was none of your business, and with all the shooting that was going on, you could have been killed yourself."

Then Rose intervened in a soft voice. "My husband, have you forgotten that Mrs. McNab saved our granddaughter's life?"

"No, and for that reason, I am pleased that she was not harmed. Is that why you saved her?" Blue Quill asked.

"I am not sure why. It happened too quickly for me to think about it."

White Bear grinned at his friend, trying to help. "Maybe for the same reason Breland went after her today. She is very good-looking, for a white woman. I might have done the same thing myself."

Jay responded to this teasing in an uncharacteristic way. He turned around abruptly and walked outside.

They were all surprised, but it was Melissa who was most shaken by the incident. Jay had taken a *terrible* chance in rescuing Catherine from the vengeful warriors! And why had he said nothing about it since then? At least to his own family? There was no reason to keep it from them, unless ... he had something to hide! Could this dearly beloved cousin of hers be somehow involved with Catherine? A *white* woman? He had, after all, given her his amulet. *No*, she told herself fiercely. It had been bad enough for her and Jim. But for a man of her people and a white woman? Unthinkable! No. Jay was far too sensible to let that happen, and Catherine ... there was an innocence about her and a natural honesty that was unmistakable. She would not betray McNab.

White Bear was bothered by the same idea. He had never asked his friend why they were protecting the white woman; good friends did not ask about things like that. But if there was something between them ... *wah!* He had talked too much. He wanted to make amends and went outside to look for Jay.

***

The fire was still burning in the centre of the camp. Some of the people were dancing but most of the men who were going to Fort Pitt were resting or getting ready for the morning. He had no trouble spotting his friend's tall figure, leaning against a tree, watching the dancers.

"Will you ride Cloudwalker tomorrow?" White Bear asked him offhandedly.

"I was thinking about that, but I want him fresh when we get to Fort Pitt. I'll take another horse and lead Cloudwalker."

"Good. I traded all but one of my horses to Lone Man. But I can borrow one and lead him too. We will have the best horses if there is a fight, eh?"

"Better a fight than what happened here." He looked his friend. "I never thought they would kill the priests."

White Bear had seldom said anything about his years with Father Lafarge, but suddenly his face was filled with both pain and anger. "I am sorry he died like that, but I feel no grief for him. You may know that everyone in my family was killed when lightening hit our lodge, and it burned to the ground. He took me in, but he was not kind. He used to tell me that they were burning in hell and would for all time, because they were heathens and not baptized. I would cry for them. They were good people, and I loved them. They did not beat children, lock them in dark closets, or send them to bed hungry when there was food to eat. The priest would do that if I spoke Cree or tried to run away. He cut off my hair and made me pray so much my knees hurt. I learned not to cry, but I was never happy. That is why I like to make the little ones laugh now." White Bear abruptly stopped talking, embarrassed. His tongue was wagging at both ends tonight! "Well," he added, pointing at the crumbling church, "he is the one who is burning tonight."

Jay gave his friend time to recover from his outburst, then threw his arm around White Bear's broad shoulders. "I have an idea. Maybe we should make sure Breland is getting ready to go with us tomorrow." White Bear's poise was restored in a flash at this hint of action, and they were off, heading for Breland's tent.

***

Breland was sitting in front of his small canvas tent on a blanket, watching the dancers. They stopped beside him, Jay's eyes glittering coldly. This man had looted Catherine's home; he was wearing McNab's coat. The dead man's dun gelding was tethered behind this tent with another horse, and just today, he had probably frightened Catherine badly. Breland's rifle was beside him. Jay moved closer to him suddenly, and picked up the weapon.

"What the hell do you think you are doing?" Breland demanded in English. Jay checked to be sure the gun was not loaded, then faced toward the firelight and squinted down the barrel. He tossed it back to the seated man.

"This gun needs cleaning. Do it before morning." Then Jay ducked his head and looked inside the tent. "What's this?" he asked in exaggerated surprise. "You are not packed up yet? Maybe we should help you then." With that, he went inside and began throwing out clothing and supplies, littering the ground. With a roar of outrage, Breland jumped to his feet. Clenching one ham fist and clubbing his gun in the other, he started for the tent only to be tripped by White Bear and sent crashing to the ground. But he was a quick and powerful man, on his feet again in a second. He made a wild swing at White Bear, just missing him. While he was still off balance, White Bear crouched and charged, butting him below the ribs with his head. The breath exploded out of the big man, doubling him over, just as Jay came out of the tent with more of Breland's possessions.

By this time, a circle of people were looking on curiously. Jay dropped his armload, then pushed a tent pole to one side, collapsing the canvas.

"I'll kill you!" shouted the Métis, glaring first at him, then at White Bear.

"No, no, my friend," scolded White Bear, wagging a finger at him. "You have it all wrong! It is *white* men you came here to fight, not us. Remember?" By this time, Wandering Spirit had joined the spectators. But he did not speak or interfere.

Breland had no idea why the two men were bedevilling him, but he was game for any fight, outnumbered or not, and now he had his breath back. He was deciding which one to go after first. When he hesitated, they both came at him, knocking him flat again, then jumped on him. It was a free-for-all after that; wild kicks and blows were launched, and some even landed. It finished with Jay and White Bear on top, one sitting astride him and one kneeling on his shoulders, pinning him down while his legs flailed and his feet beat against the ground.

They ended up right beside Wandering Spirit. Panting, White Bear looked up the war chief, his eyes all innocent.

"We just wanted to be sure he is packed and ready to move out at dawn, as you told us. We are helping him!" A smile tugged at the corners of Wandering Spirit's mouth, as he looked at Breland's strewn and disordered belongings.

"I can see that," he said, waving them away from the prone Métis. When Breland surged to his feet still fighting mad, he found himself looking straight into a pair of cold and deadly eyes an experience that had sobered and intimidated better men than him. "Get yourself ready," the war chief said quietly. "Do as they say."

"His gun needs cleaning too," said Jay with a wicked grin.

"And clean the gun," added Wandering Spirit, as he turned and walked away. Jay and White Bear also moved off, the latter wiping at a bloody cut on his cheek.

"I think he will be ready in the morning," White Bear predicted.

"He will, and looking for the first chance to get even with us." They smiled at one another, restored to good humour by the brawl, and the way it had ended.

CHAPTER TWENTY

Catherine was confused and disoriented when she opened her eyes. By the dim light, she guessed it was dawn, but there was so much *noise*! Gunshots, horses, bells and rattles, and men shouting and chanting. Scotty was at the door-flap, peering outside. Marie and Suzy Two Horse were sitting by the stove wrapped in blankets.

"Come and see this," said Scotty. "You may never see the like again. They are ready to go. Lord help the folks in Fort Pitt when they see *this* lot coming at them!" Both women moved to look outside, and Catherine decided to follow them. The sun was just over the edge of the horizon, revealing a chilling scene: an enormous circle of mounted warriors.

Snow had sifted across the camp during the night, but few of the men out there wore shirts. Instead their half-naked bodies were splashed in vivid paint: circles, jagged lines, stars, and dots. Some were wearing feathered war bonnets, others had buffalo-horned caps or tall spiky roaches and beaded eye-fringes. Some carried rifles; some of them were flourishing the terrible *pukamakuns* the steel-bladed war clubs. The horses were as gaudily painted as their riders.

The circle was revolving more swiftly by the moment. The men were yelping and shouting to one another and firing the odd shot into the air. Most of them were Plains Crees, although many Woods Crees were with them, along with rebel Métis, sedate by comparison in buckskin coats and wool caps. Bathed in the red light of the rising sun, the cavalcade was sparked by flashes from signal mirrors on thongs around the necks of the warriors.

In the centre of the circle three figures waited, unrecognizable under the paint and eye-fringes. Catherine wondered if Jay could possibly be out there in that menacing throng. She had a sudden eerie feeling that she and Dan Scott and Julia were the only white people left in the world. Then one of the men inside the ring raised his rifle over his head. An earth-shaking howl went up. The circle accelerated, opened up, and the leaders began to move toward the far side of the creek to the Fort Pitt trail, the others falling in so closely that the column assumed the appearance of a long and very deadly snake.

***

When they were out of sight, a profound silence fell. Catherine crept back into her bed. She had imagined herself numb, beyond more fear and horror, but now she was terrified for her friends in Fort Pitt. She tried to pray for them, although she was no longer sure there was a merciful God inclined to listen to her.

After a while, she heard Scotty talking quietly to Suzy and Marie. "Joe says there are still some who want to kill the two white women. I hope none of *them* stayed behind."

"Not likely; the bloody-minded ones won't want to miss out on the fighting. But I would feel better if young Clear Sky hadn't gone with them," said Marie. So, Jay *had* gone with them! Although she knew she was being unreasonable, Catherine had a sinking feeling that she had been deserted. There had been something so reassuring in knowing he was close by.

She realized that, since Ian's death, she had become far too dependent on Jay. And it was not fair, after all he had done for her. She felt close to panic. What if *he* was injured in the fighting? It was a terrible thought. She closed her eyes and clasped her hands and tried praying for him. If God *was* listening, she thought, He would certainly be confused by her conflicting loyalties!

Scotty resumed. "Speaking of Clear Sky, Joe told me last night that, when he was visiting the Indian camp, he saw him and that friend of his giving

Breland a bad time. Says they threw his stuff all over the place and knocked his tent down, then got into a knock-down brawl with him."

"Mercy! Because he tried to take off with Catherine, do you think?"

"Wouldn't be surprised. He seems to have appointed himself as her guardian angel or something. But Joe was saying there was Breland wearing poor Mac's coat, Mac's dun gelding tied up behind his tent, and probably more of their things in his tent. That maggot, as you called him; I hope those two young hellions kicked the *shit* out of him!"

"I hope so too," agreed Marie.

Had Jay done that for her too? She could not imagine why, but she was oddly comforted by the thought.

"I got a chance to talk to Louisa McRae, yesterday," said Marie. "She says Julia Simmons is carrying on like a crazy woman. Cries all the time, won't help with the work, screams and swears at the children. What is worse, she screams at any Indians who come to their tent. Louisa had to give some of her jewellery to the last pair of visitors, to keep them from shooting her then and there."

"That doesn't sound like Mrs. Simmons. She seemed like a nice quiet lady, what we knew of her," replied Scotty. There were other sounds after that: the camp stove being lit, water going into a kettle, Marie and Suzy talking quietly. Catherine's mind drifted. It would be spring in Rosemere now, with tulips, daffodils, and the first traces of green on the towering elms that lined the wide gracious streets. People out walking, rejoicing in the end of winter. She could see her father at his cluttered desk, and her mother working in the kitchen with Billy watching from his wheelchair. But no ... Billy was gone. That reminded her. Rosemere vanished and she sat up with a start.

"Mrs. Scott, what happened to that poor man they called 'the dummy'?"

"Why, I don't know, child. I'll ask Suzy." After a brief exchange in Cree with her tiny friend, she smiled at Catherine. "She has seen him, and says he looks much better. Now that the people have food, they are able to feed him, and he's been given some decent clothing."

"Thank goodness," Catherine said, relieved. "The last time I saw him, he was just a living skeleton."

"The Indians will take care of him. I think I told you once how kind and generous they are with such people."

"Kind and generous? After what happened here, you can say that? After what we saw out there this morning?"

"Now hold on, Mrs. Mac," said Scotty. "What happened to you was terrible, seeing your man killed like that, and you not doing a thing to deserve it. But you have a good head on your shoulders, and you see things straighter than most. Try to remember that the Indians have been treated real bad, and they have seen *their* loved ones die too. They'll see a lot more of that, you can bet. The whole country will be up in arms by now. Troops will swarm into the district with their big guns, and before it is all over, these people will be blasted all to hell, and we'll be here to see it too. That is if we're lucky enough to live through it ourselves."

Catherine froze; her violet eyes were dark with pain and shock. She had blanched paper-white at Scotty's grim words. Marie came to her and took her hand.

"There now," she said. "I know how you feel. I do. I hated the Battle River when it took and drowned my man, long years ago. There were times when I even hated him too, for dying and leaving me alone with all our children to raise. That passes. And the river flows and life goes on, all to the Lord's plan. Whatever lies ahead for us, we must trust Him, leave it in His hands. When you can do that, it will ease the pain and anger in you now."

That afternoon, Scotty decided it was time to put up his own tent, which he had brought back from Fort Pitt. They were very crowded in the Two Horse tent, and the camp was so quiet he felt it was safe to move around outside. By sunset, Scotty, Marie, and Catherine moved into it without attracting any undue attention from the hovering guards.

***

Two days later, Catherine was alone in the tent, mixing bannock, when she looked up to see a young woman in the doorway. She dropped the dough into the bowl in her lap.

"MaryLou! Am I seeing things or is it really you? How on earth did you get here?"

"It is me," MaryLou answered, looking closely at Catherine. "I came across country on horseback. Actually, on stolen horseback. Us Clear Skys are good at that." She paused before adding, "I'm sorry about your husband. Melissa told me what happened. I made her come over here with me, although she thinks you may not want to see her again." Now Catherine could see Melissa, standing behind MaryLou.

"Of course, I do," she answered quickly. "Melissa! I have been wondering about you. How are you now?"

"Getting over it. I've been thinking about you too, but ... well, it was Jim who started..."

Catherine stopped her. "You had nothing to do with that. It is good to see you again, both of you. I've been so lonely; can you stay for a bit?" At that moment, Marie appeared, trying to bring warmth back to her icy hands. She had been washing clothes in the creek. She hugged Melissa, then looked curiously at MaryLou.

"This is my cousin, Mrs. Scott," Melissa explained, speaking in English for Catherine's benefit. "MaryLou, Jay Clear Sky's sister. She has just arrived from Battleford."

Marie was dumbfounded. "Now, how did you manage to do that?"

"I had a lot of good company as far as Poundmaker's Reserve. I stole a good horse, and I have this," she replied, patting a pistol in her belt. "I came the rest of the way myself. It was muddy going with the spring runoff. But I made it, as you can see."

"You have a lot of nerve, just like your brother," approved Marie. "And you look like him, too. But who took you to Poundmaker's?"

"Oh, just about every male in the Battleford Agency," said the girl calmly. "They had all gone into Battleford after Poundmaker, who tried to tell the agent that rations had to be increased if he was expected to keep his people out of the rebellion. But the agent was scared; he wouldn't leave the fort. All the other white people are hiding in there too. The chief waited for hours; then night came on and some of the people got angry and began to loot and burn the empty stores and houses. I refused to go into the fort, so I was there to talk them into leaving the Appleton house alone." She looked at Catherine. "You know what a good kind man Mr. John is. Anyway, when the people went back to Cut Knife Hill in the morning I went with them. I had the pick of all the unguarded stables for a horse. I rode along with them just like a regular warrior. A lot of them were teasing me and calling me Chief Needs-a-Man, but it was fun!"

"Dear Lord! What next? Did you go past Bresaylor?"

"Yes, but there is no one in the town now."

Marie gasped. "Where are they? I have a daughter who lives there, and grandchildren..."

"They are safe," MaryLou interrupted quickly. "Some Métis came and tried to get the men to go to Batoche to help the rebels there. But no one would go, and they started to fight about it. Then Poundmaker showed up with some of his warriors and told the rebels that no one had to fight who didn't want to. The Batoche people want the chief on their side, and they backed off, but they wouldn't leave. So, the chief took the Bresaylor people back to his own camp, where he could protect them. They are there now. Safe, Mrs. Scott."

Scotty had returned while MaryLou was telling the news. He put his arm around his shaken wife. "Sit you down now, old lady. Your folks are safer with Poundmaker than we are here, maybe. Miss Clear Sky, I guess you know that most of the men in this camp have gone south to attack Fort Pitt."

"Yes, Melissa told me. But I turned north at Pipestone Creek, miles east of the fort. I didn't want to run into any police patrols."

The old trader shook his head. "It must be pure hell in that place right now."

THE AMULET

***

Despite everyone's worries, some for their men in the war party, and some for the people of Fort Pitt, there was an interval of quiet in the camps beside Pounding Creek. It gave them all time to rest and recover from the violence that had changed their lives.

The small children played their games. The elders moved outside to watch them and enjoy the first warm sun of early spring. They spread their blankets and set up their backrests, then sat to smoke or talk or just bask in comfortable silence. The boys fished, snared rabbits and gophers, and herded the remaining horses. Their sisters gathered firewood and carried water, while the younger women cooked, sewed, tended babies, and shared gossip. The guards who had been assigned to the prisoners were alert, but not intrusive or hostile.

It should have been a healing time for the three white prisoners, but for Scotty, Catherine, and Julia, the horror and numbing shock of the tragedy was still overwhelming. Scotty, who had not been there when it happened, was wracked with guilt. It did not show. The seamy-faced old trader appeared to be as cryptic and calm as ever, but again and again, he kept asking himself why he had failed to recognize the escalating danger. Now, when it was too late, he recalled the signals that should have warned him. The impassivity of dark faces that once smiled so readily. The flat black eyes that no longer met his own. Curt nods instead of friendly handshakes. Cool formality instead of jokes and small talk. To think he'd shrugged them off, putting them down to changing times, instead of understanding such typical signs of anger and resentment!

Why had he even gone to Fort Pitt? He could easily have sent Tom Adams for the merchandise shipment. Then the likeable clerk would have been alive today. And had he been on the scene, he might have found some way to avert that terrible bloodbath. But no. Doddering old fool that he was, he waited around for the damn shipment while people died in Pounding Lake. He was going to feel the pain and guilt of that for the rest of his days.

Catherine, with the natural resilience of youth, was slowly regaining her courage and innate good sense. There would always be a place in her heart for the memory of her husband, but theirs was a flawed love and marriage with too many episodes of loneliness and resentment. Perhaps, given time and the children Ian so desperately wanted, they might have grown closer. But he was gone, and she was alone, except for Scotty and Marie. They were so kind and reassuring, calm and matter-of-fact despite the pervasive danger and discomfort of their surroundings. Then, one evening, Catherine discovered how mistaken she was in assuming that.

***

Catherine and Scotty were alone in the tent. Marie was visiting her son Giles and his family. She had tried to talk Scotty into going with her, but he refused, muttering something about keeping an eye on Catherine.

After a while, Catherine scolded him mildly. "You should have gone with her, Mr. Scott. Now that the warriors and Breland are out of the way, I am safe enough. It would do you good to see the grandchildren. I'm going to have to learn to take care of myself, now that I am alone."

"Aye, alone! If I could make it up to you, I would lay my life on the line to do it, so I would." She was surprised to see his face contort and to hear a heart-wrenching groan of pain.

She stared at him, amazed. "Mr. Scott, what are you talking about? What do you mean 'make it up to me'? Surely you are not blaming yourself for what happened?"

He bent his head and covered his face with his gnarled hands. "And who else is there to blame?" Then it all came out in a ragged choked voice. "I ignored Lafarge's crazy ways. I should have reported him to the church authorities. I watched Jim Burr cruelly misusing his position, without a word of protest...I underestimated the danger and the anger of the Indians... I ran out on everyone by going to Fort Pitt and staying around down there. Waiting for my stupid shipment even after the telegraph lines went down..." It all came out: his shame, remorse, and grief. Neither Scotty nor Catherine noticed Marie, standing in the shadows by the door, her eyes filled with pain for the man she loved.

"Mr. Scott," said Catherine after a while, "if you weren't hurting so much already, I'd be tempted to pound some sense back into your head! Have you forgotten that they were all full-grown men, with eyes and ears and minds of their own, the same as you?" When he did not answer, she tried again. "What if you *had* reported Father Lafarge? It would have been put down to your dislike of the man. *That* was no secret. What good did it do when you and Inspector Kingsley and Mr. MacKenzie *all* reported Burr to the commissioner for the trouble he caused in Fort Pitt? He got a mild reprimand.

"Suppose you had gone to the agent yourself, objecting to his methods? Peter Gray tried it, and I'm damn sure that's why the agent and the priest wanted the police out of town. They were both so arrogant. They refused to tolerate *any* challenge to their authority. As for warning the townspeople, Peter tried that too, very emphatically, several times. Take Ian. Don't think for a moment that he would have listened to you. Bert warned him. Peter warned him. Gabe Berthier warned him. I quarrelled with him about it. He ignored us all, just as he would have ignored you. Like the men who died with him, he refused to see what he didn't want to see."

Scotty raised his head and looked at her intently. "Nothing will ever change the fact that I should have seen what was coming. But there is sense in your saying that my warnings would have been useless. And I thank you for helping me to see it that way."

"That is the way it was. There is no forgiving those who shot down unarmed men, but if you look back and remember the crazy things some of the Pounding Lake people did to make a bad situation worse, you can't blame the agent or the priest for it all. Even Ian. He was not as much to blame as the others, but he wouldn't try to stop them. He never saw the Indians as human beings; he was totally indifferent to their suffering. To him, they were a means to an end: making money. He looked forward to the future when they were 'dealt with', as he used to put it." Her voice was tremulous now, talking to herself as much as to Scotty.

"You can't feel like that about people without them becoming aware of it. He was like that with me, in a way. In Rosemere, I was something pretty he wanted. Out here, he forgot that. I was supposed to produce children on demand for him, and when I failed to do that, he saw our marriage as a failure too. He cared for me, as much as he could care for anyone, I'm sure. But we were not lovers or even very good friends, most of the time. I'm so sorry about that now."

At that point, Marie came out of the shadows to sit with them. "It sounds like you two are getting a lot of feelings out that have been all locked up inside. That has to be done when something very bad has happened and you have to live with it." The big woman heaved a monumental sigh. "It is the only way you can get to see things straight again."

"Old woman," said Scotty, "you say the damnedest things at times! I think you are right this time, but after all these years, I never know what to expect next."

"And you never will," retorted Marie, pleased to hear a bit of teasing in his voice, something that had been missing since his return from Fort Pitt. "Now, you'll never guess what I got for you on the way back to the tent."

He smiled at her. "I guess I won't until you give it to me."

She chuckled as she handed him two full pouches of tobacco. "I know you're nearly out. I got them you'll be pleased to hear from As-a-Child! From the look and smell of him, all covered with soot, he must have gone over to the town and poked through the ruins of the buildings."

Scotty pocketed them happily. "I'm not proud. I'll take them and no questions asked!"

They talked idly for another hour, all three of them more relaxed than they had been for a long time. Catherine slept right through the night, with no bad dreams to wrench her out of oblivion.

CHAPTER TWENTY-ONE

There was nothing anyone could do for Julia Simmons. The submissive and self-effacing woman had been so traumatized by her husband's death that she had turned into a totally different person. Bitter. Vindictive. Cruel. The next evening, Paul McRae, looking desperate, came to talk to Marie about it.

"That woman," he told her, "is making us all so unhappy that I feel like giving her back to the Indians."

"Lands sake, Paul, what is going on?"

"With our nine children packed into my tent, and with her not used to little ones, she is taking it very hard. She screams at them, slaps them, and calls them dirty little half-breeds. We ate rabbit last night, but when she saw it had been cooked with the head on, she threw her share into the fire. I had to pull it out again. It takes a *lot* of food to fill nine children! She cries at night, keeping us all awake, and she won't help Louisa with any of the work. She yells insults at the Indians who come to see us. They can't understand the words, but they know is isn't flattering. Then we have to cool them off, since they are not too happy with me still being around as it is. We are running out of things to give away to keep her safe. When we tell her that, she just says to let the Indians kill her; she wants to die. Do you think you could reason with her?"

Catherine listened with a mixture of pity and dismay. She knew Julia had loved her husband deeply. In truth, she had sometimes wondered at the way the sensitive and intelligent woman had doted on the handsome but unremarkable man. Even so, she could hardly believe that Paul was talking about the same Julia she had known.

"I'll talk to her right away," Marie replied, her eyes flashing with anger and concern. She turned to Catherine, and there was still annoyance in her voice. "You stay out of sight while I am gone. Scotty has gone fishing with Joe, but they should be back soon. I mean it now. It's not fair to make trouble for people trying to help you."

"I know that," Catherine agreed at once, "and if you can't get anywhere with her, I'll try talking to her."

"Of course, child," said Marie more gently. "I am upset for Paul and Louisa. I didn't mean to turn my anger on you."

***

Watching Marie leave, peeking out from behind the screen of the door-flap, Catherine felt an intense desire to go out into the warm sunshine. She longed to breathe in the fragrance of moist earth and new growth, to stretch her long legs and run for joy as she had done as a child, and to feel the searching wind in her hair. It seemed so long that she had been confined, allowed outside only to relieve herself, always with an anxious Marie or Suzy hovering nearby, urging her to hurry.

She thought about trying to escape and how she might do it, stealing a gun and a horse and shooting anyone in her way, like the heroine of some 'penny dreadful' novel. But she would not take one of the other prisoners' horses, and there were no weapons in their camp. The idea of running away in the night occurred to her, but where would she go? Fort Pitt was under siege, Battleford was much too far away, and their captors were expert trackers. She was sure to be caught, and then she would end up dead, or at least worse off than she was now. No, this was real life and not fiction.

She could faintly hear the rushing water of Pounding Creek, although she could not see it from her viewpoint. She went to the back of the tent and unfastened the loops at the bottom of the canvas wall from the pegs which held them. She had to lie down to get her head through the loosened wall but it was worth the effort. From the tent, the ground fell away in a long slope to the creek ravine, and she could see the water leaping and flashing, blue-green under the bright sunlight, free at last of the ice and debris that had choked it during the spring runoff. She watched it for a long time, visualizing the course of the frothing water from Pounding Lake until it was absorbed into the torrent of the North Saskatchewan.

The river so fascinated her that it took her a moment to realize that someone had entered the tent behind her. It could be Scotty, back from fishing, or Marie, but perhaps neither one of them. Moving very cautiously, she inched back and then, without moving her prone body, she raised her head just enough to peer with one eye over her bedroll. Her heart jumped. A tall man, rifle in hand and streaked with paint, was standing silhouetted in the middle of the tent, looking around. She ducked her head, but made some small sound. He whirled to face her. He dropped the gun, and his hands closed in a vice-like grip on her arms and pulled her to her feet. She struggled and kicked, and she felt her hard shoe connect solidly with the intruder's shin.

"Cate, what you are doing?" She stared wildly at him. Then with a rush of pleasure and relief, she recognized him.

"Jay! Oh, my Lord you scared me; you really did!" She took a deep breath, but she was still trembling. He was looking at her very seriously, although he spoke softly.

"You didn't do *me* any favour, either. You kick like a mule!"

"I'm so sorry," she babbled, half-laughing and half-crying. "Oh my, it *is* good to see you back safely! I was so worried. You are all right, aren't you?"

"Nothing came close to happening to me." His hands were still clamped tight on her arms, but she did not protest; she was too glad to see him. He was looking at her so strangely! She felt light and dizzy and breathless, but gradually became aware that he looked tired and very tense.

Abruptly, he released her arms and stepped back. "Has there been any trouble here?"

"No trouble, Jay. It has been very quiet. I didn't know the war party had returned."

"It's not back. They have many prisoners from Fort Pitt slowing them down. I came on ahead. Breland was missing this morning. I was afraid he might come after you again. Have you seen him?"

She shook her head. "I'm seldom out of the tent; I see hardly anyone."

"You shouldn't be left alone like this. That man would have no more trouble getting to you than I did."

"I'm not alone very often, but Scotty is out fishing and Marie got a call. They should be back soon." He frowned down at her, then picked up his rifle and went to the door. "I see no sign of either one of them."

She had followed him. "Don't go yet."

"I'm not going to leave you here alone. I haven't seen you for a week. And I know you must be anxious to hear about your friends in Fort Pitt."

"Yes, I am. You say they have prisoners?"

"All of the townspeople. The police tried to prepare the fort for siege, and everyone retreated into the barracks for protection—a wasted effort. With all our warriors, it was certain we could take it in a few hours. But Big Bear wanted no more killing, especially when women and children were in there. He talked Wandering Spirit into letting them get away unharmed before we destroyed the fort. I went to the fort with the war chief, under a flag of truce, to give them his message. But the inspector told us that his patrols had found that the Battleford trail was nothing but melting ice and mud. Horses might get through but not the wagons and carts needed for the families.

"He also told us that his men had built a big barge, hoping to get them out that way, but the river is still in flood and filled with broken ice too dangerous for them yet. Then Wandering Spirit asked the trader MacKenzie to come with us and discuss the problem with Big Bear. He agreed. The chief told him we were going to destroy the fort whatever happened, and since the people were trapped there, he could give them one other choice. They could stay there and be killed or they could come with us as prisoners. But not the policemen. They could go out on their barge and take their chances with the river. He agreed not to attack the fort that night, so they would have time to make their decision. They didn't have much choice. The offer was accepted.

"As soon as the people were out of the fort, the warriors took over and confiscated everything of value: furs, carts, bedding, and food supplies. Then they set the fires. I don't think it all burned. That night snow was blowing and some of the fires went out. My uncle found a she-dog with pups. We had to eat all of ours when we were so hungry last winter, so he is bringing them back with him. Lizabet will get one of the pups to play with. Muskwa found a glass eye. He's bringing it back for his blind brother, although I tried to tell him they don't work that way. Another man found some false teeth. But there was no whiskey left behind. They did leave some bottles of medicine. Some of my friends drank it but not me, I knew what it was from my school days in Winnipeg." He started to laugh. "They will be the last one's home; they have to keep getting off their horses, and ailing White Bear claims that his horse gets taller every time he tries to remount."

Catherine laughed with him. "Was there no shooting at all?"

"There was one bit of trouble. A three-man patrol was sent this way to find out what was going on. Coming back, they blundered right into the council going on between Mr. MacKenzie and Big Bear. The warriors thought they were leading more policemen in to attack us, so they opened fire. Lone Man killed one of them, but the other two, although wounded, made it back into the fort."

The colour drained out of Catherine's face. "Not Peter Gray! He wasn't one of them, was he?"

"No, Cowan was the one who died. I didn't recognize the other two. Your friend must be getting close to Battleford by now, if their barge held together." He paused, then added quietly, "Before he went away, he married trader MacKenzie's daughter, Ellen, outside the barracks, under the flag where we could all see them. I wanted to tell you this before you heard it from her." His eyes were searching hers.

At first surprised, she began to smile. "If that isn't just like Ellen. I'll bet it was her idea too!'

"Then you don't feel badly about it? I saw you crying when he left Pounding Lake."

She was puzzled for a moment, then she remembered. "Jay, I told you then that he was just a friend. I'm happy for them." She stepped closer to him and put her hands lightly on his chest, looking up at him as intently as he was looking down. "A friend! But not even Peter has been as kind and caring about me as you have been. You gave me your sacred amulet to keep me safe, and I'm sure it wasn't easy for you to part with it. Even today, I know it must have been a hard ride for you to get here so quickly. I don't know why, when we are... well...I suppose...on different sides in all this trouble."

"Don't you know, Cate? Do I really need to tell you?"

Catherine hesitated. "No, you already have in so many ways. Almost in words the day the policemen left. There has been something between us since the first time we saw one another. I can't put a name to it, a sort of recognition perhaps. I tried never to let myself think about it, but I did sometimes."

"It *was* there for you, then! I often wondered. As for me, I have had trouble thinking about anything else since that night in Fort Pitt. But Cate, I think we are saying too much. I can't have you, the way things are. And now we can't pretend we are just friends any more."

"Oh, Jay, I don't *want* to! At least not when we are alone like this."

There was a tense interval while they each fought a battle within themselves, trying to cling to reality and common sense. Then it was lost. Slowly, he drew her closer, and she melted into his arms with an aching pent-up need for each other that sent the world away from them. All there was left was her woman's body hard against his, her breasts yielding under the thin cotton dress to his naked chest his hands even as his arms held her, moving and caressing her shoulders ... her slim waist and hips. He buried his face in her silky hair. They could both hear their own hearts, shutting out every other sound. It was an elemental coming together, the lonely, love-starved girl and the intense, troubled young man, caught between two races and two cultures, both trapped in a time of violence and looming disaster.

Catherine turned her head up and her lips found and met his. Suddenly they were kissing in the white man's way, long and passionate and with increasing urgency that carried them beyond all emotions they had known before. It was a wild giving and taking of each other, in body and mind, that would change them both forever. Somehow, they ended the clinging embrace and drew apart.

Jay looked stunned. "How did that happen, Cate? Please believe me, I never meant it to. I don't know what to do about this." For the first time, it was him appealing to her.

She looked up into his agonized eyes and laid her hands gently on both sides of his face. "What *can* we do? Neither one of us meant this to happen, but it has. We didn't plan it Lord knows that. I guess all we can do is keep it to ourselves, a lovely and happy secret between us."

"My God! I don't know, Cate. I want you so much, I'm afraid I can't look at you without showing it."

"Yes, you can, because you must. Think what could have happened if Marie or Scotty had walked in on us a few minutes ago. We are going to need to be much more careful."

"I thought of that. I would have told them that I forced myself on you against your wishes."

"You would have told such a terrible lie? And with me looking so bliss-ful?" Suddenly they both laughed, and still were laughing as they went to sit, primly on opposite sides of the tent.

Just then, Scotty came in with several whitefish and found them together. Marie might have scolded them. By Cree custom, it was highly improper for a man and a woman to be alone and unchaperoned like this. But Scotty was too anxious to hear news of Fort Pitt to even think about it. Jay told him all that he had told Catherine about the events in the fort. And Scotty, along with everyone else, was surprised but grateful that Big Bear had been able to control the warriors.

As Jay rose to leave, Catherine spoke to him again. "You brought us happier news than we expected. Now we can tell *you* some good news. Your sister MaryLou is here from Battleford. Safe and well, and I am sure, waiting anxiously to see you."

Once again, she was fascinated by how any sudden pleasure in his dark eyes altered the stern mask of his face. Then he stepped outside and was gone.

CHAPTER TWENTY-TWO

Melissa and MaryLou were sitting in front of the Blue Quill lodge. MaryLou was beading a pair of moccasins for Jay; Melissa was knitting a sweater for Lizabet. The little girl, chattering and lively as ever, had gone off with Theresa and Rose to gather firewood. She did not yet know that her doting 'Poppa' would never come back to her. When she asked for him, as she often did, the women looked anxiously at one another. They would soon have to tell her the truth.

They were not talking. It was warm, and the two women had just about talked themselves out in the last few days. MaryLou had been full of interesting stories of what it was like working for white people. She had brought gossip about their friends and relatives on the reserve near Battleford. Now they were content to sit quietly, knowing there were not likely to be many such lulls before the fire-storm of the rebellion caught up with them again.

They were surprised by a tall figure who came around the tepee and stood there, smiling at them. MaryLou's face returned almost the identical smile, although it faded a little when she saw how thin her brother was.

"It looks like I should have brought you food instead of a package of artist's supplies," she said.

"You brought me some?" he asked, as he came to sit beside her. "I do need them and we have all the food we can use for now." They gazed at one another with open affection. It seemed such a long time since they had seen each other in Battleford.

"I heard you were in camp. How did you get here?" Jay asked. Once again, MaryLou told the story of her journey, while Melissa knitted, happy to share vicariously in the conversation. Jay told them of the taking of Fort Pitt. "The war party and their prisoners should come in soon, probably about sundown."

Melissa paused her knitting and looked at him closely. "Why did you come back ahead of them, Jay?"

He hesitated a moment before answering. "Do you remember Buck Breland?" he asked.

"The whiskey smuggler?"

"That is the one. White Bear and I had a difference of opinion with him before we left for Fort Pitt. I noticed that he was gone this morning. I thought maybe he was heading this way to make trouble. So, I came back here after him."

"A difference of opinion? Is that what you call scattering the man's belongings, pulling down his tent, and then the two of you jumping all over him?" Melissa asked.

MaryLou looked amused. "Why were you two so mad at him?"

Jay shrugged and looked away from her. "It was a personal matter. Has anyone seen him here today, do you know?"

Both girls shook their heads. But Melissa had another question. "Who told you that MaryLou was back?"

Jay shot her an annoyed look. "Why? What does it matter?"

"Because I have an idea why you are so mad at Breland. He tried to take Catherine McNab away; I have heard that story. You were afraid he was going to try it again. That is why you came back so quickly. You have been with her. She is the one who told you about MaryLou."

Melissa stood up abruptly. "Jay, I was afraid of this! White men *do* take our women as I know all too well but it can never be the other way around. It would make the most awful trouble for both of you." She dropped her knitting and ran into the lodge in tears.

Incredulous, MaryLou looked at her brother. "What is all this? What are you two talking about?" Jay picked up a stick and began absently to tap it on the ground between his feet. She waited patiently. They had always been honest with one another in the turbulent years of their childhood. But she could see he was having difficulty and began to feel uneasy. Her voice was gentle when she spoke again. "Melissa said something about McNab's wife. What does she have to do with this?"

He shrugged again, not looking at her as he answered. "Our cousin is pleased that her friend was not killed when the white men died. She does not like it though, that *I* was the one who took her friend away from the shooting and over to Mrs. Scott. But I could not leave her there to be taken by the warriors."

"I can understand that, certainly, but not why Melissa is so upset."

"We both know what a bad time she had because she married a white man. She is afraid, I think, of anything like that happening to people who are close to her. So, she wants me to stay away from Mrs. McNab."

MaryLou smiled at him. "Is that all it is? Then why worry her, Jay? Just stay away from her."

"No!"

MaryLou could not believe her ears. She stared at her brother, totally shocked.

"I'm not going to," he added. "You asked me, and I have always told you the truth."

"I know that," she assured him. "I'm trying to understand this. You *will* not or *cannot* not stay away from Catherine?"

He made an impatient sound. "You heard what Melissa said. It is true."

"What is true?"

"Look, MaryLou. What you are trying to make me say is going to hurt you. You will not like it any more than she does. Cate and I hoped it would just be something between the two of us. But I will say it if you insist. One night in Fort Pitt, I stood alone in the darkness with her. We talked and I took her hand and put my amulet in it, and nothing has been the same for me since then."

"A white woman? One who already belonged to another man?"

"How many times do you think I asked myself that, without finding any answers? But since that much has been said, I will tell you the rest of it. I will never feel for another woman the way I do about her. She is the one I will always want, always think about when I am alone, and always remember. I cannot explain it or change it. There is also nothing I can do about it … the way things are. But Cate and I are also friends. She trusts me. I will go to her whenever she needs me until she is safely back with her own people. I am sorry if you and Melissa cannot accept that. But it is the way it will be until she is gone." Jay threw the stick away with a violent gesture. "Nothing worse can happen to me after that."

MaryLou, recovering from her shock, saw such pain on the handsome face of her brother that she had to look away. He stood up, and now his voice was steadier.

"I have to see to Cloudwalker. Some of the young boys offered to rub him down and then walk him for me. He had a hard run. When I have taken care of him, can I come back and see the supplies you brought for me?"

"Oh Jay, you know you can! What else would I do with them?" She watched as he crossed the camp with that graceful loping stride of his, then went into the lodge to confront Melissa.

"I wish you had prepared me for this," MaryLou said. "I am not sure that I said any of the right things to him."

"I'm sorry," said Melissa. "I was not sure of it myself until just now. Oh, why did we let this happen? How could he?" When the other girl looked at her pointedly, she added hastily, "I know, it happens. I know that better than anyone. But what are we going to do about it? We can't let him…"

"Not a thing, we cannot change his feelings any more than he can. Anyway, it will be this rebellion against the government that will do the deciding for all of us, before it is over. I have an idea we should take any kind of happiness we can get now. There is not going to be much of it afterwards ... for those who survive."

***

The war party came in just before sunset. The sound of it was like a warning rumble in the distance at first, echoing from the hills that lifted it above the Pounding Lake trail. It grew to thunder as they came into sight. The mounted warriors preceded squealing Red River carts, groaning wagons, and drivers shouting and snapping their whips. They broke like a tidal wave over the two camps. Their families ran to meet them with shouts of welcome, and hilarious relief when they found that none of their relatives and friends were casualties.

The new lot of prisoners were directed to a broad open place close to the creek ravine. The Pounding Lake prisoners were ordered to join them right away, if they did not want the warriors to do it for them. No one wasted any time in argument. The warriors were tired and surly; the Fort Pitt people had held them up interminably on the trail.

"They will have the tents down around our ears," Marie warned Catherine, throwing everything helter-skelter, clean or dirty, onto blankets, which she bunched and dragged outside. She waved and shouted to the mounted men to indicate their compliance with the abrupt order. Dan, pulling up the tent pegs, called to Catherine to douse the camp stove and drag it outside before it burnt the collapsing canvas. They did not fold the tent, just piled the bulky shelter loosely into the wagon. While Dan hitched up the team, Catherine and Marie stored the blanket bundles over and around the tent, gasping with exertion.

"Why are they in such a hurry?" asked Catherine, eyeing the guards.

"They don't want to be bothered with us; they want to get back to their families," panted Marie. "And I guess they want us all together, so fewer men can guard us. They slash tents and scatter the goods of even their own people, if they don't obey orders to move quickly enough."

"But that's awful."

"Yes, and necessary," said Marie, still trying to get her breath. "It's wartime, and these are fighting men. Suppose this camp is attacked. Do you think the enemy is going to wait patiently while we pack up neat and proper? Slow-pokes get killed! In a way, we are getting a lesson. We will have to learn how to do it without wasting any time. If we are forced to go on the move with them, we will need to get rid of everything we don't really need."

Just then Suzy came running over to them, "Joe and I have just been told to camp with the Indians," she told Marie. "I suppose that means we are no longer considered prisoners. But I will come back to see you as soon as I can." The two women hugged one another briefly before parting.

"Come on, old lady," called Scotty. "Let me get you hoisted up on the wagon. Mrs. Mac, you can help me lead the team. It's not that far." It was nearing dusk. The flaming sunset created long black shadows across the ground. As they walked, Catherine began to feel a tenuous new freedom.

***

The new campsite was teeming with activity and people, some moving about aimlessly, bewildered by all that had happened. Others were hurrying to put up their tents, while enough light remained to see what they were doing. Scotty stopped at a gap between two other tents and helped Marie's teetering descent from the wagon. Catherine looked around, eager to see the MacKenzies.

Scotty cautioned her, "There will be time for greetings tomorrow. Right now, we need a roof over our heads." As the two women held the uprights, Scotty threw the canvas over the ridge pole and pounded pegs into each corner. Once the loops were over them, Catherine was free to help him with the other pegs. Then a complete silence fell, broken only by the wail of Daisy Bradley's baby.

Wandering Spirit, Ayimasees, and Clear Sky had just ridden into the compound and the chief was signalling to the prisoners to approach him. When they had formed a watchful circle, the chief spoke to Jay, gesturing fiercely. "Wandering Spirit has come to give you a message and a warning,"

Jay interpreted. "We'll be moving out soon. You must learn to move much more quickly than you did today. Take good care of your horses and wagons. If they break down, they will be left behind. If any one here is caught with a weapon, it will be used ... on you. None of you will be ill-treated unless you make trouble for us. That includes trying to leave messages along the way or trying to slow us down.

"The chief plans to use you as hostages. You may be exchanged for prisoners held by the whites, or for bargaining in negotiations with them. Finally, he has this to say, and I advise you to take him seriously. If one of you succeeds in getting away, one of the other prisoners will be shot and killed in your place. It could be a man, woman, or child."

There was a concerted gasp from the onlookers. They were all in shadow now except for the three men astride their horses, caught in the last light of the setting sun, so that they appeared to be floating there, over darkness. Catherine could not believe it was Jay saying such menacing words. His face was barred with fresh streaks of colour, and he was wearing a roach wolverine headdress that rippled with every movement of his restless horse. She would not have been sure that it *was* Jay, except for the deep accented voice that she now knew so well. Suddenly another voice arose from the onlookers.

Tom Bradley shook his fist at Jay. "You bloody bastard! I'm looking forward to the day when I see you swinging from the end of a rope. You and all your murdering pals here." Cloudwalker snorted and sidled as Jay slowly turned to look at Bradley. The other two Crees had shifted position and were looking menacingly at the white man.

"That may happen, Mr. Bradley," said Jay evenly, "but I assure you that, unless you quiet down, you won't live long enough to see it. These two men do not make idle threats, as one look over at the town will tell you." As though to emphasize his words, Wandering Spirit and Ayimasees edged their horses closer to Bradley, aiming their rifles at him.

Paul McRae spoke evenly, "Don't say another word, Tom. One bullet could start them all shooting ... just like before." Bradley got the message, shoved his hands into his pockets, and looked away from the two warriors. Jay's stallion suddenly snaked sideways, then reared, lashing out with his hooves and whinnying loudly. Wandering Spirit jerked his head around and spoke curtly to him as the crowd scrambled back. Jay turned his horse away from the white people. The war chief glared in his direction and then issued a brief command. All three men swung around and trotted away from the frightened prisoners.

Catherine shivered uncontrollably. This incident brought back too starkly the way Ian and the other men had died. Marie clung to Scotty while he patted her shoulder.

"Come on, old girl. They won't be coming back tonight. We'll brew up some tea and have ourselves a cup or two. Into the tent with you, Mrs. Mac; the chill is coming on."

***

Back in their tent with the lantern lit, Scotty lit a fire in the camp stove while Marie regained her composure. He brought more of their belongings inside, as Catherine put the kettle on. As the water began to heat, the women arranged the tent as it had been, laying out the bedrolls and sorting their clothing.

"Well, child," Marie remarked, "we got through that one too, eh? That big-mouth Bradley, he'll get a piece of my tongue tomorrow!"

Scotty came in with another armload just in time to hear this. He grinned at Catherine. "He'll be running to the Indians begging for help by the time she's finished with him!"

Catherine was still shaken. "That was awful, what Mr. Bradley said to Jay about hanging," she declared. "He was only saying what he was told to say. Anyone could see that!" Marie and Scotty exchanged worried looks. The kettle began to boil and Marie poured the hot water over the tea leaves in the pot.

"Jay Clear Sky is pure Indian, lass," Scotty warned her. "He is one of the Big Bears by his own choice, and he will stay one when it comes to a showdown. It is sometimes easy to forget that, since he is friendlier than most and speaks English, but it's best not to. I'll give him this though. He pulled off a smart stunt with that horse of his tonight."

"You think he did that on purpose?" asked Marie.

"Sure, he did. Hell, he can handle the stallion better than that, and the war chief knows it. But it worked, he got their attention away from Bradley. Joe says Clear Sky is a great favourite of the chief. But even, so I'd say he was pushing his luck there. One good thing though, Wandering Spirit cools down just as fast as he riles up."

"I'm damn glad of that," snapped Marie, "or there wouldn't be a live soul left in the whole district of Saskatchewan."

They were sipping their tea and eating some bannock when they heard a whispered voice at the door-flap. "It's me, Paul, Mrs. Scott. I have Mrs. Simmons here. Can we come in?"

"Dear Lord," gasped Marie. "I forgot I told him he could bring her here, now that there are more prisoners." Then she raised her voice, "Come in, Paul." The husky Métis stepped inside, pushing Julia ahead of him. The gaunt woman, her face chalk-white except for red-rimmed eyes, peered anxiously at the three of them. With a sudden cry she rushed at Catherine, threw her arms around her and began to sob.

"Oh, Catherine, when is this awful nightmare going to end? I can't take any more, I just can't!" Catherine had spilled her tea under the onslaught. She put the cup down and folded her arms around Julia's quivering body.

"There now, Julia, please calm down. It's all right."

"How can you say that? It's not all right. It never will be again. Those monsters won't let us go. You heard them out there. Why don't they just kill us now and get it over with?" In her frenzy, she pushed Catherine backwards, so she stumbled and nearly fell. Marie stepped in smartly, and pulling Julia away from Catherine, brought her around to face her. Marie raised her hand and slapped Julia's face hard, but without anger. The verbal tirade stopped abruptly.

"Now, Mrs. Simmons," said the big woman, "that's better! You aren't doing yourself, or anyone else, any good by carrying on that way." Julia began to whimper again, and Marie spoke more forcefully. "And stop that too! I've a mind to let you stay with us, but not unless you start to behave yourself."

Julia raised her hand to her flaming cheek. A sly look stole into the wide eyes, once so soft and intelligent. "You ... will let me stay? I won't have to go back to all those half-breed brats?"

Catherine winced, looking at Paul's tired face. "Mr. McRae, I'm sure she doesn't know what she is saying. She owes her life to you. She'll realize that once she is herself again."

"I know. Maybe you'll help her more than we could, Mrs. McNab. You and the other white folks from Fort Pitt. They didn't know that you two were still alive until they got here. The MacKenzie girls wanted to come to see you, but their father thought it best not to rile the Indians any more tonight. Now, Marie, have you decided about Mrs. Simmons?"

The older woman scowled at Julia. "Are you going to behave?"

"Yes. Please Mrs. Scott, I'll be quiet, I promise." With enormous relief, Paul left immediately. The drums were pounding again in the other camp and the singing climbed to a deafening level. Catherine saw Julia's eyes glazing over and hastily took her icy hand and led her to a bedroll.

"Look, Julia, this is where I sleep. We'll curl up together tonight. See how cozy we'll be? I'll help you take your dress and shoes off, then you lie down and be all warm and safe. Do you want a cup of hot tea?" Julia shook her head but did as she was told. As soon as she was under the covers she clapped her hands to her ears and closed her eyes. Catherine watched her for a while, then went back to the Scotts, feeling drained and distressed. Dan and Marie were watching Julia with sympathetic eyes. She had lost a shocking amount of weight.

"You're a good lass," Scotty said raising his voice over the din outside. Marie refilled Catherine's cup and handed it to her.

"And you two are the kindest people I have ever met."

***

Catherine hardly slept that night. Apart from the noise, Julia shuddered every so often in apparent panic, relaxing only after being patted soothingly. When Catherine did sleep she had strange dreams. At first, Jay was there holding her as he had on his return that day. But then she saw him up on his horse in the blood-red sunset, roach headdress tossing, his painted face turning away from her, even though she called out to him. She awoke with tears trickling from the corners of her eyes, desperately wanting him to be with her there in the darkness, talking to her, holding her, making love to her then a sense of shame engulfed her. *Why* was her mind playing such cruel tricks?

She tried to summon Ian's once-familiar face Ian who had died only two weeks before. But his image kept eluding her. *Dear Lord,* she thought. *Am I crazy like Julia too, only in a different way?* She lay there, eyes wide in the dark. The amulet felt very warm between her breasts. She touched it and somehow it felt comforting. Her breasts were tingling, and there was the strangest sensation in the pit of her stomach. The wanting was on her again, deep, aching and imperative.

This was impossible! It couldn't be happening ... but it was. Hot tears stung her eyes, and this time she could not stop them. At last she drifted off into exhausted sleep. When she awoke the next morning, she was still holding the amulet.

CHAPTER TWENTY-THREE

"Oh, my dear Lord! *Mercy!*" Marie reeled back from the tent flap, clutching her ample bosom, her face ashen. It was an hour after dawn. Scotty shot out from under his blanket, and Catherine sat up in alarm. Julia pulled the blankets over her head. Marie pointed outside with a trembling finger and glared at Catherine accusingly as she tried to get her breath back. Scotty, a spry, if unromantic defender in his long johns, picked up an iron frying pan the only weapon he could find and hurried to the opening.

"Child, it's that *wolf* of yours!" Marie wailed. "Bigger than ever! I nearly stepped on him! All I wanted to do was relieve myself, a small thing for anyone to ask to do in peace and quiet. And there he was, snarling with dripping fangs. And those awful yellow eyes! Oh, *mercy!*"

After peering around outside, her husband looked back at her, half-amused and half-annoyed, his hair all awry.

"Woman, he's lying down over by the corner of the tent, nowhere near the door, yawning and not even bothering to look at me."

"Well, that may be, but he did give me a terrible turn," she replied. Catherine was out of bed and pulling on her shoes.

"I'm sorry he frightened you, Marie. But honestly, he has never hurt anyone. Wait, I'll hold him while you go outside."

"I don't have to go anymore," she said crossly, sitting down.

When Catherine came out of the tent and went to her knees beside him, the wolf whined happily deep in his throat. In a familiar gesture of affection, he took her arm in his jaws, pressing the skin gently with his long white teeth. His half-closed eyes flickered at her then away, and his plumed tail swept the ground. He was still wearing his collar, and he looked fit and well fed. Muhekun had almost completed his growth. His head had broadened, his muzzle had lengthened, and his paws were no longer too big and clumsy for his powerful legs. He was nearly all white except for his black nose. Scotty, watching from the doorway, whistled in surprise.

"Lass, I'm thinking he's one of the arctic ones—the big whites that live on the tundra. If it had been a real bad winter up there, and the she-wolf had lost her mate, she could have drifted south in search of food. I've only seen a few of them in my time."

"He is beautiful," said Catherine, scratching at a favourite spot behind his ear. "But I don't know what to do with him. We can't have him scaring Marie like this."

"That woman is scared of cats, dogs, mice, and little bugs. It's only people she's not afraid of ... and should be. But I'm thinking. You used to keep him tied, didn't you?" At her nod, he went on thoughtfully. "It mightn't be a bad idea to keep him around, considering the fix we're in, no weapons and all. That wolf would never let anyone like Breland near you; maybe he'd guard the rest of us, seeing we're with you. I could drive a stake at that corner and get a rope short enough to keep him back from the door, what do you think?"

"Mr. Scott, if Muhekun makes up his mind to take off, no rope or stake is going to hold him."

Scotty grinned at her. "I know that and so do you, but Marie doesn't. Some day he will take off for good, looking for his own kind, but right now he is still attached to you. He's a bit of insurance, lass."

Like my amulet, she thought, remembering that Ian had once called it that. *My two white wolves.* She sighed, drawn and tired from her restless night.

"How is he with children?" asked Scotty.

"Who?" asked Catherine blankly.

"Why the wolf, lass," answered Scotty, looking at her closely. "Are you feeling poorly, now? Or is it Mrs. Simmons? She's upset you, maybe."

"Oh, no, I'm sorry. I was daydreaming. He never minded the children in Pounding Lake. He loves As-a-Child. The only ones to worry about are grown men. He was never very good with Ian, especially when we had a tiff. But I would just have to say 'down' and he'd back off."

Scotty ducked into the tent, reappearing with his trousers on and pulling his suspenders over his shoulders. He approached cautiously. Muhekun's ears flicked and his tail stopped wagging, but as Catherine went on scratching him, he laid his head on his forepaws and ignored the man.

"If he stands with his legs all stiff and stares right into your eyes, you should back off," she explained. "I think in wolf talk that means you are challenging him."

"Makes sense," he agreed. "Dog fights start off that way. But you talking about him not liking men reminds me of something the Indians told me. They believe that a mature wolf, raised by a woman, becomes real jealous of any man around her. The pack instinct I'd guess."

"Well, Mr. Scott," she replied, getting to her feet, "before we decide to keep him here, we will have to see how your wife feels about it." The idea horrified Marie, but when Scotty reminded her of their lack of weapons, and Catherine promised to take the wolf with her whenever she left the tent, she agreed reluctantly. After breakfast Scotty found a sturdy stake, drove it firmly into the ground and handed the rope to Catherine. The wolf allowed her to tie it to his collar, stretched out and went to sleep.

***

Later, when Ellen and Connie came out of their tent and caught sight of them, they waved frantically. Catherine looked at the guards but the nearest ones looked bored and indifferent. She ran to her friends. It was several minutes before any of them could say a thing that made sense. There were more tears and hugs and laughter as Leslie, Emma, and Daisy came to greet her.

"Oh, my dear," Leslie managed at last, wiping her eyes. "We were so sure you had been killed or…or even worse…and here you are looking as pretty as ever."

"I'm all right," Catherine assured her. "Nothing happened to me after the shooting, and I try not to think about that day." An involuntary shudder that went through her as she said it moved Leslie to change the subject quickly. "That is for the best, I'm sure. How is Mrs. Simmons?"

"Much worse than I am. She's grieving to the point of losing her mind, but it might do her good to have you around. She can't mix easily with Indians or Métis, even with Marie Scott or Louisa McRae, kind as they are." She turned to Ellen. "Is it really true that you and Peter are married?"

"Even to the ring," said Ellen sticking her hand out. "Would you believe that Inspector Kingsley gave it to us? It was his mother's. You should have seen my bridal outfit: winter coat and boots, and a bunch of paper daisies from one of mom's old summer hats. But I'm a bride in name only. I keep wondering if they got down the river safely. It was raging when they left. And where he is now? It's not knowing anything that is so hard. It must be like that for your family. The inspector sent a dispatch rider to Battleford before the fort was taken, when we got the news about Pounding Lake. We assume he got through."

George MacKenzie, with Scotty and Paul, joined them. His face lit up when he saw Catherine, and he embraced her heartily. "It's more than we dared hope for, to see you again, dear lass. And bonny as always, after all you've been through! I promise you, we'll get you ladies out of this, one way or another." He turned to Leslie. "We been talking to Big Bear with the help of Paul here. It seems we can let you women go to the creek for water and fire-wood. We men can cut a few evergreens for screening and rig up a privy. But we'll be moving out soon, heading cross country for Poundmaker's reserve."

They broke up then, after being warned by Paul to be ready to move at a moment's notice.

***

Catherine had very little to pack: Jay's blanket, a thin mattress, her worn shoes, a comb Suzy had given her, and a pair of moccasins. Marie had donated two of her print dresses. She still had her brown shawl, but had discarded the dress she had worn the day Ian was killed. She never wanted to see it again. As Julia had no more than that, Catherine made one pack for them both.

"There! If we're told to move, we just need to tie it up," Catherine said. Julia stood silently as the other two women bustled around her. "Julia, it doesn't look as though we are going to be as confined as we were. Why don't you let me take you to visit the other white women? They're very nice; I know you'll like them." No response.

Marie tried. "I just had a nice visit with Gus and Annette LaRonde from Fort Pitt. Land sakes, we talked ourselves dry! And that reminds me, we are out of water."

"I'll get some," said Catherine. "Please come with me, Julia; the walk will do you good."

This time Julia responded. "No, please don't make me go! I'll have to see Indians if I go out there." The other two women looked at each other over her bowed head.

"Leave her be," sighed Marie. "But take the wolf with you, for safety."

"Mine or yours?" teased Catherine, unable to resist.

"Get along," retorted Marie.

***

When Catherine started toward the creek, with Muhekun padding after her, she followed a faint trail made by others going for water. She hesitated when she encountered one of the guards, a burly young man with a round but not unfriendly face. He looked at her curiously, and then she remembered him. This one had helped Jay to guard them when they were still in the Two Horse tent. He stared at the wolf, and to her surprise, spoke to her in English less fluent than Jay but understandable. He asked her about the wolf.

"He was starving when I found him. A very small cub. I have kept and fed him ever since."

"A snow wolf!" he said in admiration. Then he smiled slightly. "You make ... unusual friends ... Mrs. McNab." She nodded and walked on, cheeks flushing.

The drop to the creek at this point was steep, and she was careful to keep to the path through the heavy and thorny bushes. The water was still high and beside it the ground was muddy. She nearly slipped into the creek as she leaned over to fill the pail, then noticed that Muhekun was gazing downstream, eyes intent, his tail slowly wagging.

Catherine looked in that direction and saw As-a-Child sitting on a rock, fishing with a long pole. He saw her too and his face twisted into the oddly sweet expression that meant he was happy. She picked her way toward him over stones and fallen branches. She put the pail down and shooed Muhekun away from a convenient drink.

"Go get your own, lazybones," she scolded.

As-a-Child had caught several whitefish. When she sat beside him, he slid two of them over to her. She thanked him and threaded the fish through the gills onto a handy stick. She saw when he caught the next one, that he banged it loose from the hook. Then he lifted bark from a fallen tree and dug out a white grub to re-bait his hook. She was surprised at his attention span. It was such an awkward process, with his lack of co-ordination, and she wanted to help him. But she held back, recalling how her brother had hated anyone to help him, when he could do something for himself.

It was wonderfully peaceful and serene in the little valley in the warm morning sun. Muhekun ranged idly up and down the creek bank, and her mute but happy friend was content beside her. She thought about Marie, waiting for the water, but could not resist the temptation to savour this quiet, healing moment for a while. She knew that Marie would forgive her when she saw the whitefish.

***

Jay was sitting in front of his uncle's lodge that morning, sketching on a pad, when a shadow fell over him. He looked up, closed the pad, and rose to his feet. It was Ayimasees, and he appeared uneasy.

"My father wishes to see you," he said. This usually meant that the chief wanted Jay to interpret for him, but Ayimasees surprised him with a further explanation. "He has had a dream-vision, and he is troubled." Jay followed across the camp, wondering what any of this had to do with him.

Inside Big Bear's lodge, the chief sat cross-legged looking into the small cooking fire, his ceremonial pipe resting on his lap. His eyes were unfocused, as though his thoughts were very far way. Several other members of his family sat quietly with him, the men on one side, the women on the other. They all had the same solemn look that Jay had seen on Ayimasees' face.

Ayimasees spoke to his father to get his attention, indicating that he had brought Clear Sky as requested. Big Bear slowly came out of his trance-like state and motioned for Jay to sit facing him. He whispered, so that Jay had to strain to hear him.

"There is death on the wind. It has come to me over the plains, around the hills, and up the river valleys. I see smoke and flames, blood on the ground. I hear the thunder of big guns and the screams of dying men and horses." The chief pointed to the southeast. "It comes from there. I can smell death. I feel it all around me. It has chilled the marrow in my bones that I might be dying myself."

There was a long silence and Jay, who had been warm and lazy in the sun outside, felt himself go cold, and he, too, caught the odour of smoke and blood, hot metal, and gun powder.

"Tell me what I can do for you," he asked the old man.

"Take your swift stallion and ride hard to Cut Knife Hill. "I want your eyes to see what is still hidden from my mind. Then bring it back to me. Go to my friend Poundmaker, who is in great danger. Tell him of my dream, unless it is too late for that. We will move away from here, down as far as Frenchman Butte. There we will stop and wait for the news that you bring back to us."

"I will do that," said Jay, standing. The chief's eyes were already hooded and far away.

Jay sped back across the camp. Blue Quill stood in front of the lodge, waiting for him. Jay explained quickly, then asked his uncle to get Cloudwalker, picketed nearby. He went inside for his rifle and bedroll.

"I must ride out on an errand for Big Bear," he told MaryLou, as he tied on his cartridge belt and slid his rifle into its carrying case. The women packed pemmican and bannock into a saddle bag. Outside, Blue Quill slipped the rawhide rein over the stallion's lower jaw.

"I don't know how long I will be gone," Jay said.

"Go carefully," urged his uncle.

***

Jay held the horse to a slow lope as he left the camp, though the animal was keyed up and eager to run. "We have a long way to go and wide rivers to cross," Jay cautioned him, slapping his muscled neck. As they passed the prisoners' encampment, Jay looked around, but to his acute disappointment, Cate was nowhere to be seen. He did see White Bear on guard, and they exchanged signals of acknowledgement. Dropping down into the creek ravine, Jay headed for the sandbar used as a crossing point, then reined in the stallion. Cate was there, just beyond the crossing, sitting with As-a-Child.

He felt the familiar rush of pleasure and excitement as soon as he saw her. He knew that he should keep going, but instead rode as close as he could over the tangled undergrowth and dismounted. Since she was there, he tried to convince himself that it was meant that he should speak to her. She had seen him too and came quickly to meet him. Wearing one of Marie's voluminous dresses, she had to hike it up as she stepped from stone to stone. The sun was striking golden sparks off her hair. Violet eyes were alive with pleasure as she approached him. But when she noticed the blanket roll, the saddle bags, and his cartridge belt, her happy expression faltered.

"Oh no, you're not going away again are you, Jay?"

"Yes, as a courier for Big Bear. But I'll come back as soon as I can. I wanted to see you, to promise you that."

"Will you be in danger, where you are going?"

"Maybe, but not nearly as much as I am when I'm with you." He meant it as a reassuring joke, but the words did not come out as he intended. "If anything happens while I am gone ... if things get bad ... get word to my friend White Bear. He speaks some English. He is my age, round face, big this way," he said, indicating very broad shoulders.

"Yes, I know who he is. He spoke to me as I passed him on the way here."

"Good. We are like brothers, and he knows about you."

"He knows ... what about me, Jay?"

"That I don't want anything to happen to you. Maybe he suspects it is more than that, but he would never ask." He paused. "It is so much more than that, Cate. Last night when my people were singing and dancing, I wasn't with them. I was one of the guards at your camp ... by choice. I wanted to be close to you. I go past the Scott tent on any excuse, sometimes none, hoping for even one quick look at you. I only feel alive now, when I am with you; all the rest is wasted time."

She looked at him with such a mixture of wonder and aching pleasure that her eyes teared. "Yes, it is like that for me too. I wish I had known you were one of the guards; I might have tried to see you, instead of having an awful dream."

"What dream? Do you want to tell me about it?"

"Yes. I could see you just as you were at sunset last night talking to us. I kept calling to you but you turned away from me, and I felt so lost and alone. I woke up crying, and I wanted it to be you in the bed with me, instead of Julia. I know I shouldn't tell you that. It's shameless, but I no longer care." Her face flushed, and she was close to tears again.

He took both of her hands. "I'll never turn away from you—another promise. My people believe in dreams, but maybe your dream was just a warning that I was going away today. Listen to me. I remember every time we have met, every word we have spoken. When I came back from Fort Pitt, and you were so happy to see me, I wanted to make love to you. More than anything I have ever wanted in my life. I still do."

The happiness flooded back into her eyes. "I want that too. Why not, Jay? Why can't we have each other for just a little while? A bit of time out of our lives for you and me. Who knows? When we get into the fighting, as everyone seems to think we will, one or both of us might not come through it. But if we do, we will always have that much, at least, to remember."

It was suddenly too much for him to have her so near, to see her looking at him like that, to be touching her. He pulled her close and kissed her more deeply and intensely than he had in the Scott's tent. She answered his passion, her mouth opening to his, her entire body responding. They seemed to be melting into one another. She could feel his arousal now. His one arm pulled her against him, his other hand found her breast through the thin dress that covered it, one of the lovely breasts that he had seen so very briefly.

He had never held a woman like this, so intimately and passionately. Nothing had prepared him for the reality of it, the intense sensations of love and wonder, as well as the taste of her. It was all suddenly his, after all the long months of believing it would never happen. And now he had to ride away and leave her! He forced himself to release her, stepped back and away, dividing them in two once more.

His instinct to protect her restored, he realized they were in the open. Any chance passer-by could have seen them! He looked around warily, still trying to catch his breath. He thought it so odd, when his whole world had just changed, that familiar things moved and sounded the same. The creek still ran and splashed in the sunlight; birds chirped as always. There was no one in sight except As-a-Child, absorbed with his fishing. Only the wolf noticed. He was growling deep in his throat, his hackles raised and his yellow eyes fixed on Jay. He was about twelve feet away and stealthily approaching them on stiffened legs.

Catherine saw Muhekun at the same time. She brushed her hair away from her face with an unsteady hand. She spoke sharply, ordering the wolf down, then repeated the command. The baleful eyes flickered, the hackles subsided. He sank down to a sitting position and turned his head away.

"Wah!" Jay exclaimed. "You have two wolf protectors while I am gone. Your amulet and this one. But this one doesn't think we are making any sense."

"Well, *I* do," she insisted. "This is the only thing that has happened to me for such a long time that *does* make any sense!"

He touched her cheek gently, recklessly happy. *"Amee,"* he said, his voice husky.

She was puzzled. "You mean ... friend?"

"No, in French it means friend. In Cree, it is the word for your most loved one. But I must go. When I come back, I promise we will be alone somewhere together. There will be time to make our memories."

Cate smiled back at him. He thought she looked more beautiful than ever before. She whispered, "I promise I will be waiting for you. *Amee.*"

He returned to the stallion and remounted. They locked eyes for a long moment, realizing the full implication of the promises they had just exchanged. Then he pivoted the horse away from her, splashed through the shallows, and rode up the far site of the ravine. The stallion, as though aware of his rider's mood, pounded south along the trail at a joyous headlong gallop.

CHAPTER TWENTY-FOUR

The summons to move out came two mornings later. Fully aware by now of the rough treatment inflicted on laggards, the prisoners dropped whatever they were doing and ran to hitch teams and load their belongings. Joe located Scotty's saddle horse in the herd, and quietly returned it to him after nightfall. When old Pascal offered to drive Scotty's wagon, he gratefully accepted. George MacKenzie and Tom Bradley were also still mounted, and they decided that their greater mobility could be useful, should any of the wagons break down on the trail.

The moment the prisoners were ready, they were directed into the middle of a long column with Plains Crees in the lead, and the Woods Crees and rebel Métis bringing up the rear. They were soon exhausted by the pace enforced by the warriors. It had rained the night before. The ground had turned into heavy clay-like mud, which stuck to the wagon and cart wheels and had to be scraped off every few miles. It took all of them, men and women, to do it. They were soon as caked and muddy as the well-cursed wheels they were forced to clean.

The morning was cold and blustery. When they came to creeks, they got off the wagons to lighten them. At first, they removed their footwear to keep them dry. They gave that up as stones in the creek beds lacerated their feet. Some of the water was waist deep, and soon they were soaked through and chilled to the bone. The men had to lead the balky horses and often to put their shoulders to the wheels. Women carried or piggy-backed their children across.

Whenever they moved over level ground, Julia and Catherine huddled together for warmth, under a damp blanket on the wagon seat beside Pascal. Marie rode in the back of the wagon with several of the McRae children. Pascal was as jaunty and talkative as always, though Catherine noticed that he was careful never to mention Ian and Bert. Instead he tried to divert them as they struggled along. He told them of his childhood, when his family left the Fort Garry settlements and came out to Saskatchewan for huge, organized buffalo hunts. He told them about the time he had worked as a teamster for the first North West Mounted Police in the territory. Even Julia listened to his tales of Jerry Potts, the wildly eccentric Métis guide who, drunk or sober, brought the policemen through their first harrowing years in the northwest.

Catherine appreciated his attempts to distract them, but was not always attentive. She kept thinking about Jay, longing for his return so she could at least see him now and then. She no longer questioned her passion for him. She yearned for the sound of his voice, to see his smile, to touch him again. It took her breath away to remember his virile, athletic body hard against her, as it had been on the magic morning beside Pounding Creek.

She told herself that wanting him was wrong for both of them, that it was disloyal to Ian's memory. If discovered, she knew that she would not have a white friend left in the world. But it made no difference. Danger and hardship, now part of her life, no longer mattered. She refused to think through how all this might end. Jay was her only reality.

Her thoughts were interrupted by a huge flock of Canada geese, flying very low on this overcast day. They passed above them so closely that she could catch details of dark glistening eyes, white cheek patches, black outstretched necks, and silvery feathers. The din they made was overpowering. Constant babble and swooshing of great wings, which impelled them north for hundreds of miles, filled the air all around the human cavalcade. There was a sudden up-flare of alarm. Some men began to fire at the magnificent birds, bringing down several of them. Then they were gone, just undulating lines in the sky to the north, their strident calls becoming faint, wild music in the distance.

"Bon voyage, niskuk!" Pascal called to them; then he grinned at Catherine. "I hate to see such a bird go down, but also I like to eat it. My old sister, she cooks it so good, you wouldn't believe it."

A voice lashed out behind them. "What is this 'old sister' talk I hear? And you ten years older than me, you little goat!"

The 'little goat' winked at Catherine. "I should have said *big* instead of *old*," he whispered, "and the biggest thing about her is her ears!"

***

The MacKenzies were ahead of the Scott wagon; behind them were the Wilson and Bradley families. Rain clouds were shredding, casting swift shadows over the land as the column passed a mile from Camas Lake. Smoke obscured the village; it too was burning.

Catherine felt sympathy for the people behind them. She knew how devastating it was to see your home, your only security against the merciless weather and moods of this harsh country, destroyed. It was all vanishing, along with handmade furniture, beds where children had been conceived and born, books, cherished china, hooked rugs and patchwork quilts, works of skillful and patient hands over years of hard and lonely living.

Julia, who made her own home such a warm and welcoming place, just stared with hollow eyes at the rising smoke. Again, Pascal tried to distract her. He pointed to a big black bear with two cubs shambling lazily out of their way. Although the animals were downwind, some of the horses shied and snorted as they encountered their ancient foe.

A woman passed them, going to join the Crees at the head of the line. She was riding astride, as Cree women did, pulling long poles crossed over in front of her saddle.

"That travois," said Pascal, "might look funny to you, but it's the best way to go." Catherine looked more closely. Behind the horse, the poles were joined at intervals by tied-on crosspieces. Her lodge-covering was lashed to the widest space, and other bundles to the narrower ones. A child rode on one of the bundles. "They're faster than wagons, never get stuck in the mud, and there's nothing to break down, no wheels, axles, or brakes. And best of all, Mrs. Mac ... you guess." The old man smiled at her. She tried to puzzle it out, and then shook her head. "No *noise!* And that's good out hunting or making war; see what I mean?"

"Yes, fast *and* quiet," she agreed. "But the men don't seem to be doing any work. Why don't they pull travois too, Pascal?"

"Use your pretty head! They might see game for their evening meal or they could run into an ambush. No time then to stop and unload, eh? See how they ride out from the rest of us? That's to keep the families safe and the pots full. That's the way the women want it, you bet."

***

They made camp that night on the ridge that overlooked what was left of Fort Pitt. Immediately George, Scotty, and Gus LaRonde, who spoke Cree, asked to see Big Bear. They came back after a while, looking pleased. "We told him our supplies are running out," George explained. "The chief agreed to let us take a cart and go down to the buildings to see what we can salvage. Under guard, of course." He jerked his thumb at two men on horseback waiting for him. "The chief says they had poured kerosene over a lot of the supplies, so the soldiers couldn't use them, but there may be something left. And Marie, Joe Two Horse said to tell you he has a goose for you. A few of the friendlier Indians are going to send over some ducks and rabbits. So, get the cooking fires going, ladies."

The younger women set out with pails to Pounding Creek for water. They looked down into the familiar valley, and Ellen pointed to the wooden bridge where the three policemen had blundered right into the council between her father and Big Bear. They were all saddened to see the remains of Constable Cowan and two horses lying on the valley floor, all too vividly illustrating Ellen's story.

***

When they got back to the tents, the older women had the fires going. Some of them had rigged makeshift clotheslines to dry their damp clothing. Ellen looked at the assortment of strung-up petticoats, which Métis women always wore, and tried to lighten the mood after seeing the body in the valley.

"I heard a true story once," she told them, as she eased off her wet boots. "A young white man drifted out to this country a while back and got himself married to a Métis girl. Well, on their wedding night, it took her so long to take off her petticoats that he fell asleep waiting. And when he woke up in the morning, she had started to put them all back on again. They never did have children, those two." There was a ripple of amusement, and Louisa looked up from nursing her new baby, her dark eyes sparkling.

"Métis men are not nearly so easy to discourage. I have nine examples to prove that, despite all my petticoats!"

"Or else you take them off a lot faster than that other poor girl," said Marie with a chuckle. A little later, the men who had been to the fort returned with a cart piled high with goods. Scotty looked at the expectant women and smiled cheerfully.

"You'll sure be happy when you see all the things we found, everything from a clap of thunder to a lady's fart."

"Mr. Scott!" Julia protested.

"Sorry, Mrs. Simmons, but you and Mrs. Mac are going to need a few more duds to wear. And the Indians didn't know about the dugouts under the kitchens. We found salt pork, potatoes, onions, dried beans and fruit, and more. We'll share it between us. And here's the ducks and rabbits we were promised."

Soon the women had the game cooking. Some of them made bannock, while others peeled potatoes and onions to stew with the meat. Marie was fussing over the goose Joe had sent her. She cleaned it, covered it with a cloth to keep the flies off, and hung it in a tree.

Catherine looked on dubiously. "It will be a nice change, I suppose, but back when I could afford to be picky, I found goose very greasy."

"White women don't know the trick to cooking them," retorted Marie. "I'll show you when we have time to roast it properly."

***

Another early start was called the next morning. With the sun out and the wind down, the going was somewhat easier the second day. But when they turned off the Battleford trail, they had to push through thick woods and go around mosquito-infested marshes. Whenever they got to level ground, Catherine got down and walked beside the wagon, preferring the chafing of her shoes to the jolt of the seat. It felt good to be wearing hose and under-garments again, although a chemise she had been given was uncomfortably tight across her breasts. When Ellen looked back and saw her walking, she got down and waited for her.

"I'll swear I have two big blisters where my backside used to be," she complained.

"And I'm getting webbed feet," replied Catherine. "Where do you think they are taking us, Ellen?"

"I happen to know that. Big Bear told Pa last night when they were talking. We're heading for Frenchman Butte. That's it up ahead, see? The biggest one." There was no mistaking the one she meant. Higher than the other hills, the butte shouldered wide and rugged against the skyline, streaked with coulees, bare and wind-swept on top. "We should get there by sundown," added Ellen. "The Indians are going to wait there for a message from Poundmaker. Maybe we'll get news about Peter's detachment."

"Perhaps we will. Ellen, do you remember Clear Sky, the one who used to interpret for Big Bear at times?"

"Sure, I do; all us girls noticed him! He's all right, Pa says. He used to stop and talk to him sometimes. Why?"

Catherine chose her words carefully. "I think he could be the messenger you mentioned. I haven't seen him around for the last few days. If it is him, I'm sure he would pass on any news to us. I used to talk to him occasionally at Pounding Lake."

Ellen's emerald eyes filled with tears. "Oh, for just any little bit of news! Not knowing a thing is awful. It's hard sometimes to be brave about it."

"You are wonderfully brave, Ellen. I don't know how you keep up so well."

"Look who's talking! After all the pure hell you have been through!"

Before Catherine could answer, they heard someone ride up behind them.

"You two think this is a tea party here, eh? You move your butts back to the wagons where you belong. *Now!*"

"It's *not* a tea party?" asked Ellen. "And all along I thought it was! Well, go to hell, mister. I'm not slowing anyone down." It was a Métis who had caught up with them. Catherine recognized Buck Breland, still wearing Ian's coat and riding Dundee. His face was contorted with anger at Ellen's defiance. He leaned over and pushed her so roughly that she staggered and fell. Scotty shouted from the far side of the wagon, while Pascal's hand started to move toward his concealed slingshot.

A warrior moved up beside Breland, and gave him a sharp prod with his rifle. Breland was still unbalanced and nearly fell from his horse. His hand darted for the pistol in his belt, but froze in mid-air. The warrior's rifle was in his left hand, and in the other hand a wicked-looking knife was poised to throw. Catherine acknowledged White Bear with a nod, as she helped Ellen to her feet and pulled her away. Breland and White Bear were shouting at one another in Cree. The wagons had not stopped, and the two girls had to run to catch up with them.

"Get on up here you two crazies," said Marie crossly. She was on her feet, leaning over to give them a hand up. Ellen was quite unruffled as she plopped down on the wooden seat and turned back to Marie.

"What were those two saying to one another?"

"It wasn't polite," said Marie, scowling at her. "If you are going to make trouble like that, make it by your own wagon from now on." Then she laughed. "If you must know, the Indian told Breland to keep his hands off the prisoners. That we had been taken by them, not the Métis. Breland told him to watch out, he didn't have his ugly friend handy this time to back him up.

The Indian told him he didn't need to watch out, anyone could smell Breland coming a mile away ... things like that, with other rude words I won't repeat."

Ellen giggled. "That young fellow got to Breland pretty damn quick. It looks like we have a knight in shining war paint, Catherine."

At that, Marie turned serious again. She waggled her plump forefinger at Ellen. "Don't you take the chance of talking back to them again. There are a few mean and bad men in that bunch. To them the rebellion is just an excuse to make trouble, and Breland is one of them. Catherine can tell you about him."

"What do you know about him that I don't?"

"Well, he looted our house before they burned it," Catherine told her. "That's Ian's horse he is riding and his coat he's wearing. He has my diamond pin, which he was willing to give back to me, *if* I went off with him, and of course, shared his bed as part of the deal. I chose to stay with the Indians."

"I can add to that," said Ellen, lowering her voice. "Pa told me he's not only a bootlegger, he ... consorts with fallen women." She shuddered. "And to think he came after you! I would rather crawl in with a bunch of rattlesnakes."

Pascal, who had not missed a word, chuckled. "Snakes is nice company compared to Breland, you bet. But Scotty has passed the word around about him, and I'd say he's in trouble. If we don't get to him first, the Indians might, from the look of it."

***

They made a halt at noon, just long enough to boil water for tea. They were in thick woods again. Voracious insects whined around them in clouds, so no one questioned the short rest period. While they were eating, they could hear loud crashes from along their back trail. Once they were moving again, Catherine asked Pascal about it. He told her that their captors were dropping trees over the path they had made through the woods.

"But they can't hide the tracks of all these horses and wagons, can they?"

"No, but you've got it wrong. See, they know police and soldiers are going to come looking for them sooner or later. They'll have to move all them big trees before getting their own horses and wagons through. That'll slow them down and give Indian snipers a good target too. That Wandering Spirit, he's maybe a bad man, but he's a good fighter. He knows all the tricks, just like a fox. Like where we're heading. What you'll see is a damn good camping spot. But it'll also be where they can move real quick down to the Battleford trail or north to the Beaver River, depending on what news comes in. Troops will have a hell of a time trying to pry them out of there."

***

Old Pascal's prediction of a good camp site was true. An hour before sunset, they emerged from the woods to a wide meadow beside the west bank of the Little Red Deer River, which meandered around the base of Frenchman Butte. There was good grazing for the horses, both on the flats and up on the hillside. The water was pure and there was enough wind to keep the mosquitoes down to a tolerable level. Wandering Spirit himself arrived to talk to them through Paul McRae. He told them to make their camp with easy access to the river, and said they would be free to fish and snare rabbits.

"We will be here for a while," he added. "We are going to have a Sun Dance. My men will not bother you." He seemed to be in an unusually benign mood. Noting this, George screwed up his courage and asked a question that needed to be put carefully and respectfully.

"Chief, we can see that we are slowing you down. Surely you would be better off without us. If you let us go and we got safely back to Battleford, the soldiers might not be so determined to come after you. And it could be better for you, after the fighting is finished."

Wandering Spirit glowered at him. "Trader, you take plenty for granted. The soldiers are not going to just walk over us. Some of the most famous fighting men in the Cree nation are here with me. The troops might win in the end, but if they do, it will be because they have better weapons and many more men. And if they take me, all I am going to get is the end of a rope, no matter how I treat you. So, talk sense. We don't want you with us any more than you want to be here. But you could be useful as hostages. If things get very bad, I can use you to bargain for the safety of our women and children. That's why I warned you against trying to escape." The look on his face was omen enough. "Don't try it. But you have nothing to fear, if you stay quiet. The man who made trouble today has been warned by me not to do it again." Then he left them. George looked after him thoughtfully, as the crowd broke up and went to raise their tents.

Scotty paused to put his hand on George's shoulder. "Good try! I'm not sure I would have had the nerve. Maybe it's because Marie is part Indian, but I can understand the man's way of thinking, even if I don't like it. He knows that, one way or another, he is a goner. But he'll go on fighting for his folks to the very end."

"I know, Scotty. If it wasn't for that damned massacre at Pounding Lake, I could admire the man."

CHAPTER TWENTY-FIVE

Catherine was the first one awake the next morning. For a while she lay quietly, listening to the bird songs. The night before, the peeping, trilling, whistling, and croaking of a thousand-frog orchestra was so melodious that she had stayed awake to hear it. But now she had to get up. It was cool and she shivered as she dressed and threw her shawl over her shoulders.

When she went outside, she was pleased to see Muhekun again curled up beside the tent. As she bent down to stroke the white head, she marvelled at the bond that still held this wild creature to her, even though he was free and almost mature. He padded after her when she went to relieve herself, and she was amused when he went to the same spot and squirted his own urine over it.

It really was a beautiful campsite, with wildflowers everywhere. Marsh marigolds were glowing in swaths beside the river. White star-flowers and yellow and purple violets clustered along her path, while tall puffs of hares' tails waved and bowed gracefully. The river was alive with ducks, gabbling and flapping their wings as the sun warmed them. The green heads of mallard drakes shone like living emeralds, joined by white-throated pintails and red-headed canvasbacks. Darting around and through the bigger birds were sooty black, white-billed coots. As the wolf went to lap up some water, the coots fled, squalling in panic, wings and feet working frantically.

Catherine washed, then dried herself with her shawl. Muhekun, ignoring the distressed coots, pounced on a large and luckless bullfrog. Catherine averted her eyes as he ate it alive. She could hear people stirring in the camp by this time. As she walked back, she picked up sticks and twigs along the way for firewood.

***

Scotty and Marie were outside with Julia, drinking their morning tea. She dropped the kindling, tied the wolf to a tree, and sat down beside them. Dan looked worried.

"You want to be careful, wandering off," he scolded her. "What with Buck Breland hanging around for one thing."

"I will, Mr. Scott, but I had the wolf with me. And Wandering Spirit said that he had been warned against making any more trouble."

"Aye, he did. But I don't trust the man. We're fond of you, lass; you're getting to be like a daughter. Don't go calling us Mr. and Mrs. anymore, after all we've been through." Catherine was touched. She leaned over and kissed his cheek impulsively. His eyes twinkled. "Guess I'll say that every morning."

"Marie," she asked, "what would the Indians do to Breland if he caused any more trouble?"

"Well now, the usual way, the warriors would take all his belongings and send him away on foot with no gun or food. But if he and that White Bear have a grudge going, they might decide to let them fight it out to get it over with. They can't have that, living as close as they do. Sometimes bad feeling can be smoothed over with a bit of gift-giving and a few smokes, but not always."

"I was listening to the frogs last night," said Catherine, remembering. "Just as I was going to sleep, I thought I heard screaming and then a shot not too far away. Maybe I dreamed that."

"No, lass," he said. "I heard it too, and then later there was a real ruckus going on. It sounded like a fight. Maybe Breland and White Bear did have it out."

Marie shivered. "Why would anyone pick a fight with that awful man? He is so big and strong and mean-looking."

"I recall *you* waving a teapot at Breland," Scotty reminded her. "But if it did happen, I'd put my money on the Indian. He's said to be a real scrapper. If he was smart enough to keep Buck from getting a bear hug on him, that is.

Breland's a giant all right, but he has done a lot of loose living and drinking and that fat gut of his is no help. If there was a fight, I wish I'd seen it."

"You're a blood-thirsty old devil and that's a fact," scolded Marie.

"That I am, when it's not my blood being spilled." After breakfast, Scotty dragged two fallen trees to the door-flap to serve as seats. Then he got stones to set the camp stove higher, so Marie would not need to squat to do her cooking. That done, he dug a small privy behind the tent and screened it with saplings and evergreen branches.

George, who had been doing the same thing, strolled over to join them. "Do you want to go fishing, Scotty? I'd rather eat rabbit and there's lots around here, but I don't have the knack for setting snares; do you?" Scotty was about to answer him, when a new voice came from behind them.

MaryLou, looking like a young pirate, stood with her arms folded, her raven-black hair tied back with a crimson band and a pistol stuck into her wide beaded belt. Julia gasped and ran back into the tent. She was amused by the effect of her quiet "Hello".

Catherine introduced her to Scotty and George.

MaryLou nodded to them coolly. "Setting snares is so easy our children can do it. Catherine, do you want to come out and try it with me?"

"Now wait a minute," protested George. "Are you sure it's safe for her to leave the camp, Miss Clear Sky?"

"If it's Breland you're worrying about, forget him," she replied. "He's no longer a problem to anyone." Then she looked at the other three. "She'll be safe with me. I have a gun, and we can take her wolf along."

"Do you want to go?" asked Scotty, frowning at Catherine.

"Yes, I would like to try it, if you don't mind." The Scotts agreed, reluctantly.

When the two girls were gone, Scotty looked at Marie and George shook his head.

"We've got an odd pair of them here, folks. One in the tent, hiding from the Indians, the other one all set to go off with them."

***

Catherine felt an almost giddy sense of freedom as MaryLou searched out the rabbit runs and tied snares across them. Each time she did it, she sang a song.

"I am speaking to the rabbit-spirits. We do this when we must kill or use anything. We tell of our need; then the spirit will understand and be free, perhaps to assume a new life form."

"If I am going to set snares, then I should learn that song," said Catherine.

MaryLou looked at her. "Not many whites would say that. They would laugh or mock the idea. You would make a good Indian!"

By noon, they were resting on a rock overlooking the river. Muhekun settled down between them and accepted a pat from MaryLou with lordly tolerance.

"Breland and White Bear had a terrible fight last night," said MaryLou after a while. "But the fat man looks a lot worse than White Bear does today."

"Why? Surely White Bear was not that angry just because he pushed Ellen around."

MaryLou laughed. "Oh, no, it was much more than that! Last night, Breland came after me when I walked out alone. Maybe he thought he could get even with Jay that way. I don't know. He started pulling at my clothes and got me down on the ground. But I've had to look after myself that way for some time. I started to scream and kick, and I had this with me." She patted the gun in her belt. I got a shot off at him, although it missed. Then my uncle and White Bear and some others came.

"Breland ran off, and it was hard to find him in the dark, but White Bear did. *Wah!* Was he mad! When he told Wandering Spirit what Breland had tried to do to me, the chief decided to let them fight it out. I was afraid for White Bear, but he was a crazy man. I think he could have beaten up a grizzly! In the end, the other man was unconscious. The chief sent him away to never come back."

"I thought I heard a shot," exclaimed Catherine. "No wonder White Bear was so angry! But I'm sorry you missed him with that bullet."

"Yes. I wish I had shot off his balls," said MaryLou coldly. Catherine had never heard that expression before, but she knew exactly what the other girl meant. And she laughed.

MaryLou laughed with her. "You know, back in Battleford, I thought you were such a lady, so helpless and fragile looking that you would never last out here, even if all went well. And yet here you are, widowed, your home destroyed, a prisoner, and forced to live in a way that must be very hard and rough for you. Yet, somehow, you seem untouched by it all."

"I can imagine what you must be thinking," said Catherine slowly, "that I am cold and unfeeling. I would like to be honest about that with you, because I feel so guilty, especially when people compare me with poor Julia Simmons. But she really worshipped her husband, and they were very happy together. I cared for Ian, but not like that. I'm so sorry he died, but I don't feel the grief that Julia does, and I can't pretend that I do."

"I didn't see you as the happy bride in Battleford," said MaryLou. "I saw you as terribly lonely and a bit afraid of your husband."

"I didn't know how to make him happy. All I can do is try not to think about that ... only about good things I have left. My friends, not only among the prisoners, but you and Melissa ... and Jay."

"Jay is more than that to you. I can see it in your face when you even say his name. You are going to need to watch that. Marie Scott is a very smart old lady, and she doesn't miss much. You know, of course, that he is hopelessly in love with you, too?"

"How do you know that?" asked Catherine.

"When he came back early from Fort Pitt, Melissa was sure it was because of you. When I asked him if that was true, he admitted it. To be honest, I was shocked and upset about it at first. I couldn't imagine, I still can't, how it even started between you two. But I understand it a little better now.

"You and I are after little rabbits today, but I have my eye on bigger game. Like a White Bear." She started to laugh. "He doesn't know how I feel yet, so he just keeps looking at me with those moon-eyes of his. And he can't think of a thing to say when I tease him ... and him such a big joker with everyone else! Of course, I'm not supposed to guess why he was so crazy-mad at Breland last night, either. But I am going to tell him soon."

MaryLou looked down at the river, and her eyes were suddenly very sad. "We haven't got much time, Catherine. Terrible trouble is coming at us. When I was in Battleford, I heard how troops from all over Canada are being stationed into the north-west. They've finished building the railway around Lake Superior to get them here even faster. Thousands, they say. Our band is the prime target, since the word got out about the men killed in Pounding Lake.

"The whites want to fill this country with settlers. But they won't come out here if there are powerful leaders like Big Bear, Wandering Spirit, Poundmaker, Payepot, and the others. So, they must be finished off, one way or another. This rebellion is the perfect excuse to do it by force, even though the Métis started it. Catherine, those troops will be coming at us any time now, perhaps in days, a couple of weeks at most. Maybe none of us will come through it alive. I'm going to take whatever happiness I can get before that happens. I hope you and Jay will, too. Now come along. We had better see to our rabbits."

They walked back into the woods again. Later they took some rabbits back to the Scotts and to the lodge of Blue Quill.

CHAPTER TWENTY-SIX

Marie prepared a special fireplace for the big goose. She scooped a hole in the ground and built up a pile of red coals. She plunged a spit through the bird, balanced it over the coals, and put a lid on top.

Catherine watched the preparations intently. "Is that the cooking secret you were telling me about?"

"So, you remembered, eh? Now help me turn it every so often, and I'll tell you." She handed her a knitting needle. "No, child, you don't have to knit a sweater for it! When it starts to brown, you keep poking holes in all the fat places to let the grease run out. I will catch it in a dish. *Pimi*, we call it. For the rheumatics, you heat it and rub it all over the pain. Of course, the sweat baths the Indians make are even better..."

Marie realized she had to raise her voice to be heard. The two women stood up to peer over at the other camp. A tremendous surge of sound rolled over them, as though every drum was pounding, and every man, woman, and child were singing along with the clash of bells and rattles, ear-piercing bone whistles, and the stamping of hundreds of feet.

They had grown used to the drumming and singing, but they never heard anything like this! The other prisoners came out of their tents, looking concerned. The clamour grew louder. A huge circle could be seen, dancing slowly, holding aloft their guns and war clubs. George and Leslie, with Ellen and Connie hot on their heels, ran to join Catherine and Marie as Scotty emerged from his tent.

He had to shout. "What do you make of it, George?" Before the other trader could answer, Julia bolted out of the Scott tent, screaming that they were all going to be killed. Her face was chalk-white, and her eyes were protruding in terror.

Catherine managed to catch her as she ran past. "No, Julia!" she shouted. "They're not even looking this way. It has nothing to do with us!" Julia stared at her for a moment, and then slumped against her, shaking from head to foot. Patting her shoulder, Catherine tried to comfort her.

Ellen, who had also jumped to intercept her, looked on in disgust. "You'll have to stop babying her like that. What she really needs is a good hard boot in the behind!"

Meanwhile the two men were still trying to talk over the uproar. "I figure they have had some news," said George. "Though good or bad is hard to say. I saw Clear Sky come in a while ago. Looked like he had been doing some hard and fast travelling." Catherine was careful to look disinterested, and it was just as well. Marie was looking right at her.

***

The raucous noise kept up all afternoon. Several of the Métis who could speak Cree tried to learn the reason for the excitement, but no one responded to them. Gus LaRonde reported that he had seen a party of warriors cross over to the east bank of the river. The far side of the ravine was open ground. They had been riding up and down the ledge, pointing and gesturing. Wandering Spirit had been with them.

Marie was carrying on as usual, stirring beans on the camp stove and mixing bannock, all the time grumbling to Catherine, who was dutifully piercing the roasting goose. "It's always the same old thing for women—white, Indian, Métis, and, I'm sure, black and yellow ones too, while the men get all excited, and hurry around doing the Lord knows what, the women have their same old endless tasks. And that's to feed them and then wash up. You mark my words, when the world comes to an end, and the angels are blowing the trumpets of glory, we'll have to finish the dishes first, before we ever make it through those pearly gates!"

It was not until after dinner, and the goose was reduced to a pile of bones, that the noise from the other camp began to subside.

"I suppose the brutes themselves couldn't stand it any longer," said Julia as she sipped tea. Just at that moment, Scotty came back into the tent followed by Jay Clear Sky. Catherine's heart jumped as she looked at him. He appeared drawn and tired. He glanced quickly around, his eyes locked momentarily on Catherine's, then turned to Marie.

"I have a message for you. I have just come back from Poundmaker's camp. Father Cochin was there. He wants you to know that your daughter and her family are safe and well, although there has been a big battle there. I asked him to tell her that you two and your son's family have not been harmed." Marie jumped to her feet and threw her arms around him, catching him off guard.

"God bless you for this kindness," she sobbed. "We've been so worried about them!" She dabbed her eyes and looked abashed. "I'm sorry, but this is such good news. Now, you do look very tired. Can I get you a cup of tea?" Jay hesitated, glanced at Catherine again, then nodded and sat down. Catherine poured his tea. When she gave it to him, his hand deliberately lingered for one moment on hers. It felt as though they were alone in the tent.

But Scotty had already started to question Jay, anxious not to miss out on this chance to get some news. "Your folks have been whooping it up pretty good all day. It is for any reason that you can tell me?"

"I don't see why not. Hundreds of government troops attacked Poundmaker's camp on Cut Knife hill. I got there in time to get off a few shots myself and see the end of the fight. They brought in cannons and a Gatling gun. They came with no warning, and they turned the guns on the lodges first."

Scotty's face went white. "My God, the slaughter must have been terrible!"

"It would have been, but the first shots were aimed too high, and the families had time to run for cover. Then the soldiers got stalled on the hill and let themselves get caught in a surround, just as the police did at Duck Lake. They don't learn fast, do they? We could have killed nearly all of them when they tried to retreat over Cut Knife Creek and got mired down. But Poundmaker held the warriors back and let the soldiers get away. He said there had been enough killing for one day."

"I've always thought well of that man," said Scotty reflectively. "So, it is a victory dance you've been having over there?"

"You could say so, Mr. Scott. Only six of our people died, and three were badly wounded. They sent three to four hundred men against us, and they had dead and dying men in their wagons. They left one body behind, along with a lot of supplies and ammunition."

"My God," said Scotty in horror, "I hope whoever led them into that mess won't be leading the men who come to rescue us."

Jay's face went still and cold. Catherine had never seen him look like that, except at Jim Burr, but his voice was unchanged as he spoke again. "As to that, there is also news. On my way back, I met a courier bringing a letter to Big Bear from John McDougall."

"McDougall. Isn't he the missionary to the Stoney Indians in the foothills?"

"Yes, that one. I brought the letter the rest of the way. It advised us that troops are on the way here from Edmonton, and hundreds more are about to follow them. Their purpose is to kill or capture all the Big Bear band. Soon there will be fighting here."

"Good," shouted Julia suddenly. "Now you bloody cowards will learn what it's like to be shot at rather than doing the shooting yourselves!" There was a shocked silence, then Marie turned on Julia, angrier than Catherine had ever seen her.

"You damn fool woman! This man came here out of kindness to tell me about my girl and he saved Catherine's life!"

Jay interrupted the tirade as he stood up. "It's all right, Mrs. Scott." He left the tent. Now both Scotty and Marie were chiding Julia. Catherine saw her chance to slip out after Jay. He was waiting for her, but gave her no chance to speak. He kissed her once, then whispered urgently. "Scouting parties are going out and lookouts are being posted on the hills. My place tomorrow is on Frenchman Butte, this one. I'll be on a ledge on the south side. Two tall pines very close together mark it. We can be alone there." Then he was gone.

***

Neither of the Scotts had noticed her brief absence. Marie was in mid-tirade. "If he had been any other Big Bear, you might have been shot then and there. Dear Lord, you of all people, should know what happens when the shooting starts."

Julia was still defiant. Scotty was just as angry as Marie. "Listen, I'm not having my Marie killed just because you don't care if you live or die. I'll throw you right outside first! As it is, you've probably lost us a good friend, and God knows, we need the ones we have. If there is ever any talk with Indians in this tent again, you keep right out of it. And I mean that!" Julia was beginning to wilt under their combined wrath.

For once, Catherine did not feel sorry for her. "Julia, go to bed." When she scurried into the bedroll, the other three sat uneasily together. Scotty turned down the lantern and began to talk in a much lower voice.

"When those soldiers turn their guns on these Indians, they'll be shooting at us, too. What a choice that gives us! Do we sit tight and get all shot to hell by them, or do we try to escape and get all shot to hell by the Indians? Right now, ladies, I wouldn't bet a fart in a mitt on our chances of getting out of here in one piece."

"Don't talk like that in front of Catherine," scolded Marie. "Now, do you want to know what *I* think?"

"Only you and the Lord can ever figure that out," grumbled Scotty, "and I'm not too sure about Him. So, suppose you tell us."

Catherine tried not to, but suddenly she could no longer hold back her laughter. The Scotts were incredible, one minute discussing their extreme peril, and bickering and teasing the next! "I'm sorry," she gasped as they looked at her in surprise. "I must be a bit hysterical!"

"Not you, lass," Scotty said. "Like my old lady here, you're as tough as rawhide. Just don't look it, that's all."

"That's the truth of it," agreed Marie. "But I want to tell you what I think. When the soldiers get here and things start going bad for the Indians, that devil Wandering Spirit, he'll parade us out where the troops can see us, right into the line of fire. Then he'll start bargaining and stalling while his people have a chance to scatter in all directions, like grease on a hot stove."

"Maybe," he replied. "It could happen if they run out of ammunition or supplies or they get caught in a place where they have no room to manoeuvre. But that bunch out there is full of fight and they have nothing to lose any more, to their way of thinking. No matter what, we'll be dragged through the whole damn thing with them. Now, I'm going over to see George and tell him about all this."

CHAPTER TWENTY-SEVEN

Catherine hardly slept that night, she was too excited at the thought of seeing Jay again. She was determined to go to him on the lookout, and she knew they would make love when she did. Their passion for each other was too powerful, and their time together would be too short to deny it. She wanted him desperately, even though sex had nearly always been an uncomfortable and unfulfilling experience for her. Perhaps it would be with Jay too, but she wanted him to hold her in his arms for much more than a furtive embrace; the thought of it made her body ache.

She wanted to leave as soon as she got up, but she forced herself to sit calmly and eat breakfast. She tried to think of an excuse for going off by herself. She could say she was going out again with MaryLou for rabbits. As it happened, MaryLou came to see her while she was eating.

Catherine spoke first, sending a warning glance at the same time. "I almost forgot, we had planned to snare rabbits again today. I'll get my shawl; it's still cool."

MaryLou nodded without speaking.

"You two be careful now," warned Scotty. "You won't have the wolf with you; he slipped his collar last night." Despite the warning, he did not look as doubtful as he had the last time, but Marie's eyes were wary. She had noticed the way Catherine and Clear Sky looked at each other when she served him tea the previous night.

***

As soon as they were alone, MaryLou had to ask, "Catherine, what was that all about? Have you gone rabbit-mad?"

"No. I'm going to meet your brother. I know where he is."

"So *that's* why he wanted me to walk with you this morning! He wouldn't say why, he just smiled and asked me to show you the ledge where the twin pines grow." They were south of the camp, walking quickly. "There it is," she pointed.

Catherine looked up at the broad wooded flank of the hill that rose beside their path. She could see the two pines at once. Her heartbeat picked up.

MaryLou looked at her. "I'll go with you across this meadow until you are into the trees. No one can see you then. I'll wait for you there an hour before sunset ... with some rabbits, I hope." She paused. "White Bear is up there too; they got easy work today. White Bear is still hurting from his fight with Breland, and my brother is tired from travelling. He's not all *that* tired, it seems."

When they got to the trees, they parted and Catherine went on alone. She wondered why she had not been embarrassed with MaryLou, and doubted that she would be with White Bear. Nothing else mattered but seeing Jay. There were times, though, when she found herself trembling and breathing more quickly than the exertion of her long climb warranted.

***

Jay was watching for her. When she finally reached the pine trees, he was waiting for her. He was so happy-looking and excited to see her that he seemed speechless. He took her hand, led her past the trees and up onto the ledge, and all the while they never took their eyes from one another. Then he threw his arms around her and lifted her off her feet with an exuberant bear hug. There was no sign of the tense and tired man of last night. He looked exactly what he was this morning: young and strikingly handsome, with a smile lighting up his face. He was not wearing a shirt. Her hands on his bare shoulders could feel the strength in him, as he held her in that sudden burst of affection. Then he put her down and looked beyond her.

Catherine turned, trying to catch her breath. White Bear came toward them. He looked at her curiously, and while he did not smile, he did not seem unfriendly. She saw a large and painful-looking cut on the side of his mouth, and one eye was bruised, swollen, and half-closed.

"My friend is not always this ugly," Jay assured her.

"Oh my," said Catherine. "MaryLou said you had a fight with Breland. You must be very brave."

He answered off-handedly. "Lucky too. He was drunk." Then he said something in Cree to Jay, and limped past them, into the trees.

"What did he say?"

Jay laughed. "He said that, if he stayed any longer, you might get to like him more than you do me. He is going to watch with Lone Man on the next hill." He took her hand again, and they walked along the wide shelf of the hillside to a spot close to the lookout point. On a log, she could see field glasses and a drawing pad and pencils. Jay opened the book and handed it to her.

Her own face looked back at her. It was exquisitely done and much more detailed than the portrait he had made of Jenny Appleton. In the drawing, her hair was tossed and windblown. She appeared serene, and her lips were slightly parted as though she was out of breath. Her shoulders were bare, and she was wearing the amulet.

"Oh, Jay, is this how you see me? It's much too beautiful," she whispered.

"No, it is just like you, Cate, the way I think you will look after we have made love." She felt her cheeks flush, and she did not look up from the drawing.

"I don't seem to have anything on."

Amused, he said, "Amee, would you be wearing clothes at a time like that?"

She did look at him then and smiled. "I wouldn't know, since we have not made love to each other."

"Not yet." He took the book from her, closed it, and put it back on the log. Then he picked up the field glasses. "Come over to the lookout with me. I am supposed to keep watch. You should see this country from up here."

They took a few steps closer to the rim of the ledge, and while Jay scanned to the south with the field glasses, she stood beside him, entranced. Across the miles below were thick stands of forest, with intervals of green open spaces between them. Meandering ravines cradled rivers and smaller creeks, drawing dark veins across the land, sometimes glittering where the sunlight touched the water. The camps below were not visible, although a faint haze of wood smoke from the cooking fires hung in the air above the green plumes of the trees. It looked utterly wild and lonely, a primeval wilderness with no other sign up here of people or the herds of horses. Catherine moved closer to him.

***

He lowered the field glasses and put his arm around her, pulling her even closer. He was looking down at her, his eyes searching her face. "You don't know how close we came to it … to making love beside Pounding Creek that day when I had to go away. What I wanted to do was put you up on Cloudwalker with me and go off to some hidden place. Then take away your clothes and mine and make love to you for the rest of my life!"

She leaned her head against his shoulder. "I wanted to run after you and beg you not to go, or take me with you. I might even have done that if you hadn't left so quickly."

"It was quickly or not at all." He turned toward her and put his other arm around her. "Cate, I want you to think about this. I can give you nothing more than myself, and perhaps that for only a few hours here today. I can't say that I will always be with you, though I want that more than anything in the world. I can't say that we will make children together. I will not be able to stand beside you or protect you when the fighting starts, but I will do what I can. In a few more days, it is certain that I will be shooting at white soldiers, your own people. We might not even have the chance to say goodbye after that. How are you going to feel, if you give yourself to me today?"

"I want that memory, Jay," she answered. "I've thought about all those things too, but I don't want to think about them now. I can tell you this: I will love you then as I do now. I always will, no matter what happens, for the rest of my life."

"Cate, come back to my log with me. When you look at me like that, I get dizzy, and if I fall off this ledge, the rest of your life will last about a minute, because I am not going to let go of you." They both laughed as they turned away from the lookout point, their hands clasped tightly.

"People would certainly be surprised if we fell into the middle of one of the camps together. I am supposed to be out snaring rabbits, you know."

"And I am supposed to be tired; I was before you got here. I spent all night wondering if you would come, and thinking about you," he said.

"I have spent many a night lying awake in the darkness and wanting you there beside me. I haven't had much sleep myself lately."

"If I *had* been there, you would not have slept at all."

***

They moved into each others' arms and this new intimacy was even better, a long, sweet, and unhurried coming together, full of the pent-up longing and desire and need denied until now. He slid his fingers into her hair. "Take the pins out," he told her. "Make your hair the way it is in my picture of you."

She did as he asked, and then shook it out, letting it tumble down over her shoulders. He let the tawny silken strands slip through his fingers like captured sunshine. "Now you are like the Cate in my picture. Except for that dress you have on." She smiled at him, then she took off the dress and spread it on the ground. She was wearing the chemise and a petticoat salvaged from the ruins in Fort Pitt. She had worn them today because they were lacy and feminine beneath the shapeless dress. She sat down. He stood as if transfixed for a minute, then sat down beside her. He kissed her long and hungrily. Then he looked at the chemise.

"I don't think this was made for you any more than your dress was, my Cate." He undid the buttons and took it off. He looked at her breasts, freed from their confinement. "That is a silly thing to wear," he told her. "Look, there are marks on you where it is too tight." He touched first one breast and then the other, gently tracing the faint lines where the seams had been. He held one of them while he kissed her again and her lips opened to his. All the while he stroked and fondled her and she moaned softly, her eyes closed, silently willing him never to stop. They were lying side by side. He lifted his head and touched one of her erect nipples.

"Like wild roses," he whispered. He began to brush his lips over it, softly and then more hungrily, and then his mouth took one of them in. She felt his tongue on it, a shock of pleasure surging through her, so intense it was almost painful. He heard her gasp, and he looked into her eyes, saw her flushed face.

"I can't wait much longer, Cate, are you ready?"

"Yes. Please, don't wait," she said, knowing it was true—relaxed and ready in his arms. His hands were moving down her body now. They stopped at her slim waist, and he loosened the buttons on her petticoat and undergarments. She lifted her hips a little to help him take them off. As he quickly removed his own clothing, she stared at his naked muscular body, feeling an increasing heat between her legs. He was so beautifully made, and so aroused when he turned back to her that she expected him to enter her right away. But he took her into his arms again and began to stroke her hips and buttocks. He gently eased his hand between her legs, finding them hot and wet to his touch, and she moaned again.

She threw her arms around his neck and twisting her head, sought out his lips. She could hardly breathe, and her own racing heartbeat and his were the only sounds she could hear. His hand between her legs was moving again, exploring her, parting her, and he quivered with desperate desire. He shifted his body over her. His hand was replaced by his erection, hot and hard and seeking against her. She moved under him so that he could enter her. At first, it took her breath away, then she claimed all of him and they were completely joined. The eternal miracle of love infused with passion swept through them both. He in her and she holding him into her with all the strength of her arms and legs.

He began to surge ever more deeply into the body that was arching to meet him, again and again, and Catherine heard herself gasping and muttering his name and other incoherent words. He was fierce now, crushing her against the ground, his hands and arms bearing most of his weight over her, but his mouth still moving over her face. Then it happened, seized by an almost paralyzing ecstasy, she called out to him. She heard him answer, but not the words. His whole body tensed, shuddered, then slowly relaxed. She closed her eyes as her own tension and wildness slowly drained out of her. She felt tears slide from the corners of her eyes into her hair.

After a brief time, she realized that, although he was still holding her close against him, they were apart. She touched his face gently and shivered with pleasure at the way he was looking at her. Then he buried his face in the silken heap of her hair, still trying to catch his breath.

"My beautiful Cate! How I love you!" For a long time, they lay there quietly, just looking at each other or touching tenderly as the sweat dried on their entwined bodies. This too, was new to Catherine. She had only known feeling used ... and then aching loneliness. He sat up and looked at her closely. "What is wrong?"

She touched his face and smiled at him softly. "What could possibly be wrong ... after that?"

"I don't know. I know more about making pictures of women than making love to them. I am going to do another one of you. The one I showed you is not nearly beautiful enough. And I will draw all of you this time."

"Will you show me that one too, Jay?" He kissed her in the hollow between her breasts, under the amulet.

"Just you, I won't share it with anyone else. And I will always keep it. Now about this love-making, Amee. I think in a few minutes, I am going to need more practice at it. To be sure I am doing it right."

She had to laugh at that. "Oh, you are doing it right and you know it, so don't make excuses. Anyway, you don't need excuses with me."

He was looking down at her. His glossy black hair fell around her face like a gleaming curtain. "This really *is* happening, isn't it? We're not just dreaming?"

She took his hand and guided it to her breast again. "It is a beautiful dream, and I hope it never ends. Forever we will be here, naked and making love, beyond the two tall pines, under the sun, and the endless sky."

He brought his mouth down on hers for another sweet kiss, then said, "I want to make love to you again, my Amee, but I don't know what part of you to taste or touch first. It is very hard to decide when you are so lovely."

"And you are the handsomest man in the world," she replied, sliding her arms around his waist. She caught her breath again as he moved into her, and she closed her eyes and gave herself to him with absolute and complete abandon. She melted into the earth. Soared like a hawk. She was a star flashing through the night sky. His forever.

***

The sun was approaching the western horizon when reality began to stalk the young lovers. Catherine dressed and fixed her hair, while Jay moved to the log to scan with the field glasses. As he did, he confessed, "They could have come in and shot the top off the butte with their cannon, and I wouldn't have noticed!" When he came back, the warmth of hours of shared passion was still soft on both their faces, but gradually succumbing to sadness now that it was over.

"When do you think the soldiers will get here?" she asked.

"It depends if they come by land or down the river from Edmonton. Or, if they come straight through or stop at Fort Saskatchewan, Victoria or Saddle Lake. They could turn north to Pounding Lake or go straight to Fort Pitt. My guess is that some of them, the men on foot, the heavy guns and supplies, will come on barges. The mounted men will have to come overland. Our scouts are out; we'll know soon."

He returned the glasses to the log, and they began to walk back toward the pine trees. "Another thing ... there are still many soldiers in Battleford, maybe more have come in. They could also come at us from that direction."

She looked up at him. "It's going to be very bad, isn't it?"

"Yes." He took her hand. "Isn't it strange that your people and mine are going to do all this fighting and killing, yet they would see our love for each other as something wrong? I want so much to take you off somewhere, away from what is going to happen. But these are my people, my family and friends. It won't, in the end, make any difference if I am here to stand with them or not ... but I can't run away. Do you understand that, Cate?"

"Yes, I do. The way we feel about each other does not change who we are. I can't run away either, if it means that someone else, a child perhaps, would be killed if I did. There would never be any happiness for me if that happened, even with you."

Jay looked deeply into her eyes, knowing what he must ask of her, and searching for the strength. "Cate ... *Amee* ... I cannot go into the battles that are sure to come unless I know that you are safe. Please, promise me, when the time comes ... if I ask you to ... you *will* go. You will run far from here and make a life for yourself. For me ... because if you are no longer in this world, I will lose the strength to fight and the will to survive."

She searched his eyes, feeling desolate. "I might never see you again! How could I ..." Tears filled her eyes. "When you ask me like that, you force me to say I'll do as you wish. But my heart will never leave you and it will be broken forever." She brushed angrily at her wet face. "Do you think we can be together again, before that happens?"

He took her in his arms and held her. "We can try. The scouts go out in turns. I could be sent out tomorrow or the next day. But I will come to you if I can, I promise you that."

For one precious moment, their lips met again. Then Catherine pushed herself away and turned, half-running, paying little heed to where she was going. She left him standing beside the pine trees, silent and alone as he watched her disappear out of sight.

CHAPTER TWENTY-EIGHT

The Cree scouts watched the advance of General Strange's army, as hundreds of men came downstream through the valley of the North Saskatchewan River. Jay and White Bear, along with others, were concealed in a thick stand of poplars when the soldiers stopped briefly at Saddle Lake. There, the 65th Carabinier, who had marched to that point, exchanged places with the Winnipeg Light Infantry on the barges.

The Crees, accustomed to silent travel, could hardly believe the noise. The cavalry, infantry, and artillery units, with their boats and barges and long wagon trains of supplies and ammunition, could be heard for miles.

White Bear pointed to a huge cannon jutting starkly from a raft. "I want to be there when they try to pull that thing through the trees and swamps. We should have some good sniping then!"

Little Poplar looked at the younger man. "*Wah!* I hope you will not shoot them all. Save a few for me."

Jay grinned. "We will take the ones in green. You older men can see the ones in the red coats better!"

"Thank you," said Little Poplar sourly, as the other scouts chuckled. But there was no amusement when they returned to Frenchman's Butte. The Sun Dance was over, but most of the men were still gathering in the brush-covered ceremonial lodge out of the hot sun. A courier had just arrived with news, and it was all bad. Batoche had fallen after a four-day battle. It was in charred-and-smoking ruins, and the surrounding fields were littered with the bodies of the men who had died fighting for them. The surviving Métis were either in hiding, or like their leader, Louis Riel, on the way to trial and prison. "I must also tell you this," said the courier, speaking with difficulty. "Chief Poundmaker and all of those who follow him are on the way into Battleford, where they will lay down their weapons and surrender." There was a dead silence.

Wandering Spirit broke it angrily. "But why? They won the fight at Cut Knife Hill!"

"He thinks once the whites have him and his people are disarmed, the families will be allowed to go quietly back to their homes." The Métis from Batoche were silent, in stunned shock, wondering if they had families or homes to return to, but the Crees were talking quietly. Their own plans needed to be decided immediately. The leading men were asked to speak.

Big Bear had nothing to say; he looked shattered and broken. "I am old and my life is ending, no matter what happens. I ask Blue Quill to speak in my place."

Jay's uncle was composed. "We have no choice, as I see it. We know by MacDougall's letter that the army is coming to kill or capture us all. I do not want to let them do it easily. We can move around faster than our enemies; we know the country and we are well led. Our war chief learned his fighting skills in the old days, and he has forgotten nothing. If two armies are coming at us, we cannot win against such odds, but we can make it so costly for them that they might offer terms to end the fighting. Poundmaker has made a bad mistake; he has always trusted white men too much. There will be no mercy for his people once they are helpless. Or for him."

"If you decide to fight," said Wandering Spirit, "I will lead you to the end. If you want to surrender, I will accept your decision, but I would rather die fighting than at the end of a rope."

Ayimasees was more specific. "The life we have had for the past few years was no life at all. But bad as it was, it will be far worse if we surrender. I will fight the soldiers, if I have to fight them alone!"

Lone Man, who never wasted words, held up his hand. "I fight." All the other Rattlers concurred. One Woods Cree did not. He proposed that they should scatter off in all directions immediately.

One old warrior shook his war club. "I would rather die than live in the way they have planned for us. We are men, not cattle."

When the will of the gathering was clear, Wandering Spirit spoke again. "We will make our first stand here, harassing them with ambushes and snipers as they come in. Then we will lead them through bogs and quicksand and forests so thick they will have to cut roads to follow us. But everything will depend on how fast we can move. Those who cannot keep up must be left behind. Are you willing to face that?" There was a roar of agreement as the listeners, quiet and intent up to this point, stood and began to shrill their war cries. An hour later, the Crees crossed the Little Red Deer River and began to dig rifle pits on the treeless eastern bank. Jay was dispatched to instruct the prisoners on the plans.

***

The prisoners were restless and uneasy. They watched as scouts came and went constantly. They knew that the troop from Edmonton must be close by this time, yet their conviction persisted that the rest of the world had forgotten all about *them*. The anxiety and tension in their camp was almost unbearable. When Jay appeared, they clustered around him, all asking questions at once.

"We are going to take you across to the other side of the river in the morning. You must leave the heavy wagons behind, although the two-wheeled carts can go. I advise you to make travois as we do, to carry your children, tents, and supplies. We'll cut poles for you, and help you to make them if you wish. But you must move out at dawn."

The prisoners looked at each other with mixed dread and excitement. Perhaps rescue was only a few miles away!

"Clear Sky," George asked, "can you tell us what is going on?"

"The soldiers are coming, and we are going to fight them. They have made camp six miles east of Fort Pitt and an advance party is on the way here. You will hear shooting soon; our snipers are waiting."

It was the first time Catherine had seen Jay since their day together. She was standing quietly with the others, and he had not looked at her, but she knew he was aware of her. He managed to give her one quick glance as he dismounted, then several more in the hours that followed, as the guards helped to rig the new travois. It was a small comfort to her in the chaos of getting ready.

That evening, the guards, Jay among them, pulled back but remained within sight of the compound, circling it slowly. They were singing. It was a slow, cadenced sound that seemed to have in it the rush of wind, of calling wolves, of easy laughter, and sighing grass, all timed to the stepping of the slowly moving horses.

"That is the song of the night riders," Marie told her. "I first heard it as a child when we went to visit our relatives. The riders form circles around the camp, each one farther out, with the best warriors on the outside. They sing partly to amuse themselves and keep awake but also to let the families know all is well. If one circle is suddenly silent, the others know that something is wrong. We children were all snug and warm in our beds with the firelight flickering. It was a fine way to drift off to sleep."

Catherine tried to listen, but she was distracted. Jay was out there, but where would he be tomorrow? Would he get through the fighting uninjured? And if the soldiers rescued them, she would never see him again. Both thoughts were so gut-wrenching that she felt physically ill.

Marie was looking at her with concern. "You look tired, child. I think we should go to bed early. It won't be an easy day tomorrow."

***

Marie's prediction was accurate. The ravine of the Little Red Deer River was the steepest they had yet negotiated. For once, the guards did not hurry them. Pascal, concerned for his sister, talked one of the Métis families into parting with a Red River cart, and with the big woman on the seat beside him, he drove carefully down the slope with Julia and Catherine walking beside them, hanging on. Once down, the bottom land was covered with thick mud that sent them sliding and slipping. The women fell several times and soon they, the carts, and the horses were all covered with the foul-smelling slime. It was a relief to get to the water. It was swift but not very deep and rinsed off most of the mud by the time they got to the far side.

On the opposite side of the ravine, the climb was very steep. The women led the straining horses up while the men pushed and levered the carts from behind. Those with travois made it up more easily. Finally at the top, they rested, exhausted. All along the top of the river bank, as far as they could see, there were armed men and boys in rifle pits. Just then, with the carts stopped and everything quiet, they heard faint sounds of gunfire and artillery to the west. Jay took this chance to look at Catherine. This, he knew, could be the end for them. She looked incredibly beautiful in the clear morning light, as slim and graceful as a doe. Her dress was soaked, and the wind had plastered it back against her breasts, slim waist, and softly rounded hips. In his mind, he saw her lying naked and warm on that same dress, responding to every touch and eager for his love-making.

He noticed George hovering nearby, so he fought against the longing and pain as the trader approached him. "What are we supposed to do now?"

"We're going to take you upstream, until we can find you another camp-site. It would be safer for you back in the woods. But I don't think you could stand the mosquitoes." Shortly, they stopped in a level clearing, bisected by a creek, and there they set up their tents again under the watchful eyes of the guards. Except for Jay, their guards were unhappy to have this tedious duty instead of sniping or manning the rifle pits.

Later that day, the warriors' families moved upstream and settled close to the prisoners' camp. By now the deep booming roar of the nine-pounder cannon sounded even closer. Incoming soldiers were raking the forest ahead of them, trying to clear out the snipers, who were watching and waiting for them.

***

General Thomas Strange cut a dashing figure in his frock-coat, sword, and hat turned up on one side, just as he had worn it when serving with the

British army in India. But even he was dismayed by the terrain, as they traversed the obstacle-ridden trail. Whenever they had to stop to move fallen trees, snipers maintained an unceasing fire on the sweating men and horses.

Strange had three hundred men of various units with him. He had left one hundred of the Carabinier east of Fort Pitt, to intercept any warriors going that way, but after several costly ambushes, he decided to send for them. As soon as they arrived, he moved on again at first dawn. It was May 28th.

The early light was turning the eastern sky into a flame of rose and gold when his army passed the former camp and the abandoned wagons. The Sun Dance lodge was still standing, brooding and silent in the shadows of the trees. They halted on the west bank of the Little Red Deer. The general scanned the east bank with his field glasses. They were over there; he caught the odd glint of metal and signal mirrors. He ordered the artillery into position on the trail where they had crossed the river. Then the soldiers began to filter down through the trees to the river. It was exactly seven o'clock. He signalled to the crew of the field guns.

The eerie silence of that fateful morning was shattered as the nine-pounder opened up, exploding great gouts of earth out of the east bank. Then, as the soldiers emerged from the trees, a deadly opposition fire broke over them. Strange was alarmed when they began to bog down in the treacherous mud that was not apparent from his vantage point. The Gatling crews moved up quickly to cover them, but their range was too short to carry across the river. The cannon did not dislodge the warriors. They were firing steadily at the exposed men struggling through the mud to the water's edge. His casualties would be horrendous if he sent them across the open water and up the bare far side toward their entrenched opponents. He called for a temporary halt.

Major Sam Steele's Scouts, a paramilitary unit composed of members of the North West Mounted Police, civilian scouts, and members of the Alberta Mounted Rifles, were ordered by General Strange to move to the north. Then he sent a company of Carabinier to cover the ground the Scouts had vacated. All this time, the artillery kept pounding and rifle fire continued from both sides of the river. It annihilated the tranquility of this wilderness previously untouched through centuries.

***

The first roar of the cannon tumbled the prisoners from their beds. They now stood helplessly outside their tents as rifles cracked over the din of shouting men and intermittent bugle calls. Some of them were jubilant, pounding backs or dancing jigs of excitement, sure that rescue would come in a matter of hours. Others were worried. The sound of battle was getting closer. It became earth-shaking, and parents picked up their terrified children. Steele's Scouts were across the river, firing at them! Their guards came on the gallop, with Jay shouting at them to move back into the woods with the families. One bullet struck a guard's horse, knocking the screaming animal down and dislodging his rider, who lay crumpled in a motionless heap. Jay jumped off Cloudwalker to look at him. He shook his head and remounted again.

There was no time to pack anything, just a moment to snatch at whatever was at hand. Bullets whined around them as they fled back toward the woods, stumbling over stones and driftwood, struggling through knee-deep swamp. They were goaded on by the yelling guards, who paused at intervals to shoot back at the soldiers, clearly visible across-stream in their brightly coloured uniforms. Somehow, in all the panic, Scotty managed to get the cart hitched up and Marie into it. Catherine and Julia ran beside it, hanging on for support and not looking where they were going.

The MacKenzies were just ahead of them. Catherine saw Ellen swerve suddenly. She broke away from the others, ignoring the angry shouts of the guards. Fiery red hair streaming in the wind, Ellen ran back toward the river, where on the opposite side, several policemen had jumped into the water to get across. Ellen's father, ashen-faced, went after her on his horse. He seized her arm and dragged her back to the others. One of the guards had raised his gun, but he lowered it again as George caught her. They made it to the impenetrable woods. Catherine peered around frantically, but could no longer see Jay and Cloudwalker.

There was no track to follow through the woods. A way could have been picked through, given time, but in this headlong flight, Scotty's cart struck a rock with jarring force. It twisted, teetered, and rolled over, throwing Marie heavily to the ground. A wheel came loose, spun crazily, and fell on top of her. Scotty and Catherine got to her at the same moment and pulled the wheel aside, trying to get her to her feet. But Marie lay there stunned, eyes glassy, nose bleeding and gasping for breath. Scotty tried to urge her to move, but the crashing sounds of the gunfire drowned out his words. He looked pleadingly at Catherine, and she stared back at him, completely helpless.

Pascal and Paul McRae arrived on the run with a horse and travois. They spread a blanket on the travois and eased the semi-conscious woman onto it, and tied her there securely. With Pascal leading the horse, they headed farther into the woods, harassed by swarming clouds of mosquitoes.

***

Catherine stood there, dazed and trembling. Where was Jay? Had he been shot down like the other guard? A bullet plucked at a fold of her skirt, others buzzed around her like angry hornets. She had lost sight of her friends and began to follow their tracks; with hands scraped and bleeding, she flailed at the clouds of mosquitoes around her head. As she ran, the ground fell away, and she rolled down into a depression, landing on some stones at the bottom. A searing pain shot up her leg from her ankle. After a bit, she tried to crawl up and out of it, but tears of pain and sweat blurred her vision.

Someone was pulling at her. She could hear a voice, although the words were unintelligible. Wiping at her eyes with the back of her hand, she looked up. It was As-a-Child, doing an oddly distressed dance and holding his hands out to her imploringly. Reaching up, she got a grip on one hand and he pulled her out of the hole with surprising strength. She struggled to her feet, clinging to him. Despite her own terror and pain, she saw that his eyes were fixed on her, pleading, adoring, and wild with fear. She tried to smile reassuringly, but just at that moment, he flew violently backwards, lifted off his feet, limbs flailing like a broken doll. He slammed against the ground, shuddered once, and lay still.

She screamed and hobbled to him. A hideous red stain oozed across his chest. Great sobs began to wrack her, as she took the lifeless hand that had just helped her. Her grief was unbearable, and not only because it was

As-a-Child lying there, broken and dead. Somehow, it was her beloved brother Billy too. In the stress and pain and terror all around her, they turned into one in her mind. She knew that she would never see his oddly sweet smile again. The gentle voice was stilled forever, the kind eyes glazed under the cruel mid-morning sun. She tenderly brushed the ragged hair back from his forehead and saw her tears drip onto his face. She told him that it was all right now. There would be no more pain and bewilderment. No more fear, loneliness, cold, or hunger, not ever again. Then she slumped over his body, and the noise, light, and pain faded into darkness.

***

Major Steele reported back to General Strange. The warriors were dug in for over a mile to the north, and although they had fired at them, beyond that point, they had not been able to cross the river. As they spoke, a panting messenger joined them from the Mounted Rifles. A party of warriors had outflanked them and were about to open fire on the wagon corral!

Strange could see no way now to dislodge the warriors from their rifle pits without losing too many of his own men. There would be few left to make a further advance. They needed troops to move up behind their opponents, and to do that, they would have to wait for the troops coming from Battleford with General Middleton. He made his decision and recalled the men trying to cross the river. As soon as the last sweating, mud-caked, and insect-bitten man was out of the ravine, Strange ordered a cease fire. After three hours of furious noise and sustained battle, the valley of the Little Red Deer River was suddenly deathly quiet again.

The soldiers went back the way they had come in, taking their dead and wounded with them. By nightfall, they were back in their camp near Fort Pitt.

***

Gabe Berthier found Catherine. He lifted her to her feet, ignoring her muddled protests.

"But I can't leave the poor man here like that. He was my friend. Please wait." She took off her ragged shawl and laid it over the dead slack face, already crawling with flies. Gabe patted her shoulder, shaking his head at this crazy behaviour. Then, noticing her hobbling, he picked her up in his powerful arms and carried her to a clearing where the prisoners were huddled together. Neither of them had seen Muhekun slip silently through the brush and settle down near As-a-Child, beside his friend.

There were no guards on them now, none of these people were going any-where! Shaken, stunned, and haggard, some injured, they sat or sprawled on the ground, trying to recover from their ordeal. The sun was flooded over them, the trees rustled in the breeze, and a brave bird sang somewhere close by. There was no more rifle fire. The artillery was silent. And then they heard the warriors up and down the river calling out and cheering wildly. Paul McRae could make out some of the words. His face was tight and drawn as he passed the news along to them. The soldiers were retreating to Fort Pitt. The first battle was over.

CHAPTER TWENTY-NINE

The scouts reported the arrival of troops and supplies from Battleford at the military camp east of Fort Pitt. Wandering Spirit, knowing that now they were in danger of a 'surround,' decided to move to the north.

By this time, the prisoners were back in their camp beside the river, trying to salvage what remained of their belongings. They were ragged and down-hearted, their faces swollen from insect bites and sunburn, their boots and shoes worn through. When the summons came to move out again, they obeyed sluggishly, packed what little they had left, knowing a further ordeal awaited them. Many of them were bitter, feeling the soldiers had heartlessly abandoned them to their fate.

Jay had only seen Catherine for brief minutes when he delivered the message, but he was stricken when he saw the woman he loved. Scratched and bruised, she was limping in obvious pain, her lovely hair snarled and tangled. Even so, she managed a whispered word to him about As-a-Child and where his body was.

As he had warned, Wandering Spirit led them around the edges of invisible bogs and quicksand, through thick forests, across muskeg, creeks, and rivers while the warriors fought a rearguard action, ambushing and harassing Steele's Scouts who still followed them. Food was scarce. There was no time to hunt, fish, or snare. Carts broke down and were left behind. People, mostly the elderly and those seriously wounded, died along the way and were quickly buried with no time to mourn them properly.

***

One day at noon, the warriors and their prisoners arrived at a ridge over-looking large bodies of water, known as The Two Lakes. A forested peninsula jutted from the north side, into the one known as Loon Lake. They made rafts and laboriously crossed the water to the spit of land. When Steele's Scouts kept up a steady fire on those making the crossing, they suffered some casualties, but as soon as the families reached land, the warriors returned to the southern shore to shoot back.

As nightfall came and the shooting continued, the captives, suffering from exposure, exhaustion, hunger, and despair searched frantically for shelter. The men dug trenches, but the water table was high; within three feet of the surface, they began to fill with water. Branches were thrown in and the children were hustled into the meagre shelters and wrapped in blankets. To make matters worse, a thunderstorm started to rage overhead, and blankets were soon soaked through. Tents and other such luxuries had been long since left behind, along with everything else of value they had once owned.

Marie Scott had injured her back and broken some ribs in her fall from the cart. Although she seldom complained, her once plump and smiling face was haggard with pain. Every movement was agony, and more than once, she had begged her husband to leave her behind. But Scotty and Catherine, who limped along with the help of a stout stick, kept her going.

On this nightmarish evening, Marie lay exhausted on the ground, with rain pouring down over her face and the lightning flaring. Scotty, Julia, and Catherine worked as quickly as they could to enlarge a hollow they had found in the side of a hill. When they got Marie inside, with Scotty on one side and Julia on the other, there was no more room. Scotty offered Catherine his place, but she refused, knowing it was better for Marie to have her husband with her. Even though she was chilled to the bone, with her hair plastered down over her head and shoulders and the ragged dress stuck to her shivering body, Catherine was reluctant to join them. She told them she would crawl in with one of the other families, and that she knew where the MacKenzies were.

***

Despite warnings, Ellen had left notes for Peter in several places on the brutal forced march after the battle. He must be with the police, she kept insisting. With his wife a captive, he wouldn't be assigned to any other duty, would he? But why hadn't he make a sign or signal that he was there?

George scoffed at this, telling Ellen she was being impractical. "What the hell type of a signal could he have made in the midst of running battles? Sure, Peter was there," he told her, "but so were a lot of other men, all following orders and not gallivanting around on business of their own." But Ellen had lost her cheeky aplomb. There was a strained look in her once-merry eyes. Like the rest of them, she was scratched, bitten, and too thin.

Catherine knew something the MacKenzies did not. She had talked to Jay several times. Everyone was so worn out by the daily struggle to survive that no one noticed them. Jay had often been their only guard, but no one thought of him as that any more. Once, after hours of searching, he had found and returned a lost child to the McRaes. He was just there, accepted or ignored.

Once Catherine and Jay had been alone for over an hour, while she huddled against him. He told her that he knew about the notes Ellen had been leaving, but he had done nothing about them. After all, what could Ellen say that was not already known to their pursuers? Then he told her that he had seen two police corporals wounded and possibly dead, during the battle at Cut Knife Hill, one too far away to recognize, the other with a disfiguring head wound. Catherine knew that he would not have told her this, unless he suspected one of the fallen corporals had been Peter Gray.

She tried not to think about it. Dear, steady, caring Peter with the laughter in his sky-blue eyes and his fair hair shining like gold ... *no!* He was too strong, and full of life and love for Ellen, to be dead or maimed. But it was becoming more difficult to go on reassuring Ellen with the necessary conviction. She had too little of her own strength left. And so, she stood there in the driving rain, inert and numb with misery. Suddenly there was a searing flash of lightning and a crash of thunder that shook the ground under her feet and left her ears ringing.

***

Someone took her arm, and with another stroke of lightning, she knew it was Jay. He leaned over and shouted directly into Catherine's ear. "Come!"

With no hesitation, she took his hand and soon they were into the trees. He had found a small cave and piled up branches to screen the opening. They crawled into it, removed their drenched clothing, and lay down together on the dry floor, holding each other close, listening to the wind and rain and the rolling echoing thunder. They lay that way for a long time, warming each other slowly, somehow comforted during chaos.

After a while, Jay stroked the tangled strands of hair away from Catherine's face, and kissed her gently. She sighed like a tired child, and although she would never have dreamed it possible, she felt herself responding to his touch. Only this mattered. The pain, fighting, hunger, fear, and despair all vanished. They knew once again the breath-taking magic of their desire and love for one another. Knowing that it would soon be finished for them made it more poignant. This brief enchantment had to be deeply sensed and forever remembered like a haunting melody. They knew they would have to move on, going their separate and lonely ways, where nothing like this would ever happen to them again. And so, throughout the night she told him of her love and heard him tell it back to her. Sometimes there was lovemaking, him coming into her and she holding him in an ecstasy of giving and taking; affirmation of life amid all this death.

The storm receded slowly. Only Jay was awake when dawn came; the trees were dripping slow tears, pattering on leaves torn loose by the storm around their shelter. He had not been able to hold back the dawn after all. He looked at the woman in his arms. Her hair was matted but her mouth was the same, soft and sweet and vulnerable, her body silken and feminine against him. After all that had happened, how could she still be so beautiful? What a wild and improbable fate it was, he thought, that had brought them to this one overwhelming moment on a menacing morning in mid-June.

"Cate," he whispered, "it is morning now." She stirred reluctantly, moved even closer to him, and opened her luminous eyes, so close to the colour of spring violets. "Amee, you must listen to me very carefully, but don't look at me, or I won't be able to say this." Obediently, she snuggled her face in under his chin, kissed his throat and waited.

"Our scouts have brought in word that this whole country is teeming with soldiers. There are three big steamboats on the river south of us. They have landed many more, ready to come up and join the ones who are shooting at us here. But worse than that, some of our best warriors are dead, and we are nearly out of ammunition." Jay found it very hard to go on saying these things. He paused to be sure his voice remained steady and calm. "It is almost finished, Cate. Although we will fight on as long as we can, we will soon have to break up. The Woods Crees lost Chief Cut Arm in the fighting yesterday, and are talking about surrender. The Métis from Batoche are going make a run for the border. Some of my people, who are not well-known to the whites, will slip into the reserves around Battleford, and others will go west to Chief Crowfoot, who has promised us refuge. Big Bear says that he is too old and tired to run. He will let them take him."

Catherine had gone very still as she listened to him. "What are *you* going to do, *Amee?*"

"I haven't decided yet. First, I want to see you safely out of here." Just as he finished saying that, there was a volley of shooting that wrecked the dawn stillness, silencing birds just into their morning songs. Jay sat up, listening intently. The shots were coming from the southern shore of Loon Lake.

"Cate," he said during a lull. "You must go away today, while we are still fighting, when the warriors will be too busy to miss you for a while. Now that we're going to break up, you are of no use as hostages any more, and I'm not sure how you might be treated. If you go, I don't think anyone will bother to follow you. You can't go back the way we came here, with the shooting still going on. But that is not the best way to go, even if you could. We put the lake between us and the soldiers to slow them down. You can head south through the woods to the east of the lake. If you go far enough, you will hit our back trail, and then you can follow it to where the steamboats are."

She looked up at him, and her eyes were spilling tears. "I would rather stay here and die with you."

He frowned at her. "You promised me that you would go when I asked you to. You *said* you would do it for *me*."

She touched the amulet between her breasts and was silent for a while. "Well, I still have this, and unless you want it back, I will never take it off, or part with it. Maybe it still has power, Jay. Feel how warm it is."

He touched it and pulled her close again for one last long unbearable embrace; his heart filled with pain. "It will protect you. Go back to the Scotts, Cate. Now! I'll tell Mr. MacKenzie how to go by the overland trail. Go quickly please, Cate."

She followed him out of their shelter, pulling on her wet and tattered dress. She started back for the dugout where she had left Scotty and Marie. Jay watched as she limped along, her head down. He knew that she was crying as she went. Then she was gone, swallowed up by the trees. His dearest loved one ... his *Amee*.

***

The Scotts had awakened from the firing, now increasing in ferocity. "Well, lass," Scotty greeted Catherine wearily, climbing out of the small dugout. Julia was already standing with her hands over her ears. "I hope you found a place to get some rest. You look mighty peaked. Is it the ankle that's worse, then?" Catherine shook her head, and then sat down beside Marie her throat so constricted she could not speak. Marie looked at her searchingly, then took Catherine's icy hand in both of her own rough ones.

"You have said goodbye to him then," she said softly. "I am so sorry, child. If things were different, you could have been so good together. He is a fine young man, that one." Catherine stared at her, momentarily shocked out of her grief, her face drained of all colour. Marie nodded, "Yes, I have known for a while now. I have lived for a long time, and I know the look of a woman who has been with her lover."

"Oh, Marie," she replied, "I could take all the rest of it and get through somehow, but I can't bear the pain of this." She began to sob, and then she buried her face in the older woman's ample bosom, causing a spasm of pain to cross Marie's face. She put her comforting arms around Catherine, soothing her as she would have held a distraught and desolate child. Both Julia and Scotty looked at them in surprise. Marie shook her head at them and waved them away. She continued to hold Catherine until the convulsive sobbing subsided and she was spent.

Now and then, Marie shook her head again. "Maybe some day people will stop hating one another," she said, talking to herself as much as Catherine. "Maybe, but when, I don't know. I'm afraid it won't happen in our lifetime, child."

***

The captives left the camp in an hour, able to move that quickly because they had so little left to pack up. George led the way, following Jay's directions. They had rigged a few travois with the horses they had left, to carry the injured and the children. Catherine rode the horse pulling Marie's travois. Tom Bradley, Gabe Berthier, Gus LaRonde, Paul McRae, and Giles Dumas formed a rear guard. They had no weapons other than knives or wooden clubs. But back of them was old Pascal, slingshot in his hand and a bag of stones at his belt. At close range, the stones were as deadly as bullets and they were glad to have him.

Reverend Wilson, the only dissenter to their sudden flight, had sullenly refused to go out in front with George or with the rear guard. Scotty walked along beside the travois, doing what he could to make Marie comfortable. But no one followed them or stood in their way.

***

Three days later, the rag-tag band of prisoners met an advance party from General Middleton's oncoming army.

"Dear God in heaven! Is it really you, Mrs. McNab?" Catherine pushed her matted hair back from her dirty, tired face and looked up at the officer who had dismounted and hurried over to her.

"Superintendent Cooke? Yes, I guess it's me." She looked down at her dress, which was hardly whole enough to cover her decently. She tried to clutch it around her more tightly, and Cooke immediately took off his field tunic and put it around her shoulders.

"My dear girl, we had given up hope of ever finding you alive after all this time."

Some dumbfounded soldiers were gathering around the gaunt and staggering refugees. Many of the women were sobbing in relief. Julia had slumped to the ground in a faint. The men were shaking hands and pounding shoulders with tight smiles, as they struggled to believe that their ordeal had finally ended.

"Off-load some of the wagons for these people," ordered Cooke sharply. "Get Doctor Murdoch up here." He turned back to George. "How long has it been since you've had something to eat?"

"We ran out of everything yesterday morning, sir. We need a few rations, if you could spare us some."

"Just bully-beef and hardtack, but there is a good supply of it, and we'll have coffee and tea for you in no time. Cooke gave some further orders, then looked at Catherine. "Mrs. McNab, there were rumours that both you and Mrs. Simmons had been tortured and perhaps killed. It has been in all the newspapers. Everyone, indeed the whole country, has been waiting anxiously for news of you."

She gave him a vaguely puzzled look, noticing the livid scar on his cheek, from the wound he received at Duck Lake. "They have? Well, we had some very bad moments, but none of us were personally hurt. In fact, some of them were very kind to us." Cooke appeared stunned by that remark.

George suddenly realized Ellen was interrogating a group of policemen. "Sir, my son-in-law is Corporal Peter Gray. Is he with you? Can you tell me where he is?"

Cooke's face went pale at the question. He cleared his throat nervously. "I'm afraid he is not, Mr. MacKenzie. I deeply regret having to inform you that Corporal Gray died bravely on the field of battle at Cut Knife Hill. He was buried, with full military honours, along with the other men we lost, beside the fort in Battleford."

They stared in shock and horror at the sorrowful face of the police officer, unable to speak or move for a moment. Catherine tugged urgently on George's arm, "Mr. MacKenzie, you had better get to Ellen before she hears this from someone else."

"Aye," he answered in a choked voice. "I'll do that. My God, is there never to be an end to this slaughter?" He hurried first to get his wife, then they went to the group of policemen standing around Ellen.

Catherine had no tears left, not even for Peter. She just stood there, waves of misery washing over her. She was aware that Ellen had run up to them, face as white as chalk under her vivid mane of red hair, emerald eyes blazing with fury at Superintendent Cooke.

"Well, that should just about do it, eh? You've got nearly all the best men in the country killed off, and now you've got this big army going to finish off the poor savages you tricked and starved and abused into bloodshed, and then it'll be all over and you'll be patting yourselves on the back and getting medals for doing it, and to hell with what it cost!"

"Ellen, stop it!" cried her father. "This man is not running the country, he..."

"*You* shut up, Pa!" she shouted. "Not *me!* Not with my darling Peter lying dead and buried and God knows how many others, and then you look at all these men and weapons and try to tell me that they didn't cost more than it would have to give the Métis their own little scraps of land, or keep their bloody promises to feed the Indians enough to keep them alive? How many times did you say that to yourself? You saw it coming long before it happened, and so did anyone with half a brain, but this is what they wanted, and this is what they got. So, you'd better lock me up, Superintendent, because if you don't, I'm going after that fancy Lieutenant-Governor, sitting all safe and smug in his nice big office, and he'll find out what it's like be scared silly, and to die, and go hungry, and broken-hearted, and robbed..."

Catherine grabbed Ellen by the shoulders and shook her violently, stunning the frantic girl into silence. She put her arms around her, holding Ellen tightly, unaware that Cooke's field tunic had fallen to the ground. "Hush, now Ellen! Hush I tell you! This won't bring your Peter back, or Ian, or Bert, or any of the rest of them. It won't put our hearts and lives back together again. It's not this man's fault, any more than it is your father's." She paused and looked at Superintendent Cooke. "Have you any brandy? She's stiff as a board, and ice-cold."

The medical officer who had been tending to Julia had her up on her feet again.

"Doctor Murdoch!" Cooke called out, his face full of pain and his eyes over-bright. George, Leslie and Connie were standing by, all of them weeping openly as the doctor hurried up. He took one look at Ellen, and then bent down to open his black bag.

CHAPTER THIRTY

Catherine, Julia, and Ellen were on the steamboat, *Northcote*, heading for Battleford. Dressed in an odd assortment of donated clothing, they stood at the stern railing watching as the frothy wake smoothed out, leaving no sign of their passage. Several missionaries and other dignitaries escorted them. But the three widows had asked for privacy, and the other passengers respected their wishes.

Some of the former prisoners had returned to Fort Pitt. George, Leslie, and Connie MacKenzie were already there, starting the work of rebuilding their home and store to resume the trading business. Scotty helped them while Marie rested, recovering from her injuries. None of them would ever go back to Pounding Lake.

It had been another wrench for Catherine to leave these dear friends behind. Only Marie had not assumed it was forever. "Something tells me different, child," she said, as she hugged her. "But maybe I'm just a crazy old lady."

By now, Catherine felt like a puppet, eating, sleeping, dressing, sitting, standing ... doing whatever she was asked or told to do. The only thing she had done on her own, since Loon Lake, was to request an interview with General Middleton when the steamer stopped at the army camp to pick up some wounded and drop off prisoners.

***

General Middleton received Catherine immediately with both kindness and concern. When she requested that a certain man, one known as Clear Sky, be treated with consideration if captured, he harrumphed and tried to change the subject. But Catherine was insistent.

"General, he saved my life at the risk of his own, when my husband was killed. There were a hundred things he did to make it easier for the prisoners. I know Mr. MacKenzie and Mr. Scott will back me up on that. He found a lost child and returned it to his parents. He was the one who planned our escape during the fight at Loon Lake. And he kept me safe whenever that awful Buck Breland was in the camp."

"Breland, you say?" asked the general in surprise. "He claims he was your protector during your captivity."

"Breland looted our home before it was burned," she answered wearily. "He rode my dead husband's horse, while I walked. He wore Ian's warm clothes while I froze. He even tried to buy me with my own sapphire and diamond pin with the worst of intentions toward me. If you search his belongings you should find it."

The crusty general's face darkened with his famous temper. "I will order his arrest immediately, Mrs. McNab. As for this Indian, what's his name, Clear Sky, you say?" He went to his desk and wrote Jay's name and description as Catherine gave it to him. "I will see to it personally that he gets full amnesty."

That done, Catherine retreated into silence again. All she could think of was the distance increasing between her and the man she loved. She was not the heroine everyone was assuming she was and she knew it ... but could not deny it. To them, she was Ian McNab's grieving widow, and she had to play that part, for Jay's sake. She would never regret the intimate and passionate hours she had spent with him. She felt no guilt about it. But her heart was so sorrowful that she was tempted to step over the railing and drop into the cold embrace of the river below her, except that she knew what it would do to Jay if he should ever hear about it. The *Northcote* landed on the 10th of June.

***

It looked as though the entire population of Battleford was waiting at the dock to meet them! The police band was playing and people cheered and waved as the three widows came down the gangplank. There were speeches of welcome and generous gifts. But those who knew them personally were silent, seeing in their faces the reality of war, the broken hearts, shattered lives, unborn children, and long-lost dreams. Once engulfed by the welcoming throng, they were separated.

John and Jennie Appleton finally managed to get Catherine into their carriage and headed toward their home, which, thanks to MaryLou, had been spared during the rebellion. Jenny was driving the team of horses, and Catherine suddenly noticed that John, pale and thin, had an empty sleeve where his arm had been. He saw her shock.

"The rest of me is somewhere out on Cut Knife Hill, my dear. But I am still alive and kicking, which is more than can be said for a lot of brave lads."

"As though you need to tell *her* that, John, dear," chided Jenny. Her voice was softer than Catherine remembered it. The awful conflict had affected this assertive woman too. She looked older, shrunken, and the round sharp eyes that Catherine once likened to 'little grey mice' were dull. She knew that Jenny had cared very much for Ian, so she answered John, but what she said was meant as much for Jenny.

"Yes, you are alive and I thank God for that, and so would Ian, I know. As his closest friends, it might help you to know that he died at once. I don't think there was any time for pain at all. And while some of the other bodies were left out there where they fell, I managed to talk Big Bear into placing Ian's body in the church, before they burned it. I think we can say he is resting in hallowed ground."

John looked at her gratefully, and Jenny dabbed at tears in her eyes. "You are a brave girl to tell us that, my dear, and we do thank you."

***

In the privacy of the Appleton home, sitting in the same room that Ian and she had shared less than a year ago, Catherine read the letters from home accumulated over the past three months. Her parents had written faithfully, although she could sense the fear that their only remaining child might never receive the loving and concerned words they wrote.

Catherine was saddened to read in one letter that old Jamie McNab, Ian's father, had died of a heart seizure upon hearing of Ian's death. As his widow and only survivor, her father wrote, she would inherit the entire McNab estate, a substantial one. Although their home and the Pounding Lake store had been lost, the Battleford Bank advised her that Ian's savings ran into five figures. She was now a wealthy woman.

***

Sergeant William Porter had been assigned to accompany Ellen and Catherine (who wanted to come with her), to the cemetery beside the fort in Battleford, where Peter had been buried. Porter, the former 'mother hen' of Fort Pitt, had asked for the assignment, but his face was splotched with emotion, and his pale eyes blinked rapidly in the morning light. He led them to the neat rows of wooden crosses. Jenny Appleton had given each woman some roses from her garden, and now they silently placed them beneath the simple white cross.

Ellen stood for a long time looking at Peter's marker. She told them in a trembling voice that she had not, until now, been able to believe that she would never see him again.

"Oh, my love," Ellen whispered. After a while, she looked over at the sergeant. "Do you remember those silly paper daisies I carried when we were married, Sergeant?" At his nod, she explained to Catherine. "I took them off one of Ma's old hats. A bride needs flowers. You should have seen Peter laugh when he saw them!"

Porter hesitated, then made up his mind and cleared his throat. "As to that, Mrs. Gray, I ... well, I took rather a liberty, I'm afraid. You see I was with him when he fell during the fight. I saw to it that he was on one of the wagons when we pulled out of there. The paper flowers were in his pocket, and I ... well, I don't really know how to say this, but they are with him still."

Ellen stared at the stolid policeman, then she put both of her arms around him and kissed him firmly on his ruddy cheek. "This is from both Peter and me," she said, "although I know it is a silly little reward for being such a true and wonderful friend."

"It means more to me than any tin medal would, ma'am."

Catherine had to walk away from them. She had not cried since parting from Jay, but she was afraid she was very close to it now, and that would not help Ellen. To divert her mind, she looked at some of the other names on the white crosses. Then she stopped up short, in pain and surprise. Inspector David H. Kingsley!

Another friend gone, she thought sadly, remembering the kindly officer with the clipped British accent and the genuinely warm smile. The sergeant came to join her, leaving Ellen alone for a few minutes at her request. He looked at Catherine's sad face and answered her unspoken question.

"The cold and wet on the barge coming to Battleford did him in, Mrs. McNab. That, and the way the malaria had been undermining him since his service in India. He died several days after we landed, worrying to the end about you prisoners. You especially, ma'am, if I may say so. I wish he could have known that you were going to get out safely; it would have made his going easier. He ... cared for you. He had a bad fever making him talk maybe, but that was the last thing he said to me."

Catherine returned his gaze directly. "I am very honoured to have had his regard. David Kingsley was everything an officer and a gentleman should be, but for all that a lonely man, I think. Were you with him when he died?"

"I was, Mrs. McNab."

"I wish I could have been there too," she said. They left the cemetery then, the two young widows, clad in black, walking slowly arm in arm. The police-man escorted them as proudly and respectfully as he would have escorted the old British monarch herself.

***

Catherine became increasingly restless that afternoon. She was still thin and weak but went for a walk across the bridge and back to the cemetery. On her knees beside Peter's grave, she clasped her hands. "Poor dear man, you were so kind and strong, different and yet in some ways like the one I love. Now you, at least, are beyond all the passion and pain, love and loss that we must still endure. You are past it forever, and there is nothing that even your beloved Ellen can do to change that.

"You see, Peter, my dearest one brought me through all that hell back there. Why were we brought together and allowed to love each other so much? Why were our lives spared then, only to be parted now as cruelly as you and Ellen?" Catherine did not notice the slender figure in black standing behind her. Ellen, too, had been drawn back to Peter's grave. "Are there no reasons for the things that happen? I feel there is something so wrong about all this, but I don't know what to do about it. We both accepted the idea that what other people thought was what we had to think too; we never questioned it. But seeing your grave here today has made me question all that now."

"Catherine, my Peter can have no answers for you any more. But would you like to tell me what you are talking about? I shouldn't have listened, but I was too surprised to move."

Catherine froze. How long had Ellen been there; how much had she heard? She tried to think of something to say, but failed.

Ellen sat beside her and took her hand. "You sound terribly troubled. You were never really in love with Ian, were you?"

"No, but I didn't know it then. I respected him, I cared about him, but our marriage was not a very good one. I would have been loyal and faithful to him if he had lived, and still wanted me as his wife."

She looked away from Ellen. "I can't tell you more, I'm sorry."

"Can't you trust me? It sounded to me that you need very much to talk to some one who *can* listen to you."

"Of course, I trust you. But I must protect him."

"From me?" asked Ellen in disbelief. She stayed very quiet for several minutes. "I think I am beginning to understand this. One or twice I wondered, but forgot about it because I was so worried about Peter. All this is about Jay Clear Sky. You don't even need to answer, I'm sure it is. You poor kid!"

Catherine had expected almost any reaction but sympathy. "We are," she said, then corrected herself, "we were, so desperately in love," she whispered. "I would rather have stayed there and died with him. But he made me leave him, because he cared more for me than he did about himself."

"Oh Catherine, Jay isn't dead! There is word in Fort Pitt that he survived the conflict. But he and White Bear were caught by a police patrol last month. Jay was released the next morning, thanks to General Middleton. He even got Cloudwalker back, much to the disgust of the soldiers. White Bear was sentenced to three months in jail."

"I didn't know!" said Catherine, astonished at the news. "I'm almost afraid to believe it, in case it's not true!"

"Whew!" said Ellen, shaking her head. "And I thought I was the expert at getting into trouble! I can understand it though. He saved your life. There's something about you that makes men want to protect you. One thing leads quickly to another, I think, in war time. Next thing you know you're in love."

"What would you do if you were me, Ellen?"

"Lord knows. Look what I did! I married a man, and we never even had the chance to... But I don't think I'd go back east, if I were you. Not yet, unless you are sure that you can close the door forever on him and on that part of your life. Why don't you stay with the Appletons for a while? They're obviously fond of you. It's still too soon. We've both been through so much to be thinking clearly yet." She touched the white cross with trembling fingers. "I wonder if I ever will."

"You will, Ellen. I remember what Marie said to me about the death of her first husband. He drowned, you know, leaving her alone with children to raise. She said, 'That passes. The river flows and life goes on, all to the Lord's plan. Whatever lies ahead for us, we must trust Him, leave it in His hands.

When you can do that, it will ease the pain and anger that is in you now.' Peter would want that for you, Ellen."

"Yes, I know he would. Oh, Catherine, I'm so tired. I'm going home."

"Do that, Ellen. And I'll stay on here a while. I must find my own answers, one way or another."

***

In August, Ellen came back to Battleford to meet Peter's parents. She had sent a letter from Fort Pitt to say she was coming. Catherine and John Appleton met her at the landing with his carriage.

John bluntly vetoed her plan to stay at a hotel. "Nonsense, Ellen. The hotels in town are no place for a young woman alone. You'll stay with us, and no argument about it!"

"Thank you, Mr. Appleton, I'm not really anxious to be alone, since I feel so nervous about meeting Peter's parents. They've come all this way to see Peter's grave and then to meet me. I understand they are very prominent and wealthy people. What on earth are they going to think of a country bumpkin like me?"

"Their son fell in love with you, and so will they," said Catherine. "They are staying with Judge Rouleau and his wife. You're going to meet them there this evening."

"Yes, but how did *you* know?"

"Mrs. Rouleau suspected you might want a little moral support, so she very kindly invited me to come along, too."

"Oh, bless her! Having you with me will help, Catherine." The Rouleau house, the largest one in Battleford, was a short walk from the Appleton home. It too had escaped destruction during the rebellion. Mrs. Rouleau met the two young widows at the door, and led them into a large and ornately furnished drawing room. A distinguished-looking couple rose and came at once to meet Ellen. Henry Gray was a tall, white-haired man with a clipped moustache and a keen, sharply-chiselled face. His wife, Elizabeth, was a short delicate woman with

Peter's sky-blue eyes and warm smile, although now her lips trembled. She held out both hands to Ellen as Mrs. Rouleau introduced them.

"Oh, my dear, you are as lovely as Peter told us you were in his letters." There were tears in her eyes. "Please excuse me, this has been an emotional day for us, seeing Peter's resting place, so far away from home. But this is where I'm sure he would want to be."

Henry Gray shook her hand, looking tired and sad, but pleased to see her. "Ellen Gray! We have heard nothing but the finest things about you." Then Ellen and Catherine both froze. All the colour drained out of Ellen's face as a man, talking to the judge in a corner, turned and came to meet them. He looked so much like Peter that neither woman could speak.

"This is our eldest son, Richard," said Mr. Gray, seeing their shock. "There was always a strong family resemblance between our two boys." Mrs. Rouleau smoothed over the awkward moment by introducing Catherine to the Grays.

"Of course," said Henry, bowing to her. "I think the whole country was praying for you and Mrs. Simmons after the tragedy at Pounding Lake."

"There were a lot of tragedies besides our own," said Catherine, "on both sides."

Richard was still looking at Ellen, but he replied to Catherine. "The more I talk to people, the more I'm beginning to realize how bungled affairs were out here. The Prime Minister and his appointees in this territory were hopelessly remiss in their responsibilities. I'm a lawyer, and involved in Ottawa politics. I'm going to do a lot more probing and investigating before I'm through."

"I hope you do," said Ellen quietly.

"I have some business to take care of in Ottawa. I'll see my parents home safely, finish up there, and then come back out here and get to work on it. Why don't you come with us, Ellen? You can see Peter's childhood home, get to know us better, and then come back with me. We had planned to invite you, if we liked you." He smiled at her. "I'm sure I can say it for the three of us. We do."

Ellen was astonished. "Why I…I don't know… I never thought…"

"Please think about it, Ellen," said Elizabeth Gray. "You've been through such an ordeal, and with grief for Peter on top of it all. A change and a rest would do you a world of good."

"We can make you very comfortable," added Henry Gray. "Our private railway car is waiting for us on a siding at Swift Current."

"Oh, my!" said Ellen, looking dazed. "What do you think, Catherine?"

"I think you should go. I'm sure your parents would say the same thing. We both have to go on with our lives, one way or another."

***

Ellen and Catherine were sharing the Appleton's guest room. After they turned off the lamp that night, they lay awake in the darkness.

"I think I will go with the Grays," said Ellen. "Anything is better than constantly fighting this awful emptiness inside me and crying so much. I'm making everyone else unhappy. What about you, Catherine? Have you found any of your answers yet?"

"I think I have. I heard that Julia Simmons has gone back to her home in Ontario, but I don't believe that's right for me. I'm going to go back and look for Jay, unless he sends me away again. I know people will be scandalized, and I will lose most of my friends, certainly the Appletons, and my parents will never understand. I have accepted that. I can live with it, if I have Jay."

"You won't lose me or Connie. And Marie and Scotty really love you, Catherine. Then there's MaryLou. She's staying with the Scotts. Marie says MaryLou is expecting White Bear's baby, so that's a good place for her to wait until they let him out. Jay sometimes goes there to see her, so you may not need to look for him."

"Then I'll take the steamboat to Fort Pitt. Until I see Jay, I'll say it's just a visit."

"Yes, don't go overland. It's not safe. The Indians are still quite hostile and some of the soldiers' patrols are no better."

***

A few days later, Ellen left with the Grays for Swift Current. As Judge Rouleau's carriage stopped at the Appleton house to pick her up, Richard Gray was out of it immediately to take Ellen's luggage and assist her inside. There was no disguising the admiration on his face as he looked at her. Suddenly, Catherine had the distinct impression that her lovely friend was no longer alone, and that Richard Gray would be there for her when she was ready for happiness again. Catherine's eyes teared up as the gleaming carriage rolled away from her.

The next morning, the Appletons drove Catherine to the dock to board the *Northcote* for her visit to Fort Pitt. She hugged them both goodbye without further explanation, not knowing if she would ever see them again.

She spent her first day in Fort Pitt with George, Leslie, and Connie, telling them about the Grays. "They loved Ellen right away, you could see that, and I'm sure they will take wonderful care of her. She'll even be travelling in a private railway car once she gets to Swift Current!" They were all surprised to learn that Peter, so unassuming, was from such a wealthy family.

"I'm so glad she went with them," said Leslie. "That wasn't our laughing little hellion creeping around here for the last few weeks, just a shadow of the daughter we had before."

***

The next day, Catherine went to see the Scotts ... and MaryLou. There were hugs and tears and kisses of greeting.

"I said you would come back, didn't I, child? Remember?" asked Marie, dabbing at her eyes.

"Yes, and I came for this visit just to make your prediction come true," teased Catherine. "How is your back, Marie? You're looking much better than when I saw you last."

"Well, so are *you*. I am much better, but I'll never ride in a Red River cart again, and that's the truth," replied Marie. Scotty was looking on, smiling widely as pipe-smoke wreathed his head.

Catherine turned to MaryLou. "So, you caught your White Bear after all!"

"He was a very willing victim, but we didn't have long together before the soldiers caught him, too."

"Long enough," said Marie, "she's going to have a little bear cub, a few months from now."

"Are you terribly upset about him being in jail?" asked Catherine.

"No, it was a light sentence compared to most, and when he gets out, we won't need to be hiding and running from the police and soldiers any more. He is being well-treated. Clicker Lang, do you remember him? One of the policemen in Pounding Lake? Well, he got ordered back here to look for some of the horses the police left behind when they evacuated Fort Pitt on the barge. He told me that White Bear is well-liked by the policemen who guard the prisoners. You know what a talker he is! He tells them all kinds of tall stories and jokes. He says he is on vacation, and praises the white man for cooking him such good meals and looking after him so well! I know how he's really feeling, but he's far too proud to let the white men see it."

***

Catherine wanted to wait until they were alone before asking MaryLou about Jay. Perhaps Marie sensed it. She suggested to Scotty that they needed water and followed him outside.

"How is he?" she asked MaryLou.

She hesitated, then Catherine caught a flash of anger in MaryLou's dark eyes. "He is hurting in his heart. I pray he doesn't come here to see me until you are gone. Losing you once was bad enough. To have it happen again would be terrible for him. I don't know what he would do. Why did you come here, Catherine?"

"I have come back to him. I too have a breaking heart. He won't lose me unless he sends me away again, as he did last time. He thought it was best for me, but it wasn't. What is best for me is to be with him. And I think, for him to be with me. Nothing else matters."

"I suppose you mean that. But have you any idea how your own people will turn on you, if they find out that you love my brother and want to live with him?"

"That is what I have been thinking about, instead of going back to the east as expected. Thinking about it very carefully, until I was sure. MaryLou, I'm not going to let the same people who allowed all these terrible things to happen this past year and for years before that decide for *me* what is right or wrong. If love is wrong for Jay and me, only he can tell me that."

For a long time, MaryLou was quiet, skeptical, her eyes searching Catherine's face, thinking over what she had heard. Finally, she decided.

"Yes, he has the right to do that. You know that lookout point on Frenchman Butte? He has built a place there, a large one, so he has room for his painting and drawing. And White Bear started one for us when Jay's was finished. That's what they were doing when the police patrol caught them, cutting logs down in the valley to take them up the hill. Blue Quill and his family were there, too, but not down in the valley, so the policemen missed them. Since then, they have moved to Blackfoot Crossing, where Chief Crowfoot has taken them in."

"Jay is living in this cabin, now?"

"Yes, and White Bear and I will go there when he can come back to me again. For now, Jay is alone. I don't know when he will be back; he was just here a week ago."

"I'm not waiting around," said Catherine. "I will go to him. I'll buy a horse and some supplies from Mr. MacKenzie and then go to Frenchman Butte. I know the way by now."

"You're out of your mind! You'll run into desperate men trying to get to the border. They'll let no one, certainly not a lone woman, stand in their way. Or you'll run into army patrols. A lot of them hate this duty here. They loot whatever they can get away with. A lot of them would take your horse, your supplies, and then you."

"I'm going," insisted Catherine. "I'll take the best horse I can get. I'll keep off the trails and dress like a boy. But I'm *going*, MaryLou!"

"Don't you *ever* listen to anyone?"

"Look who's talking!" said Catherine. "It seems to me the person I'm looking at came across-country all by herself from Battleford to Pounding Lake. In the middle of the rebellion!"

"That was different."

"How?"

"Oh, there's no use trying to reason with you! When you go, take my horse then, the mare I stole in Battleford. She is well rested and very fast ... I chose her well." She took her ever-present pistol out of its hiding place in her belt. "Do you know how to load and shoot one like this?" Catherine shook her head. "Then I will show you. Jay can bring them back to me, *if* you get to him safely."

"It's not all that far," Catherine reminded her. "Six miles east, a few more miles north ... less than a day's ride, even if I have to avoid the trails and keep to cover. But I won't take your horse and gun. I have all the money I need to buy my own and more."

"You *will* take mine! You try buying anything like that from Mr. MacKenzie and neither he nor Mr. Scott would let you out of sight for a minute. Give me a little money. I will buy a few supplies for you, not enough to make them suspicious. But what will I tell them after you are gone?"

"The truth, I think," said Catherine slowly. "I'm sure Marie already knows why I came back, and perhaps Scotty, too. Maybe even Connie, because Ellen knew."

MaryLou grinned at her suddenly—her flashing reckless smile that reminded Catherine so much of Jay. "I think I should feel sorry for anyone who gets in your way!"

CHAPTER THIRTY-ONE

Two days later, Catherine slipped away from Fort Pitt just before dawn. MaryLou's mare was indeed a joy to ride, eager and easy-gaited. Catherine wore riding boots, trousers, and a plaid shirt, her hair shoved under a wide-brimmed felt hat. She headed northeast, keeping to the higher ground, but off-trail as she had planned. By the time the sun was well up, Catherine could see the brooding outline of Frenchman Butte. Looking down, she could still make out the trail so laboriously hacked out of the primeval forest, already a little grown over.

It was perhaps four o'clock, judging by the angle of the sun, when Catherine came to the site of the former camp, where the tepees had been. The Sun Dance lodge was still intact, with a polished buffalo skull gleaming from the top of the tall lodge pole in the middle. There was no sign of another living creature, other than a hawk circling high overhead.

Catherine passed the place where the prisoners had camped. Broken-down wagons were the only markers here. She paused on the bank of the Little Red Deer River. On the forest floor, shell casings were scattered here and there. On the far side, she could see craters where the artillery fire had torn open the earth and shaken their world.

At last, she shaded her eyes with her hands, looked up, and saw the two huge pines high above her, guarding the place where she and Jay had first consummated their love. The path that led upward through the trees was clearly marked now, from hauling the cabin-making materials. The woods were silent and serene all around her. The amulet rested warm in her cleavage.

Her heart was racing, and she was almost breathless with apprehension. The mare snorted loudly. The shrill whinny of a stallion challenged her.

***

Jay's cabin was set back against the hillside, sheltered by trees. Catherine dismounted, and tied the mare's reins to a low-hanging branch. She started toward the cabin.

Jay stepped outside, not as bone-thin as he had been, but every bit as athletic, seemingly puzzled as she continued making her way to him. MaryLou's horse ... but it was not MaryLou.

Cate!

He stood rooted to the spot until she was just yards away, then came to his senses. He ran to her, lifted her high into his arms, as he had done on that day when she had claimed his heart, knocking her felt hat off and allowing her blond hair to cascade down her back.

"I'm dreaming," he said, his voice cracking. "I'm making this up in my mind, but you feel so *real* ... tell me you are, Cate! I want to believe it!"

"I'm real. I'm real!" she said through tears. He buried his face in her hair and kissed her neck. She returned his kisses, and they were both shaking and holding each other so tightly that they could hardly breathe. After a while, they calmed down a little ... enough to hear a growling sound behind them. Yellow eyes impaled her—froze her in place.

She quickly recovered. "Muhekun! Down!" She had to repeat it, sharply. Clearly offended, the wolf sat down and turned his head away.

"After I have been feeding him for months, he talks to me like that!" said Jay. Still holding her close, he brushed her hair back and kissed her again. "He's been waiting for you. He knew you would come back, even though I was fool enough to send you away."

"You won't do it again?"

"No more than I would hold back the river, or banish the sun from the sky. Because I can't, my *Amee!*"

***

Muhekun intruded on this emotional reunion, emitting a high-pitched whine of greeting, then crawling forward to flop at her feet. He rolled to expose his belly, tail frantically lashing in anticipation. She knelt and happily obliged him with long overdue scratches and belly-rubs as even more tears were shed.

Then, with Muhekun padding along, Jay led Catherine to a small grave-site between the cabin and the horse corral. "As-a-Child," Jay told her. "He has been waiting, too."

***

Moonlight flooded through the windows of the cabin. Catherine awoke to find Jay resting his head on one elbow, gazing at her. They had spent hours trading gentle affection and loving words with sudden bursts of raw passion, clinging to each other as if they might be torn apart at any moment. Now she was warm and comfortable, her body against his, totally relaxed.

"What are you thinking about?"

"Remembering," he replied. "About long ago when I was a child. It was the last time I saw my father, the day he gave me the amulet. He was dying, and he tried to explain ... in words that a child could understand: 'There are three things in this life that you must be able to love and trust, *Mikosis*, my small son,' he said, 'your woman, your brother-friend, and your land. If you lose any one of them, you can never be whole again.' I found out what he was trying to tell me when I sent you away, when the soldiers took White Bear to jail, and when the treaties took our homeland and only gave us back little bits and pieces of it, and none to the people of Big Bear."

She put her arms around his. "But now, I can go on from here. White Bear will come back. And with the money from my artwork, I will buy this place ... in the white man's way. So no one can take it from our children."

"I hope I *can* give you children, Jay."

"You will, *Amee.*"

***

Many months later, Jay and Catherine bent over a small cradle and tenderly fastened the amulet around the plump warm neck of their sleeping infant son. It was time to pass it on to this beloved child who would surely need its mystical power of protection in the years ahead.

AUTHOR'S NOTE

The Amulet is a work of fiction, and Pounding Lake is a fictitious place. But this novel is closely based upon historical events which happened at Frog Lake.

> *"Although it was not a military engagement, the incident known as the Frog Lake Massacre proved to be one of the most influential events associated with the North-West Resistance. Incited by hunger and mistreatment rather than political motives, a breakaway element of the Plains Cree murdered nine white men on the morning of April 2, 1885, in Frog Lake (now Alberta but then in the District of Saskatchewan, North-West Territories).*
>
> *Big Bear, chief of the Plains Cree in the region, sought improved conditions for Treaty Indians through peaceful means and unity among the tribes. However, the food shortage that followed the virtual extinction of the buffalo left his people near starvation and weakened his authority.*
>
> *Disaffection focused upon Thomas Quinn, an Indian agent who treated the Cree with harshness and arrogance. Before dawn on April 2, a party of warriors captured Quinn at his home. The Cree, led by war chief Wandering Spirit and Ayimasees, Big Bear's son, took more prisoners as they occupied the village. Shortly before 11 a.m., the prisoners were ordered to move to an encampment about two kilometres from Frog Lake.*
>
> *When Quinn obstinately refused, Wandering Spirit shot him in the head. In the short minutes of panic that followed, eight more*

prisoners were shot dead: sawmill operator John Gowanlock, farming instructor John Delaney, Catholic priests Rev. Leon Fafard and Felix Marchand, clerk William Gilchrist, trader George Dill, carpenter Charles Gouin, and John Williscroft, Father Fafard's lay assistant. Cree women hid William Cameron, a Hudson's Bay clerk, beneath a large shawl and thereby saved his life. Cameron, Theresa Delaney, and Theresa Gowanlock, widows of two of the slain men, their families, and others from the settlement, numbering 70 in all, were taken as captives."[1]

Catherine and Ian McNab, Jay Clear Sky, Corporal Peter Gray, and Inspector David Kingsley are fictitious characters. Wandering Spirit, Big Bear, Poundmaker, Ayimasees, and their enemy combatants, General Frederick Middleton and Major Sam Steele were real people involved at the time, as were Louis Riel, the political leader, and Gabriel Dumont, the military leader of the Métis involved in the North-West Rebellion at Duck Lake, Battleford, and Batoche.

Wandering Spirit surrendered near Loon Lake. Wandering Spirit and five other Crees, plus two Métis, were hanged in November 1885. Big Bear avoided capture but later surrendered at Fort Carlson in July 1885; he was tried and convicted and served two years before early release for medical reasons in 1887, and died ten months later in 1888. Ayimasees was never charged. Poundmaker surrendered his arms at Batoche and was tried and sentenced to serve three years in prison, but only served 10 months, due to poor health; he died in 1886. Louis Riel was tried and convicted of treason, and hanged. Gabriel Dumont was exiled to the United States, and died in 1906 in Saskatchewan.

Today, Frog Lake is a small Cree community, approximately 207 kilometres east of Edmonton, Alberta, Canada.

---

1   Chaput, John. "Frog Lake Massacre." *Encyclopedia of Saskatchewan: A Living Legacy*. Regina, SK: University of Regina Press, 2005.

Big Bear and Poundmaker, Glenbow Archives NA-1234-5

ACKNOWLEDGEMENTS

I didn't know when I started this project that it would become more than just a project, it has become a sentimental journey into truly appreciating my mother as *an author*. I couldn't have done it alone.

I would like to thank all the staff of Friesen Press of Altona, Manitoba for their guidance and patience while I navigated the learning curve and for their impeccable layout and design.

Thank you to Doug Dance, wildlife photographer and author himself, for the mesmerizing cover photo of "Muhekun".

I would also like to thank my early beta readers Barbara Rutherford (Manitoba), Vera and Glenn Osborn (Saskatchewan) for their insights and input.

Of course, thanks to my life-partner Wilf, who encouraged this project from conception and is a valued sounding board, motivator, and in-house editor.

More recently, I would like to thank associate editor and virtual assistant Laurie MacNevin (Manitoba), who arrived just in the nick of time to do the final edit, format the documents and images, and to ensure the project got over the finish line.

Thank you for taking the time to read this book. How did you feel about it?
Do you have comments, ideas, questions? We'd love to hear from you!
We truly appreciate honest reader feedback.
Join the conversation and leave an honest review by visiting our website at:
HistoricalFiction.ca/books/the-amulet and click on "Review on Amazon"

To find other books by Norma Sluman go to:
HistoricalFiction.ca/books

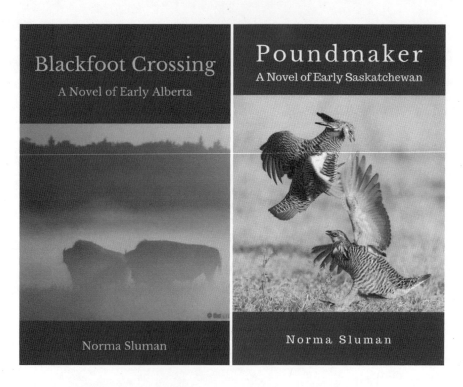

Blackfoot Crossing   Poundmaker

Be part of the Historical Fiction community!
Subscribe to our blog and join our Free Book of the Month Club at:
HistoricalFiction.ca/free-book-of-the-month-club

Each month we will feature one outstanding book by or about a Canadian author, photographer, artist, poet, historian, etc. We'll randomly draw from our subscriber list and give away one copy of that book.

Printed in Canada